Halfway to the Holidays

Complete 3 Book Holiday Boxset

The Halfway Series

Steena Holmes

Elena Aitken

Welcome to Halfway

Welcome to Halfway, a small town where family holiday traditions are the center of every relationship.

Meet the women of Halfway, in this sweet collection of small-town friendships.

In this collection are three stories all set in the town of Halfway:

Halfway to Nowhere

There's a reason Nikki hasn't been back to Halfway in over a decade, and it has everything to do with her secret son and her best friend. But, she's soon finding out that when it comes to small towns and their secrets – there's no place to hide. Especially when everyone can finally see the truth of the secret she can no longer keep.

Halfway in Between

Nikki Landon is settling back into life in her hometown of

Halfway, even helping to organize the annual Pumpkin Festival, and everything feels close to perfect, especially with the bloom of new love and a relationship with Parker Rhodes. Despite growing closer, Nikki can't help but feel that there's something —or someone—coming between them.

Halfway to Christmas

Whether it's a new love or a new baby...a joyful homecoming, or a stressful return in a difficult season, Christmas brings out all of the strongest emotions. Join the women of Halfway, Montana as they celebrate love, friendship and the benchmarks of life this holiday season while learning some hard life lessons along the way.

Dear Reader

Steena and Elena here!

When we decided to join forces and write a story together from two different viewpoints, we thought it would be a lot of fun. And it was! It was also an incredibly interesting and emotional story line to explore. We are both thrilled with the result, and it's our sincerest hope that you fall in love with Nikki and Becky and their experience as much as we did.

We both love to connect with readers and chat about our love for books which means we'd love for you to sign up for our newsletters so we can stay in touch (plus we're both giving away copies of one of our own individual series...so you know you want to sign up!)

For Steena's website: www.steenaholmes.com

For Elena's website: www.elenaaitken.com

We can't wait to hear from you!

Steena & Elena

NEW YORK TIMES & USA TODAY
BESTSELLING AUTHORS

STEENA HOLMES

and ELENA AITKEN

HALFWAY
to nowhere

Chapter One

~Nikki~

Nikki Landon hadn't been down the main street in Halfway, Montana for ten years, but it might as well have been yesterday for all the changes there were. She pulled up to a single flashing red light. That was new. *Okay, maybe some things did change.* She adjusted the rearview mirror and peeked into the back seat at her son, Ryan. *Definitely,* she thought as she stole a glance at his blond hair and sparkling blue eyes taking in everything outside his window. *Some things changed a whole lot.*

She tapped her brake pedal, but with no other cars in sight, Nikki eased her vehicle through the intersection and continued down the street.

"That's Grounds," she said to Ryan. She rapped on the glass, pointing to the coffee shop where she'd spent many hours, pretending to do homework.

"Do they have hot chocolate?"

"Of course." She smiled. "They also have the best macchiato I've ever tasted. Maybe we can stop in and get one sometime?"

Nikki bit her lip, regretting the words the second they left her mouth. She didn't plan to be in Halfway long enough to start visiting her old haunts. With any luck at all, she'd be able to deal with her mother's house and get out before anyone noticed. As if that would be possible in a town the size of Halfway.

Nikki tried not to dwell on all the reasons she didn't want to be there; the list would be way too long. She needed to stay focused, close up her mother's estate, and say goodbye to her past once and for all.

But first, food. She pulled her car into an open space on the street in front of the Evergreen Grocer and looked in the mirror again. "Will you be okay for a few minutes? I just need to grab us a few things for dinner because I'm not sure what Grandma had in the..." She drifted off when she saw Ryan's face crumple.

Nikki twisted around in her seat the best she could and grabbed her son's hand. "Hey, buddy. It's okay to be sad, you know?"

He nodded and sucked in his lips, trying to hold back the tears.

Nikki blinked hard. She refused to cry in front of Ryan. "Grandma was very special and I miss her too." She squeezed Ryan's hand. "And when we get to the house, I'll be able to show you the cool collection of spoons she had."

"Spoons?" He raised his eyebrow, clearly not believing her.

"It's true," she said. "Grandma collected spoons from all over. And you'll be able to see them, as soon as we get there." Nikki let go of his hand and patted his knee. "But first, we need food. How does frozen pizza sound?"

Ryan's eyes lit up the way she knew they would. "And fries?"

She shook her head, but said, "Okay. But you have to have milk with dinner."

"Deal."

Satisfied for the time being, Nikki left Ryan to play on his tablet and got out of the car. She froze for a minute before walking into the Evergreen. The problem with trying to sneak into a small town you'd run away from ten years earlier was that it was impossible. Everyone knew everyone and everyone's business. She had as much chance of sneaking into town undetected as a kitten cuddling up in a wolf den. Not that she was some helpless kitten. No, Nikki could hold her own. And besides, there were only two people she needed to avoid.

The bells jingled overhead as she pushed her way into the store and Nikki cringed. She scanned the space, but no one was looking her way. Yet. Needing to hurry, she grabbed a wire basket from the rack by the door and moved down the first aisle. She was counting on the fact that the Wilsons still owned the store and hadn't changed the layout, and from what she could tell, it was exactly the same.

Nikki located the frozen food section and tossed in a pepperoni pizza, a bag of fries and at the last minute, a box of ice cream sandwiches. *Might as well go all out with the junk food.* Voices in the next aisle stopped her in her tracks. It may have been ten years, but she'd recognize the voice of her childhood best friend anywhere.

Dammit. As frozen as the pizza in her basket, Nikki stood and listened but didn't actually hear the words Becky said to the other woman. She absorbed the sound of her friend's voice. Nikki longed to circle around the shelves of cereal and pull the woman who she used to tell everything to into her arms. But common sense prevailed and she snapped out of her daze.

As quietly as she could, she closed the freezer door and was halfway to the till when Nikki remembered her promise to Ryan that he'd be drinking milk with his dinner of junk food. She looked at the basket. *Forget it; there was dairy in the ice cream.*

"Hello there," the cashier said. Nikki loaded the items on

5

the counter and nodded in reply. She glanced at the girl's name tag. *Natalie*. She looked about sixteen or seventeen, which meant she would be too young to remember Nikki.

"Is that all for you?" Natalie snapped her gum and stuffed the food into a plastic bag. "We have a two for one on—"

"No. That'll be all."

"Okay." Natalie drew out the word and rolled her eyes.

"Sorry." Nikki handed the girl her credit card. "I'm in sort of a hurry." She snuck a glance towards the back of the store where she'd heard Becky. The aisle was empty.

"No one's ever in a hurry in Halfway," Natalie said. She swiped the card and looked at the name. "It's the slowest town...hey," she said, changing tracks the way teenagers are wont to do. "Are you related to Mrs. Landon? That was a wicked brutal accident. I heard that the car got totally crunched and—"

"I am," Nikki said. She signed her name on the electronic pad and snatched her credit card from Natalie's hand. "She was my mother."

"Oh, oops. My mom's always saying I talk too much, but I..."

Nikki didn't hear anything else the girl said. She turned and fled from the store, desperately needing air. Her eyes burned with the tears that for the last few days she'd held back. She would not cry. Not in front of Ryan.

She stopped for a moment to compose herself before getting back in the car. Ryan was in the backseat, his head still bent over his tablet, totally oblivious of anything going on around him. She usually hated it when he spent so much time on screens and was constantly yanking them away, forcing him to look out the window and take in his surroundings. But as far as she was concerned, for the next few days, he could spend as much time as he wanted playing Minecraft or whatever the current game craze was. It would keep him busy, his mind off losing his grandma, and with any luck, his questions about the town she grew up in to a minimum.

Just a few more days, she told herself. Just long enough to wrap up her mother's affairs, and put the house up for sale. She'd hire someone to pack it up. The sooner she could get Ryan and herself out of Halfway and back to Seattle, the better. But first, dinner.

Dammit. Nikki looked down at her empty hands. In her haste to get away from the cashier, she'd left her bags behind. For a second, Nikki considered abandoning her purchases and ordering pizza. It would certainly be easier, and it would all but eliminate the chance of running into Becky, who was no doubt still in the store. The only problem with that plan was that as far as she knew, there was nowhere to order pizza in Halfway.

With a sigh, she turned around and walked back into the store. Natalie, looking very apologetic, and blushing all the way to the roots in her hair, had Nikki's bags in her hands and ran over to her.

"I'm so sorry," Natalie said. "I really don't mean to say such stupid things."

"It's okay. It was my fault. I'm really in a hurry and—"

"No way!"

Nikki tightened her grip on the plastic bags and steeled herself. She turned around slowly, and was immediately crushed in a hug.

"Nicole Landon, I should kill you for taking off on me like that." Becky Grant, or rather Jennings now that she's married, was the closest friend she'd ever had, released her from the hug and smacked her lightly on the arm. "But I won't, only because I'm so happy to see you. How are you?" Becky's beautiful smile turned down in a frown and she added, "I'm so sorry about your mom. Such a terrible tragedy. But it did bring you back, and sometimes in times like this, we need to take whatever good we can. When did you get in? I can't even imagine what you're going through...and look at me, not even giving you a chance to speak."

She laughed at herself, and for a moment, Nikki was transported back in time to when they were sixteen. Becky hadn't changed a bit. Opposite in every way to Nikki, Becky was only five foot four. The much taller Nikki had always felt it was a grave injustice. Becky's blond hair was draped down her back, and in jeans and a down-filled coat, she looked exactly the same as the last time Nikki'd seen her. The biggest change was the diamond ring that flashed on her left hand.

Nikki looked away. It wasn't a secret that Becky had married Matt Jennings right after high school. She'd been invited to the wedding, of course. Not that she'd gone.

"I'm doing well," Nikki finally answered. "It's been a hard few days and of course, I have so much to do while I'm here." She hoped maybe that would be enough to get away from any further prying, but Nikki should've known better.

"Of course you do," Becky said. "And one of those things you have to do is come over for dinner. I know Matt will want to see you, too."

Nikki flinched at the mention of his name and hoped Becky didn't notice.

"I really don't know. I mean, I have—"

"I won't take no for an answer." Becky stared at her with those deep green eyes that used to be able to see her secrets. "Besides, you owe me."

The blood drained from her face and for a horrifying second, Nikki thought she might pass out. *There was no way Becky could know. No one knew.*

"Relax," Becky said with a laugh. "You owe me an explanation for where the hell you've been all these years. I'm pissed with you, ya know? You can't just take off and expect me not to be a little upset."

Nikki nodded and relief flooded through her. She glanced back towards the car and Ryan. She needed to hurry. Even with a video game, Ryan wouldn't wait forever without coming in to look for her.

"I know I was a total jerk," she said. "I really am sorry but—"

"Good," Becky said. "Tomorrow night then. It's settled." Becky scribbled her number on a piece of paper and handed it to Nikki before grabbing another wire basket from the stack. "It looks like I have some more shopping to do. Matt will be thrilled when I tell him I ran into you. So, six o'clock? We're at the Jennings' farm. You heard that Matt took over for his dad, right?" Nikki nodded. She remembered well. "Great," Becky continued. "See you then. You remember how to get there?"

She nodded again. "See you then," Nikki muttered, as Becky walked away.

In a daze, she cursed herself all the way to the car, being sure to get in quickly and drive away before she was spotted by anyone else.

"Did you get the pizza, Mom?"

Pasting a smile she didn't feel on her face, Nikki looked into the mirror. "Pepperoni, your favorite."

"You rock, Mom." Ryan smiled, revealing the dimples she loved so much, the ones that never failed to remind her of his father.

Chapter Two

~Becky~

Becky hummed to herself as she dropped the bags of groceries into the trunk of her SUV. She couldn't believe Nikki was finally home. It'd been too long. Way too long.

Her fingers drummed on the steering wheel as she pulled out of the Evergreen Grocer parking lot and turned onto the main street. She waved to Mr. and Mrs. Redwood as they ambled across the street ahead of her. She didn't even mind that they seemed to be slower than the turtles in her pond back at the farm today. Nothing was going to ruin the rest of her day: not the Redwoods or the fact that she was going to get stuck at the only red light in a town with no traffic because they took so long to cross the street, nor the fact that she was about to go see Norma, her mother.

Nope. She'd begged for a bit of sunshine in her day today and she got it.

A smile spread across her face as she thought about seeing Nikki again for the first time in years. She looked good. Better than good, if she were being honest. She looked fabulous. They'd always been polar opposites in their looks. Although Becky was petite and blond and always teased about her doll-like looks, Nikki had been the Amazonian: tall, muscular, and gorgeous with her thick brown hair. Except, back then there'd been no heavy bags beneath the eyes or a forced smile.

Yeah, Becky had caught that smile, but chose to ignore it. She'd make it her goal, her mission to bring the real smile back to Nikki's face, and she knew exactly how to do it, too.

As she pulled into the town's small hospital, Becky mentally sorted through the hundreds of recipes she had and began the process of creating a meal for tomorrow night when the perfect idea hit her. She'd spent the morning trying to come up with a theme for this month's blog posts on her website, Sweet Spoons and Bites. What if she did a Girls Night Out theme? She could start it off with a story about the time she and Nikki had decided to make brownies from scratch one night and came up with a recipe that literally changed Becky's life when she entered it into a contest run by Hershey a few years ago. She could also do a test run of that lava cake recipe she'd found online and post the results tonight on her blog. She was due to post a test recipe on the site, anyways.

She pulled out the bags of food and supplies Norma had demanded she bring today from the back of her vehicle and literally skipped her way up to the front steps of County General.

"Someone's in a good mood today." Dennis Hobs, a local retiree who deemed it his life's mission to greet anyone who came into the hospital with a smile, held the door open for her.

"The sun is shining, I had my coffee already, and Nikki Landon is back in town." Becky planted a quick kiss on Dennis's cheek, something she did every time she ran into her uncle and smiled.

"Well, well, the dynamic duo is back together. I remember the shenanigans you two used to get into." Dennis patted her hand as they walked down the hallway together. "Sad news about her mom, though. Things aren't going to be the same without Marie around to boss your mother about."

"Or the other way around." Becky frowned. "Which reminds me, I'd better hurry..." She lifted up the bags and Dennis waved her away.

County General was a one-floor hospital that consisted of three main areas: the doctors' offices, the patients' wing, and the urgent care center. Becky headed towards the patients' wing where her mother's room was located.

She smiled at the nurses as she walked past and made a quick stop at the nurses' desk to leave a container full of freshly baked chocolate chip cookies. God knows the nurses all deserved a little treat for putting up with Norma this past week.

Becky stood outside the door that led into her mother's private room and took a deep breath. She held it for a few seconds before slowly releasing it. *I will remain calm and cheerful, and not let her get to me. I will remain calm and cheerful—*

"Are you coming in or are you going to stand out there all day?" Norma Grant, yelled.

And not let her get to me. Becky forced a smile on her face. She really couldn't blame her mom for being so cantankerous and obnoxious at the same time. She'd just lost her best friend, she was confined to a hospital bed, and she'd been forced to eat cafeteria food.

Her husband, Matthew, told her that she needed to have an extra dose of patience for her mother right now. And he was right. She did. There could have been two tragic deaths that fateful night, just over a week ago, instead of one. She needed to count her blessings. At least she still had a parent alive, unlike Nikki...

"Your face is all scrunched up," her mother admonished her. "That's how you get wrinkles you know."

Becky just shook her head. "Then don't yell at me." She smiled. "Someone's in a good mood today it seems." Becky placed the bags she'd been carrying on the chair beside the bed and leaned down to kiss Norma's cheek. She was pleased to see some color back in her mother's face. It looked like Sally, the local beautician, had made it in to wash her hair and style it a bit.

"It's hard to be in a good mood in here when all people want to do is poke and prod in places they should just leave alone. It's my hip that is broken, nothing else," her mother grumbled.

"I'm sure they want you out just as much as you want to be out." Becky reached into one of the bags and took out a warm wool cardigan. "I like what Sally did to your hair."

"She did okay." She patted her shoulder-length gray hair before she shook her head. "That's not the one I wanted. I said the green one. That isn't green." Norma's lips pursed together as she leaned forward and let Becky drape the sweater across her back and over her shoulders.

"The green one needed to be washed. I'll bring it in tomorrow." She reached into the bag and pulled out a couple pairs of socks and fingerless mitts. "Before you say anything, I couldn't find the socks you wanted so I brought you some of mine. They have extra layers in them to keep your toes warm."

"I wasn't going to say a word." A hint of a smile appeared on Norma's face as she drew the gloves over her hands and leaned back against her pillow.

Becky unpacked the rest of the items in the bag, placing a book and notepad on the small table beside the bed, along with a smaller container of cookies, and then sat down.

"What did the doctor say this morning?"

Her mother snorted. "It's what the fool didn't say."

"I told you he wouldn't let you out today." As long as she was out by the weekend, that would leave her plenty of time to—

"That's not all..."

Maybe it was the way her mother refused to look at her, or the way her hands knotted together. Whatever she had to say, it was bad.

"Has she told you she won't be leaving till after the festival?" A deep voice behind Becky broke the news. She twisted in her chair to find Dr. Richard behind her, holding a clipboard in his hand.

That was the news she'd been dreading.

"What do you mean, she can't leave till after the festival?"

"The old fool thinks I'll overdo it so he's keeping me here," Norma muttered.

Becky blinked a few times as she gathered her thoughts. From the disheartened look on her mother's face to the sympathetic smile on Dr. Richard's, Becky figured Norma had already tried to change his mind and failed.

"But...but..." Becky stumbled over her words as the full realization of what the news meant.

She stood and paced the small room. "Who's going to organize the festival this year? It's only a few weeks away and there's still a lot to do. Trust me—I'm the one fielding the calls from everyone wanting to know what's going on."

"Perfect." Dr. Richard stepped into the room and stood beside her chair.

"Excuse me? There's nothing perfect about this situation. This day was supposed to be full of sunshine and happy thoughts. *Happy thoughts.*" Becky pointed at both her mother and the doctor. "Why do I have a feeling you're about to ruin that happiness?"

"Oh, stop being so melodramatic, Rebecca. You'll just have to be the organizer this year and that's that."

Becky looked to Dr. Richard for help but he only shrugged.

"Does she really need to stay here?" Becky didn't even try to hide the whine in her voice.

The older gentleman only nodded while her mother crossed her arms over her chest. "I'm afraid she does. I know your mother too well. She's more stubborn than a mule. She'll do too much and overtax her body and she'll wind back up in here but in worse shape than she is now. Trust me. I know it's the last thing you or the nurses want to hear but she's not going anywhere until after the festival."

Becky's world as she knew it just ended. Although she'd always helped her mother organize the festival, her role barely made a dent in all the behind-the-scenes things her mother and Marie, Nikki's mom, took care of.

"How am I going to do the job of two people? When I offered to help you earlier, it was because you couldn't do it by yourself. Even you admitted that. So how am I supposed to?"

"Oh for Pete's sake." Clearly her mother was more than a little annoyed with her.

For a few seconds, there was silence in the room before Dr. Richard slowly backed out of the room. Becky glared at him for leaving her like this. This was all his fault. When he shut the door behind him, she pursed her lips and turned her attention to her mother.

"I'm sorry but—"

Her mother raised a hand and cut her off. Becky clamped her lips together and counted to three.

"Rebecca Jennings, there is no way that this festival is not going to happen, so pull up your big girl panties and do what needs to be done. It's not like you don't have time. All you do is piddle with recipes and post them online. There's a meeting scheduled for next week with all the participants. The preliminary stuff is done, so you just need to delegate some tasks to all the other volunteers."

"I do more than just piddle," Becky mumbled while she sank down in her chair as the weight of what was entailed rested on her shoulders.

This festival wasn't just a small town gathering. What once used to be a small town tree lighting ceremony had turned into a statewide celebration. Now, there was an annual contest to see which tree farm from the surrounding counties would have the honor of having their tree selected as the tree for the year.

The festival was a whole weekend affair with a winter carnival, food contests, and a plethora of showcase booths from local artisans. This was also the busiest weekend for their family tree farm as families from all over came to select their own personal Christmas tree.

"I'm not in a bad mood," her mother grumbled while a small smile teased her lips. "Okay, maybe a little, but the point is," her mother grabbed her notebook from the small bed table beside her and opened it up, "you won't be doing this alone. I'm here. All you need to do is enlist a couple of your friends to help you with some of the tasks Marie used to take care of and you'll be fine."

"Oh," Becky straightened in the chair, "now that you mention it, you'll never believe who I ran into on my way here?"

Norma opened her eyeglass case and propped her bifocals on the edge of her nose.

"Come on, three guesses." She would love to see a smile on her mother's normally stern face. She used to complain that Nikki was her second daughter because the girls spent so much time together.

"Rebecca..."

Becky hated it when her mother used that tone on her. She

felt as if she were back in grade school all over again. "Fine. The least you could have done was attempted a guess." She waited for her mother to look at her. "Nikki's home."

Norma only shrugged. "Well, of course she would be. Someone needs to see to Marie's things. Don't expect her to stick around, though."

"Why not? I've already invited her over for dinner tomorrow night." She planned to do everything she could to delay Nikki returning to wherever she lived now. She knew it was doubtful Nikki would return home for good, but was it too much for her to hope that their friendship could be rekindled? She missed her best friend more than anyone could possibly know.

"Don't get your hopes up, girl. I'd hate to see you get disappointed again."

Becky scooted to the edge of her seat and leaned forward. "I've never believed any of those rumors and you know it."

"One day you'll take off those rose-colored glasses of yours. I just hope you're prepared for a world of hurt when you do."

That was it. She'd had enough of her mother attempting to bring her down. She would let her mother stew in her own self-pity—because that's exactly what it was—and she'd go off and pick up some fresh baked bread from Carla's cafe and get her spaghetti sauce simmering on the stove.

"I'm not naive, Mother. You, of all people, should know that."

She leaned down and laid a soft kiss on her mother's cheek. "I'll be by to see you tomorrow and maybe then we can talk about this festival. Who knows, I might even convince Nikki to help me." She gathered her purse and other bags.

"Don't ask—just tell her she needs to help you. God knows, she owes you that, at least."

Chapter Three

~Nikki~

The next day dawned bright and cheery, the exact opposite of Nikki's mood. After setting Ryan up in the guest bedroom the night before, Nikki had gone straight to bed herself. There was so much to do, too much. But she couldn't bring herself to start sorting through her mother's things. Not yet.

As it turned out, she probably should have, for all the sleep she got. Lying in her childhood bed in her old room, she couldn't settle. Too many memories surrounded her. Everywhere she turned, there was another reminder of the life she'd had, the one she'd run from.

As soon as the sun started peeking through the blinds, she'd gotten out of bed, tied her old robe around her, and padded down to the kitchen. There was no point waking Ryan. He needed his sleep. Losing his grandma so suddenly had been difficult for him. On both of them. And that was an understatement.

Her mother had been the only link Nikki had with her past. And the only one who knew the truth.

She went to the cupboard and pulled out the coffee grounds, exactly where her mom had always kept them. She measured out the perfect amount, filled the water, and set it to brew. While she waited, she wandered into the living room. Her mother's knitting sat, half-finished, on the side table next to her chair with a half cup of water. Nikki picked up the yarn, and let it slide through her fingers. She'd been making slippers, probably for Ryan for Christmas.

Tears pricked at Nikki's eyes and her sinuses burned as she tried to hold them back. Ryan needed her to be strong. She was the only one he had now.

Not the only one.

The thought came out of nowhere, surprising her. She shook it away and sniffed loudly. "No," she said aloud. "That's not going to happen."

Even as she said the words, doubt filled her. How could she be back in Halfway and keep her secret? Wasn't that the whole reason she'd left?

She wandered to the mantel and scanned the photos. Most of them were of Nikki and her mother on her visits over the years, with a few of Nikki as a child scattered about. There were none of Ryan. She'd made her mother promise, and she'd kept her word. No one could know about Ryan. Nikki's heart cramped at the hurt it must have caused her mom to hide pictures of her only grandson. Not to mention what Ryan would think if he noticed the absence of photos.

Without thinking, she started gathering the frames off the mantel. Nikki piled them face down on the coffee table and as she reached for the last one, she froze. It was a shot of her and Becky on their prom night. Nikki picked up the picture and walked over to the sofa, where she sank into the cushions.

She remembered exactly when the picture was taken. They'd decided to get ready at Nikki's house and have the boys pick them up there. Of course, Becky was going to prom with Matt. They'd been together for over a year by that time, with the exception of an important but brief breakup, and were almost completely inseparable. From the moment Becky declared she was interested in Matt, Nikki knew her best friend would get exactly what she wanted. Which was why she'd stepped back and shoved her own feelings for him to the side. Becky was a force of nature when she set her sights on something. And seeing them together, Nikki'd always known she'd made the right decision to back off. They were her closest friends, and they were perfect together.

Nikki had gone to prom with Parker. They'd dated a few times, and he wanted it to be more, but she just couldn't convince herself it was anything serious. He'd been a fun date, though, and prom night was amazing. When the girls had come down the stairs together and her mother had snapped the picture, Nikki had never been happier. Everything was perfect.

After the summer, Becky and Nikki were going to go to college together and be roommates while Matt stayed in the boy's dorm. They were all going to get out of Halfway, and start their lives. Prom night was the celebration of the start of the rest of their lives. Thinking back on that night, Nikki had to blink back the tears that were threatening to spill over. It was one of the best nights of her life. How was she to know that it would be the last night that everything would be okay?

The next day, with her period already two months late, Nikki took the test she'd been putting off. Less than two weeks later, she was gone.

Nikki ran a finger across the glass at the happy girls in the photo. Hadn't she already known on prom night? She was just delaying the inevitable, just as she was doing now. With a sigh,

Nikki got up from the couch and went to the phone. She punched in the number Becky had given her the day before and held her breath.

Secretly, she was hoping for the answering machine. *Maybe Becky was still sleeping? What if Matt answered?*

"Shit." She hadn't considered the fact that Matt might answer the phone. She couldn't talk to him. Not yet. Nikki pulled the phone away from her ear and almost hit the button to disconnect when a voice came over the line.

"Hello?"

It was Becky.

"Hello?" Becky said again.

Nikki shook her head and put the phone up to her ear. "Hi, Becky. It's Nikki. Sorry to be calling so early."

"Early?" Becky laughed. "It's not early for me. Not when I have the Tree Festival to singlehandedly organize. Did you know that your mother and my mother always do this together and now with my mother barking orders from the hospital and your mom—oh, Nikki. I'm so sorry. I didn't mean to—"

"It's okay." Nikki turned and stared out the window at the pink sunrise that was making the sky glow. "I know, and it's fine, really," she said and meant it. "So, your mom has you taking over all the planning? Sounds fun."

Unfortunately, Becky missed the sarcasm in her voice and only picked up on the words. "Do you think so? It could be fun," she said. "If you help me."

"What? No, I can't—"

"It'll be fun. The next generation of best friends working together. I was actually going to suggest it, and since you think it's a good idea, too, it'll be perfect."

Nikki shook her head even though Becky couldn't see her. There was no way she could work side by side with her on this. *No way. It wasn't happening.* "I wish I could, Becky," she said.

"But I really have so much to do with the house and I can't stay in town very long. I just don't think it would work."

That was an understatement, Nikki thought.

"Please, Nikki. I really need you and you're so good with organizing. Besides, you should stay. It'll be good for you to have a little fun," Becky said. "And didn't I hear that you work from home, anyway? Mom said something about a computer thing."

"I design websites," she said. "But I really can't—"

"We'll talk about it tonight," Becky said as if the matter was settled. "I'm working on this great recipe. Did I tell you about my website? Maybe you could look at it when you come over and give me a few tips?"

Nikki swallowed hard. Becky wasn't going to take it well, but she had to cancel. She couldn't leave Ryan alone and there was absolutely no way she was taking him over to Matt and Becky's house. That wasn't going to happen in a million years. "About tonight," she started. "I'm so sorry, but I just don't think I'm going to be up to it. I'm a little overwhelmed with everything I have to do here at the house and to make arrangements and everything. I just don't think it's a good idea, tonight."

"Oh."

"It's not that I don't want to," Nikki added quickly. Becky always was sensitive when she canceled plans, and the last thing Nikki wanted was to make her old friend feel worse. If she wasn't careful, there'd be a lot more hurt coming for everyone before she left town. "I do, Becky. I just don't think it's a good idea tonight. I need to get things packed up is all."

"Well, if you're sure."

"I'm sorry, Becky."

"It's okay. Maybe we can do it in a few days?" She heard Becky take a deep breath on the other end of the line. "Oh, and speaking of packing up, I thought you might need a few more boxes, so I had Matt load them up in the truck for you."

A knot of panic formed in Nikki's chest.

"He said he'd bring them over for you later," Becky continued.

"That's not necessary." Nikki turned when she heard a creak on the stairs. Ryan, still in his pajamas, his blond hair mussed and standing up at strange angles, was walking downstairs, rubbing his eyes. She held up her finger to her lips. "Really, Becky. I don't need any boxes. I'm good and I don't want to trouble Matt with anything. I know how busy he must be at this time of year. The last thing he needs is to be coming all the way out here on a silly errand."

Becky chuckled, totally oblivious of the rising panic Nikki was feeling. "It's no trouble at all," she said. "He's actually on his way over right now. He had to run out and grab some coffee from Grounds since I forgot to pick some up yesterday. So he said he'd run over right away before you got started packing. We both thought you'd be up and at it already."

Nikki spun around, unsure of what she was looking for. *Matt couldn't come here. No.* Ryan sat at the table and plopped his tired head in his hands. "Becky, I have to go. I'll talk to you soon, okay?"

"Okay, maybe I'll—"

Nikki hung up on whatever it was Becky was going to say. She couldn't think. She ran her hands through her hair and pulled at the roots. If Matt was on his way over, he would be there soon. She didn't have much time. She needed to do something. Anything. Her heart raced. A bead of sweat broke over her brow and she grabbed the counter to support herself because she wasn't sure her legs could hold her up for another moment.

"Mom?"

Ryan.

Through a veil of hair, she looked at her son. She had to get a hold of herself. She couldn't fall apart, not now. She took a deep breath. She was strong. She'd been through worse. She could make it through this. With a deep breath, she stood up straight and pushed away from the counter.

"I'm fine, Ryan." She walked over to him and ruffled his hair. "Did you sleep okay? You look tired." She forced a lightness into her voice and hoped he didn't notice as she glanced out the window. If Matt was going to stop by, maybe she could head him off at the door.

"Why don't you have some cereal for breakfast?" She opened the cupboard on the off chance that her mom had some cereal that wasn't totally bran. She pulled out a box of Cheerios. "Here you go."

Everything was exactly where she remembered it and it only took a few seconds for her to find a bowl and a spoon. Ryan was happily munching away when she heard the truck pull into the driveway. Her heart automatically picked up the pace and Nikki had to force herself to calm down. She picked up her coffee cup, took a sip and slowly walked to the kitchen door.

"Hey, buddy?" Ryan lifted his head, the spoon halfway to his mouth. "I'm just going to be outside for a second, okay? You just finish your breakfast. I'll be in in a second, okay?"

Ryan shrugged and continued to eat, so Nikki slipped from the room, walked through the living room and opened the front door just as Matt was pulling a stack of folded cardboard from the back of his pick-up. She closed the door behind her and gripped the coffee mug to keep her hands from shaking. She wasn't ready. It'd been so long.

And then, he turned. His eyes met hers and she started at the familiar deep blue. When his face split into a smile, and his dimples deepened into his cheeks, Nikki shook so violently, hot coffee spilled onto her hand.

She wiped it on her pants and forced a smile to her face. "Hi, Matt."

"Nikki." He all but sprinted up the stairs to the porch, balancing the awkward stack of boxes. "It's so good to see you." She knew he meant it, too. Matt didn't have an insincere bone in his body. "I'm so sorry about your mom." His smile faltered. "What a tragedy it all was, and...well, it shouldn't have happened. I'm so sorry."

"Thanks, Matt," she said. "That means a lot."

"I'm glad you're back, though. I really want to give you a hug." He jostled the boxes around again, trying to shift them to one arm. "Is there somewhere I can drop these for you?"

"No."

Matt looked at her and raised an eyebrow. "You don't need them?"

"I...um..." Nikki desperately searched her brain for something to tell him. "I do," she said finally, because anything else would be a lie and he'd know it.

"Okay." He drew the word out slowly. "Let me take them inside for you."

"No," she said with a little more force than she intended. When Matt tilted his head and gave her a strange look, she added, "That's fine. You can just leave them on the porch." She put her coffee mug down and moved a chair, trying to clear a place. "Here, I'll just move a few—"

"Nonsense," Matt said. "I'll just take them in." Before Nikki could stop him, he shifted the load to his left hand and used his right to open the door and all she could do was pick up her coffee mug and helplessly follow him inside.

"Just put them here," she said. Nikki glanced in the direction of the kitchen and said a silent prayer that Ryan was having a second helping of cereal.

Matt dropped the boxes and straightened up. Before she

25

could object, he wrapped his arms around her and squeezed. Her coffee sloshed over the side, splashing on both of them, but Matt didn't seem to care. He only pulled her tighter. "It really is good to see you, Nikki." He spoke into her hair and she closed her eyes, fighting the overwhelming rush of emotions that were crashing into her just by being close to him.

She tried to wiggle out of his embrace. "Matt, I—"

"I've missed you, Nik," he said, using his nickname for her. "It hasn't been the same, since—"

"Mom?"

Her blood drained from her face, and if Matt hadn't been holding on to her, she would have fallen over. For an instant the world stopped, and there was nothing but a roar in her head. Matt released her, and only by instinct, she grabbed the couch to hold herself up. She watched as Matt's face changed from shock to slow realization as he took in the miniature version of himself that stood before him.

Seeing them together, it was undeniable. From their mussed blond hair, to their ice blue eyes and the matching dimples in their cheeks.

In slow motion, Nikki turned to face Ryan. "Hey, buddy. Can you go back in the kitchen? I just need to finish talking to... Mr. Jennings. I'll be done in a minute."

"Wait," Matt said. "You have a son." It wasn't a question, but there was something in his voice that asked a lot more.

She nodded but wouldn't look at him.

"Nikki," he spoke softly, but firmly. "How old is he?"

She shook her head, willing Matt to take his questions and go away. She focused on her son. "Go finish breakfast, Ryan." She kept her face as neutral as possible until he left the room.

"Nikki," Matt said again. "How old?" He grabbed her shoulder and spun her around so she was facing him. Despite the questions on his lips, there was no denying the clarity in his eyes. Matt was a smart man and it wouldn't take a genius to figure out what was plain for anyone to see. "Tell me, Nikki," he said, giving her shoulders a small shake.

Tears pricked her eyes, but she forced them away. There was no room for that. Not now. She took a deep breath and set her jaw before she said, "Do I really need to answer that?"

Chapter Four

~Becky~

Becky sat down at her office desk and turned her computer on. She checked her phone again to see whether Matt had texted her back since she'd first sent him a message to pick up some sugar while grabbing the coffee. That had been an hour ago. He should have been home by now. *How long did it take to drop off boxes?*

Instead of the coffee she craved, she sipped on a cup of homemade hot chocolate with shaved milk chocolate, cocoa, sugar, and heavy cream that she'd simmered on the stove. She'd been trying out a few variations of the homemade mix because she wanted to use these as gifts in some gift baskets she was going to give out on her website and to friends and family around town. So far, this one was the best recipe she'd tried— except it could use a little bit more sugar.

She had a list of things to accomplish today but she couldn't get motivated. All she could think about was how Nikki couldn't hide the fact she'd wanted to get off the phone with her. She knew, no matter what Nikki had said, that she would never come over for dinner, and there was no doubt in her mind that she was trying to figure out how to get out of town as quickly as she could before Becky found out.

Well, that wasn't going to happen. Not again.

Back in high school, they'd both had dreams and aspirations. Being the wife of a tree farmer wasn't exactly what Becky had in mind when she thought about her future, but then neither had being a baker with her own cookbook and a growing fan base. She'd wanted to explore the world, to experience history first-hand and maybe even become an anthropologist. Anything that would take her away from Halfway and her mother.

But then Nikki had vanished just as summer began and Matt's father had his first stroke. Heading off to college alone wasn't something Becky had wanted to do and with Nikki gone...she'd felt alone. When Matt broke the news that he had to enroll in the local college and help out more with the family farm, Becky had made the impulse decision to do the same. They married a month after graduation.

"Funny how plans change," Becky muttered to herself as she scrolled through a social media site and looked at the recent baby photos one of her online followers had posted. Becky made a mental note to post some homemade baby food recipes and diet-friendly desserts.

Her heart ached as she paused on an image of the mother holding her child close. Being a mother was a dream Becky had always had, but after multiple miscarriages, she'd finally let go of that wish. Matt had broached the subject of adoption, but she wasn't sure she was ready for that. Her last miscarriage had only been a few months ago and the pain was still too...fresh.

She closed the browser and leaned back in her chair. They'd been so close last time, almost making it to the twelve-week mark, the longest she'd ever carried one of her babies. Her gaze strayed to the bookshelf in her office where she kept the journals she'd bought after each pregnancy. The first book, with a soft cream cover, was full of her hopes and dreams for their child. Every feeling, every sensation, even every episode of morning sickness was recorded. Then, after that miscarriage, every tear, heartbreak, and question for God was recorded. She'd bought another journal for her second pregnancy, but this time her joy was more reflective and the pages were full of prayers for a healthy pregnancy. In total, there were four journals. She didn't think she could handle buying another one, even if it were for an adopted child.

She heard the sound of a door slamming and pushed herself up from the chair. Finally, Matt was home. She went to see whether he needed help with the grocery bags but he came into the house empty-handed and walked past her with barely a word.

"Matt?"

He turned to look at her, but it was as if he saw right through her.

"Are you okay?" He gave his head a little shake but didn't say anything. "Did you get the coffee and sugar?"

"Sugar?" His shoulders deflated.

"I sent you a text." She knew he got it. It showed as read on her phone.

"Yeah, sorry...I totally forgot. I can go back into town and get it later, okay?" He sank down on a bar stool at their kitchen counter and pulled his phone out of his pocket.

"I kind of needed it now. Nikki canceled dinner tonight"— Matt's head popped up—"so I thought I'd make her something and take it into her. Maybe help her pack."

"No. I mean..." Matt shook his head. "I'll take it in."

Becky grabbed a recipe book off the shelf of her curio cabinet and thumbed through the pages. "Why? I thought you told me this morning you needed to be down in the field for the day, which is why you went into town this morning for me."

"Do you think that's a good idea?"

She lifted her gaze from the recipe book to her husband and noticed that he wasn't looking at her. "Why wouldn't it be?"

He licked his lips before pocketing his phone and rose. "Nikki...I think she just wants to be left alone."

Becky winced at his words. "What she wants and what she needs are two different things. She just lost her mother—being alone right now isn't what she needs. She needs to know she's still loved and accepted and that the past is behind us." She leaned her elbows down on the counter. "We were best friends, Matt. Best friends. No matter what happened that drove her away, that has never changed."

She watched as her husband stepped towards her and held out his arms. She gladly went into them. She loved the feel of his arms around her, knowing how safe and protected she was.

"Sometimes the past is best left alone," he whispered into her hair before he laid a kiss on her forehead.

Becky looked up into his eyes and was confused by what she saw in there. Fear, hope, uncertainty. His forehead knitted together before he blinked and pulled away.

"Oh trust me, I don't plan to dredge up the past. I'm just happy she's back. I plan to do all I can to make sure she knows it, too." Becky smiled as an idea came to her.

"What?" Matt must have recognized the look in her eyes.

"All Nikki needs to know is that she's not alone, and I know the perfect way to prove that."

Matt shook his head. "Becky, I don't think—"

She held up her hand to stop him. "Trust me, okay?" It would work. All Nikki needed was a reason to stay. One person can't change all that much. Nikki was always the type to step in when someone needed help, whether it was someone needing a last-minute babysitter or a volunteer at the hospital.

Well, Becky needed her to help with the Tree Festival. But that wasn't all. She knew the perfect way for Nikki to use her computer skills to help not only the festival but the town itself.

Now all she needed to do was convince her best friend of this.

###

Becky pushed open the door to the *Halfway Herald* front office and breathed in the deep scent of aspen pine. A large tree sat in the middle of the large front window but the floor around it was strewn with opened boxes of tree ornaments. Melissa Trait, owner of the paper, stood behind the counter and handed a stack of printed flyers to her daughter.

"This time, make sure you leave only one in each mailbox." Melissa frowned as her daughter plugged her ears with plugs that blared with music from her iPod. "Shay, I mean it." Her daughter stuffed the papers into her backpack and almost knocked into Becky as she rushed out the front door.

"I swear, sometime that kid will be the death of me," Melissa mumbled as she watched her daughter cross the street with her head down, barely noticing the car that slowed down for her to cross. Melissa grabbed a small shoe box from the counter and held it out.

Becky reached for it. "I can't believe how big she's gotten." Melissa had been left to raise her daughter when her husband skipped town a few years ago. Being a single mother hadn't been easy for Melissa, and Becky was so thankful she wasn't in her shoes.

"Yesterday she stuffed twenty flyers into ten mailboxes. Twenty! The phone rang all day with people complaining. All she wants to do is listen to her music and hang out with her friends." Melissa's arms folded across her ample chest as she stared out the window until her daughter was out of sight.

"She's a kid. I remember us being like that too. In fact"—Becky juggled the box she held in her hands until she was able to get her purse off her shoulder and place it on the counter—"I seem to remember helping you burn a few hundred flyers your father gave you to pass out into mailboxes a few times."

"The trouble I used to get in..." The expression on Melissa's face softened as her shoulders relaxed and she turned towards Becky. "I've been trying to decorate this tree all morning." She glanced down at the box in Becky's hands. "You can help."

Becky rolled her eyes at the command but opened the box to reveal a variety of small glass ornaments in the shape of Christmas trees in the box. "I thought you had the trees last year?"

It had become a tradition years ago, back when her mother had taken over organizing the yearly festival, to have a town ornament created in the shape of a tree. One class from the elementary school would design it and one store along Main Street would host the tree adorned with all the ornaments.

"Your mom never got around to assigning which store got the tree this year, so I figured I'd just put it up again. How's she doing, by the way?"

Becky shrugged. "You know Mom. She's giving Dr. Richard a hard time for keeping her in the hospital until the festival is over. I totally forgot she did that every year—assign the tree to a different store, I mean."

"Well, who else would do it? It's part of the festival. Which reminds me," Melissa's lips quirked, "who's going to run it this year?"

33

"Me." Becky pursed her lip. The first tree she'd pulled out of the box was the one she'd designed back in grade six. She turned the tree over and searched for her initials she'd placed on the star and smiled at the memory of how much trouble she'd gotten into that year for doing that. She smiled at the memory. The star on the top of the ornament was always to remain unadorned and was to look like the tree they used each year to top their town tree, but that year, just before her teacher had submitted the design, Becky had scribbled her initials at the tip of one of the star points.

"You?" Doubt filled her friend's tone.

She rolled her neck to get rid of a kink. "I'll need help, of course."

"Of course. Your mother and Marie Landon were the dynamic duo when it came to this festival. Between the two of them, nothing dared to go wrong. Such a shame what happened." Melissa sighed. "You know, your mother usually had the flyers all prepared by now." Melissa stepped away from the tree and reached over the old oak counter and pulled out a large scrapbook from beneath. It contained every single flyer ever printed, a practice her father had started when he began the *Halfway Herald*.

Becky rummaged through her purse and pulled out a notebook. "Flyers. Right. That's on the list."

Melissa's brows rose. "It should be at the very top of the list. Becky, you need to get those out, right and quick. I'd offer to do them but I'm up to my eyeballs in other work and Lorraine is on holidays."

Becky was surprised to hear this. Lorraine was one of those women who was always around and the type to fill in anywhere and everywhere. She'd pitch in for Sunday School classes if someone didn't show up, she'd volunteer at the community center, help the local florist with deliveries, drop by someone's home and bring a meal if they were sick...Lorraine pretty much never left town.

"Lorraine never takes a vacation. Where did she go?"

"Her daughter showed up last week and literally dragged her away. Something about a fourteen-day cruise." She sighed. "If anyone deserved a vacation, it's Lorraine. But it was last minute and left me in the lurch."

Becky bit back her smile. *This was perfect.*

"So basically, I need someone to take on the design aspect for this festival. Anything other than the flyers?"

Melissa tapped her chin with a pen. "Well, there's the ad I put in the paper, the notices that go up all over town..."

Becky leaned forward. "What about a website?"

Melissa shook her head. "Our town website hasn't been updated in...years. I know Norma has talked about having a website created for the festival but no one ever volunteered to take it on."

Becky plucked the pen out of Melissa's hand and jotted down a few notes in her book. "What if I said I knew of someone who could update this for us?"

"Do you now?" A smile grew across Melissa's face. Becky knew she was thinking of all the different ways an updated website could be used.

"I do. And just think—that spotlight you always wanted on the town's website for upcoming news and a community calendar, well, she could probably do that too." All that and more. Why, it would probably become a full-time position, keeping the town's website up and running. Halfway might be a little town stuck in the middle of nowhere but that didn't mean nothing happened around here.

"She? Who do you know that could do this? You know the council already squashed the idea of hiring an outside firm to do this. They want it to be someone local."

Becky nodded. Maintaining local resources was crucial to the town's wellbeing.

"Well, spill. Who could do this?"

Becky let out a long sigh. She knew this plan would work. It had to.

"Let's just say an old friend is back in town and she just happens to run a website design company."

Melissa wasn't just the owner of the town's only newspaper. She was also one of the busiest gossips around. Once word spread that there was someone in town will skills that could help the community...there was no way Nikki could leave.

Chapter Five

~Nikki~

After Matt left, Nikki followed him out to the porch. To do what? She didn't know. When he realized the truth, Nikki'd seen it cross his face. But he didn't say anything. He'd just stared at Ryan before turning and storming out without a word.

She'd left Ryan standing in the living room while she went to watch as Matt got in his truck and spun out of her drive. She didn't call out to him or try to explain. And even if he had stayed, there was nothing she could say to him. An apology wasn't enough, and after ten years, what was the point?

"Mom?" Ryan startled her and she broke out of her daze. Her son looked at her with his father's eyes, and just as it always did when she looked at him, she felt the flicker of sorrow. Only this time, the feeling was magnified. "Who was that?"

She reached out and brushed the hair off his forehead. "Just an old friend."

"Do I know him?"

She shook her head and forced a small smile. "No." Nikki paused. "No, you don't know him."

She knew coming home to Halfway was a risk. She knew there was a chance of Matt finding out. Or Ryan asking questions. But there hadn't been a choice. She'd had to come home. And now all she could do was finish up and leave town as quickly as possible. "Come on," she said, and grabbed Ryan's hand. "I bet Grandma had some cookies or something in the freezer."

She led Ryan back into the kitchen, and distracted him with baked goods, which she knew would work. At least for a little while. Ryan barely got any fresh baking, unless her mother had come to visit. She couldn't seem to get anything to turn out, so she stuck to store bought—it was safer that way.

With her son settled for the moment in front of the television, Nikki got to work. She only had a few days to clear up whatever details she could and then she needed to go. Especially now that Matt knew the truth, the faster she could get finished up, the better.

In the kitchen, she flipped through her mother's papers until she found the town directory, right where it'd always been kept. She dialed the number for the funeral home and leaned against the counter, giving herself a moment to close her eyes before Levi Jenkins picked up.

"Levi? It's Nicole Landon. I'm calling—"

"Nikki. I've been expecting your call. I'm so sorry about your mother. She was a fine lady." The familiar voice washed over her, soothing her frayed nerves. There was a reason Levi owned the only funeral home in town. There was something so naturally comforting about him, you couldn't help but feel better in his presence. He also had the strangest resemblance to Santa Claus, and even when Nikki was a child, she'd thought he was old enough to be her grandfather. But he was still in Halfway, and for that, Nikki was grateful.

"Thank you, Levi." She swallowed the sadness that she didn't have time for. "There's so much to do," she said. "I suppose I'll need to come by and take care of some details."

"That's not necessary, Nikki. You mother took care of everything before her passing. She said that she wanted to make it as easy for you as possible, because she wasn't sure if you'd come back to town in the event of her passing."

A flash of guilt and surprise went through her. "What?"

"I didn't ask for the details," Levi said. "After all, that's not my job. But she seemed set on taking care of the details, so it's all arranged. All I need from you is an outfit for the—"

"Okay." Nikki nodded her head, still trying to process what he'd said. "I can do that. And since there won't be a service, I'll—"

"Oh, there'll be a service."

"But, I have to—"

"Your mother wanted a service, Nikki," Levi said, firmly. "And that's what she'll get. I have her requests for music and flowers and—"

"But, I really can't stay. I don't think it will—"

"Nicole Landon. Your mother was not only a valued customer, but she was also one of my dear friends, and if she wanted a service, that is what she'll get and given the timing, I've scheduled it for Friday."

Nikki's head spun and she rubbed her eyes for a moment before looking at the calendar her mother had hanging on the wall. "Friday? But that's almost a week away." Her finger found the day. And the bold words written in the square next to it. "And the day before the Tree Festival."

"Yes," Levi said. "I think she'd like that, don't you?"

Nikki nodded despite the fact he couldn't see it. "Yes, she would. But—"

"Good. Then it's settled. I'll need the outfit whenever you can find it. I look forward to seeing you, Nikki."

She hung up the phone and stared at it for a moment before returning her gaze to the calendar. The Tree Festival? A week away. She couldn't stay in Halfway for an entire week.

Nikki gave herself one more minute to feel sorry for herself before springing into action. If her mother wanted a service, there was no way she was going to resist it. She'd been selfish enough where her mother was concerned and Lord knows her mom had sacrificed more than enough where Nikki was concerned.

She peeked in on Ryan in the living room. He seemed settled enough, watching cartoons. "I'm going to start packing," she said. He only raised his hand in recognition, but didn't move. "Ryan?" She took a few steps towards him. "Are you okay?"

Nikki perched on the arm of the sofa and tried to stroke his blond hair but he jerked away.

"I'm good."

She tried not to be hurt. It wasn't like him to pull away from her. "I know it's been hard, buddy. You know if you want to talk, you can come to me, right?"

He turned to her. "I know, Mom. I'm fine. Honestly. I'm just watching TV."

Her motherly instincts were on high alert, but she knew better than to push it. "Okay," she said after a moment. Nikki smacked her palms on her lap and pushed up from the couch. "I'll be upstairs if you need me."

She took one more look at him before she made her way up the stairs. His gaze didn't leave the screen, so she shook her head and went up to her mother's room.

. . .

Her mother's room looked exactly the way Nikki remembered it. As if she hadn't changed a thing since she'd been a child. The smell of her mom's vanilla-scented perfume hung in the air and for a moment, Nikki closed her eyes and let the familiar scent wash over her. Tears burned her eyes and she swiped at them.

"No," she said aloud. "I can't do this now." She wouldn't let herself fall apart. Not when there was so much to do. She couldn't.

The wall on the far side of the room caught Nikki's attention. That was different from the last time she'd been home. She moved closer to look at what was a photo wall dedicated to Ryan. Pictures from when he was a baby, all the way up to the most recent shot Nikki had mailed of Ryan on his bike, covered in mud after getting caught out in a storm. Each picture was framed and hung neatly.

She couldn't hold the tears back and her heart broke at the thought of her mom having to hide her only grandson away from her friends in such a way. Nikki ran her fingers down the frames, one at a time, pausing at a photo of Ryan and his grandma that she herself had taken the last time she'd come to visit.

"Oh, Mom. I'm so sorry." She took the photo off the wall and hugged it to her chest.

Never once had her mom complained or protested about Nikki's choice to keep Ryan a secret. Even when Nikki told her the truth about who Ryan's father was. But not once had Nikki ever considered how hard keeping the secret would have been for her mom. She'd been incredibly selfish. She knew that. She'd always known that. But she'd also done it for a reason. For Becky. The truth would destroy her best friend.

And they were best friends. Despite Nikki's poor choices and everything that had come after. A friend of the heart didn't just go away because there was distance between you. Becky couldn't know the truth.

But Matt knew.

Nikki shook her head, trying to block the reality she needed to face.

Putting the photo down, she sniffed and wiped her eyes with the back of her hand. She needed to pull herself together. Without another look at the picture wall, Nikki went to the closet and selected a beautiful blue skirt and jacket set. It would be a lovely color for her mom. And it wasn't black, which her mother would have hated.

She went to the jewelry box on the dresser to choose some jewelry when a voice startled her.

"Who was that man?"

Nikki jumped and then froze when Ryan's words sank in. Something in the way he asked got her attention.

She turned slowly and looked at him. "I told you," she said. "He's just an old friend."

"I feel like I know him." Ryan didn't look at her when he spoke. Instead, he walked to the far side of the room and stared at the wall of pictures.

She watched him as he looked at each of the pictures, but she didn't say anything. She waited until he turned to her and spoke again. "I do know him," he said. "Don't I?"

She didn't make it a practice to lie to her son. In fact, Nikki had always believed it was best to be as honest with Ryan as possible. Except for one area. In that, she couldn't tell him the truth. She'd always told Ryan his dad was from her town but had moved away and they'd lost touch. How could she tell him the truth about who his father was and then explain why he couldn't see him? It wasn't an option. It never had been. Until now.

Nikki took a breath and assessed her son, so much like his father it couldn't be denied for much longer. "Ryan." She shook her head. "I don't think—"

"Why won't you tell me the truth?" The anger behind his words startled her and she took a step back. "I know that I know him, Mom. And I know that you're lying to me."

"Ryan." She took a step towards him, wanting to close the gap between them. They'd always been so close. A team. But in only a few days, she could feel the distance between them. It was Halfway. It was this place. Being home. The secrets. The lies. "I need you to understand, buddy." She reached out to touch him, but he pulled away.

"I'm not a kid anymore, Mom."

She wanted to smile. He was still a kid. After all, he was only ten. And that still meant he was a kid, didn't it? She opened her mouth, but couldn't find the words to tell him what she knew he wanted to hear.

His eyes traveled back to the wall and Nikki watched while his focus changed and he fell apart. "I miss her, Mom." Ryan's head fell and his shoulders started to shake with the tears she knew he had to have been holding in.

In one step, she was at his side, and had her arms wrapped around him. There were still so many questions she didn't know how to answer. But comfort was one thing she could give.

"I know, Ryan," Nikki said as she rubbed his back. "I miss her, too. So much."

She let him cry for a few minutes, because sometimes that's what needed to be done. And when his sobs began to subside, she pulled away and wiped his tears with her thumb. "It's not fair that we had to lose her," she said. "But you have to know that Grandma loved you more than anything else in the world. You know that, right?"

He nodded.

Nikki reached past him to the bed and picked up the photo she'd dropped their earlier. "In fact," she said. "Why don't we take this picture downstairs and put it on the mantel while we're here? Would you like that?"

Ryan nodded and wiped his nose with the back of his arm.

"I think Grandma would have liked that, too. Very much."

Chapter Six

~Becky~

Becky pulled up in front of Nikki's mother's front walkway and looked out her window. She knew coming unannounced was a risky move to make, but she needed to have a plan in place for the festival before she headed over to the hospital to see her mother. This was her chance to prove to Norma that...that what? That she was better than the typical wife who stayed home and cooked all day? Not once had her mother acknowledged what Becky had accomplished in her life. Instead, all she heard about was how she threw her dreams away for love. It was almost as if having her own cookbook published was beneath her.

No matter what she did, it always felt like she could never earn her mother's approval. Didn't mean she wouldn't keep trying, though.

Her phone vibrated in the cup holder with a text from Matt. *Heading to north corner in back field. Will be late.*

That was odd. There was nothing back there. That back field was being left alone for another year, to give the ground some rest before they planted more trees. He should be in their southern fields, marking the trees for customers to cut down. They only had a week left before the gates opened for the season.

Her fingers tapped the phone. *Something wrong?* Her mind raced with possible scenarios of what would take him back there. There was a neighboring farm off that lot, but they'd never had issues in the past.

Just checking out the old cabin. See you for dinner.

Becky shook her head at his text. That old cabin needed to be torn down but Matt wouldn't hear of it. His great-grandfather had built that cabin, the original homestead, back in the day. Matt's father had left it alone, using it as an old camping site for the local Boy Scout group in Halfway. A few years ago, Matt had put a stop to that as the cabin fell apart and was unsafe. He'd started talking about fixing it up again and making it livable. They could rent it out to groups or campers, adding another source of income. But that was a project for the spring, not a week before the tree-cutting season was to start.

She gathered her purse, stuffing her phone inside, and opened her door. She'd made a casserole for Nikki to reheat for dinner and had grabbed an apple pie from Sweet 'n Savory, the local bakery. She would have made it herself, but without the sugar...it wouldn't have been worth it.

As she walked up the front walkway, Nikki met her on the porch with a guarded look on her face.

"Since you won't come to my house for dinner, I brought dinner to you." Becky held out the casserole dish and waited for the deer-in-headlights look to fade from Nikki's gaze.

"You didn't have to do that." Nikki stared at the dish but didn't reach for it.

"I know. But it beats the frozen pizza you probably would have eaten, right?" She set the casserole dish down on the wicker table by the front door when it became evident that Nikki wasn't going to take it and pushed her hands deep into her jacket pockets.

From the way Nikki stood guard in front of the front door, it was a good thing the weather had warmed up. Becky zipped up her jacket and then sat down on the porch swing.

"Remember when we used to sit out here for hours during the summer? We'd daydream about our futures and how we were going to change the world?"

"That's not quite how I remember it."

Becky hid her smile as her friend finally moved away from the door and sat down in the chair opposite her.

"Really?"

"We'd sit out here for hours only because you were too scared to book it home and face the wrath of your mother once she caught wind of your shenanigans."

Becky's brow rose. "Shenanigans? Really, Nik? You sound just like both our mothers combined right there."

Nikki shrugged. "You were always getting into some sort of trouble."

Becky shook her head as she leaned back. "And yet I was never alone." She winked and was pleased to see a smile grace her friend's face. Between the two of them, Becky had been the more adventurous type but Nikki always tagged along for the ride.

"We had a lot of fun, didn't we?" The smile left Nikki's face as she gazed into the front window of her mother's home.

"We did. It's too bad it had to end, especially the way it did."

An uncomfortable silence grew between them. Becky had hoped maybe Nikki would apologize and attempt to give some sort of explanation of why she left...but she didn't. In fact, she just sat there, refusing to even look at her.

Becky sighed. *Fine then.* "Do you need help?" The front room held the boxes Matt had brought by earlier.

Nikki shook her head. "I'm good. But thank you."

Becky caught the way her hands gripped the edge of the seat. "Good," she said, forcing a lighthearted tone to her voice. "'Cause I need your help and I'll do anything, even bribe you with meals, if that's what it will take."

There was a look in Nikki's eyes, as if she were about to bolt. Becky leaned forward and took a deep breath. She had no idea what was going on, but she needed to figure out a way to keep Nikki seated and hopefully get her talking.

"Listen, I know now probably isn't the best timing, but I could really use your help with this festival."

Nikki snorted. "You do realize how long it's been since I was even at the festival, right?"

"I know, I know. But just hear me out." She pulled out her notepad. "The festival is one week away and I just found out today that I need to create a flyer and design an ad for the town paper. Except, I have no idea how to do any of that."

The skeptical look on Nikki's face told her what she thought of that.

"I bake and cook. That's as far as my talents go. But you... you do websites, so you must be good at graphics, right? We don't need anything fancy. And here," she pulled out samples she'd gotten from Melissa earlier, "this is all my mother did last year for the paper. And then this was the flyer." She unfolded the copy Melissa had made for her and spread it out for Nikki to see.

"As easy as those look, I really don't think I'll have the time. I want to put this house up on the market as soon as possible and Mom's funeral is on Friday."

Becky straightened. "Friday?" The timing couldn't be more perfect. "That's the day before the festival."

"Yeah. Mom had it all planned out, I guess, and Levi thought it would be a nice touch."

"Leave it to Levi. You know he had a crush on her, right?"

"He did not!" Nikki's eyes grew round moments before she started to chuckle. "She never said a word."

"I doubt she knew. I overheard Norma tease him a few years ago about it."

Nikki's grip on the chair relaxed. "Could you imagine having Santa as a stepfather?"

"The kids love him, that's for sure. I'm not sure what this town will do when he's not around to put on the red suit. You should see him in action these past few years. Do you remember Elizabeth Preening? She married Derek Banner a year after I married Matt. Anyways, she picked up photography as a hobby and it turns out she's pretty good at it. She does it for a living now—has her own shop just off the main street and takes all the Santa photos with the kids now."

There was nothing Becky had loved more, in the past, than to watch those little kids see Santa up close and have their picture taken with him. The expression of wonder on their faces...and the smile on Levi's. She'd once overheard him say to her mother that there was nothing more worthwhile to him than to see someone smile at him with joy rather than with sorrow.

"Hopefully he'll be around long enough for you to get your babies' pictures taken." Nikki glanced away from her and stared down at the porch floor. "I thought you would have had a few of your own by now."

Becky sighed. "So did I." She blinked past the tears that gathered in her eyes.

Sitting there, with Nikki again, brought back so many memories. Despite the distance between them, there was still a bond. She thought back to all the times when she'd wished Nikki were with her, to help her get through all the hard times. She hadn't really realized just how much she missed not having her there.

"One day, though, right?" There was a desperate sound of hope in Nikki's voice. Almost as if she knew that something was wrong.

Becky shook her head. "I don't think so. My body doesn't seem to like the idea of having children, no matter how many times we've tried. I've had a few...miscarriages. Matt would like to adopt one day." Becky sucked in a deep breath. "We'll see. He'd make a wonderful father and there's nothing he wants more in life than to be a dad."

And yet, the thought of adopting, as wonderful as it was, made her feel like she'd failed in some way. Like she wasn't good enough to be a mother. Maybe the miscarriages were her body's way of telling her that.

"I'm so sorry." Nikki's voice dropped into almost a whisper. "I had no idea. My mom never said anything."

"Probably because she didn't know." That was one thing her and Matt did agree upon: keeping her miscarriages a secret. They didn't want the pitying looks from everyone. Norma knew about the first two losses, but that was it. After that, they'd agreed to wait until she'd passed the three-month mark before they told anyone.

Nikki's face had completely drained of color, almost to the point where Becky thought she'd pass out. "What's wrong? Are you okay?"

Nikki held up her hand, stopping Becky as she rose from her chair. "I'm fine. I'm fine. I just...I never knew. I just assumed you were waiting. You'd always said you wanted to focus on a career before kids, so I just thought..."

Becky's shoulder muscles tightened. "Things change. I'd also wanted to be an archeologist and never thought children would fit into my lifestyle. Now I'm a tree farmer's wife, living in a house with empty bedrooms that should be full of childish laughter." She frowned. "Fate has a funny way of playing tricks on a person."

A sudden breeze blew through the porch and Becky shivered. When Nikki glanced down at her watch, Becky got the impression that it was time to leave.

"Listen, no matter what happened between us, I could really use your help right about now. Please?" Nikki was her only option at this point. Time was running out.

"Nothing happened between us. Life just got in the way," Nikki whispered. She reached for the flyer Becky had set down on the table between them. "Sure, I can help. This won't take me long and will give me a break from packing. Why don't I work on it tonight and forward it to Melissa by morning? That should give her enough time to do whatever she needs to do with it, right?"

A wave of relief swept over Becky at Nikki's words.

"Thank you. Seriously, you are my lifesaver. And I was serious about the casseroles. Consider your meals taken care of while you do what needs to be done." Becky stood and grabbed her purse. She'd bake the woman so many casseroles she wouldn't know what hit her, if that's what it took.

"I, ah...you don't need to do that. Seriously."

Becky shrugged. "Then come over for dinners. There's no need to be eating alone, especially in a house full of memories." She leaned forward and gave her old friend a quick hug. "Whatever happened in the past, I've missed you, Nikki, and I want my friend back."

She waited for Nikki to say something, anything, but she

didn't. Once again, at the subject of their past, there was only silence.

She tried really hard to not let it bother her as she headed back down towards her vehicle, but it did.

It really, really did.

Chapter Seven

~Nikki~

Nikki poured herself another cup of coffee and watched the sunrise out the window. The night before, she'd managed to get a lot more packed than she thought she would. Of course, after Becky's surprise visit, she'd been spooled up. And there really was no chance of doing anything else for the rest of the day besides pack. And, as it turned out, most of the night, because there was no way she could sleep. She was even able to quickly do up the flyers for the festival and send them off to Melissa.

The last thing she'd expected after Matt's surprise visit and subsequent discovery was for Becky to show up on her porch. She'd expected her old friend would be home with her husband, hearing all about the illegitimate child he hadn't known he had and the terrible person Nikki was for keeping it from all of them.

Nikki had definitely expected a visit from Becky, all right. She just hadn't expected the one she got. Clearly, Matt hadn't told her anything about Ryan. If he had, a very different Becky would have shown up. Of that, she had no doubt. But why hadn't he told his wife about Ryan? Why hadn't he asked her more questions? And if he had, would she have answered them?

She turned away from the window and sipped at her coffee. So many questions. And there really weren't any answers. Not any that she'd want to hear, anyway. There was no point dwelling on it. Matt knew about Ryan; she couldn't change that. And if she was forced to be honest with herself, she wasn't sure whether she wanted to. Keeping the secret for ten years had been exhausting. Clearly, it had taken a toll on her mother as well. She didn't want to admit it, even to herself, but ever since Matt's visit the day before, a weight had definitely been lifted.

The sound of footsteps on the floor above reminded her that there was still someone who didn't know the truth. She'd have to tell Ryan about his dad. Especially because it was clear he already suspected something. Ryan was a smart kid. She couldn't hide forever.

"Hey, Mom."

She turned and her mood instantly shifted when she saw her son, freshly showered and dressed for the day, standing in front of her.

"Good morning," she said, moving to kiss him on the head. He dodged the kiss, and she pretended not to be bothered by it. "What's gotten into you this morning?"

She watched while Ryan moved to the cupboard and pulled out a coffee cup. "What do you mean?"

"I mean," she said slowly, not taking her eyes off him. "It's not like you to shower and get dressed without a little nagging. What's up?"

He took the pot and poured himself a cup of coffee and although Nikki's eyes widened in surprise, she still didn't say anything.

"I thought I'd help out a bit more today," he said and raised the cup to his lips. Nikki watched and waited. "Like I said, I'm not a kid anymore."

"No," she said. "You're not."

Ryan took a sip of the coffee and Nikki forced herself not to laugh when his face wrinkled up in response. She raised her own mug to hide her smile.

"How can you drink that stuff?" Ryan asked when he recovered. "It's terrible."

"You get used to it." Nikki moved to the refrigerator, pulled out the jug of orange juice and poured him a glass. He took it readily and gulped it down. "Why did you want to drink coffee anyway?"

Ryan wiped his face with the sleeve of his shirt and Nikki forced herself not to say anything about it. "I wanted to show you that I'm not a kid anymore. I'm ten now. That's practically a teenager and a teenager is practically grown up."

Nikki raised her eyebrows. "You think so, do you?"

"Mom. I'm serious." He was trying so hard to make his point, Nikki relented.

"Okay," she said. "I know you're growing up. But you're not grown up yet. So lay off the coffee, okay?"

"Not a problem."

She grabbed him a bowl and poured him some cereal before sitting across from him at the table. A feeling of nostalgia washed over her as she remembered so many similar mornings where she'd sat with her own mother, just the way they were.

"Are you sad?" Ryan asked through a mouth full of cereal.

Nikki wiped her face and the tears she hadn't meant to cry. "I was just thinking of Grandma," she said. "But I'm okay now."

"Are we going to her funeral? Declan, in my class, he went to his grandpa's funeral last year. He said lots of people cried and told stories about his grandpa. And they played songs and stuff. Are they going to do that for Grandma?"

"They are."

"And we're gonna go?"

"I don't know, Ryan. I think..." Her voice drifted off as she assessed her son. Her mother had wanted a funeral. Levi told her as much. But there was no way they could go, even if Levi did insist on going through with it. Everyone would see Ryan. They'd know. He'd know. Panic pricked at the back of her neck and she squeezed her mug a little tighter.

But Matt already knew. He knew.

"Mom?" Ryan dropped his spoon with a clatter in the bowl.

Nikki looked up with a start.

"So are we going?"

Nikki let out a breath. "Would you like that?" she asked. "Or would it make you sad?"

He looked down into his bowl. "I'm sad anyway." His small voice cracked. Nikki's heart broke a bit more. "But I think we should go. Grandma would want us to go."

He was right. There was nothing her mother would have wanted more than for Nikki to be in Halfway with her son. After everything, it was the least she could do for her mom. She nodded.

"You're right. She would have wanted it very much."

"So we'll go?"

"We'll go." Nikki forced a smile she didn't feel. She'd work out the details later. She'd have to.

###

She didn't like the idea of taking Ryan out of the house and into town. Despite what they may have decided on, she still wasn't ready to introduce him to the general population of Halfway.

The funeral was still days away and surely Matt would have said something to Becky by then.

She couldn't be the one to tell her about Ryan. Especially not after hearing that they weren't able to have children of their own. When Becky had shared that with her the day before, it was all Nikki could do to continue sitting there on the porch with her. Becky wanted to forgive her for running away from their friendship. But how could she sit there and pretend she hadn't betrayed her in the worst way possible, all the while knowing that she had the one thing her friend would never have: Matt's child?

It was unthinkable. And she hated herself more the longer she stayed in the small town. The day after the funeral, they'd be gone. Nikki looked in the rearview mirror at her son.

But for now, she had details to take care of and she couldn't leave Ryan in a strange house with no one to watch him. There was no getting around it. She had to risk it.

"Where's your tablet? I thought you were going to bring it."

"The battery was dead," Ryan said. "I can come in with you. I want to see."

"It's a funeral home, buddy. Not a toy store." She tried to keep her voice light. "I just need to drop Grandma's clothes off and then we'll go."

"I want to see."

"There's nothing to see."

"Mom, I'm not going to break anything."

"I know. It'll just be faster if I run in, okay?"

"I'm not slow."

"Ryan," she snapped. "That's enough. Just wait in the car, okay?" They'd pulled up to Levi's and she put the car in park before looking in the mirror again. Ryan was biting his lip, trying not to cry.

She sighed. Just because she was losing control of everything did not mean she had to lose it on him. "Come on," she said with a sigh. "Let's go."

By the time Nikki grabbed her mother's clothes out of the back, Ryan was already waiting on the sidewalk, with a smile on his face.

"It's really not that exciting," she mumbled as she led the way up the walk.

She pushed the door open, and the gentle ring of a bell announced their arrival. Levi operated his funeral home out of an old historical house on Main Street. He had a small apartment on the upper floor where he lived, and she could hear him shuffling around above her.

"I'll be right there," he called.

"Don't touch anything," Nikki whispered to Ryan, who was already moving around the room, looking at the few display coffins and silk flower arrangements.

She didn't have time to say anything else, because Levi appeared in the doorway.

"Nikki Landon. Look at you." He held out his arms. She put the package she was holding down on a nearby table and accepted his embrace. It felt good to be hugged by someone she'd known her whole life and Nikki almost let herself give in to her grief.

"Levi," she said when she stepped back. "You look the same as always. You haven't changed a bit."

"Neither have you," he said in his familiar rumbling voice. "You're still as beautiful as the last time I saw you."

Nikki blushed. "Levi, you old flirt. I'm ten years older and it shows."

"You're still a looker," he said. "Just like your mama was."

At the mention of her mother, Levi's eyes welled up with tears, but he blinked them away before she could say anything. A noise from the corner of the room caught their attention, and

Nikki whipped around to see Ryan trying to catch a flower display he'd knocked over.

"Oh, Ryan." She darted over and grabbed the vase before it could crash to the ground. "I told you to be careful."

"No trouble," Levi said, coming up behind them. "And who's this?"

Nikki straightened the vase and stood behind Ryan. It was the moment she'd dreaded since returning to Halfway. But there was no other option. She took a deep breath. "Levi, this is my son, Ryan."

Like a little man, Ryan shot his hand out and said, "It's nice to meet you, sir."

Nikki smiled and if the situation would have been any different, she would have been able to appreciate her son's impeccable manners.

Levi shook Ryan's hand, and Nikki watched the old man's face transform as he looked first to the little boy and then to Nikki. And back. "It's nice to meet you," he said to Ryan. To Nikki, he added, "Your mother didn't say anything about a grandson."

Nikki saw the hurt on his face and she immediately regretted introducing Ryan to him in such a way. Levi and her mother were friends. Hadn't Becky said she thought he had a crush on her mom? Of course he'd be hurt if he discovered the woman he cared about had kept such a secret from him. How could she be so careless?

"Ryan, do you see those cards over there?" Nikki pointed to a shelf on the other side of the room. "Could you go pick out a design that we can use for Grandma's program?"

He nodded and, happy to have a task, headed off to take care of it. As soon as he was out of earshot, Nikki turned to Levi and whispered, "It's not that she didn't want to tell you. It's my fault."

His face was muddled with confusion.

"I asked her not to say anything to anyone in town about Ryan," Nikki tried to explain. "As you know, this is the first time we've been to visit. And, well, I just didn't want anyone to know my business, I guess."

"You didn't want your friends to know you had a son?" Levi pulled on his beard and stared intently at Ryan.

"It's complicated, Levi. I can't really get into it right now."

"Mom," Ryan called. He turned in their direction, holding up a card. "I found one I think Grandma would've liked. It has lilacs on it. She liked those the best."

Next to her, she heard Levi take a sharp breath. And she knew he'd seen the resemblance and figured it out. There was no way it could be missed.

Emotion flooded Nikki, but it wasn't her who answered Ryan.

"Yes," Levi said. He walked to Ryan and squatted so he was at the same height. "You're absolutely right. Lilacs were her favorite. I think it's a perfect choice."

When he stood and returned to Nikki, the card in his hand, he didn't say any more about the subject. He simply nodded, and she knew he understood, even if he didn't agree.

###

When they got back in the car, Nikki wasn't ready to go back to the house. Nothing but memories and boxes were waiting for her there. Feeling bolder after their visit with Levi, she spun around in her seat. "What do you think about stopping by Grounds and getting one of those hot chocolates I told you about?"

"Can we?" Ryan's face lit up the way she knew it would. He wasn't going to turn down a treat. "Really?"

"Really."

She faced front and turned the key in the ignition. There was no point hiding. Matt knew the truth, and now so did Levi. It was only a matter of time before word got out. And when it did, she would handle it. But she was done hiding.

Nikki steered the car down the icy streets towards Grounds and pulled up in front. Ryan bounded from the car before she had a chance to grab her purse and get her door open. She laughed as she joined him on the sidewalk.

"If I didn't know better, I'd think you'd never had a hot chocolate before the way you're acting."

Ryan rubbed his stomach. "I love it."

"Are you sure you don't want a coffee?" she teased.

He blushed, one of the few traits he'd inherited from her, and shook his head. "I think I'm done with coffee for a while."

"Good." Nikki put her hand on his shoulder, noting how tall he was getting and spun him around to face the shop. But instead of taking a step down the sidewalk, she froze.

"Matt."

"Nikki." He nodded at her but she didn't miss the way his gaze lingered on her son. Their son. "Ryan? It's...it's nice to see you both." He stumbled over his words and looked up at her again. His eyes were full of emotions Nikki couldn't decipher, and it pained her to realize there once was a time when she would have known exactly what he was feeling.

"We were just about to get a hot chocolate," Nikki said.

"Do you want one?" Ryan blurted out the question and both Nikki and Matt stared at him.

"No," Matt said after a moment, and then added, "Not this time."

"Next time then," Ryan said confidently. He looked up at Nikki. "Ready?"

Nikki's head spun with the poignancy of the situation. But she needed to be strong. There wasn't another choice. She reached into her purse and handed Ryan a twenty. "You know what, buddy? Since you're so grown up and all, why don't you go place the order? I need to talk to Matt about something."

He didn't need to be asked twice. Ryan, clearly pumped about the opportunity to show his maturity, grabbed the money and headed into the store. Before he slipped inside, he turned and said, "Maybe we'll see you again, Matt?"

"Yeah." Matt nodded. "I think so."

Satisfied, Ryan went inside to complete his task.

"What are you thinking?" Matt asked the moment he was gone. "You can't bring him here."

As if she'd been slapped, Nikki stepped back. Whatever she'd expected, she didn't expect that response from Matt. "Bring him to Grounds? Are you kidding me?"

"Nikki, people will see him. And he looks...he looks...well, he looks just like me," he finished. "What are people going to think?"

Anger flared through her. For all the mistakes she'd made, her first priority had always been Ryan. And that hadn't changed. She stepped up and straightened her shoulders. "They're going to think the same thing you did when you saw him. That he's your son."

"But, I—"

"And they'll be right," Nikki said, not backing down. "He's your son, Matt. And I'm sorry I didn't tell you. I have made mistakes. I'll admit that. And we can talk about that. You deserve that from me, I know that. But this isn't the time or the place for that conversation."

"Nikki." He scrubbed a hand over his face. "This is crazy. I don't know what to do here."

"You were right when you said people were going to notice the resemblance, Matt. And I'm not going to hide him. He's my child and I'm done with secrets." She pulled her purse higher on her shoulder. "So may I suggest that before your wife makes the same connection, you be the one to tell her that you have a child? He's ten and his name is Ryan."

Chapter Eight

~Becky~

Becky's fingers tapped on the counter as she checked off things from the new to-do list Norma had given her at the hospital earlier. Instead of the praise over what she had completed, she'd had a long list of items thrust at her and then given a stern lecture on how certain things needed to be done.

Like normal. Why would she have expected anything different?

Just once, she'd like her mother to tell her what a great job she was doing. Because she was. Everything was on schedule, no issues had popped up last minute, and everyone was ready for this festival to begin. It helped that everyone knew Norma was in the hospital so they all stepped up to ensure things ran smoothly, just like a small town would. That was one of the benefits of living in a town like Halfway.

She tried really hard not to look at the clock or her phone. A plate of cold spaghetti and meatballs sat at the kitchen table for Matt for whenever he decided to come home. Last night, she'd gone to bed alone and she'd woken up the same way. She had a feeling Matt had slept in the spare bedroom rather than wake her up when he climbed into bed. He often did that when he was out in the fields late and it was something she'd just gotten used to over the years.

What she wasn't used to was his silence. Sure, he might have slept in a separate bed, but he always left her a note on the counter for her to find or sent her texts throughout the day. She'd sent him a few but when he didn't respond by noon, she figured he was busy.

She didn't figure that anymore. Something was wrong. She knew it.

Sure, they were behind on some bills, but they weren't the only ones. And yes, having her mom in the hospital added a bit more stress than normal at this time of the year, but again, that was something they could deal with. Or normally would deal with together.

They were known as a power couple in town. The high school sweethearts. The ones who would make it through, no matter what. A lot of their friends were either divorced or separated or just trying to find a way to make it through another day while raising a family.

But not her and Matt. Their love was just as strong as it had been when they started dating in high school. Stronger even. They'd weathered their own storms but made it through and Becky had no doubt no matter what came their way, they'd be just fine.

Just fine. So why did the thought feel like a heavy burden?

A light outside caught her attention and she turned to watch the headlights from Matt's truck illuminate the driveway.

The tight vice-like grip around her heart disappeared now that he was home. She inhaled, breathing in the crisp air and then slowly exhaled.

On her way to the door, she flipped the switch on the coffee maker. By the time he got in and was settled, the coffee would be brewed. She looked forward to a quiet night with him; it had been a while since they'd had one and it would probably be their last night with both of them at home until Christmas Day.

She stood and watched as he crossed the driveway towards her. His arms were laced behind him so she held the screen open for him and tried to peek over his shoulder to see what he was carrying.

"I'm sorry," he said as he held a bouquet of flowers in one hand and a bottle of red wine in his other.

Becky searched his gaze. He had nothing to apologize for, but there was something in his look, something that had her swallow back her words. She nodded as she took the bouquet and headed towards the kitchen.

She busied herself with finding a vase and filling it with the flowers. She added a teaspoon of sugar to the water before cutting the stems on an angle and placing them inside the vase. Matt sat at the counter and watched her. It was a bit disconcerting.

"Is everything almost ready?" She figured his day must have been spent getting the tree lot organized.

"Just about. The fences went up today and Bob is organizing a schedule. We'll wait as long as we can before we start cutting down the trees." The trees they sent down South or up to Canada were always cut earlier in the season, but the local trees were saved for last. "What smells so good?" Matt rubbed at his face.

Becky poured coffee into his mug and set it in front of him. "Cinnamon buns. I wasn't sure if you'd be hungry or not." She pointed towards the plate of spaghetti on the table.

"I totally forgot to send you a text. Bob asked me to join him at the pub for a burger and we went over the schedule. I'm sorry."

"I'd almost think you were trying to avoid me." She stared at him, hands on her hips. "You're not, are you?"

When Matt didn't respond, Becky's hand fisted together before she went to grab the dinner she'd left for Matt and cover it with wrap before placing it in the fridge.

"I'm going to go have a shower," Matt muttered before he drank the last of his coffee and stood.

"Excuse me?"

"I won't be long."

Becky shook her head. "That's not the point. I haven't seen you for two days but the minute you're home, it seems like you're trying to find ways to not be around me."

Matt pulled her into his arms and held her tightly. "I'm not avoiding you, I promise."

She pushed him away as she wrinkled her nose. "Then go have your shower. There's nothing worse than sharing my cinnamon buns with a stinky man." She attempted to smile while he gave her a searching look before he placed a small kiss on her cheek and left the room.

Becky puttered around the kitchen, tidying it up while responding to emails on her phone regarding the festival. There were so many last-minute things to consider, like making sure the bulbs in the lights that strung around the tree all worked. She'd have to dig them out of her mother's garage and go through them tomorrow.

She tried really hard not to think about the fact her husband was obviously avoiding her. In the past, anytime he stayed in town for something to eat, he always asked her to join him. This was the first, that she knew of, where she hadn't been welcomed. It hurt.

Why was her husband pulling away so suddenly? Everything had been fine between them until yesterday.

Just as she heard the water turn off from the upstairs bathroom, the oven dinged to let her know her pastry was done. She pulled the tray out of the oven and set it on a wire rack to cool before she headed into her office for her camera. She liked to take various images of her baked goods, sometimes even taking pictures of the whole process. But tonight she just wanted an image of the golden brown crust before the cream cheese icing went on to post on the various social websites she visited.

She listened for the thud of Matt's footsteps on the stairs before she headed into the kitchen with her camera. Her grip was tight and she fumbled with the lens as she attempted to find the right light for the shot. Her nerves were on end and there was a heaviness to the room when he sat at the table.

She went to reach for her coffee cup but bypassed it when she caught sight of the bottle of wine he'd brought home. She poured some through an aerator into her glass and while it sat, she prepared two cinnamon buns. She needed to keep her hands busy while Matt just sat there, watching her with a look on his face like his world was about to end.

"Mom will be out of the hospital soon," she said to break the silence.

"Is she coming to stay with us, like we planned, or back to her place?"

"Her place. You know how she is." Stubborn, that's what her mother was. "She's already got home care set up to help her, too." Which was ridiculous because Becky planned to be there as much as she could to help out.

"Have you talked to Nikki?" Matt blurted.

"Not since yesterday. I stopped by to chat and talk about the festival. I thought...well, I thought we'd be able to pick up where we left off, but I guess she just needs a bit more time."

"Did you...did you meet her son?"

Becky had the wine glass raised to her lips and paused. *Her son?*

"No..." But it would explain why she'd been so focused on looking through the window and why she'd never been invited into the house. *A son?* Nikki had a child. The thought crushed her. "Did you?"

Matt nodded.

"How old is he? A baby?" Her voice squeaked.

He shook his head.

"I can't believe she has a child. She never said anything. Mom never said anything. How could I not know this?"

"Maybe your mom didn't know."

Becky snorted. "As if. Mom knows everything. And it's not like Marie would have kept this from her. They were practically sisters."

"She might have had her reasons for keeping the secret."

"Why didn't she say anything to me? We even talked about having kids," Becky muttered to herself as she took a sip of her wine.

"How old is he? What's his name? How did you meet him?" Becky barraged her husband with questions. It wasn't fair that he knew the answers before she did. Nikki had been her best friend. Not his. Well, technically they had all been close, but still, it wasn't fair.

"Ryan. His name is Ryan. And I," he cleared his throat, "I don't think Nikki meant for me to see him."

"When? Today?"

Matt had a telltale sign when he was upset. A little spot in his cheek became indented whenever he ground his teeth together.

"The other day."

Her brow rose. "You've known she had a child for days now and you're just telling me?"

Why? It didn't make sense. Was that why she'd canceled dinner for the other night? Because she hadn't wanted them to meet her son? Why the secrecy?

"How old is he?"

"Ten."

Her best friend had a ten-year-old son that no one in Halfway had known about.

"Oh my..." That's when it hit her. "Someone from here must be the father. That's why she left like she did and has never come back."

At the stricken look on Matt's face, she knew she'd guessed correctly. "Do you know who?"

Becky tried to think back. She'd gone to prom with Parker and then left shortly after.

"I can't believe she would have kept something like that a secret from me." For years, she'd wondered why Nikki had run off the way she did. She couldn't have imagined what Nikki had gone through, finding out she was pregnant at such a young age. But why did she leave? Hadn't she known that she would have been supported, that Becky would have stood by her, no matter what?

And why keep it a secret for ten years? Did the father even know? Was that why she never came back, because she didn't want him to know? Or did she tell him and he didn't want the baby? Was that why she'd left?

"Whatever you're thinking, stop." Matt reached for her hand and grabbed hold. "There's something you need to know."

"Like what?" She stilled and she could feel her heart slow down until the sound of it thudded in her ears.

"I love you—you know that, right?" Matt tightened his grip.

"Of course. I love you, too."

"It's always been you. There's never been anyone else in my life. Never. From the moment I first saw you, I knew you would be mine."

Becky nodded. She knew that. She'd always known that. There had never been anyone else for her either. They'd started out as best friends and remained that way throughout everything. Matt had been her first love, her first kiss, and her first lover.

Just as she'd been his.

"But there was that time when we'd broken up, just before finals and school ended. Remember?"

Remember? How could she forget? That had been the worst month of her life. Matt's dad had his first stroke and instead of letting Becky be there for him, Matt had pushed her away. He'd told her that his life would be forever tethered to Halfway and Becky deserved more, deserved to see the world, like she'd always dreamed about. So he broke up with her. She'd been heartbroken and locked herself in her room for weeks. She wouldn't even see Nikki, not at first. But then when she'd been ready and realized that she needed to fight for her and Matt, Nikki hadn't wanted to see her. She'd become distant for a while. Until...until she and Matt had gotten back together.

"I made a mistake. It was one time and I'll forever regret it, but..."

Becky's knees buckled from beneath her and she gripped the counter for support. She'd wrenched her hand out from under her husband's, not wanting his touch.

The room spun around her and she barely heard the words Matt said. She saw his mouth move, but everything was garbled.

It didn't matter, though. "Don't say it," she pleaded. Her voice had dulled and when he reached out towards her, she stepped back. "No, don't. Please, just don't."

He was the father. Matt. Her husband.

"Becky..." His voice broke and she saw the torment in his eyes but it didn't matter to her, not right then.

"No. I don't want to hear it. Please..." *If he said the words, then they'd be true, right?* Maybe she was exaggerating. Maybe it wasn't this at all—maybe...

"How? How could you and not tell me? Why wouldn't you tell me? How could you lie about something like this?" Her stomach twisted at the thought of Matt and Nikki together, all those years ago. How could she not have known?

"I didn't know. Please, I need you to believe me." His voice cracked. "I didn't know."

Becky's eyes stung. "Didn't know? How could you not? You slept with her!" Her voice rose until she was yelling. "You slept with my best friend and never told me. How could you?"

"I'm sorry," he whispered. "I'm so sorry."

She backed away from him, not wanting to be near him, not wanting to see his face, to see the emotions written so plainly for anyone to see.

She wasn't sure what hurt her the most: the fact that he'd betrayed her or that the realization that he was a father of a child who wasn't hers.

Chapter Nine

~Nikki~

After more or less announcing Ryan to the town of Halfway, Nikki expected to feel exhausted or anxious. Instead, she returned to her childhood home feeling better than she had in a long time. As if a weight had been lifted off her, a very heavy weight of lies and secrets. It was freeing that Matt finally knew the truth. But at the same time, it was terrifying.

Clearly Matt hadn't told Becky about her son. *Their son,* she mentally corrected herself. But he would soon. She was sure of that now. And when he did, Nikki had a feeling she wasn't going to be feeling such a sense of relief anymore. So for the moment, she was going to enjoy the peace.

When they got back to the house, Ryan wanted to explore in the attic, and he promised that he would even pack up a few boxes if Nikki let him play with any of her old toys that they found. There was no way she could say no to that offer, so they each grabbed a stack of flattened boxes and made their way upstairs.

Growing up in an old-style home with a traditional attic had been fun for her as a child, and it was nice to see that Ryan enjoyed it the same way she once had, hiding in the nooks and crannies, digging through her mother's trunks of old clothes, and discovering all kinds of unique treasures.

As an adult, especially one who was trying to pack up an entire house full of memories and a lifetime full of stuff, Nikki wasn't enjoying the attic as much as she once had. The space was packed with boxes and trunks of God knows what. "What are we going to do with all this stuff?" she asked Ryan, who had his head stuck into a chest and was pulling out trophies.

"It's cool," was his mumbled response. "I didn't know you were a track star." He emerged from the chest holding one of the larger trophies she'd earned.

"I would hardly say I was a star." She crossed the space and took the trophy from his hand, running her fingers over the engraved 1st Place State Meet lettering. "But I guess I did win a few races. I ran cross country. Sprinting wasn't my thing."

Ryan wrinkled up his nose. "I hate running."

"You get that from your father," she said, remembering how Matt would avoid any type of long-distance running.

"My dad?"

Nikki realized her mistake a moment too late. She squeezed her eyes shut and swallowed hard.

"What else did my dad hate?" Ryan asked.

She didn't like to lie to her son, but she also knew she couldn't tell him the truth. Not yet. It was one thing for Matt to know the truth and even for some of the other townspeople to figure it out on their own. But she couldn't tell Ryan. Not until she knew how Matt and Becky were going to handle the situation. She'd tell him. Just not yet. So she resorted to her usual tactic of avoidance.

"Why don't we see what else is in here?"

Ryan opened his mouth to say something, but thankfully he didn't push the issue. He usually didn't. It was almost as if he could sense that it was a sore subject for his mother. He was a smart kid and a sensitive one, too. She needed to handle the situation carefully. Especially considering she'd already made such a mess of it.

"Look at this," Nikki said, pulling out a large book. "This is my old yearbook. I can show you a picture of me earning that trophy."

Ryan seemed momentarily satisfied with that, and slid closer so he could look at the book.

Nikki knew exactly where to turn and she flipped the pages until she found the shot she was looking for. It was her, crossing the finish line at the state track meet. Her hands were in the air, a huge smile on her face—complete bliss. The girl in that picture had no idea how her life would change in only a few short weeks. For that Nikki, everything was right in the world.

Ryan pointed at the picture and laughed. "Did you really wear socks like that?"

"What's wrong with those socks?"

"They're huge, Mom."

They were huge. Nikki turned her attention back to the picture, although she didn't need to in order to remember those socks. Becky had given them to her as a good luck gift. The black-and-white picture didn't show it, but they were rainbow striped, and so bright that Nikki was sure she probably blinded half the competition.

"My best friend gave me those," she told Ryan. "They were for good luck."

"For luck?" Ryan gave his mom a doubtful look.

"They worked, didn't they? I have the trophy to prove it."

"True." Ryan nodded slowly and took the book from her hands. "Is there a picture of your friend? Can I see her?"

There was no harm in showing her son pictures, especially because she had a feeling that in some way, although she didn't know how yet, Becky was going to be a part of his life. Nikki flipped through the pages until she got to the senior class. "That's Becky." She pointed to a portrait that, even though it was in black and white, showcased a stunning girl. Becky was one of the prettiest girls in their class, if not the whole town. Every boy wanted to date her and she could have had her pick.

But she didn't pick any boy, Nikki reminded herself. She'd picked Matt.

"You know what, Ryan? I think those socks are probably in a box over there. I think I saw one labeled 'Nikki's Things.' Why don't you go dig through there?" Ryan didn't need to be asked twice. He jumped up and eagerly started digging through boxes.

Nikki returned her attention to the yearbook and flipped the page until she saw the picture of the boy she'd loved back then. Matt Jennings. She'd loved him first. And maybe things would have been different, too, if she'd spoken up. But she hadn't.

There'd been a time when Matt loved her, too. Or at least she thought he had. There'd been flirting, phone calls, and even a date that ended with a kiss. Nikki couldn't remember being so happy. But then Becky announced that she liked Matt. To be fair, Nikki didn't tell Becky how she felt. She'd kept it quiet, enjoying the secret she had.

But Becky was a force of nature, and whenever she wanted something, she went after it. Once she set her sights on Matt, Nikki knew there was no point. Her best friend always got the guy. It was a fact.

So she'd stepped aside.

Except that one night.

Her mom was out with Norma at some sort of charity meeting and she'd been catching up on homework when the doorbell rang. Matt was standing on the porch, looking lost and utterly broken. Of course she'd invited him in and they'd talked. A lot. He'd just come from Becky's house, where he'd broken up with her, and when Matt kissed her, Nikki knew she should have pushed him away. She knew in her heart he wasn't kissing her for anything more than comfort and it was wrong. But she'd let her heart lead the way and soon the kisses turned into more and—

"Mom! I found them."

Nikki closed the yearbook and looked up to see that in fact, Ryan had indeed found the socks.

She laughed and went to join him across the room. "I can't believe she kept them." She shook her head. "Well, actually I can. Mom kept everything."

"You should wear them, Mom. They're awesome."

"Weren't you making fun of them a minute ago?"

"That's before I knew they were lucky. Can I wear them?"

Nikki laughed. "You can have them."

"Awesome." Ryan tugged the socks on over his jeans.

Ryan got up and danced around the small space, causing Nikki to break into laughter. The type of deep belly laughing that took her breath away in a very good, long overdue way. When she was finally able to pull herself together, she wiped her eyes with the corner of her t-shirt, and asked, "What do you need luck for, anyway?"

Ryan dropped to his knees in front of the box he'd just been digging through. "What don't I need luck for? Maybe I'll find something really cool in here. Do you have anything that was my dad's?"

Nikki froze. She'd only ever touched on the truth with Ryan. She'd told him that she'd gone to high school with his dad and then they'd lost touch. It was partially true. And Ryan had always been too young to want to know too much more. She'd spent years deflecting his questions and putting him off, until he'd stopped asking much. At least until they'd come back to Halfway. She wasn't stupid, and she knew she'd made some huge mistakes where Ryan was concerned. And he was old enough to know the truth. That much she had decided on.

It was just a matter of when to tell him.

She blinked hard and watched as Ryan started unearthing random items from the box. Her mother truly had kept everything. "I don't know what you'll find in there," she answered honestly.

"Do you think my dad knows you're back in town, Mom?"

She took a deep breath and nodded slowly. "I think he probably knows."

"Will he want to come and meet me? I think I'd like to meet him."

Her chest ached, thinking of the mess she'd made. "I think he might, buddy. But we need to remember why we're here, okay?"

The pain intensified when she saw the disappointment on his face. He was just a kid who expected the best from everyone, and so far his mother had been the one to let him down. "Come here, Ryan."

Ryan shuffled over on his knees and fell into his mom's arms, where she held him and stroked his hair. He was getting so big—it wasn't often that he let her get a cuddle in, and she relished those moments. "Why don't we see if we can find a snack downstairs? I think that's enough organizing for right now." She looked around the space, and the piles they'd made. There was still so much to do, she wasn't sure how she'd ever get it finished. But that didn't matter. Not right now.

Together they went downstairs and rummaged in the cupboards until she came up with a bag of cookies. Nikki watched Ryan dig into the treat and knew that food wasn't going to distract him for very long. She'd need to face the truth, sooner rather than later. Not for the first time, she found herself wishing her mother was still around so she could get some advice.

"I'll be in the living room, buddy, okay?"

Ryan looked up long enough to nod and Nikki moved through the door, straight to the photo he'd put on the mantel of him with his grandma. She'd never pushed Nikki to tell the truth or come clean with anybody involved. In fact, she'd never said anything one way or the other about Nikki's choice. Sure, Nikki knew her opinion, or at least she'd thought she did. She ran her finger along the image of her mother. Maybe Nikki hadn't known how her mother really felt about her choices after all. She'd never asked.

It didn't matter, because now that Nikki wanted to know, and wanted her mother's advice, she couldn't get it. She was all alone.

A knock on the door startled her and she wiped at her face and the tear that had slipped from her eye. Without returning the photo to the mantel, she answered the door, looking through the glass as she turned the handle.

"Levi," she said as she opened the door wide. "What can I do for you? Did I forget something earlier? I thought I'd—"

"Oh, no, you brought everything." His smile was warm and Nikki had the overwhelming urge to hug him. "But you left before I could tell you that if you needed anything while you were here, you just have to ask."

"Thank you. That means a lot."

He stuffed his hands in his pockets awkwardly and shuffled from side to side. "I mean it, Nikki. I know there's a lot I don't know about, and your mother...well, I'm sure she had her reasons for keeping secrets, but—"

"Levi. That was my fault." Nikki stepped out onto the

porch. "I asked her to keep the secret. It wasn't her choice. I'm sure she would have told you, but…"

He nodded, understanding, but Nikki could still see the lingering hurt there. "She meant a lot to me, your mother."

"I can see that." She smiled and handed him the photo she still held. "I think it would have made her very happy for you to see this."

She watched as he took the photo and just as she had earlier, ran his fingers along the outline of her mother's image. "She looks so happy here," he said after a moment.

"Ryan made her very happy. Nobody loved him the way she did. It was wrong of me to—"

"That's enough, now," Levi cut her off. "You had your reasons. And what's done is done. You can't look back anymore. There's nothing to be gained from that. Okay?"

She nodded.

"Can I use this photo at the service?"

Nikki didn't even hesitate when she answered. "Of course. I think she would like that very much."

"I think you're right, but…well, you're sure about it?"

She knew what he was asking. The old man was perceptive and it didn't take much to figure out the truth and what using the photo would mean. But it didn't matter.

She nodded. "I'm sure. It's time. It's way past time."

Levi smiled and tugged on his beard. "I know your mother would be very proud of you right now."

Tears sprang to her eyes and she sniffed them back as much as she could.

"But that's not the only reason I came here," Levi said, his voice shifting, becoming lighter. "I was going to go down and watch the ice carving. I don't know if you remember, but every year the McPherson brothers get their chainsaws out and try to out-do each other in preparation for the festival."

Nikki smiled with the memory. "I remember. I used to love watching that."

"Well, your mother liked it, too. It was actually something we always did together and I thought that maybe this year...well, maybe the boy would like to come with me."

Nikki's heart almost burst with appreciation and love for the man. She didn't even bother wiping her tears this time but instead threw her arms around a shocked Levi, and gave him a hug. After a moment, his arms wrapped around her and stroked the back of her head while she cried.

"Now, now," he mumbled. "Crying won't fix anything. But you go right ahead and get it out. Everything will be okay."

Nikki gave herself over to the tears and emotion, and wished she could believe him.

Chapter Ten

~Becky~

With automated motions, Becky prepared a lunch for Matt and filled up his thermos with coffee before he headed out back to mark more trees to be cut. The house was silent; barely a word had been spoken between the two of them since Matt's bombshell from last night. She couldn't look him in the eye, couldn't fathom his betrayal...couldn't handle her guilt, knowing someone else had given him a child when her own body wouldn't.

She wasn't sure whom she was madder at: Matt for betraying her with Nikki or Nikki for betraying their friendship by sleeping with Matt and then running away with his child.

Was she even mad at Matt? She wasn't sure whether her anger was even valid. He'd tried to explain that it had been a lapse in judgment, that it had happened while they'd broken up and that he'd instantly regretted it. Was it right of her to hold something that happened more than ten years ago over his head like that? Was it even fair to think she had the right to be angry about that?

All night, while she lay in their bed alone, she tried to remember how things had been back then, during their breakup. Nikki's actions now made sense, why she backed away from her. Had she been waiting all along for them to break up so she could swoop in and seduce her husband?

Just the thought made her blood boil.

How could she do that to her? They were supposed to have been best friends. Like sisters.

Her heart continued to splinter apart as she thought about it. She'd mourned the loss of her friend for too long. She'd been so naive in thinking they could start over, that they could pick up from where they'd left off.

There was no picking up the pieces of this shattered dream. Their friendship was over and it was time for Becky to grow up and realize it had been for a long, long time.

What did this boy, Ryan, look like? Did he look more like Matt or Nikki? Would she be able to tell right away he was Matt's child?

As she drove into town to visit her mother at the hospital, she was tempted to drive past Nikki's place, to see whether she could catch a glimpse of the boy. But she didn't.

How could Nikki have kept such a thing a secret?

After parking in front of the doors of the hospital, Becky leaned her head back against the seat. She needed to get her act together. She needed to push this out of her mind, for now, and focus on the festival, when all she wanted to do was cry on her mother's shoulder.

She could imagine what Norma would say. *Life doesn't always play favorites, so deal with it.* Well, she was tired of having to *deal with it*. With every miscarriage, she'd tried to *deal with it* and look where it left her—barren.

"Do you need help?" Uncle Dennis stood at her car door and knocked on the window. Becky pasted a smile on her face and shook her head. Dennis opened the door for her and she gathered her purse and notebook before she took his offered hand and got out of her vehicle.

"What's up, lil' missy?"

She shook her head. She wasn't even sure how to handle this.

"Your mother's about to be released, from what I hear. Good thing, too. I think her nurses are due a vacation." He chuckled as he led her up the stairs and opened the door for her.

"What will she do when she gets old?" Becky placed a small kiss on her uncle's cheek.

"Your mother doesn't know what that word means. She'll outlive us all, with her crotchetiness."

She was able to keep her emotions in check until she stepped into her mother's room. Her mother sat there with an expectant look. The weariness that had hung over her was gone and the pale pallor that was in her face had transformed to an almost healthy color. Tears welled up in Becky's eyes and it was all she could do to not sob. She sank down in the chair beside her mom's bed and leaned forward, placing her head in her hands.

"What's wrong?" her mom asked.

Becky just shook her head, not trusting herself to speak.

"Did something happen? Is it Matt?"

Again, Becky shook her head but hearing the concern in her mother's voice seemed to bolster her, and she was able to sit back without letting the tears fall.

"Did you know Nikki had a child?" She stared up at the ceiling light and blinked. When Norma didn't respond, a stone settled in Becky's stomach and she felt ready to get sick. "You knew?"

Norma gave her head a tiny shake but then she nodded. "I knew. But not from Marie. I saw pictures one time, a few years ago, of Nikki with a little boy."

"And you never said anything?"

"Wasn't for me to say. Marie had her reasons, I'm sure, for keeping such a thing a secret." She rubbed her hands together.

Becky snorted. "Of course she did."

"Rebecca."

"No. You don't get to sound like that. It wasn't fair of Nikki or her mother to keep such a thing a secret."

"Is that why you're mad? Because Nikki kept it a secret from you?"

Becky shook her head. *If only her mother knew.*

"So you don't know his name or how old he is or even who the father is?"

Norma's lips thinned. "What do you think? Marie had her reasons. I knew she'd tell me if she needed to. I figured something had to have happened to make her bolt the way she did and never return." Norma sighed as she leaned back against her pillow. "Being a single mother, especially a teenage mother, had to have been hard. I never understood how she could cut herself off from everyone, especially you, like she did, but once I saw those photos, I figured she had her reasons."

Becky pushed herself up from her chair. The anger that bubbled beneath the surface of her heart boiled over listening to her mother stand up for Nikki.

"Her reasons? You want to know what her reasons were? Our sweet Nikki, the one everyone thought to be an angel, seduced my husband and ended up pregnant." She went to the window and leaned her hip against the wall, staring out into the park that was across the road. The same park where she had to start setting up for the festival later.

"What do you mean, seduced your husband?"

Becky whirled to stare at her mother. "Remember when Matt and I split up for that short period of time? Well, my best friend swooped in and tried to steal him from me."

"Oh, Becky," Norma sighed, "you guys were only dating back then. You can't be mad at her for that mistake."

Becky's brows rose. "I can't? Why can't I? She was my best friend, Mom. My"—her voice broke—"best friend." This time the tears did run down her cheeks.

Norma patted a spot on the bed beside her and Becky almost ran to it. She sat down and let her mother gather her in her arms. With her head on her mother's shoulder, Becky gave in to all the emotions that ran through her and cried.

After a few minutes, her mother pushed her away. "Is that what you're really upset about?"

Becky looked at her in confusion. Of course that was the reason.

"Being a mother has been a strong desire for you for a long time. I can't imagine how hard this must be for you, knowing someone else gave your husband something you've tried to do but can't." The sympathy in her mother's eyes softened her words. But not by much.

"I can still give him a child. I'll still be a mother, one day." She knew in her heart it was a moot point but she still needed to say it.

"Oh honey, you might think I haven't noticed, but I'm still your mother. I know the signs. I have my own angel babies, remember. But I think you're forgetting something."

"What?" She didn't want to think about her angels. Not now.

"You already are a mother."

Becky pushed herself up, away from her mother and shook her head.

"He's not my child. He's Matt's and Nikki's. He's theirs.

Not mine."

"Rebecca Jennings, I raised you better than that. If he's Matt's child, then he's yours as well."

Becky wrapped her arms around her body. "But I...but he... oh my..." She sighed deep. She hadn't thought about that aspect. Well, to be honest, she hadn't wanted to. The idea had brushed her thoughts all night but she refused to think about it. That she was now a mother. Maybe not the kind of mother she had wanted to be, nor was Ryan the child she dreamed of...

"How does Matt feel about all this?"

Becky shrugged. "We haven't really talked about that." But they needed to. They would. They had no choice.

"What happens when Nikki leaves again?"

"Well...she can't. Can she?" At Norma's shrug, a tight fist grabbed Becky's heart. "She can't take Matt's child away from him, not now, not like this. He's ten years old, Mom. Ten. There's no way Matt's going to be willing to lose any more time with him than he already has."

Norma gave a deep nod. "Good. Good. So why don't you go find your husband and talk about this? I doubt you have much time left. Marie's funeral is in a few days. Levi's managed to convince that girl to stay for her own mother's funeral but I doubt she'll stick around long after. If you want to be part of that boy's life, you'd better do something about it now."

Renewed with a sense of purpose, one that she didn't have before, she grabbed her purse, gave her mother a quick kiss and hug, and then left the room.

"But don't forget to check all the lights first!" Her mother's voice followed her down the hallway.

###

. . .

We need to talk. I'm sorry I wasn't ready to last night. Becky sent Matt a text. *Meet for hot chocolate? Heading to the park to go through the lights.*

Matt deserved a better apology, and she knew that. But she'd wait until they were face to face to give it to him. Last night she'd been selfish and nursed her wounded ego, not once considering what her husband must have been going through to realize he had a child he'd never known about.

She was still angry that he hadn't been faithful to her but if she were to be honest, it was a moot point now. It wasn't right of her to hold that indiscretion over his head, not after all these years. She'd never doubted him before and wouldn't let this creep up into their marriage to cause an issue.

As she made her way to the park carrying the Tupperware containers of lights, she knew they needed to be a strong unit in this, just like they'd always been in the past.

"There you are. Here, let me take those." Gus, from the hardware shop, grabbed the containers from her and hefted them in his arms. "Is this all there is? I thought Norma had more?"

Becky groaned. "She does. But I didn't have room. The rest are still in her garage."

"Give me the keys and I'll go grab them." Gus set the containers down by the pavilion in the middle of the park while Becky dug out her mother's house keys from her purse.

"If you take a look in her freezer, you might just find a container of jam with your name on it." Becky smiled her thanks as a grin crossed Gus's face as he took the keys, whistled to his son and headed towards his pick-up truck.

She was hoping she could sweet-talk someone into helping her with those lights. She couldn't believe how many containers her mother had stored in the rafters.

Her phone buzzed in her pocket. *Almost there. Need to set up area for trees. See you soon.*

Becky glanced around the park and smiled. This was probably her favorite time of the year, or one of them. Everything and anything that happened in this town was held in this park. In the summers, there were day camps, picnics, fruit markets, and sing-along nights. In the winter, there was the Tree Festival, and then Christmas markets, snowmen contests, snow fort contests and even ice sculpting...which reminded her...

"Oops, excuse me." She was nudged in the back and pushed forward. When she turned around, she found Nikki standing before her.

Everything Becky had thought of saying to Nikki last night vanished. She couldn't say anything. Her mouth opened and closed before she managed to say one word.

"No." It was whispered softly and she wasn't even sure Nikki heard her. "No," she said louder.

"I'm sorry?" Nikki stepped back with a confused look on her face. In her hands were stacks of paper.

"I won't excuse you. I've done it for too long. Ten years, to be exact."

She knew Nikki understood when her friend's eyes widened.

"You know," Becky gritted her teeth, "I waited for you to come home for years. Did your mom ever give you those letters I wrote in the beginning? Did she ever tell you how many times I dropped by to see if she'd heard from you?"

She'd be lying if she didn't admit to some sort of satisfaction when Nikki's gaze dropped to the snow-covered ground and her shoulders stooped.

"How could you?" She rolled her shoulders as tension knotted her muscles. She reminded herself to keep her voice low, to not bring unwanted attention to them. All it would take was one raised voice, one word of discord and all eyes would be on them.

"I'm sorry." Nikki sighed.

Becky snorted. *As if that would help in any way.* Her apology was ten years too late.

"Hey." Nikki straightened, her face hardening. "I know running away like I did wasn't the smartest move, but I can't change that now. You can be mad, but before you judge me, just remember, you don't know me anymore, Becky. You have no idea the sacrifices I had to make, how hard staying away has been. How hard all of it has been."

"You're right. I don't know you, and I obviously didn't know you back then either. I thought we were best friends, Nik. But best friends don't backstab one another, they don't sleep with the other's boyfriend and they sure as hell," by this time she'd started to yell and didn't care who heard, "don't keep the son of said friend's husband a secret."

She watched as a change came over the woman in front of her. Her stance relaxed and she even had the audacity to smile. *To smile?* That angered Becky more than anything.

"You're right. You obviously didn't know me. Because if you had, you would have known that I loved Matt even before you knew his name. You also would have known that I would have done anything for you and in fact did, when I stepped aside when you decided you liked him."

What?

"Since when did you like Matt?" Becky couldn't believe what she was hearing.

"Funny, how that's what you focus on. It doesn't matter, does it? You married him. You are the one he loves. I've grown up, moved on and realized he wasn't worth whatever feelings I'd had for him."

Becky bristled at that. She stepped forward until she invaded Nikki's personal space.

"Not worth it? He wasn't the one who ran away. He," she jabbed her finger into the down of Nikki's coat, "wasn't the one who kept his child away from him."

"No, he wasn't," she said softly. "That was me. All me."

All of Becky's anger dissipated at Nikki's admission. She had expected more...more excuses, more apologies, but not this. She stepped back and struggled to get her bearings. She glanced around the park and noticed how everyone had literally stopped what they were doing and had edged closer.

"Here are some copies of the flyers I made up. I figured you'd want to see them. I sent them to Melissa, too, but I made a few variations. I wasn't sure what you wanted."

Wordlessly, Becky took the stack of papers from Nikki's hands and watched as the person she once called her best friend turned and started to walk away from her.

"Nik?" she called out. "Nikki?"

Nikki stopped but didn't turn. Becky took a few steps towards her. "Listen, I'm sorry. I...Matt just told me, and I..."

Nikki then turned. "No need to apologize. Trust me."

Becky blushed. "But I do." She couldn't believe how upset she'd gotten. That wasn't like her. "And apparently for more than I realized."

Nikki just watched her, waiting.

"We need to talk. About your son. About Ryan. All of us—you, me, and Matt. And I'd like to meet him. Your son—"

"Our son." Matt appeared at her side and wrapped his arm around her waist. "Our son. We'd like to meet him and be introduced to him, properly, this time."

Becky watched as Nikki's face blanched at his words and was thankful that Matt had said what she couldn't say.

Chapter Eleven

~Nikki~

Meet Ryan? They wanted to meet Ryan? Nikki shook her head, but she couldn't be sure who she was shaking it at.

Of course, she'd known it was a possibility. It was more than a possibility and she'd always known it, even if she'd denied it to herself. Matt and Becky were good people; of course they were going to want to know their son.

But he wasn't their son. He was hers.

Ryan was hers.

She looked at them both in turn. Matt looked exhausted. His handsome features were clouded with an obvious lack of sleep, making him look a lot older than his years. But it was Becky's face that made her heart clench. She'd have to be blind not to see the hurt in her eyes. The pain that was all over her face. It may have been years since Nikki had called her best friend, but she still hurt with her. And she knew she'd deeply wounded her friend. Which is exactly what she'd been trying to avoid.

"Yes, Nikki," Becky said, breaking through her fog. "We want to meet him."

"He's not here," she said automatically.

Matt glanced around. "Where would he be? He's only ten, right?"

Her hackles went up. "I didn't leave him alone, if that's what you're implying. He's with—" She stopped herself. If she told them where Ryan was or who he was with, there'd be nothing stopping them from finding him on their own and she couldn't let that happen. Not before she could talk to him.

"Well," Becky said. "Where is he, Nikki? We want to meet him. He's our son."

Her words triggered something inside Nikki. "No," she said, and then pulling herself up and taking a deep breath, she said it again. Stronger this time. "No."

Becky took a step back and Matt caught her, wrapping a protective arm around her. Just like he used to. Hadn't it always eaten Nikki up to see the way he took care of her and worshipped the very ground Becky walked on, while she stood by, the third wheel best friend? When it was her heart that broke every time she saw the love between them. It could have been her. It should have been her.

No. She shook her head again. She hadn't felt that way in years. And despite everything, she didn't feel that way now. But she still wasn't going to stand by and let them take what was hers.

"Nikki, you're—"

"No," she said again, cutting Matt off. "He's not your son. He's mine."

"Nikki," Matt tried again. "You said...I mean, he's obviously mine."

Next to him, Becky seemed to sink into herself at his words.

So he hadn't told her that Ryan was a spitting image of him, then.

"That doesn't make him your son," she said. "Not more than blood. It doesn't work that way."

"And whose fault is that?" Becky said, clearly regaining some of the anger she'd had earlier. "You kept him from us. You ran and hid like—"

"Like what?" Nikki challenged her. She'd always backed down to her best friend. Always given in to whatever Becky wanted, whatever it was Becky needed. That was before. She had more important things to worry about now.

Becky narrowed her eyes at her. "Like a coward," she finished.

The word hit her like a slap and fury burned through her. She took a step up to Becky, the first time she'd ever stood up to her, and spoke through clenched teeth. "A coward? Is that what you think I am?" She didn't give Becky a chance to answer. "Did you stop for one moment to think about why I left? Why, at barely eighteen years old, I might think it was a good idea to leave everything and everyone I knew to raise a baby by myself? Did you stop to think about it?"

Becky didn't answer, but her strong eyes didn't leave Nikki's.

"I did it for you," Nikki said, her voice softer now. "I did everything for you. I never told you how I felt about Matt because I knew it would hurt you to know the truth. And when I...we..." She glanced to Matt and then back to Becky. "Well, I didn't mean for that to happen. But it did and I didn't know how to tell you. And when I found out I was pregnant, I knew it would destroy you."

"It wouldn't have—"

"Yes it would have." Her voice was firm but gentle. "You loved him so much and you thought you had it all figured out.

You were going to have a life together and have babies." Nikki didn't miss Becky's flinch when she spoke. "If I announced I was pregnant, all of that would have changed. All of it." She let her words sink in for a moment before she added, "I couldn't do that to you. I loved you too much. So I left. And no, it was definitely not the coward's way out."

Becky shook her head as if she didn't want to hear what Nikki was saying. "But you could have—"

"No. I wanted you to have everything you wanted. Everything you deserved out of life. And that wouldn't have happened if I'd stayed. You didn't deserve to suffer because of my choice."

"A mistake." Matt turned to his wife, holding her by the shoulders. "I told you it was a mistake and I'd take it back if I could. Becky, I never thought in a million years this would happen. I never would have..."

Nikki stopped listening. She couldn't bear to hear his words. Yes, she'd regretted the way things happened. But she'd never once considered what she'd done with Matt a mistake. He'd been split up from Becky and the two of them had always been close. That night when he came over to talk, it wasn't like they'd been drinking or not known what they were doing. They did. They both did. Even if it wasn't the same as what he felt for Becky, Nikki knew Matt loved her. At least a little. And never would she think that what they'd done together was a mistake. Not when that one night had given her Ryan.

"I'm sorry things turned out the way they did," Nikki interrupted their private moment. "I never meant for things to play out this way."

Matt faced Nikki again, but didn't let go of Becky's hand. "We can't change the past," he said. "But we can change how we go forward from here. We'd really like to meet Ryan."

"Before you leave," Becky added.

"Leave?"

Nikki looked at the ground and kicked at a chunk of ice. "I have to go home," she said.

"You can't leave," Matt said. "Not now."

"I have a job," she said. "A life. Ryan has school." Even as she spoke the words, she knew it was a lie. Sure, she had a job and Ryan had school. But they could do those things anywhere. She wouldn't admit it, not even to herself, but she didn't have anything real to go back to. Not really.

"When are you leaving?"

"Right after Mom's service," Nikki said. "We really have to get back."

"Before the festival?" Becky sounded horrified. "No. You have to stay. It's tradition."

"I haven't been in years, Becky." Nikki wrapped her arms around herself, the chill starting to get to her. "It's hardly my tradition."

"Then we'll start a new one."

Nikki tried to smile at her friend's eagerness, and her open heart, so willing to accept them. A motion from the corner of her eye caught her attention. The ice carving was taking place on the far side of the square and she knew Levi and Ryan were there watching. It was too soon. She couldn't risk them running into Becky and Matt. Not yet. A knot in her stomach formed at the thought of telling Ryan about his dad. Obviously, it wasn't something she could put off much longer. "Look," she said, the need to be away from them overwhelming her. "I can't deal with this right now." Unwanted tears sprang to her eyes and she blinked hard, hoping they wouldn't notice. "Everything that's been going on, I just can't...look, I need to talk to Ryan first."

"We can—"

"No." She held up her hand, cutting Matt off. "I need to talk to him first. He's only a kid and this is a lot to take in." She swiped at her face and sniffed loudly. "I'll tell him," she added, more to convince herself than Becky and Matt. "Just promise me you'll leave him alone until I do."

"Nikki," Becky started. She took a step forward as if she was going to, what? Hug her? Fortunately, she stopped before the moment got any more awkward. "We'll figure this out," she said. "Together."

Nikki's first instinct was to snap back at her. She wanted to tell Becky that it wasn't her problem to figure out. But that would be a lie. The secret was out. She had an overwhelming fear over how Ryan would react to the truth, but as she nodded, turned and walked away, there was also a sense of relief that washed over her. Secrets were a heavy load to carry and with her mom gone, there was no one left to help.

After leaving Matt and Becky standing in the square, Nikki didn't know what to do with herself. Ryan would still be a few hours with Levi and even though the loneliness was over-whelming her, she wouldn't ruin his day. He'd been so excited when Levi offered to take him to watch the ice carvers. He was just a boy and he needed a little fun. Lord knows she wasn't very much fun to be around lately. Not with everything. Besides, for everything Halfway wasn't, it was a very fun little town that knew how to throw a festival. Ryan would have a good day.

Nikki found herself walking aimlessly down the main street, staring in the windows of the shops she used to know so well. There were a few changes, but there was enough that was familiar that Nikki instantly felt comfortable. No matter how long she'd been gone, Halfway was home. Nowhere else she'd lived since leaving had ever had the same feeling. Even the small townhouse they lived in now, with the neatly groomed yard and bike lying in the walk, didn't feel as right as Halfway did.

She'd told Becky and Matt she had to get back. But the truth was, she worked from home. Designing websites was a pretty portable job and it had been perfect for a single mom with no one to depend on. She'd been able to create a successful little business on her own while being available for Ryan. Of course, a home office had its own set of drawbacks. She didn't get out very much. Not unless you counted a PTA meeting. And Nikki didn't. She couldn't remember the last time she'd had a date, either. And she knew that wasn't fair. Ryan deserved a father in his life.

A pang of guilt hit her as she remembered the look on Matt's face.

Ryan had a father.

She pushed those thoughts out of the way. She'd tell Ryan later. She said she would do it, and she would. She'd made enough mistakes, and she didn't need to compound them. But she also wasn't going to let Becky and Matt pressure her into doing it before either of them was ready. No. She knew her son better than anyone else in the world. She'd do what was best.

"Hey, careful."

At the last minute, Nikki sidestepped a man carrying a large box with pine boughs sticking out the top.

"I'm so sorry," the man behind the box said. "I can't see very well around this thing." He shifted his load and looked at her. "Nikki Landon?"

She smiled at the familiar voice. "Oh my God, Parker? Is that you?"

Parker Rhodes put the box down on the sidewalk and in the next instant, pulled Nikki into a crushing hug. His arms were warm, and strangely enough, he smelled the same way he had in high school, like fresh cut flowers. Despite herself, Nikki closed her eyes and enjoyed the moment of familiarity and comfort.

When he released her, Parker took a step back and said, "I heard you were in town and I'm so sorry about your mother. Levi has the shop doing all the arrangements for the service, and...I'm sorry."

"Don't be. I'm glad you're doing the flowers." Parker's family had always run the local flower shop, which meant on the few dates they'd had, he'd always presented her with the most beautiful flower arrangements. "And obviously, you're still at the shop. How are your parents?"

"Dad passed a few years back, but Mom's still doing the arranging. I help out where I can, but I'm teaching at the high school now. Can you believe it? In the very halls where we used to get in trouble. I'm the one handing out the detentions now. It's pretty crazy."

Nikki laughed and surprised herself by feeling lighthearted for the first time in days. Parker's presence always did have that effect on her, but she'd been too consumed with her feelings for Matt to notice when they were kids. "It's so good to see you," she said genuinely.

"I can't think of anyone I would've preferred to run into myself." Parker smiled and his green eyes crinkled up at the edges the way they used to. "Hey. Do you have time for a coffee? Or maybe a hot chocolate? I just need to run these boughs over to the square, but then I'd love to catch up."

"Oh, I..." She shifted from foot to foot. "Are you sure you don't have to be home for dinner or anything?"

He laughed. "I'm sure my dog can eat without me. He's pretty self-sufficient that way."

"You're not married?" She'd just assumed that a great guy like Parker would have been snatched up by now. Especially in a small town like Halfway. Just because she'd been too preoccupied to notice how amazing he was back in high school didn't mean every other girl hadn't wanted to be with him.

Parker shook his head. "I never did get over you, Nikki. You ruined me for any other."

Nikki joined in his laughter, enjoying the lighthearted flirting. "Uh huh, you smooth talker, you."

"So yes to the coffee?"

She glanced at her watch. Levi said he'd get Ryan a hotdog from the cafe for dinner, so she had at least another hour before she needed to be home. Besides, it would be nice to spend some time thinking about anything else but her real life, and she couldn't deny the draw she felt towards Parker.

She nodded and grinned. "Absolutely."

Chapter Twelve

~Becky~

The air was brisk as they walked hand in hand to the cafe for their long-delayed hot chocolate. It took four hours to get it all right, but at least when she called her mother tonight, she could say that all the lights worked.

The cafe was crowded by the time they'd completed all the little things that needed to be taken care of in the park but Becky managed to snag a table in the far back corner while Matt ordered two hot chocolates at the counter. She wasn't sure why they came in and sat when they probably should have headed home to have their talk, but Matt insisted.

"Here you go, peppermint mocha and a biscotti." Matt handed her the mug before he sat down. The silence lengthened between them as they sat there sipping their drinks. Becky smiled at various people who came into the cafe for their own hot beverage but quickly glanced away if they seemed inclined to come and talk to them.

"Do you think he was there?" Matt finally broke the silence between them.

She shrugged. "I would imagine so, but I doubt I'd recognize him even if he stood right next to me."

"You would. He's the spitting image of how I looked at his age." A soft smile grew across his face and the anxiety that had lingered in his eyes disappeared. "I wish my parents had known about him." The wistfulness to his tone, the longing stuck a dagger in Becky's heart.

She reached across the table and placed her hand over his. "I'm sorry, Matt. I'm sorry that we never had a baby for them to hold, to see smile or even to spoil as he or she got older." She rubbed his hand while he stared at the table. He blinked a few times before he looked at her.

"And I'm sorry that you missed out on all of that with Ryan," she said.

"I'm a father," Matt whispered. He turned his gaze upwards and Becky caught sight of the tears that pooled in his eyes.

That's what she loved most about Matt. His soft heart. He cried during commercials and his heart broke along with anyone else's if they experienced a loss. He was kind, gentle, and yet a giant at the same time.

"Yes, yes you are." She could put her hurt aside for the moment. Maybe it was time to stop looking inward and feeling sorry for herself for not being able to give Matt something he'd always desired—something he already had.

"How could I not know? Aren't you supposed to know these things as a parent?"

Becky didn't respond. She didn't really need to. She had no idea what you were supposed to know or not know as a parent. This was new territory for her, for them.

"You know now." She took a sip of her mocha. "How did you find out?"

Matt glanced behind him, out onto the street. "It was when I dropped those boxes off. I saw him and knew right away."

Becky tried to smile, but she couldn't. She suddenly had an image of Matt with Nikki and it sent shivers down her spine. That also explained why he'd come home unnerved that day and she couldn't figure out what had been wrong. She struggled not to show her emotions in her face. Even then, when he'd first found out, he'd kept it a secret from her. She swallowed past the hurt.

"Honey, I'm so sorry. It's the one thing I've regretted the most since the moment it happened." He must have caught the tremble of her hands.

"You should have told me." There was nothing else she could say. Her mom was right. They were broken up when it happened and it was in the past. Now is what mattered. Them. Their marriage. The fact they now have a son they never knew about.

"I should have. I can't...I don't even..." Matt struggled to get the words out. She knew what he was trying to say, knew where his heart was. Making him say it out loud was just torture. So she stopped him.

"It's okay." She gave her head a slight shake. "It's in the past and as much as I think I would like to know all the details, I really don't. It's enough to know it happened. I wish it hadn't, but it did. Just do me a favor, don't belittle what happened. Earlier, you said it had been a mistake—"

"And it was," Matt interrupted her.

Yes, it had been, but he didn't see the expression on Nikki's face when he said that in front of her. She obviously didn't see it that way. She didn't doubt Nikki's words about the feelings she'd had for Matt and if truth be told, Becky hadn't been as oblivious of those feelings as she might have pretended to be. But she didn't want to acknowledge them back then either.

"But there had to have been feelings involved for you to sleep with her." She held up her hand as Matt moved to object. "No, we don't need to go there, but I just don't want you to negate something that did happen. And...no matter what, Ryan was not and will never be a mistake. Not to Nikki."

"Or to me," he said. "Not now that I know." Matt lifted her hand and brought it to his lips and placed a small kiss in her palm. "I love you."

She just smiled. "So, what do we do now?"

"We wait, I guess." He scrubbed the back of his neck. "I don't know what else we can do. She asked for time."

"What if she leaves?"

"She won't. She can't. She wouldn't skip her mother's funeral."

Becky rubbed her eyes and pinched the top of her nose. "She could. She ran once, remember? And we have no idea where she lives. She could leave with Ryan and there's nothing you could do to stop her." Part of her was worried that was exactly what Nikki would do—leave.

"Not if I have anything to do about it." Levi's friendly voice startled them both. He pulled up a chair and sat down. "That girl isn't going anywhere, not with that little boy."

"What do you mean?" Matt leaned forward and pushed his coffee mug out of the way.

"We all need to grow up one time or another. Anyone with eyes can see he's your child and running isn't the answer anymore. Not for her and not for that little boy of yours. He needs a man in his life, a father."

"He's got one." Becky squeezed her husband's hand.

"That little girl has had to think alone for long enough. Marie should have put a stop to it a long time ago. I'll never understand why she didn't."

Becky sat back as she caught the haunted look in Levi's eyes.

For as long as she'd known him, he'd been a staple of the community, a solid fixture. But today, he looked...old and happy at the same time. It didn't make sense to her.

"I've loved that woman since the day I first laid eyes on her. But her daughter always came first. She should have known I would have loved Nikki as if she were my own." He cleared his throat. "I thought maybe when you girls went off to school I might have a chance, but when Nikki left so suddenly and Marie went away on those road trips of hers for lengths at a time, I knew I'd have to bide my time. I knew there was something, something she wasn't telling me...but it wasn't until I saw that little boy that I knew." He smiled at Matt. "He's something, that boy. She did a good job raising him. I know this has to be tough and no doubt there's a lot of anger inside you right now, but he's a good kid." He dipped his head down to his chest and thumped his heart.

"I don't know how I'm feeling right now, to be honest, Levi," Matt admitted, his voice low. "My life"—he glanced at Becky—"*our* lives just changed without warning. I'm angry that I lost out on ten years, I'm amazed to discover I'm a father, guilt is eating away at me for keeping what happened between Nik and me a secret..." His Adam's apple bobbed. Becky knew he was struggling to contain the tears.

"Let go of that guilt. It's not a part of this right now. We'll deal with that later. Right now, this is about Ryan." Becky knew in her heart it was the right thing to do—to focus on what was important and to let the other stuff fall by the wayside.

"You're a good man, Matthew Jennings. A good man. I'm proud to call you friend." Levi pushed his chair back and cleared his throat. "You two," Becky smiled when he leaned over and placed his hand on her shoulder, "you will make good parents to that special boy."

As Levi walked out of the cafe, Becky toyed with the word

in her mind. *Parent*. Most parents have months to prepare for their child to enter their lives, but they only had days, if that. It's one thing to know about Ryan, but another to be a parent. Would she love him? Could she love him? What if she couldn't? What if she saw Nikki and the betrayal in his face every time she looked at him?

Oh God, that made her sound horrible. A monster. Ryan wasn't one of the children in her Sunday School class—he was her husband's child. Matt said he was his spitting image, so she knew she'd fall in love with him the minute she saw him. How could she not? And Nikki...she had to be a good mother. Becky knew that deep in her soul.

She would love this boy with all her heart. And, if this was the only child she ever had, then that had to be enough. It had to be.

Chapter Thirteen

~Nikki~

The day was overcast; the clouds that hung over the town were heavy with the threat of snow and absolutely perfect for a funeral. The weather matched Nikki's mood as she zipped herself into her black dress and pulled her hair back in a bun. When she was ready, she walked down the hall to see whether Ryan needed any help with his tie.

Nikki peeked into his room. "Hey, buddy, are—"

He wasn't there.

"Ryan?"

With a quick scan around the guest room, which Ryan had taken over, it was clear he wasn't hiding anywhere in the sparsely decorated space. He must already be downstairs. They only had thirty minutes or so before they needed to start making their way to Levi's. And even if she'd spent her morning procrastinating and packing for their planned departure tomorrow, Ryan had actually been mostly dressed for hours. He seemed oddly excited for the service.

But then again, to a little boy who'd never been to a funeral before, his expectations of what was actually going to happen were probably very different from reality. Nikki was just about to go down the stairs, when a noise coming from her mother's room captured her attention. She backtracked quickly and pushed the door open.

Ryan was sitting cross-legged on his grandmother's bed, staring at the wall of pictures Nikki hadn't brought herself to take down yet.

"Do you think she knows that today's her funeral?" Ryan asked without turning around.

The question caught her off guard and it took Nikki a few moments to form a response. She crossed the room and sat on the floral bedspread next to him. "I'd like to think that wherever she is, she's watching us and yes," Nikki said, "I think she knows it's her funeral today. In fact, I bet she's looking forward to the celebration she's planned. Grandma always did like a party."

"She did?" Ryan asked. "I never knew that."

Nikki's chest squeezed, seeming to compress her heart at his words. Of course he'd never known that. Ryan had never had the chance to see the way his grandma liked to organize events, and work the room, smiling and laughing with her friends. *Just like at the Tree Festival*, she thought, but before the idea could take root, she pushed it out of her head. *No.* No matter what Becky and Matt said, she wouldn't be going to the Tree Festival.

"She used to tell me I looked just like my dad."

Nikki's breath caught in her throat and she had to remind herself to breathe. She stared at her son, looking for any kind of indication that he knew the truth, any hint that he'd already figured it out. But there was nothing. He kept staring at the wall in front of him.

"I didn't know you used to talk about that with Grandma," she said when she felt more in control of herself. She knew she had to tell Ryan the truth. That's all she'd thought about as she'd packed and organized and basically thrown herself into everything that could keep her distracted from the reality of what she had to do. But no matter what logical argument she used against herself, no matter how many ways she played out the scenario in her head, she couldn't bring herself to do it. Not yet. Not before they buried his grandmother.

She stared at her son's profile. So much like his father's it made her heart hurt. Everyone else would see it in only a few hours. Nobody in Halfway would be able to ignore the resemblance. She was a fool for thinking she could walk into a room of people who'd known her and Matt their whole lives and hide anything.

"You do," Nikki said before she could change her mind. "You look just like him. Sometimes when I look at you, I think I'm seeing him when he was your age."

Ryan turned away from the wall and looked at her, his eyes shining with excitement. "Really? You knew him when you were kids?"

"I've known him my whole life, buddy." She smiled even though she wanted to cry. "And there's something I should tell you. I think you're finally old enough to know."

"My dad? You're going to tell me his name?" He bounced up onto his knees, reminding Nikki of the child he really was. She could have cried at his innocence, his blind faith that everything would not only be okay but be better than before as soon as he found out who his father was. He had no idea that his entire world would change in a few hours.

"I thought maybe I should wait until after the service." Ryan's face fell with disappointment and she added, "But, even though the timing is less than perfect, I think you should know." She paused and took a deep breath. She'd thought about this moment in her head for years. Planned out what she might say, how he'd react. How they'd move on afterwards. She'd never intended to keep the truth from him for so long. But she'd also never intended him to find out like this. Nikki exhaled. "Your dad will be there today."

She squeezed her eyes shut, not wanting to see the excitement in her son's eyes. She'd always wanted to be enough for him. And for a few years, she thought maybe she was. She counted to five in her head, waiting for his squeal of delight. His excitement.

Nothing.

Nikki opened her eyes to see Ryan staring at her blankly. "Ryan?" She reached out to touch his arm, to feel a connection with him. "Are you okay?"

After a moment, he nodded. "He's here? In this town?"

"Yes. He lives here."

"And I can meet him? For real?"

"Yes." Nikki swallowed hard. "For real."

Ryan nodded again, his face a mask of seriousness. "Okay."

"Are you going to be okay, buddy? I mean, if you don't want to—"

"I do." He grabbed her arm and she had to swallow a genuine smile at the enthusiasm he was trying to hide. "I mean, if it's okay."

"Of course it's okay." Nikki pulled her son into her arms and held him tightly. She stroked his silky blond hair and tried to hold the tears back as she repeated, "Everything will be okay. It'll all be okay." But she couldn't be sure who she was trying to convince: Ryan or herself.

###

. . .

Half the town must have turned out for her mom's service and as Nikki peeked out of the back room that was reserved for families only, she tried to slow her breath and not hyperventilate at the idea of walking through that room full of people from her past. People who knew her and had known her for her whole life.

She turned and looked at Ryan, who was studying the program Levi had printed out. His little shoulders were hunched over and every few moments, she could see his body shake a bit, as if he was holding in his tears. Nikki's heart broke for her son. There'd been too much sadness and confusion in his young life. Way more than there should have been.

She sat down next to him and slid her arm around his small shoulders. "I know it's tough, buddy. It's never easy to say goodbye." He looked up into her eyes and Nikki had to pull on strength she didn't know she had to keep from crying at the pain she saw there. "But we have to remember that it's not really about saying goodbye today. It's more of a celebration of her life and what a great woman she was. You should see all the people out there. A lot of people loved Grandma. I wish you could have known her here."

"In Halfway?"

She nodded. "She was really something." She smiled, remembering the way everyone in town would stop and want to chat no matter where they were. Her mother had a way about her that made people want to open up and spill their problems. When she was younger, it would irritate Nikki to no end that they'd always be late wherever they were going, or she'd have to pretend not to be listening while she waited for her mom to finish giving advice or offering a shoulder to cry on, or even just a hug. "Everyone liked her," Nikki said, swallowing the lump in throat.

"Why didn't we ever come visit?" Ryan shifted until he was facing her. "When she was alive, I mean. We never came."

It wasn't the first time she'd heard the question, and it definitely wasn't the first time she'd given the same answer. She opened her mouth to repeat it, but no words came out. Fortunately, before Ryan could push the issue, Levi walked into the room.

He placed his big hand on Nikki's shoulder and said, "Are you ready? It's time to start."

Nikki nodded. "Are you ready to do this, buddy?"

Like the little man he was becoming, Ryan jumped to his feet and straightened his jacket. "I'm ready, Mom."

"Hey." Levi put his hand on Ryan's shoulder. "Why don't you run to the bathroom so I can talk to your mom for a minute?"

Ryan glanced between them and then did as he was told. When the door closed behind him, Levi turned to Nikki. "How you doing, kiddo? Are you ready for this?"

"Can you ever be ready to say goodbye to your mom?"

He put his hand on her shoulder and squeezed. "I wasn't talking about your mom."

Nikki looked at her feet and twisted her hands. She knew exactly what he was talking about. "That's going to be hard, too. Really hard."

"You're doing the right thing and everyone is going to understand."

"No." Nikki shook her head. "No one is going to understand." She swung around, determination in her eyes. "But I don't care. I'm sick of running. I'm sick of hiding my son. It's not fair to him, it wasn't fair to my mom, and—"

"It's not fair to you, Nikki."

"That doesn't matter."

"Yes," Levi said, his voice soft. "It does. And I hope this means that you're staying. Going to give that boy a home."

"He has a home. He's always had a home."

"This is his home, Nikki. He belongs here. You both do."

Her head spun with what he was saying and what was waiting for them beyond the walls of the private room. It was easy for Levi to think that everything would be okay and the citizens of Halfway would accept them with open arms. But he wasn't the one who had to face them.

Just then, Ryan came out of the bathroom and Nikki knew she couldn't put it off any longer. She held her hand out for her son, took a deep breath and nodded her head at Levi. "Let's do this."

Whatever was going to happen, and no matter how people were going to react, Nikki didn't care. She couldn't. Today was about her mom and her son. And that was all that mattered.

The moment they walked in, the room fell silent and all eyes were on Nikki and Ryan as they made their way down the aisle to the front row. She tried to ignore the gentle murmuring that started up and wrapped her arm around Ryan a little tighter, wanting to shield him from the whispering and rumors that would undoubtedly start to spread through the crowd. When they got to the front of the room, she made Ryan sit first, so she could sit on the end and block him from view. When she was settled, she glanced over to her left and directly into the eyes of Matt, who was watching them intently. Averting her gaze, she caught the way Becky's pretty face was clouded with hurt, and she saw the tears swimming in her eyes.

She knew that although Becky was probably sad for the real reason they were there, that wasn't the reason for the tears. She couldn't move her gaze from Ryan, and Nikki couldn't even begin to imagine what was going through her friend's head. She averted her eyes and focused on Levi, who was starting the service.

Somehow she made it through the next forty-five minutes. Her mother and Levi had done a beautiful job of designing the service and choosing the songs. But not even her mother could have planned the amazing speeches and tributes her friends and neighbors prepared for her. They brought tears to her eyes, but she wouldn't let them spill. She had to stay strong for Ryan because the hardest part of the day hadn't even started yet.

As soon as the final hymn began to play, Levi closed his book, left it on the table and walked down the aisle, stopping in front of her. She blinked and took his outstretched hand, gratefully gripping it like an anchor in the swirling sea of chaos. She tucked her arm in his and took Ryan's hand, letting Levi lead them through the room. She could feel everyone's eyes on them as they made their way slowly. The urge to flee was strong. But she could feel Becky and Matt's eyes watching her. She glanced down at her son, tears streaking his face, and she knew she couldn't run. As much as she wanted to leave all the heartache behind her, she owed it to her little boy.

She took a deep breath, fortifying herself and moved into the reception area where everyone would gather to offer her condolences, eat finger sandwiches, and sip tea. She could handle the well-wishers; she just hoped she could handle Matt and Becky.

Chapter Fourteen

~*Becky*~

He really was Matt's son. That's the only thing Becky could think when she first caught sight of Ryan as he walked down the aisle with Nikki. Her chest hurt as she struggled to contain all the emotions that threatened to break loose. She reached for Matt's hand and held tightly as she struggled to not stare. From the little curl in his hair to the shade of blue in his eyes, there was no doubt. And from the low murmur behind her, she knew others had noticed too.

Matt's legs twitched beside hers, and she knew he wanted to go over and sit with his son, introduce himself and just be there. She also knew that he heard the voices behind them as well.

She forced herself to focus on Levi, who stood at the front, but it was difficult. She glanced over at her mother, who sat in her wheelchair at the end of the pew and tried to smile at her. She'd had a long talk with Norma earlier today as she signed her out of the hospital and took her home.

"Today is a time to celebrate Marie's life. To honor her love for her family, for her friends, and for this town. She was the mother everyone wanted, the friend you never thought you deserved, the woman with a heart large enough to take every stray in and love them as her own." Levi had put down his paper and spoke from his heart.

Becky struggled to listen to his words, knowing how difficult today must be for him. But it was hard. All she could think about was afterwards. Surely afterwards Nikki would let Matt spend some time with his son, introduce them and not hide Ryan away anymore. She had to. Right?

Norma had warned her not to rush things, especially today. They were here to honor Marie, not to guilt Nikki into staying in town so Matt could be with his son, no matter how much Becky had wanted that to be the case. A million arguments rolled through her mind, things she could say to Nikki to help her see reason, but they all ended up being lame and selfish.

Look at it through Nikki's heart, her mother had advised. And she'd tried. She really, really had, but she couldn't. She would never have left, not like that, not without saying goodbye first. Nor did she think she had the strength to raise a child, all alone, without ever once asking for help. As much as she hated to admit it, Becky was a homebody at heart. She would have stayed, faced the criticism of being a pregnant and unwed teenager and figured out a way to make it work.

Nikki's reasons for leaving the way she had hurt more ways than she'd wanted to admit. What kind of a friend had she been to Nikki back then? Had she really been that shallow? That selfish?

As she listened to the stories that people told of Marie, how one woman had touched their lives in a way that would never be forgotten, Becky knew that if today had been her funeral, those same stories wouldn't have been said.

When Uncle Dennis stood and shuffled his way out past her

mother's wheelchair, Becky wondered what story her uncle would have to share, so she was caught a little off guard when he began to push Norma towards the front.

Tears smarted in her eyes as she watched her mother unfold a sheet of paper and place it in her lap.

"If Marie were here today, she'd be telling us all to shush up and enjoy a piece of her homemade baking. If there ever was a woman who hated to be praised, it was her. And yet, I don't think I've ever known a woman who deserved it more."

Becky caught the way Levi smiled as he sat beside the podium.

"Marie saved my life, literally, and in more ways that I could even describe. She was there for me when I lost my babies all those years ago. She stood by me as I watched Levi here lower my husband's body into his grave and she sheltered me as best she could before we were hit by that truck on the road. Those last few moments together," her mother's voice caught, "they play through my mind, over and over. We were talking about our daughters, and how proud of them we were." Norma smiled at Becky before she turned her attention to Nikki. "Girl, your mother loved you with all her heart. You were her reason for getting up every day and doing everything she did, even though you were living somewhere else. There wasn't a mother more proud of her daughter than Marie."

As Norma paused, the sound of sniffles filled the room. Becky reached for a new tissue from the box beside her as she watched her mother compose herself.

"I lost my sister that day. I wish there had been something I could have done to stop her death. Maybe I could have stopped for that coffee she'd suggested instead of wanting to rush home after our shopping trip, or even traded places with her even though I knew she was too tired to drive. She saw that truck first, but rather than try to protect herself, she leaned over and sheltered my body with hers even as the truck hit us." Norma's head dropped and her hands twisted together in her lap as she sat there, in front of everyone, struggling not to cry.

"Tomorrow is our town's Tree Festival and you all know how much Marie loved our annual tradition. Even though she won't be there with us in person, her spirit will be and I know she would be so proud of the fact that our two daughters had worked on it together." She smiled at Becky and then raised her chin. "I'm not saying goodbye today. I don't believe in them. I'll be seeing my best friend soon enough. She knows how I like things to be done, so I'm sure after she's done her exploring of heaven up there, she'll be working on getting things ready for me. But until that day, I don't plan to waste one more moment— if anything is to be taken from this day, from the stories told by everyone here, it's that we all need to be more like Marie, and that's exactly what I plan to do. Starting now."

Becky leaned her head against Matt's shoulder at her mother's words. She was right, as usual. She looked up at her husband and mouthed *I love you* to him as Levi ended the service with one of Marie's quotes and then the final instructions Marie had given him.

"Now, you all know Marie loved a good party, so please, if you'll all join us in the reception hall, there are platters of Marie's favorite sandwiches and treats, as well as a special gift for everyone. There's a table as you enter with these gifts. Please, take one. But don't open it. What Marie would like is for you to give that little gift to someone else—someone not here today. The idea is to spread a little bit of love around, and what better time than this, during the holiday season."

Levi headed down the aisle, but stopped beside Nikki and offered her his arm. Becky's heart broke for her old friend. Nikki's face had blanched and there was a hollow look to her eyes as she reached towards Levi. She held her other hand out and waited for her son to take it and then walked beside Levi towards the back of the room. Becky waited for Matt to stand, but he didn't move; he just sat there, his body angled to watch Nikki and Ryan. There was an uncomfortable silence in the room before Matt turned around and focused on the front. Becky looked behind her and nodded to the people who watched them with concerned glances.

"Matt, we should go," Becky whispered. As if in a daze, Matt stood. She couldn't read what was going through his mind, but she could imagine. She reached for his hand and pulled him down towards the other end of the pew where her mother waited.

With bags beneath her eyes, Norma looked as if she was ready to fall asleep. "Do you want Uncle Dennis to take you home?" Just fresh out of the hospital, her mother did not need to be overdoing it, no matter how much medication she was on.

"Not yet. But when I'm ready, Dennis will take me home, don't worry."

"I do worry. You need to be resting."

"I'll rest when I'm dead." Norma's lips thinned. "Just remember what I said earlier. Don't force things in there. Let Nikki make the first move."

Becky glanced at Matt. He wasn't paying them any attention. "I'm not sure if that's even possible. I don't think Matt will see anyone else in the room but his—"

"Then make it possible," Norma interrupted. "This is not the time. There's enough pressure on her as it is. Don't you think others are going to be seeing the connection?"

Becky's shoulders dropped. Everyone knew, the moment Nikki had walked down the aisle with her son, that he was Matt's. They'd have to be blind not to see the resemblance.

"Come on." Matt pulled her arm. "It's time." Becky doubted he'd heard a single word her mother had said. She followed him out of the room and into the reception area, where everyone stood, waiting for this moment.

###

The look Nikki gave Becky as she stood at the other end of the reception hall surrounded by people who only wanted to wish her well reminded Becky of a time from when they'd been kids attending a summer camp.

Nikki's name had been called to take part of an impromptu skit during their nightly fire camp time. Not one to bask in the spotlight, Nikki had frozen while everyone started to chant her name.

She looked the exact same way right now. Frozen. A weak smile was plastered on her face and she had her arm wrapped around her son's shoulders. Becky could tell she wanted to get away from those who surrounded them but couldn't.

So Becky reacted as only she could. She dropped Matt's hand and marched across the room to her friend's defense, calling out her name in a loud voice.

"Nikki." She had no idea what she was going to say but anything would work. "My..."—she glanced around the room and saw Norma by the door—"mom is going to be heading home soon. I don't think you've seen her yet since you've been home." She nudged her way between a couple who were giving pointed stares at Ryan and hooked her arm through her friend's. "Excuse us," she said as they shouldered past.

"Thank you," Nikki whispered.

"Don't mention it. And don't mention how tired my mom looks either when you see her. She was just released this morning but you know her..." Her voice drifted off as they stopped in front of Norma.

Nikki dropped down to her knees and reached for Norma's hand.

"I'm so sorry I haven't been by to see you," she said. "I was too..."

"Shhh, it's okay. I know." Her mother leaned forward slightly and rested her free hand against Nikki's cheek. She glanced over at Ryan and gave a soft smile. "Now, before we both get too muddled with tears, why don't you introduce me to this young man?"

Becky took a step back and gave her mother a questioning glare. *What happened to letting Nikki take the lead?*

"This is Ryan, my son." Nikki's voice grew in strength as she stared at the boy. She raised herself off her knees and placed her arm around Ryan's shoulders.

"Well now." Norma sat back and placed her hands together in her lap. Her head tilted to the side and then she chuckled. "You remind me of your grandma, did you know that? I think it's the nose and maybe the smile, but I'm not sure about that. I'd have to see it first." Her eyes sparkled as Ryan looked up at Nikki in surprise.

"I do?" he said.

Nikki nodded. "You do. I never noticed that before."

"Now," Norma held out her plate to Ryan, "why don't you be a good boy and go get me a few more of those brownies and anything else that looks sweet. I've been eating hospital food for too long." Ryan looked at his mom for approval before he took the plate and made his way to the table.

Becky found herself turning to watch him. She told herself it was to make sure no one else bothered him while Norma was talking to Nikki but she knew it was also because she wouldn't have been able to keep her eyes off him even if she'd tried.

This is Matt's son. She still couldn't believe it.

"Did my mother ever say anything about..." Nikki's voice trailed off.

"About her grandchild? No." Norma shook her head. "She kept your secrets, child."

"I'm sorry."

"You don't need to apologize to me. I'm sure you both had your reasons. God knows, I have my share of secrets too." Norma reached out and grabbed hold of both Nikki's and Becky's hand. Becky's stomach churned. She had no idea what her mother was doing. "Between your mother and me, we had one regret and that was the fallout between you two. It was something we'd been talking about that day as well, how we wish you two would find a way back to each other. I know there is a lot of hurt and distance between you two, but please, try to find a way to make it work. If not for yourselves, then for Marie and that little boy you've got." Norma dropped their hands, cleared her throat and swiped at the tears that flowed down her weathered cheeks as Ryan came to stand beside his mother and handed her a plate that overflowed with sweets.

"This is exactly what I needed, thank you." Norma reached out for the plate and smiled. "Now I think it's time for Dennis to take me home. I'm a bit tired."

Becky leaned down and placed a soft kiss on her mother's cheek. "Do you want me to stop in before we head home?"

"No need. Just come by in the morning to pick me up." Before Dennis wheeled her away, she placed her hand on Ryan's arm. "You come see me tomorrow, by the big tree, okay? I have something for you that was your grandmother's."

"But we..." Nikki's voice trailed off as Dennis pushed Norma out of the reception room.

"Don't say you won't be there." Becky turned to face her

friend. "You have to be there. Ryan would love it." She smiled down at Matt's son.

At Nikki's sharp intake of breath, Becky turned just as Matt came to stand at her side.

"Would like what?" he said.

Trying to act nonchalant, Becky gave Matt a bright but tense smile. "I was saying how much Nikki's son would love the festival tomorrow." She hoped he understood the undercurrent going on between them. Becky would do anything and everything she could to get Nikki to stay, even if just for an extra day.

Matt's eyes narrowed. "You're not thinking of leaving, are you?"

Before Nikki could respond, Ryan stepped in front of his mom and faced her. "But we can't. Grandma's friend said she had something for me."

"And there's a lot of kids' activities planned that Ryan should enjoy," Becky interjected while Nikki shook her head.

"I don't...there's still so much..." Nikki sighed in defeat. "We'll see, okay?" She gave a pointed look to both Becky and Matt while she ruffled Ryan's hair. He stepped back from her touch and attempted to fix his hair without looking embarrassed and Becky struggled not to smile. A boy trying to be a man.

There was an awkward silence between the four of them before Ryan took a good look at Matt and smiled.

"You came over to the house, didn't you? You're mom's friend."

Matt smiled. "Sure am. I've known your mom since she was...well, I've known her my whole life."

"Your whole life?" When Ryan looked at Nikki, Becky almost choked back a chuckle. You could tell mother and son had a silent language and that Ryan was practically yelling at her. Nikki winced before she glanced up at the ceiling.

"I need your help, Mom." Becky heard Nikki's soft prayer

before she squatted down so she was eye level with her son and reached for his hands.

"Okay, buddy, remember how I was telling you that...well, that your...This is Matt. Your—"

"Father," both Matt and Ryan said together.

Becky choked up and had to turn her head in hopes no one would have noticed. The way they said it at the same time, combined with the look of desperation in Nikki's eyes, just about floored her. Becky felt like a bystander, someone with vivid interest in the scene before her but with little or no impact to what was happening. The look of understanding and hope that flared in Ryan's eyes broke her heart. How long had this boy wondered about his father? How long did Nikki think she could continue with the facade?

Matt held out his hand to Ryan and waited for the young boy to take it. Once he did, Matt shook it, holding tightly to his son's fingers.

"I'm Matt and this," Matt reached for Becky's hand and held tightly, "is my wife and your mother's best friend, Becky. And Ryan," Matt had to clear his voice before he could speak again, "it's really nice to finally meet you."

Chapter Fifteen

~Nikki~

Nikki wasn't sure how she'd feel when the truth was finally all out there. But when Matt and Ryan looked at each other, father and son finally understanding their connection with each other, Nikki did not expect the rush of emotion that crashed over her. When her knees buckled, thankfully someone was there at her side, holding her up before she could cause a scene. She turned to see who her savior had been because everyone else was intent on watching the reaction between Matt and Ryan.

"Oh," Nikki said when she saw Parker Rhodes at her side, his arm hooked under her elbow, subtly keeping her from falling. "Thank you. I didn't even know you were here." The truth was, Nikki hadn't seen anyone. She'd been so focused on saying goodbye to her mom and the impending meeting, she had barely registered the speeches, let alone the mourners in attendance.

He smiled gently. "I wouldn't miss it. Are you okay?"

Nikki nodded. "I am, thank you. It's been a rough day and,"

she gestured with her head to the little meeting that was going on next to them, "it's far from over."

"I can see that." He raised his eyebrows and Nikki knew he wouldn't press for details. He didn't have to. Certainly he could see the truth just as well as everyone else in the room. "I think you could use a tea," he said. "If you're sure you can stand on your own, I'll go grab you one."

"Thank you, Parker."

He nodded again and disappeared into the crowd, giving Nikki a chance to focus on Ryan and Matt, who had fallen into easy conversation. She should have been surprised that her ten-year-old son who'd just met his father for the first time was capable of having a casual conversation about video games, but she wasn't. That's just the way Ryan was. Just like his dad.

She let out a breath she hadn't realized she'd been holding and looked past the big smile on Matt's face to Becky. She was watching the two of them intently with a strange look on her face. But it wasn't a bad expression. Instead, Becky looked almost happy. Could she be pleased about Matt's illegitimate child? No. Not *pleased* about that, but knowing Becky, she was just happy for her husband, because there was no denying the pleasure in his face while he was talking to his child.

Thank you. Becky mouthed the words to Nikki.

Becky didn't have to thank her. *No.* Nikki shook her head. It should be her thanking Becky for being so understanding. Why was she? The Becky Nikki had known in high school would have lost her mind to find out about Ryan. This was one scene that would not have played out ten years ago.

But it wasn't ten years ago. And things changed. But could things change that much?

Nikki looked around the room at the gathering of towns-people who'd come to pay their respects. More than a few of them had noticed the scene playing out between Matt and

Ryan. And no doubt they'd all put together the pieces of the puzzle. So far, no one had come to offer Nikki her condolences. They were waiting. Likely because there was more interesting things happening.

She hated that she was so cynical, but small towns were all the same and even if some things changed, they wouldn't have changed that much. She felt as if she were moving in a fog, but she turned her attention back to what Ryan and Matt were talking about. They were still on the subject of video games, and Ryan was giving Matt the detailed play-by-play of his favorite game, Minecraft.

"Have you heard of it?" Ryan asked Matt, who'd pulled up two chairs so they were sitting across from each other. "It's all about creating worlds, but there are griefers and they like to destroy everything you create. It sucks."

"I bet it does," Matt said, his voice laced with sincerity. "When I was your age, I liked to play Mario Brothers. And Bowser was always trying to destroy everything."

"Mario Brothers? No way? My friend has that one. It's so cool."

Matt laughed. "I think the game you're thinking of is a bit newer than the one I used to play."

"Would you like to play with me sometime, Da—Ma—"

Nikki froze, and she wasn't the only one. Matt's grin faded, and a look of panic came over his face, as Ryan tried to finish his sentence.

"Um," he mumbled and looked around at the adults. "What should I call you?"

Matt looked to Nikki for help, but she couldn't offer any assistance. She was still frozen to the spot. A roaring filled her head as the noise of the room seemed to pick up volume. Her legs threatened to give out again, causing her to grip the table.

Thankfully, it was Becky who saved them all from the

increasingly awkward moment. "Why don't you call him Matt for now?" she suggested gently. "And you can call me Becky. This is all pretty new to all of us, so we can figure it out as we go, don't you think?"

Ryan seemed satisfied with that answer and in true ten-year-old-boy fashion, completely changed the subject. "There's cake over there. Did you know my grandma loved cake? It didn't even matter what kind it was. She liked all of it."

Nikki's eyes filled up with tears at the reminder of why they were all gathered there. "Why don't you go get some?" she suggested.

"Really?"

"Of course." She tousled his hair. "And you know what? I think I could really use some cake, too."

"But you never eat cake!"

"Well, today is an exception, I guess." She forced a smile. "And I think I'd like the biggest piece you can find me. Do you think you can do that?"

Ryan set off on his mission and suddenly Nikki didn't know what she was doing standing there with Matt and Becky. She glanced around uncomfortably, wishing someone, anyone at all, would come up to offer her a kind word about her mother, or a hug, or...

"He's amazing," Matt said.

Nikki blinked and focused on him. Matt had stood from his chair and was standing next to Becky, his arm around her waist.

"He really is, Nikki," Becky chimed in. "He's so well-spoken and such a polite little boy. I can't believe he's ten."

Silence fell over them as they all thought about her words. Of course he was ten. That was the entire reason they were all in the position they were in.

Nikki broke the tension. "Well, I'm glad you like him," she said. "He really is a good kid and so smart."

"Just like his dad was at that age," Becky said.

"Becky, I don't think..." Matt glanced at Nikki. "Is this weird?"

She nodded and answered truthfully. "Yes. But she's right. He's so much like you. Every day I feel like I'm looking at a mini version of you. The way he talks, his interests, even the way he wrinkles up his nose when he laughs. Sometimes I wonder if there's any of me in him at all."

Nikki didn't miss the way Becky straightened and squared her shoulders. No doubt this was difficult on her. How could it not be?

"I know today is hard," Matt said. "But even with everything going on, thank you for doing this."

She shrugged. "It was time. And it's not like he didn't already figure it out, right? I told you, he's a smart kid." She looked around and saw a woman she recognized as one of her mom's many friends heading in her direction. "I really should go talk to some people. Can we continue this later?"

"Of course," Matt said and Becky nodded. They were so in tune with each other that Nikki couldn't help but feel a small pinch of envy at their closeness.

"Good." She moved to turn away when Becky's words stopped her.

"Now that we've found him," she said, "we're really looking forward to having Ryan be part of our lives. I guess we'll have to talk about what that looks like."

Icy fear pricked along her spine and a knot twisted in Nikki's stomach. Finally, unsure of how she made her head move, she nodded. "Yes," was all she said before turning away, desperate to find her son and make the rounds so she could leave and the day could be over.

· · ·

###

Nikki led the way up the porch, kicking herself for not leaving a porch light on, while Parker carried a sleeping Ryan in his arms. She unlocked the door and held it as he went inside.

"You can put him down on the couch," she said. "He's probably getting heavy."

Parker shook his head and used it to gesture to the stairs.

"No," Nikki whispered. "He's too heavy—you'll hurt yourself."

With a grin, Parker hefted the sleeping boy a bit higher in his arms and headed towards the stairs. Nikki shook her head and followed after them. "First door on the right."

Parker slipped Ryan onto the bed without disturbing him. Nikki was able to pull his shoes and jacket off before covering him with his blanket. He might as well sleep in his clothes. He'd had a big day, and there was no way Nikki would risk waking him up just for pajamas.

"Come on," she whispered to Parker and ushered him out of the room, clicking the door shut behind them.

Once they were downstairs, Parker didn't make any move to leave, and suddenly the idea of being alone didn't seem all that appealing to Nikki, either. "Would you like a coffee or maybe something stronger? It's been that kind of day."

Parker laughed. "Something stronger sounds great."

In the kitchen, Nikki found a surprisingly well-stocked liquor cabinet, if you liked liqueurs, that was. She shrugged apologetically to Parker. "Sorry, it seems I only have Grand Marnier, Amaretto, and some creamy pink stuff."

"Hmm, as enticing as the creamy pink stuff sounds, a glass of Amaretto over ice would be perfect."

She poured them two glasses and they went back to the

living room, where Nikki curled up on one end of the couch, pulling an afghan over her legs.

"Thank you for today," she said.

He smiled and she liked that he didn't even pretend not to know what she was thanking him for. "It's what friends do," he said. "I am truly sorry that you had to go through this today. I know when I lost my dad, it was really hard."

"Thanks, Parker. That means a lot."

They each sipped their drinks and Nikki waited for him to ask the question that had to be weighing on his mind. After a few minutes of silence, Parker said, "So, that's why you left." It wasn't a question, but Nikki nodded nonetheless.

"I knew it had to be something big," he continued. "It wasn't like you to just up and take off, and I know some people thought you were running away, but—"

"There were stories?" She asked the question even though she knew that of course there'd be a variety of rumors floating around about her departure.

Parker laughed and Nikki couldn't help but notice the way his eyes sparkled when he was relaxed. "Oh, you should have heard some of the rumors, Nik. The people of Halfway could have won awards for their creative storytelling. It really was impressive. But my favorite was that you'd run away with the carnival and eventually settled in California, where you lived in a commune."

She laughed along with him and it surprised her with how good it felt. "That was your favorite?"

"Well, I did like the idea of you being happy," he said, the laughter dying on his lips. "I always wanted you to be happy, Nik."

She looked down at her lap and rolled the glass between her hands.

"I see now that I never had a chance," Parker said softly. "It was Matt all along, wasn't it?"

Nikki nodded. "It was."

"I get it."

She looked up. "You do?"

"Well, sort of." He shrugged. "I get how you could love someone who couldn't love you back."

Nikki's heart cracked for him as she realized what he was saying. "I'm sorry, Parker. I didn't realize."

"I know you didn't." He chuckled again. "That was the whole problem. But, hey. That was a long time ago."

"It was." She nodded. It would have been so much easier if she'd fallen in love with Parker all those years ago. And then the whole mess never would have happened. But she never would have had Ryan. And despite all the drama and hurt her actions had caused, she didn't regret it. She couldn't.

"Well, I'm glad you're back." Parker raised his glass.

"Oh, I'm not back."

"You're sitting here."

"No. Well, yes. But I'm not back. Not for good."

"What about..." He tipped his head. "You can't really mean that you're going to leave. Now? What does Matt say about it?"

She shook her head. She couldn't think about it. She couldn't make a decision. Not right away. But Becky's words kept ringing in her ears. No matter how she tried to distract herself all afternoon, she couldn't stop thinking about what Becky had said. She wanted Ryan to be part of their lives, and of course she did. But how? She couldn't give up her son. The thought was terrifying. No, she wouldn't just hand Ryan over to them every second weekend. It was unthinkable.

"Hey," Parker said. He'd moved to the couch so he was sitting next to her. His hand on her arm calmed her. Nikki hadn't realized how worked up she'd gotten just thinking of the possibilities. "I didn't mean to freak you out," he said. "I just thought you would have talked about it. Or at least thought about it."

She shook her head again. "No. I didn't. I mean, I did. But not really and..." Her words were lost as sobs took over and shook her body.

Parker took her glass from her and a moment later, he pulled her into his arms. It didn't matter that they hadn't seen each other for ten years or that as sort of high school sweethearts it should have been awkward. It wasn't. And at that moment, Nikki couldn't imagine anything feeling safer than being in Parker's arms.

He stroked her hair and murmured things she couldn't make out, consoling her until her tears dried up. When she felt she might have even a basic control over herself, she pulled away and wiped at her eyes. "I'm sorry," she said. "I don't know where that came from."

"I do." He handed her a tissue from the nearby box. "You've had a hell of a day. Heck, you've had a hell of a week. Not to mention what you must have gone through as a single mom. Nikki, it's okay. You're allowed to cry."

"I know." She sniffed. "It's just that, quite honestly, I don't usually get the chance to...you know..."

"Not be strong?"

She nodded.

He handed her the glass of Amaretto again, and she took a big swallow of the cool liquid. "I know you don't want to stay," he said. "But I, for one, would really like to get the chance to spend more time with you if you do."

"How do you know I don't want to stay?"

He raised his eyebrow at her and took a sip of his drink

before answering. "Besides the fact that you've said as much? It's written all over you. And did you know that I'm really good at reading people?" He grinned and his goofiness had the desired effect.

Nikki laughed. "Are you now?"

"I am," he said with mock seriousness. "Let me tell you about the time that I tried to tell Mrs. McGregor how she was feeling. She came into the shop to order some carnations, but by the time she left, I'd figured out all her secrets. And let me tell you, there are some things I don't even think Mr. McGregor knows about Mrs. McGregor."

Nikki laughed again. It felt good and she let herself get lost in Parker's stories.

###

It wasn't until she was tucked into her bed, hours later, the lingering effects of the Amaretto flowing through her veins, that she once again thought about her choices. She could follow her instinct, and take Ryan far from Halfway and from his father. He'd be upset with her; that went without saying. But he'd be with her. There would be absolutely no risk of Becky and Matt trying to take him from her. And who knew what they wanted? Could she risk it?

Nikki knew Ryan wanted to stay. At least for the festival. Especially after meeting Becky's mom and hearing she had something for him. Besides, what kid didn't like a festival? And now that he'd met his dad...but if they stayed for the festival, Ryan would for sure want to stay longer, and the longer they were here, it would only get harder to leave.

The options swirled through her head as she weighed the pros and cons of each decision. She was a mature, responsible woman. And sure, she knew what she should do. And she knew what was right. But what if what was right wasn't the right choice?

Chapter Sixteen

~Becky~

With her hands wrapped tight around the mug of hot cocoa she'd just been handed by one of the volunteers, Becky made her way down through the market stalls and took the time to stop at every display and chat with those who stood behind the tables. The air was a bit nippy this morning but the weather forecast promised for bright sun and slightly warmer temperatures and Becky hoped it would be true. Even with the bright red scarf wrapped around her neck, her warm jacket and earmuffs, she was still freezing.

Unlike Matt, who wore only a long-sleeved sweater while he hefted bundled trees into place. He lifted a hand in a wave as she made her way towards him before he reached for another tree off the truck and placed it in a pile of other trees in the front of his display. If this year was like previous years, all those trees would soon be found in someone's home by the end of the night.

Becky stopped at a booth stocked with Christmas cookies and mugs of hot water and coffee. She set her cup down and filled up a new cup with coffee for Matt. They'd barely slept last night and she knew he wouldn't say no to another dose of caffeine.

"Most of the single women are salivating right about now, watching that husband of yours."

"As long as they remain hands-off, they can look all they want." Becky smiled at Susan, who stood beside her and filled her own mug. Susan was someone she'd gone to high school with but never really gelled with. They'd nod and say hi if they passed one another in the street and were always friendly, but it would be a long time before Becky invited Susan over for dessert and coffee. "He does look good though, doesn't he?" Even after all these years, she still loved to watch him in action. Even with a sweater, his muscles were still noticeable.

"Quite a shock yesterday, seeing Nikki's son." Susan peered down at her over the rim of her coffee cup.

Becky stiffened, but forced herself to remain relaxed. They'd talked about this last night, how they would react when people brought Ryan up, because they both knew it would happen. They'd agreed that their first priority had to be protecting their family—and that included Nikki as well. They wouldn't slander her, gossip about her, or make any reference to the fact that she'd kept Matt's son away for so long.

"I'm just glad she's finally home." Becky's voice remained friendly and light before she turned and pulled out some cash. "These cookies look delicious." She reached for a plastic-wrapped tray of sugar cookies cut out in tree shapes and decorated with candy balls. "I think it's time Matt stopped for a snack and I've never known him to turn down a cookie." The girl behind the table blushed as she took the money.

"I could swear, he's the spitting image of Matt when he was a kid." Susan stuck close to her side as she left the table and made her way towards her husband.

"He's a cute kid, that's for sure," Becky agreed while inwardly groaning. Susan wasn't the type to let go of anything until she discovered every tasty morsel of gossip she could.

"So is he?"

Becky stopped. "Is he what?" She knew exactly what Susan was after. "If you have any questions, then why not ask Nikki herself? He is, after all, her child." She then left Susan behind, gaping like a dying fish with her mouth wide open as Matt waited for her at the side of the truck.

"Well, hi there, gorgeous." He leaned down and placed a kiss on her lips and then grinned while the guys on top of the truck bed started to whistle. Becky blushed like a school girl.

"Did you really have to do that?" she whispered to him.

"Kiss my wife? Sure did. Your cheeks match the color of your scarf, did you know that? So does your nose." His eyes twinkled.

Becky loved to see him like this—happy, carefree...it'd been awhile and it was all due to Ryan. He'd fairly glowed last night after they came home and it was all he could talk about. She knew he looked forward to today, to when Ryan would arrive and Matt could spend more time with him.

As she'd walked the aisles of the market, she'd kept looking for Nikki or her son and prayed they would arrive. There was a lingering fear that they might not, that Nikki would find an excuse to leave before anyone had a chance to say goodbye or discuss how their lives had changed now. She was tempted to drive over to the house and make sure Nikki would show, but when she'd mentioned it to her mother earlier, she knew it would be a bad idea.

This had to be Nikki's choice. She had to feel the freedom to make her own decision, even though essentially she was making the decision for everyone.

"Have you seen him yet?" Matt asked, his voice lowered so no one else could hear them.

Becky shook her head before she handed him the coffee and cookies. "He'll be here. It's still early."

"I know, it's just..."

"You've got trees to sell before you're allowed to go play," she teased him. "I don't want any of these trees coming home with us tonight."

"Yes ma'am." Matt dug into the cookies and took one out. He bit into it and slowly chewed it. "It's good, but not as good as yours."

"Better not be." She winked at him before she waved to the guys unloading the truck and walked away.

###

The next few hours passed by in a blur as Becky made her rounds through the park to see if anyone needed anything and to make sure her mother didn't overtax herself, but it warmed her heart to watch Norma smile even though she knew today would be hard. This was the first festival where Marie wasn't beside her mother, ensuring everything went smooth, and it would be the first year where their annual post-festival holiday trip to someplace warm didn't happen.

But maybe it was time to start new traditions.

She thought about the tree they'd left at home to decorate tonight. Maybe they should see whether Ryan and Nikki could come over and decorate it with them. Maybe Nikki would even help her make some cookies this year. She'd invite her mother and Uncle Dennis and make a nice evening of it.

It bothered her that she hadn't seen Nikki yet but there was still time.

"Hey beautiful." Arms wrapped around her waist as she stood at the edge of the pavilion where the local school choir was warming up to sing.

"Hey yourself. How's the tree sales?" She rested her head on his chest.

"Sold over half the trees already. But it's lunch time. Can I treat you to a sausage?"

Becky turned in his arms and laughed before they walked off, hand in hand, to where the local hotdog stand was selling farm fresh sausages. Matt had teased her this morning that he'd treat her to the best lunch in town and she should have known this was his idea of what a great lunch was, considering their freezer was stocked with these same sausages and it was Matt's favorite thing to cook on the barbecue.

As they stood in line to order, Matt suddenly dropped her arm and started to wave. She shielded her eyes to see who he was waving at and noticed Ryan standing alone.

"Go on, I'll order for us." Becky nudged him and he took off running across the park.

She caught the wide smile on Ryan's face as Matt made it to his side and then watched as they jogged back towards her. She looked around to see where Nikki was but she couldn't find her.

"Look who's joining us for lunch."

Ryan stood beside Matt with a half-smile on his face, as if he wasn't sure it was okay that he was joining them.

"I hope you like sausages, 'cause they happen to be Matt's favorite food group."

"They're not a food group." Ryan's brow rose and Becky chuckled while Matt pretended to be offended.

"Shhh. Don't say that too loudly," Becky teased. "Should I order your mom one too?"

Ryan shook his head but it was Matt who answered for him. "Nikki will be here later. She's still packing things up in the house." She knew, by the tone in his voice, that he'd really hoped she would have stuck around a little bit longer.

Once they gathered their sausages, Becky hung back while Matt pointed out different things to Ryan in the park. This was the moment he'd been waiting for, to spend some time with his son, and although she knew she wasn't in the way, she didn't want to intrude on their time. But Matt seemed to have other ideas.

"Come on, slowpoke. Ryan has a date he doesn't want to miss." He reached for Becky's hand and pulled her along until she walked by his side. Ryan leaned forward a bit and smiled at her and she smiled back.

"That's right. My mom has something for you, doesn't she?"

Ryan's eyes widened at her words. "That's your mom?"

Becky nodded.

"So she's like, my grandmother?" he asked. A look of wonder filled his face as if he'd never thought about having an extended family now that he'd met his father.

"I guess she would be." Becky shrugged. She really wished Nikki were here right now. *How would she want this to be handled?*

"Do I call her Grandma then?"

Becky caught sight of her mother's wheelchair by the large Christmas tree in the center of the park.

"Why don't you ask her yourself?" She reached for Ryan's hand and waited till he reached out to grab hold of it.

The feel of Ryan's hand in hers caught her a bit off guard. She hadn't thought of what this would feel like, having this type of connection with him, but the moment he threaded his fingers through hers, she knew it felt right. She stared down at their joined hands and then at Matt, who smiled at her.

This was her son. Hers. No, he might not be of her blood, but he was Matt's and that was good enough. She knew the term would be stepmom, but she didn't want to think of it that way. She'd rather he be the son of her heart and right now, she had no problem imagining that to be a possible future.

Norma sat there with a box in her lap and a nostalgic look on her face as they walked towards her.

"You came," she said.

"Yes ma'am." Ryan shuffled his feet and bowed his head.

Norma's brow rose. "What's with this 'ma'am' business? You know who I am by now, don't you?"

Ryan nodded.

"Well then, let's try this again, shall we?"

Ryan blinked a few times before he looked up at Matt.

"It's okay, buddy; there's no pressure here."

It was hard for Becky to keep silent and she glanced around the park again, hoping for a glimpse of Nikki. *Where was she?* She couldn't imagine Nikki letting Ryan come here alone.

"Was my grandma really your best friend?" Ryan eyed the box in her lap.

"Did she ever tell you about me?"

Ryan nodded.

"Well, then you should know she was more than just my best friend. She was the sister of my heart. Much like your mom and my daughter were, when they were growing up."

Ryan stuck his hands in his coat pocket. "Would you mind if I called you Grandma, then, too? I...I really miss her."

A smile wreathed Norma's face as she let go of the box she held in her lap and reached both of her hands out to Ryan. He took hold of them, and she pulled him close until she gave him an awkward hug.

"This dang wheelchair. Once I'm out of it, I'll give you a

proper hug, okay?" She swiped at the tears that gathered in the wrinkled folds on her cheek and smiled. "Now, I promised you that I had a gift for you. And here it is. But..." She stopped Ryan when he went to reach for it. "I want you to promise me something first."

Ryan's hands dropped to his sides. "Like what?"

Smart kid, Becky thought. She knew Matt thought the same thing when he reached for her hand and squeezed. Never promise something until you know what it is, that's what Matt always said.

Norma rolled her eyes. "Just like your father," she muttered. "All I want is for you to promise that you'll finish the thing in here that your grandmother never got to start. But," she paused, "we have to do it together. Okay?"

Becky knew right away what was in the box.

Every year, Norma and Marie would do a puzzle together. They would take turns buying a puzzle to put together but they would never open it until the day after the festival so that it would remain a surprise. Becky never understood how they could wait that long to open the gift to see what kind of puzzle it would be, but they did.

"Whose turn was it?" Becky asked.

"This," Norma cradled the box in her hands, "was Marie's gift to me. I already had mine picked out for her. I found it in the summer when you took me to that baking competition in the city." Her voice tapered off.

Becky knelt down. "Maybe you and I could do that one together?" she suggested.

"I'm confused," Ryan said.

Both Becky and Norma smiled. Norma held out the box to Ryan. "Maybe your mom can explain and then you can come see me tomorrow. A tradition is a tradition, you know. And," she looked up into the sky, "just because you are gone, doesn't mean it's okay for you to break tradition this year. Our grandson, here, will have to pick up your slack."

Ryan glanced over at Matt with a confused look on his face.

"It's okay, buddy. I think it's time Norma took some more pain meds, huh?" He gave a pointed look to Becky. "And we should probably start looking for your mom. I'm surprised she's not here yet."

Ryan's head dropped and Becky's stomach twisted. *Oh dear...*

"Ryan, where is your mom? Does she know you're here?" *Please let him say yes, please let him say yes.*

He shrugged. "Well, she knew I wanted to come here..."

Matt squatted down and looked Ryan in the eye.

"But did she know you left the house to come here?"

Silence. Becky dug out her phone and knew she needed to rectify this. She could only imagine what Nikki must be thinking right about now, wondering where Ryan was.

"Okay, so you didn't tell her you left, but she knew you had wanted to come to the festival. So she should be on her way once she realized you were gone." Matt stood. "Right?" he said as he looked at her.

"I hope so," Becky whispered. The phone rang in her ear and she tapped her leg with her free hand as she waited for the line to be picked up.

Who knows how Nikki would react. Was she still planning to leave? Would she blame her and Matt for Ryan taking off? Could this backfire on them? Would she take Ryan away from them for good?

She knew Matt was thinking the exact same thing as they both looked down at their son, who hung his head in shame.

Chapter Seventeen

~Nikki~

Nikki dropped the last bag in the trunk of the car and headed back into the house to get Ryan. No doubt he was still angry with her for making the decision to leave instead of going to the festival. They'd had a heck of a fight and it wasn't like Ryan to yell at her or really have an outburst of any kind. He was usually such an easygoing kid. But when she'd told him her decision, he hadn't reacted well at all. After bursting into tears and arguing with her, he'd run off to his room, and instead of going after him, Nikki'd left him alone to his thoughts.

But what else could she do? After a sleepless night, she'd finally decided that she couldn't do it. As much as Ryan thought he wanted to go to the festival and see Matt and Becky, he didn't realize what that decision would really mean for them and the life they knew. She was making the right decision by leaving. At least, she hoped she was. She didn't even want to think of how Becky and Matt would react to find out she was gone. It wasn't fair to them to take off, she knew that. She wasn't totally heartless. But a mother's instincts were strong and she had to protect her baby.

Or was it herself she was trying to protect?

She paused on the porch before going inside to collect Ryan. It wasn't too late to change her mind. She could still swing by the festival on her way out of town and then...*Matt would make her stay*, she finished her own thought.

Her mind made up, Nikki pushed through the front door, hollering, "Ryan. It's time to go."

She moved through to the kitchen and surveyed everything that was left to do. She'd have to hire a company to come and pack up the rest of the house. She couldn't do it. Not if it meant staying one day longer. When she didn't hear footsteps above her, Nikki moved to the bottom of the stairs and called again.

"Ryan! Come on, buddy."

When there was still no answer, Nikki started up the stairs. With every step she took, the sense that something was wrong grew. It wasn't like Ryan to ignore her. Even if he was angry, he'd still answer her. She quickened her pace and took the stairs two at a time.

"Ryan? Come on, kiddo. Let's talk." Nikki didn't bother knocking; instead, she flung open the door to Ryan's room. "That's enough, Ryan. We need to get moving. Ryan—" The room was empty.

The hairs on the back of her neck stood up, and Nikki knew even before she searched under the bed and in the closet Ryan wasn't there. Without wasting any more time, she ran through the house, even checking the attic where Ryan had enjoyed playing the other day. But she knew he wasn't there. And with every second that passed, the feeling of dread in the pit of her stomach grew. Not because she didn't know where her son was, but because she was fairly sure she did.

Right as she was about to go flying out the door to grab him and force him to leave with her, the phone on the wall rang. She snatched it up. "Hello?"

"Nikki. Oh, thank God. I caught you." Becky's voice came over the line. "You must be going crazy."

"I am. Where's Ryan? Is he okay?"

"Of course he's okay. Why wouldn't he be?"

"I just...he's not here...and...where are you?"

"We're downtown," Becky said slowly. "Just in the main square. We'll wait here."

Nikki swirled around in the cord, twisting herself up with her mother's old-fashioned phone. She was just about to hang up when Becky added, "Oh, and Nikki?"

Nikki waited, but didn't say anything.

"He came on his own. We had nothing to do with it."

"I...I just can't—"

"But we're glad he did."

Nikki couldn't listen to any more. She hung up, grabbed her purse and was out the door a second later.

###

The town square looked amazing. It always did for the Tree Festival. It'd been so long, Nikki'd almost managed to forget how the town of Halfway went all out for the festival that not only celebrated the season, but also their main industry. She tried not to dwell too much on the decorations, lights, and happy people everywhere she looked. Instead, she kept a keen eye out for Ryan and it wasn't long before she spotted him standing next to Matt near the town tree.

Her breath caught in her throat and she froze. *Would she ever get used to seeing them together?*

Ryan was laughing at something Matt was saying, and even though she wasn't close enough to see it, Nikki knew that both of them would be smiling and their dimples would be on full display. Anyone with two eyes in their head could see they were father and son. And watching them together, Nikki's heart hurt. Clearly, Ryan wanted to be with Matt. He'd run away just to see him, for goodness' sake. Hot tears stung her eyes, and she hastily swiped them away. She would not cry. Not in the middle of town.

Before she could move forward, a voice startled her.

"Nikki. There you are."

Nikki spun around and looked into Becky's eyes that were full of concern and something else. Joy? That was it. She looked happy. Her whole face was glowing, and even Nikki could see it wasn't from the cool air.

"Sorry," Becky said. "I didn't mean to sneak up on you. I was just getting the boys a refill on their hot chocolate."

"The boys?" Something about the casual way Becky referred to Matt and Ryan irked her. "I hope you don't mean Ryan. Because he probably shouldn't have too much sugar. I don't like him to fill up on sweets."

Becky smiled. "Oh, surely a few cups won't hurt. It's a festival, after all."

"Yes," Nikki said. "A few cups most certainly will hurt. But I don't expect you to know that."

When she saw Becky's face fall, Nikki had a flicker of regret. She knew she was being a bitch. Becky didn't deserve her anger, or her fear, or whatever it was she was feeling. But she couldn't seem to stop herself.

"Nik, that wasn't—"

"Fair? You know what's not fair, Becky? Is you trying to steal my son."

"We didn't—"

"Do you have any idea how worried I was when I realized he was gone?" Becky opened her mouth to say something, but before she could, Nikki delivered the blow she knew would hurt the most. "Of course you don't," she spat. "You don't have any children of your own. There's no way you could possibly know how it feels."

She knew the words would hurt. And in all her life, Nikki had never said anything so cruel, especially not to her best friend. The second the words were out of her mouth and Becky recoiled, seeming to collapse on herself, she wanted to take them back. But it was too late. Becky turned and ran, dumping the cups of hot chocolate in a nearby garbage can as she made her escape.

Nikki was rooted to the spot, unable to move. Her chest heaved and she struggled to catch her breath. It took a moment for her to look around. People were staring, and she hadn't even realized she'd raised her voice. But of course people were watching them. Nikki and her illegitimate child must be the talk of the town. Her eyes floated across the crowd, not registering on any one face until they landed on Matt.

She couldn't quite make out his expression, but by the way his mouth was set in a firm line and his arm wrapped around Ryan, pulling him close, she could guess what he was thinking. She had to get out of there. She couldn't just stand in the middle of the town square, acting as the entertainment for everyone. But, still, she couldn't move.

An arm clamped down on her shoulder, and a gentle voice said, "Nikki. Come with me."

She nodded numbly and let the owner of the voice lead her away. The crowd parted for them as they walked and Nikki was glad for the strong arm that held on to her, because she didn't trust her legs to hold her up. It wasn't until she was sitting in a chair behind one of the many craft huts that lined the square, and a foam cup of coffee was put in her hands, that she bothered to look at her savior.

Santa Claus.

Of course. She recognized the voice on some level.

"Thank you, Levi," she said.

"Just drink that and calm yourself down," he said, gruffly. "You're not going to be any good until you get a hold of your emotions."

Nikki almost smiled at the older man as he shook his head and muttered something about women and their moods. He looked almost comical, pacing in his big red suit in front of her.

"Ryan? I should—"

"He's with Matt," Levi said. He pulled up a chair and sat across from her. "I think it's best if he stays there for a bit longer, don't you?"

She nodded, and then a thought hit her. "Oh no. Did he see me...I can't believe...what does—"

"It's okay, Nikki. I don't know how much he saw, but he's a smart kid, that boy. He knows something's up and sometimes it's good for a child to see their mama be human. He'll be okay."

She shook her head and inhaled the hot coffee, using the moment to calm down. "I'm sorry," she said after a moment. "I shouldn't have said any of that. I didn't really mean it."

"I'm sure you didn't," Levi said. "But it's not me who needs apologizing to. And I think you know that."

"I do," she whispered. "I just want what's best for Ryan." Nikki looked up into Levi's kind eyes. "I just wish I knew what that was."

"I think you know." He patted her leg. "You're a good mama, Nikki. And sometimes being a good mama means making the tough decisions."

She smiled weakly. "How do you know all this?"

Levi's smile grew sad and his voice dropped when he said,

"For more than fifteen years after your dad passed, I watched your mama do right by you. She was something."

"Yes she was." Nikki's eyes filled with tears again. "I wish she was here now. She'd know what to do."

They sat in silence for a moment, each of them lost in their own thoughts, while Nikki sipped at her coffee. It was Levi who broke the silence. "What do you think she would have said, Nikki?"

Nikki didn't hesitate when she answered. "She would have told me to stay." A tear slid down her cheek and she didn't bother to wipe it away before another fell. "She never said, but that's all she ever wanted."

Levi nodded. The old man's own eyes glistened with unshed tears.

Nikki knew what she wanted. And she knew what was right. "I think," she said, "maybe I could stay. At least for a little while," she added quickly. "I owe it to Matt and Ryan. They need to get to know each other. And, after everything she did for me, I owe it to my mom, too."

A sob overtook her, and Nikki gave herself over to the tears she'd been holding in for too long.

Levi's warm, safe arms wrapped around her and held her while she cried. "And you, Nikki," he whispered gruffly in her ear. "You owe this to yourself, too."

###

After her tears were spent, Nikki pulled herself together and set out to find Matt and Ryan. But first, she had an apology to make and it was long overdue. It didn't take long to find Becky. Nikki knew her old friend well, and she hadn't changed that much in ten years.

Just as she'd guessed, Becky was standing at the bake sale table, taking in the goodies and fresh baked treats for sale. Ever since they were kids, Becky'd always used chocolate to feel better. And from what she understood, it had served her well in life with her successful baking blog. Becky didn't know it, but ever since her mom told her about it, Nikki had become one of Becky's most faithful followers.

She took a deep breath before she approached her. People were watching, but she didn't care. Nothing else mattered except making right what she'd broken so many years ago.

"Becky?"

Her friend stiffened, and turned slowly. Her eyes were red and her make-up smudged, but she was still the same beautiful Becky.

"Can we talk?" Nikki asked.

Becky nodded and in a vain effort to give them some privacy, Nikki led them to a small bench. "I'm sorry," she said without waiting. "I was totally out of line and I need you to know that I didn't mean any of that. I just—"

"You're scared."

Nikki let out a long breath. "Yes," she said. "I'm terrified."

"I know this is hard." Becky's lips turned up in a small smile. She took Nikki's hand. "Heck, it's hard for all of us. But you don't have to be scared, Nik. We're family."

It took her a minute to process what Becky was saying.

"And we don't want to take Ryan away from you," Becky continued. "We would never do that."

Nikki nodded.

"But we do want to know him and be part of his life."

"Of course." Nikki thought of earlier when she'd seen Matt

and Ryan laughing together. "I want that, too," she said, and meant it.

Becky's smile got bigger and she said, "Should we go find the—Matt and Ryan?" She caught herself, no doubt remembering the way Nikki had flown off the handle the last time she referred to them so casually.

Nikki nodded. "But first..." She pulled Becky into a hug and held her old friend tightly. "I'm so, so sorry, Becky," she said without releasing her. "I never wanted to hurt you and—"

"It's okay."

"No. It's not. I can't change it. Any of it. But I need you to know that, okay?"

Becky nodded and pulled away. There were tears shining in her eyes. "I know it, Nik. I do. And you're right, we can't change it. So, what do you say we move forward, together?"

"I'd like that." Nikki's own eyes filled up again. "Damn tears," she said with a laugh. "Come on, let's go find the boys."

Epilogue

~Nikki~

Bags in hand, Nikki stepped out of the Evergreen Grocer and onto the sidewalk. She inhaled deeply, letting her lungs fill with the fresh spring air. She'd always loved this time of year in Halfway, when the snow was melting, the trees were budding, and everything was slowly starting to come to life again. She took her time walking down the sidewalk, letting her mind drift. When she reached her car, she dropped her groceries off before continuing down the street to her next destination.

What was meant to be a few days in Halfway turned into a few weeks. And finally, it just made sense to enroll Ryan in classes. The longer they spent in town, the more they both felt as if they were home. Not to mention the way Ryan and Matt were together. At first there'd been a bit of awkwardness between them as they tried to figure out their roles with each other. But Nikki couldn't believe how quickly even that vanished as they easily slipped into a comfortable father-son relationship. It made Nikki's heart happy to see them together.

And with each day that passed, she knew she would never take it away from them.

The bells over the door tinkled as she walked into the flower shop. She couldn't hide the smile when Parker called from the back of the shop. "I'll be right there," he said.

Nikki didn't say anything as she picked out a small bouquet of yellow roses and went to the counter to wait for him.

"Sorry," Parker said as he came out of the back room. "I was just finish—Nikki?" His handsome face split into a grin at the sight of her. "What are you doing here?"

She held up the bouquet. "It's my mom's birthday today. Yellow roses were her favorite."

Parker's smile fell. "I'm sorry," he said and moved around the corner to pull her into his arms.

"It's okay," she said when he released her. "Honestly. I'm fine." And she was. For the first time in a long time, Nikki felt good about things and even though there was an ache in her heart every time she thought of her mother, it was okay. "I just wanted to get her some flowers," she said. "It felt right."

"Of course." Parker took another look at her, likely making sure she really was okay and wasn't going to melt down into a puddle of tears, before heading around to the other side of the counter. "But there's no charge." He took the flowers and wrapped them up. "Not for Marie."

Nikki smiled gratefully and took the bouquet. "Thank you," she whispered.

He shrugged and the smile appeared on his face again. "But we're still on for later, right?"

"Absolutely." Nikki straightened up and tossed her hair behind her shoulder in an effort to flirt. "I can't wait to cook you my specialty. Chicken parmesan." She didn't point out that it wasn't really her specialty. In fact, she'd never actually cooked it before, but she really wanted their date to be special. They'd been seeing each other for a few months, but with their busy schedules and Ryan of course, they couldn't seem to find much time to be alone. But that was all about to change. With Ryan staying over at Matt and Becky's, Nikki was determined to make their first night alone together as special as possible.

"You know, we can go out." Parker looked down at the counter, wiping some unseen smudge off the glass. "I heard the Spruce Grill has a new pasta dish that's supposed to be really good."

"Parker, I—"

"If you don't want pasta, their steak sandwich is—"

"Parker," she said with more force behind her voice. "I'm going to cook. I want to. I already bought the groceries."

"Okay," he said, his voice laced with doubt. "If you really want to. But I'm bringing dessert, so we have something to eat." He added the last part with a mumble under his breath.

"Hey." She put her hands on her hips. "I don't know what you think you know about my cooking. But I'll have you know that I'm pretty good in the kitchen."

"That's not the way I remember it."

She stopped to think for a minute about what he could possibly be talking about. When the realization hit her, she burst into laughter. "Wait," she said, trying to gulp back her giggle. "Are you talking about the chili I made in senior year?"

He nodded, looking at her with worry.

"Parker. That was ten years ago. I'm a much better cook than that now. I was just a kid."

"A guy doesn't get over that many chili peppers." His voice was completely serious, but his face split into a smile. "But you're right, that was a long time ago," he said.

Parker's words were heavy with meaning, and Nikki nodded. "Yes. It was. And a lot can change in ten years."

As if to prove her point, she leaned across the counter and

took his face into her hands, placing a soft, sweet kiss directly on his lips.

"I'll see you later." With a small wave, she took the flowers and left the shop. She had two more stops to make before she could head home and start cooking for her date.

It was a short drive to the Jennings' farm, and Nikki hopped out of the car without hesitation. Becky would be waiting for her, and she didn't have much time. She didn't bother knocking as she opened the door and called, "Hey. I'm here."

"In the kitchen."

Nikki smiled. *As if Becky would be anywhere else.*

Her friend was behind the counter, covered in flour, with a big smile on her face and a mouthwatering smell coming from the oven. "What are you baking? It smells amazing."

"Ryan's favorite. A triple chocolate fudge cake," she said. "Here, try this." She held out a bowl and Nikki stuck her finger in the icing. Her eyes closed and she let out a small groan of pleasure.

"No wonder that's Ryan's favorite. It's seriously the most delicious thing ever. Way better than the ones I used to pick up from the grocery store."

"Oh no." Becky looked horrified. "You did not feed that poor boy grocery store cakes. No wonder he's insatiable for my baking."

Nikki laughed. "The kitchen has always been your strong suit," she said. "Not mine." She looked around. "Where are the boys?"

"Matt's got them out checking the fields," Becky said. "I think they're mostly looking to see if the streams are all thawed. But they won't admit that. When they found out Ryan had never been fishing before, Levi got it in his head that they need to fix that problem as soon as possible."

A flush of shame crossed Nikki's face. Of course Ryan

would like to go fishing. She'd never thought that he might be missing out on that by not having a father in his life. But now that he had a father in Matt and an unexpected grandfather figure in Levi, there was no doubt they'd catch him up on everything he'd missed.

"Stop that," Becky said, waving her towel in Nikki's direction. "There's nothing to be upset about. Here, have some more icing." Becky thrust the bowl at her again, and Nikki happily took a large finger full.

"Yummy. You seriously have to teach me to make that."

"One thing at a time." Becky laughed and wiped her hands on her apron. She reached for her giant binder that Nikki knew was her cookbook and dropped it on the counter between them. "Here's the recipe." She opened the rings and carefully withdrew the page. "It's super easy to follow and you shouldn't be able to screw it up."

Nikki raised her eyebrow.

"I said, you *shouldn't* but you have to follow the directions. Did you get all the ingredients I told you to?"

Nikki nodded.

"Good. Then you'll be fine."

"I hope so," Nikki said, taking the paper. "It's kind of an important dinner."

"Is it?" Becky wiggled her eyebrows and Nikki swatted at her. "Well, it's about time," Becky said. "Parker's great. You know I want you to be happy."

"I know."

"It's all I've ever wanted, Nik."

They locked eyes across the counter and it was Nikki who reached out and squeezed her friend's hand. "I know," she said. "And I am. I really am."

"So am I. You have no idea how much it means to me that you're—"

"Me too." Nikki cut her off, not needing her to finish the sentence. "I'm glad I'm here, too."

They stared at each other for another minute before Becky broke the serious moment. "Okay. That's enough of this blubbering. You have a big night ahead of you, so look over the recipe and make sure you know what to do. Chicken parmesan isn't hard. But if someone's going to screw it up, it's going to be you. I love you, Nik, but..."

"I know, I know."

After a few more instructions from Becky, Nikki was on her way with only one more stop to make before she went home to start preparing for her date. She glanced over at the bouquet of roses that sat on her front seat. *Yes*, she thought. *One more very important stop.*

The graveyard was quiet as Nikki made her way through the still brown grass, to the spot where they'd buried her mother, right where she wanted to be: under a large spruce tree, next to Nikki's father, who'd died when Nikki herself was just three years old.

She knelt on the ground, still cold from the thaw, and laid the flowers down. "Happy birthday, Mom. I know it's not much of a celebration this year, but I wanted you to know I didn't forget. I know you'd probably want a big party, but I don't think any of us are ready for that this year." She smiled a little. "We still miss you too much. But I brought you your favorite flowers, and I did get you a present."

Nikki hugged her knees close and looked up to the sky, taking her time. "I know you already know what it is," she said. "But I wanted to make sure you know that we're here, in Halfway. Ryan and me. And you know what, Mom? We're happy. We should have come years ago, but...it wasn't time. I guess in a weird way, I have you to thank for bringing me back."

The idea that her mother's death was the catalyst for her

happiness wasn't a new one. But Nikki couldn't let herself feel guilty, and she knew her mother wouldn't have wanted it. All her mother ever wanted was for her to come home and be happy. It wouldn't have mattered to her how it happened.

"I'm home, Mom," Nikki whispered to the sky. "I'm finally home."

~Want to know more? Find out what happens during the next festival in Halfway...Turn the page...~

NEW YORK TIMES & USA TODAY
BESTSELLING AUTHORS

STEENA HOLMES
and ELENA AITKEN

HALFWAY
in between

Chapter One

Melissa

Melissa glanced up at the clock again and ground her teeth. They were late, again. She tapped her fingers on the counter and inwardly groaned when she realized she'd forgotten to wipe them down from dinner. Last night had been an evening of working on her computer while Abby sat at the table and worked on homework. They'd both been so focused on other things...as usual.

As if she could hear the seconds tick away, she focused on the clock again.

"Abigail Rhodes if you don't get your butt down those stairs within the next five seconds, I'm going to..."

It was a good thing she stopped when she did because Abby appeared before she could finish. They both knew her threats were groundless.

She really shouldn't have been surprised to see the earbuds attached to her daughter's ears; they were almost a permanent accessory lately. Since when did thirteen-year-old girls listen to music non-stop? When she was thirteen, she...listened to music too.

"Is it time to go?" Abby jumped the last three steps and placed a sweet kiss on Melissa's cheek.

Melissa tugged at the earbuds until they both popped out and shook her head when the music blared.

"Yes, it's time to go. We're late, again." She thought about commenting on her daughter's outfit but decided against it. She knew when to pick her battles with Abby and this wasn't one of them. She'd raised her daughter to be a free thinker, proud of who she was and to never take gruff from anyone. Who was she to point out that her socks didn't match or that the sweater she wore was a little on the big side? At least her jeans were clean and unripped.

There was something about that sweater...

Abby shrugged. "I only have gym."

"And I only have a meeting." Which she'd be lucky to get to on time, especially when she needed to stop and get a coffee first.

"Oops." Her daughter had the decency to grimace before she grabbed a banana from the fruit bowl on the cupboard and reached for her backpack.

"Oops, my foot. Sometimes I think you plan this," Melissa muttered as she grabbed a pear and followed after her.

To be fair, they were both at fault. The power had gone out last night and left their alarm settings off. Melissa, generally not a morning person, did happen to wake up early, but rolled over and decided to sleep for only a few minutes longer. Unfortunately, those few minutes turned into thirty, so they both rushed this morning to get ready in time. She should have gone to bed earlier but she'd started to read a new book last night and it was too good to put down.

"Gym is my favorite class; you should know that by now."

Abby's sarcastic nature shone through her words. Gym was the only class she had that she hated. Melissa didn't blame her; she'd hated that class too. Probably had something to do with the teacher, Mrs. Hannigan, who, oddly enough, was Abby's teacher.

Abby stuck the earbuds back in while Melissa drove towards the school. She went through her schedule for the day. First off was a meeting with Nikki Landon, regarding help with creating ads and the town website. Now that Nikki was a permanent fixture in town, Melissa wanted to see whether she could talk her into helping out. After that, she had to sit down and finish the community newsletter she'd started last night. It was due by Friday and she also needed to print off the flyers for Abby to deliver after school.

"What would you like for supper?" Last night consisted of grilled cheese and tomato soup. From a can. None of that home-made stuff. She really needed to start menu planning. This last-minute stuff was killing her. Maybe she should start a recipe column in the weekly paper.

"Pizza?"

"Again?" That seemed like their weekly go-to meal, except they ate it more than they should.

Abby shrugged. "We can make our own this time?"

Melissa gave her daughter a look. "Do I look like Becky Jennings to you?" Becky was an old school friend who married her high school sweetheart and they lived the fairy-tale dream every woman wished for. Matt Jennings was a tree farmer while Becky used her passion for cooking and created an online presence, complete with a website and cookbook. To say Melissa was jealous was an understatement.

Oh...she should ask Becky whether she'd be interested in doing that menu column. Why didn't she think of that earlier?

Melissa pulled up to the school grounds and pulled up to

the sidewalk. Thankfully there were a few other parents dropping off their kids and the school bus was still parked out front, which meant Abby wouldn't be too late and Melissa shouldn't have to write a note.

"I'll figure something out. Maybe there will be some ready-made casserole at the grocery store today." Greta Wilson had started a *Bring Dinner Home* campaign a few years ago to help raise funds for the seniors' home. The idea became a hit, so she kept it up. Each week she would make dozens of casseroles and sell them from the deli counter at their grocery store.

"Oh, see if she has her perogies this time. Maybe Uncle Parker will come over?" Abby's eyes lit up at the suggestion before she gave her door a slight shove to open it. "See you after school." She hip checked the door closed and walked off.

Melissa sat there for a few moments to watch her daughter. Multiple thoughts went through her mind. She needed to take the vehicle in and get the dent out of the passenger door. During the Tree Festival, a tractor had *nudged* her door by accident and since then the dang thing didn't like to open and shut properly. She wasn't sure whether Parker would be available to come over, and even if he did, she doubted she'd make it to the grocery store in time to see whether there would be any casseroles. If there were some, they didn't come out until mid-afternoon.

Unless she asked Parker to pick up dinner? He might do that. Before Nikki Landon had come back to town, Parker was over at their place at least three times a week for dinner. But lately, they'd seen him less and less and although Melissa understood what was going on, Abby didn't. She probably should talk to him about it. No doubt the man never thought of how his absence would affect them.

Melissa was so wrapped up in her thoughts, she almost didn't see Abby stop at the post box and slide an envelope through its opening. The furtive action caught her attention, the way she checked to see whether Melissa was watching. Thankfully, Melissa's head was down so her daughter couldn't see that she was looking. What was she mailing and to whom?

The mysterious envelope puzzled Melissa as she drove away from the school and headed back towards Main Street. She parked behind her shop but headed directly to Grounds, the best and only coffee shop in town. She needed her caffeine fix and she only had a few minutes before Nikki was scheduled to show up. Who knows, maybe if she was lucky, Nikki was late getting her son, Ryan, off to school this morning as well.

She pushed the door open to Grounds and inhaled the bittersweet smell of freshly ground coffee. She smiled to a few of the people who occupied the tables and purveyed the selection of fresh pastries and muffins as she waited in line. She'd started a new diet last week and had so far managed to not succumb to the temptation. But her stomach growled and that pear she'd grabbed from home wasn't going to cut it. Maybe if she chose a healthier muffin and ate salad for lunch, it wouldn't hurt her. She had at least twenty pounds to shed and she was determined to do it—this time.

Melissa's life consisted of yo-yo diets, ever since she was a teenager. She'd never been a skinny type. Her bones were big, her calves huge from all the biking she did, and she'd never had a skinny waist, but it never stopped her from trying. She'd always been the *fat one* in the group at school, the one to stand at the back of the group photos.

"Your regular?" Muriel Oaks, owner of Grounds, asked.

Melissa shook her head. "I need a double shot today. Please." Double shot espresso should just about do it.

Muriel's brow rose at that. "Bad night?"

Melissa shrugged. "Late night, late morning, and a busy day ahead. I'll probably be back for another round in a few hours."

The banana muffin looked very tempting, as well as the pumpkin spice.

"You'll want the pumpkin spice. Trust me." Muriel caught her looking at the muffin and grinned. At Melissa's nod, she bagged the muffin for her and handed it over the counter before she wrote some notes on the cup and set it to the side.

"You're not helping my diet at all, you know."

"What you need to do is stop focusing on the diet and just eat healthier. Fall in love with yourself and stop worrying what the rest of the world has to say about it."

Melissa just nodded. She knew better than to argue with Muriel; she'd learned the hard way years ago. Muriel was one of the women in Halfway who didn't hesitate to speak her mind and would often write letters to the editor to make sure everyone else knew it too.

"You're right. As usual." She moved off to the side to wait for her coffee to be made and happened to glance out the window.

Shoot. Nikki was early. Melissa glanced at her watch. Make that on time. She'd just pulled up out front of her door. Yesterday, when she'd imagined the conversation she'd have with Nikki about helping out, she'd been the one in control of the situation. Nikki would walk in and see Melissa hard at work and would be impressed with how she ran the paper.

She was a dreamer. She should have known she'd never make it on time to something she was less than comfortable with. Nikki was someone Melissa used to envy once upon a time. Even being two years older, Melissa had always wanted to be included in that elusive friendship bond Nikki had with Matt, Parker, and Becky. Of course, Nikki and Parker hadn't been dating back then, but even so, they were all so close. Sure, she'd had Nyah Henderson, but it wasn't the same.

"Here you go," Muriel said. "Come back around lunch hour. I'm making some chicken wraps for lunch."

Melissa grabbed her coffee from the counter and smiled at Muriel. She took a sip and caught the subtle flavor of chocolate.

"You really aren't helping me, you do realize that, right?"

Muriel shrugged. "What's life if you don't enjoy every moment of it? I'll see you at lunch, with a healthy wrap." She shooed her away as she turned to the next customer.

She was ready to chuck the diet out the window anyways. She was tired of being hungry all the time and sick of eating carrots and celery. Maybe she'd look online and see what the latest diet fad was. Who knows, it might be something that included pizza and ice cream.

Nikki stood outside the door to the *Halfway Herald*. Melissa raised her coffee cup high as a greeting as she crossed the road.

"So sorry I'm late. It's been one of those mornings."

She caught the way Nikki eyed her coffee and had a sudden moment of guilt for not even thinking of buying her one. Which she should have. As a friendly gesture and all.

Shoot.

Chapter Two

Nikki

Nikki Landon watched her old friend cross the street, coffee and pastry in hand. She should have thought to grab breakfast herself, and another coffee would be more than welcome. The single cup she'd guzzled down before she got Ryan off to school hadn't cut it. Not since she'd had another late night working on her client's websites after Parker had finally gone home. She smiled to herself. It'd been worth it.

In the months since she'd decided to stay in Halfway, Parker had definitely become one of her favorite parts of getting used to small town living again. They were taking their relationship slowly, getting to know each other all over again, and dating had been fun. Especially considering Nikki couldn't remember the last time she'd done any.

"Good morning," she said to Melissa, as the other woman finally made her way over to her.

"I'm sorry, Nikki." Melissa juggled her coffee in an attempt to fish her keys from her purse. "I meant to be here early to open up, and—"

"Here." Nikki took the coffee from her hand. "Let me help you."

Melissa shot her a look, but her smile was warm. "Thank you."

Once she got the key in the lock, the two ladies stepped into the offices of the *Halfway Herald*. Nikki followed Melissa through the room as she flipped on lights and made her way to her small office.

"I'm glad we had a chance to sit down and talk." Melissa pulled her chair up and grabbed a notebook. "I feel like you've been here for ages now and I've been meaning to get you in here so we could brainstorm. I mean, these flyers you did for the Festival were just great."

Nikki shrugged. It had been a last-minute job to help Melissa out with the Christmas Tree Festival. At the time, it had been the last thing she wanted to do. In fact, she hadn't wanted anything to do with her hometown, Halfway, Montana, except to finish up with her mother's things and get out of there, leaving the past securely behind her. Things had a funny way of working out. "It's fine," she said. "It's been a crazy few months getting moved and settled. Ryan started school after Christmas, and he's really enjoying it, even making some friends."

"So, you're glad you're back?"

"I am." It was the truth. "But if you'd asked me six months ago if I ever thought I'd be living here again, I would have laughed at you. But now, I can't imagine it any other way. And having Becky and Matt in Ryan's life, well..." She drifted off. She didn't know Melissa well enough to be telling her such personal things and they'd never really been close. With Melissa a few years ahead of them in school, Nikki hadn't really spent any time with her. And in the few months she'd been back in Halfway, she could hardly say she'd received a warm welcome from the other woman. Or any welcome at all, really. She shook her head at herself. She really must be sleep deprived. That didn't mean anything. Melissa was a busy woman, just like she was. She couldn't expect her to drop everything just because she'd decided to move back. "It's good to be back." She changed tacks. "So what's going on with you? How's Abby? How old is she now?"

"Thirteen." Melissa shook her head slightly. "And every bit a teenager. Let me tell you, enjoy Ryan now before he hits this stage."

"I get it," Nikki said. "It's hard sometimes doing it all on your own, isn't it?" They had that in common. Single parenting. Maybe Nikki could use that to find some common ground. She leaned across the desk. "There have definitely been times when I questioned my sanity for doing it alone." The second the words came out of her mouth, Nikki regretted it. She didn't know much about Melissa's circumstances, but she did know that unlike herself, Melissa didn't choose single parenting.

The other woman's back stiffened and her lips pressed into a hard line. "It was hardly my choice." She spoke the words through clenched teeth. "Not all of us made the decisions you did."

Nikki flinched, but didn't say anything. She'd been the one who was insensitive. It was no secret that Melissa's husband Wade had run off over nine years ago and left her to raise their daughter on her own.

"And I've hardly been alone," Melissa added. "Parker's been a huge help. I don't know where we'd be without him." Something about the way Melissa looked at her put Nikki on the defensive, which was ridiculous because she hadn't done anything wrong. "Abby really relies on her Uncle Parker, you know? His presence has been very important to her."

"Of course." She nodded, but she'd completely forgotten that Parker was Wade's brother. The two of them were complete opposites. Even in high school, Nikki had a hard time associating Parker with his older, slightly more serious brother. "I can imagine that Parker's a great uncle for Abby."

"He is." Melissa stared at her a moment longer before something changed in her expression and she reached for her coffee. A smile replaced the seriousness, making the woman's harried, yet beautiful, face light up. "I'm sure you're very busy. We should get down to business."

* * *

By the time Nikki left Melissa's office, she was more than ready for a coffee of her own. Or a drink. But considering it was way too early for alcohol, she had to settle for caffeine before she headed back to work. Besides that, the aroma coming out of Melissa's cup had driven her crazy for their entire meeting. It would have been nice if Melissa had grabbed her one, but...

She crossed the street to Grounds. It didn't matter. Not really. Besides, Melissa had a lot going on; the oversight likely wasn't personal. But that thought dogged her thoughts, even after she'd ordered her own mocha and let Muriel talk her into a scone. Twenty minutes later, fuelled on Muriel's yummy treat and a coffee of her own, the slight was forgotten as she walked into her house and up to her old bedroom that she'd converted to a home office.

When Nikki'd decided to stay in Halfway, she knew she couldn't live with the memories in her old house. It was time for a new start and to that end, she'd moved into her mother's room and packed away most of her mom's things. She let Ryan pick out his paint and together they'd painted his room a vivid green. As for her childhood bedroom, the only thing she'd left the same was the bulletin board full of pictures of herself, Becky, Matt, and even Parker, when they were younger. They made her smile while she worked.

And work was what she had to do. She'd wasted enough time in town talking to Melissa. Although, she had to admit, Melissa had some great ideas about building the newspaper's website and taking the paper online. She was also going to put her in touch with Mayor Robertson about doing up a site for the town as well. Nikki could hardly believe that they'd all survived as long as they had without a website. It was a great opportunity for everyone involved, and she'd work on the proposal, just as soon as she finished things up with her current clients.

Just as she settled down to get to work, her cell phone rang. Parker. A smile split into her face as she answered. It didn't matter how busy she was; there was time.

"Shouldn't you be enlightening the minds of our youth, Mr. Tait?"

"I had to give them a break. I didn't want to overwhelm their young minds with all the knowledge I have to share." Parker was a popular teacher at Halfway High, which always made Nikki laugh because she knew exactly how much trouble he used to get into with Matt when he was the same age as the kids he was now teaching. "Besides," he added. "It's lunch. And I couldn't go another minute without talking to you."

"Now I know you're full of it." She laughed though. Despite the fact that he was joking, there was some truth to his words. They'd spent an increasing amount of time together over the last few months, and yet it never felt like enough. If she wasn't careful, she might even start to think things with Parker might be going somewhere further.

"Okay, okay. But seriously," he said. "Are we on for dinner tonight?"

"Absolutely. I'm making pork chops." She made a mental note to go to the store and pick up supplies.

"I love pork chops."

"I lo—" She stopped herself. "I love that you love pork chops. Even ones that I cook." What was she thinking? She mentally scolded herself. It's not as though she'd never been in a relationship before. Okay, well, she hadn't. Not a serious one. But still, she should know better than to blurt out stupid things like that, especially when they were talking about pork chops. "Hey, I saw Melissa this morning."

"Did you?" Was there a hesitancy in his voice, or did she imagine it? "Did you run into her?"

"No. She asked me to come in and talk about doing some work for the paper and maybe even the town."

There was a pause on the other end of the line before Parker said, "Sounds like a good opportunity."

"You don't sound so sure." Nikki tapped her keyboard while she spoke and brought the monitor to life.

"Sorry," Parker said. "I'm just a little distracted. I thought I just saw Abby walk by. I should go talk to her."

"Abby? Melissa's daughter?"

"Ya, I'm a little...tell me all about it later, okay?"

He hung up before Nikki could say anything more. A wash of jealousy filled her, which was ridiculous because he'd hung up to go talk to a thirteen-year-old girl. His niece.

Determined to get some work done before she had to pick up Ryan from school, Nikki forced herself to focus on the computer screen and the design elements for her latest client, Jennings Family Tree Farm. She'd talked Matt and Becky into a website for their Christmas tree farm, or more accurately, talked Matt into it. Becky was doing great with her own website, combining blogging and baking. Her friend was an amazing baker, and her site was really starting to take off. But Nikki had been watching and she had some ideas for Becky that would really help her take things to the next level.

But one thing at a time. First she needed to finish Matt's site and prove to him that having a website for a Christmas tree farm was actually a profitable venture. And it would be, as soon as she finished creating the best website he'd ever seen. Which meant focusing. She didn't have any time to dwell on what may or may not be going on with Parker. Or, more to the point, what she wanted to be going on with Parker. They'd been taking things slow. Maybe too slow. Nikki knew he was just trying to be respectful of Ryan and her single mom status, but she couldn't help feeling as if there was something more behind it.

Melissa. She'd tried to push the other woman from her mind, but despite the fact that Melissa had called her about business opportunities to develop websites, Nikki had the nagging feeling if there had been anyone else to call, she would have. They'd never been close when they were young. It wasn't that she didn't like Melissa; she'd just never known her very well. Being a few years older and dating Wade, she kind of kept to herself.

Maybe she was shy?

Nikki tried out the idea, but it didn't fly. Melissa was the editor of the town paper for goodness' sake; shy was definitely not the problem. No, Nikki tapped her pen against her desk and bit her lip. Shyness was not the problem. But she was pretty sure what was.

Chapter Three

Melissa

Melissa tapped her pen against the counter and eyed the coffee in front of her. She knew going for that third coffee had been a mistake and the heartburn she now experienced only proved it. But she'd gotten swamped fast and actually stopping to eat anything that required more than nibbles here and there had been out of the question.

Which was why she was on her third coffee and had eaten a healthy granola cookie that Muriel forced on her rather than the salad she should have bought.

But after the day she'd had, she could have used something more substantive.

The clock was ticking and the Halfway Pumpkin Festival was going to be here before she was ready, before the town was ready. Why did it seem like this year they were behind on everything?

For the Tree Festival last year, Becky Jennings had taken over from her mom in organizing the event and it had gone off without a hitch. After that, Norma Grant, Becky's mom, retook control and things hadn't run as smoothly for the two other festivals they held—the seed and strawberry events. Maybe it was because Marie Landon, her partner in crime, wasn't there to help her. No one would ask that, though...it was a touchy subject.

Melissa hoped things would be different for this festival, but so far...they were behind again. In more ways than were okay. The printing, the advertising...even organizing the volunteers. Maybe she should talk to Becky about it.

Not my monkey, not my circus. That was her new mantra... except, it was her monkey and her circus in a way. She was involved in the planning of the festivals and she'd slacked off this year. But Norma was a force most didn't want to disrupt. Herself included.

The bell over the door rang and Melissa glanced up, a forced smile on her face. She was ready for the disruption, eager to tackle the next thing to come her way, now that the issue of the newspaper she'd been working on was done, although, if it was anything more than simple photocopying of a document, she couldn't promise to maintain her sanity.

Her heart sank when she saw Norma Grant, the force of nature she'd just been thinking about.

"Melissa Tait-Rhodes, I would have thought you'd have too much work on your hands to be daydreaming?"

Melissa forced that ready smile on her face to maintain its position. She also tried very, very hard to remain calm. Very, very hard. Norma was the only person who called her by her whole name.

"Not daydreaming, Norma. I'm trying to figure something out."

Norma set her purse down on the counter, right on top of the paper Melissa had been working on, leaned her cane up against the wall and pulled out a folder.

"Well, I need you to do some work for me."

Melissa pushed herself up from her leaning position and glanced down at the folder labeled Pumpkin Festival in thick black marker.

"What can I help you with?"

Norma pushed the folder towards Melissa. "This." She jabbed her finger down on the folder and waited, clearly, for Melissa to open it.

She didn't oblige.

"The Halfway Pumpkin Festival. Are you ready to get working on it?" she asked instead.

"Of course I am. What a stupid question to ask." Norma huffed as she opened the folder and pulled out a sheet of paper Melissa instantly recognized.

It was the flyer she'd created last year for the festival. A pretty good one, if she said so herself. Every year she tried to do something different with the designs. The one she'd created this year was even better, though.

"This was last year's flyer."

"I know."

"What would you like me to do with it?" Melissa was a little puzzled now.

"Create a new one. But use this design. It's good."

Melissa shook her head. "I've already designed one for this year."

"No you haven't."

"I have."

Norma folded her arms over her chest and gave Melissa that *don't bother to mess with me* look.

"Norma, I submitted my design to the festival committee months ago. They've already placed their order for flyers to be printed for next week. It's all been approved."

"Not by me, it hasn't."

Well...crap. This was not a fight Melissa wanted to take on.

Not my monkey, not my circus, right? Apparently she was wrong.

"But it has been by the committee. I'm not sure what to tell you." She tried to infuse her voice with a semblance of an apology, but when it came to Norma, the moment you showed any sign of weakness, you were done for.

"Show me the design."

Melissa stepped back and headed to her cabinet where she retained copies of all her files, but stopped. "I don't really have time to change it. You do realize that, right?"

"Show me." Norma's words were clipped, her lips pulled tight and the way her face flushed, Melissa knew she had no choice but to get the design she'd submitted and show her.

She made sure to choose the one that had *approved* stamped at the top, with the signature from one of the committee members on there. She handed it to Norma, who raised it up and stared at it and waited.

And waited.

The silence grew between them until the sound of the tick-tock of her wall clock seemed to grow in volume. Finally Norma set it down, took in a deep breath and slowly let it out.

"I like last year's design better," was all the woman said.

"But you don't dislike this one, right?" Something inside of Melissa wanted—no, needed—Norma to approve of her design. This had been the only year her first attempt had been approved. The usual process had Melissa submitting multiple versions before Norma finally gave her approval and presented it to the committee. It had felt too easy this year, but Melissa blamed that on the fact that she'd worked extra hard on it.

"It's fine, Melissa. You, of course, did a lovely job. There are a few things I would have liked changed, for instance, the color of the font...why in heaven's name would you choose that shade of green?" Norma waved her hand at Melissa. "Never mind.

What's done is done. But please, in the future, come to me first with your designs."

"Sure. You know I always enjoy our collaborations, Norma." Lie. All lies. She hated every single moment of them. But, that was all part of her job and she could almost hear her father's voice reminding her to smile. Just smile and pretend you're throwing a dart.

She thought of the dartboard area in the back and did smile. Norma didn't need to know that it was often her name on the piece of paper attached to the large corkboard in the spare closet. It was something her father had shown her, years ago. At night, after the shop was closed and the lights were out, if he had a particularly difficult customer that day, he'd write either their name down on a piece of paper or the project name and then throw darts at it with as much force as possible. This was how he dealt with his anger and it was one way that she dealt with hers.

"When is the printing date?" Norma pulled out her calendar.

"Next week. Don't worry, we're right on track."

"Good. I have a few other ideas for this year that I'll need your help with, so the fact you've already created the flyers is a good thing."

"What kind of ideas, Norma?" Again, this was par for the course. Melissa had learned the hard way to expect these little projects to come her way before any of their festivals.

"Recipe cards." A smile grew on Norma's face as she said the words and in that moment, there was a softness to Norma that was rarely seen.

"Recipe cards?"

"Yes. Or maybe, a recipe book. Throughout the years we've collected a lot of great pumpkin recipes, ones you've even show-cased in your paper, and I thought it would be a great idea to either create recipe cards with these recipes on them or do up a book that we can sell."

"Whoa. Those are two very different projects that will take a lot of work." And yet, the idea had her excited. Very excited. She could already picture what the recipe cards would look like and the idea of holding a contest to find the top three or more recipes grew.

"I know. But we have more than enough time. Now, here's what I was thinking..."

* * *

"Hey Mom." Abby tossed her school bag down and plopped down in the chair beside her desk. Her earbuds were wrapped loose around her neck but Melissa could hear the music she was listening to loud and clear.

Abby blew a large pink bubble and popped it. "Got the flyers ready?"

"You walked right by them." Melissa pointed to the large and unmistakable stack that sat on the edge of the counter. The same counter Melissa always placed the flyers that Abby needed to deliver.

"What's for dinner?" Abby crossed her legs and leaned back in the chair.

Melissa took her hands away from the keyboard and half turned in her chair so she faced her daughter.

"What? No *how was your day, my day was great*, today?"

Abby shrugged. "Day was okay. How was yours?" She blew another bubble and it took everything inside Melissa not to poke at it with her finger.

"Mrs. Grant came in to see me, and I had a nice chat with Nikki Landon."

"The one Uncle Parker is seeing?"

Melissa wasn't sure how to respond to that. Were they dating? Probably. But how did Abby know?

"Did you call Uncle Parker to see if he'd come for dinner?"

Melissa groaned. She knew she'd forgotten to do something. "I'll call him now."

She reached for the phone but Abby leaned forward and took it from her. "Let me ask him, okay?"

Melissa dialed the number and sat back. She half focused on what was on her computer screen while she listened in on the conversation.

"Hey, Uncle Parker. I was kind of hoping you could come over for dinner tonight."

When Abby jumped up from her seat, Melissa knew he'd said yes.

"Awesome! I'll even make brownies for you tonight. See you later." Abby thrust the phone back to Melissa and headed towards the flyers. "I'll get these dropped off and meet you at home. Don't forget to see if Mrs. Wilson has some casseroles ready. Or do you want me to drop in and ask her to put some aside?"

Melissa chuckled. "Go ahead. See you later," she called out to her daughter, but she had a feeling Abby hadn't heard her— those darn earbuds were back in.

With a smile, she put the phone to her ear. "So you're coming for dinner I hear."

"Yeah, thanks for the invite. It's been awhile. Sorry about that."

The words *don't worry about it* almost came out, but she stopped herself. "It has been awhile and your niece has noticed. Things must be getting pretty serious between you and Nikki, I gather."

"A little."

"A little? That's all you've got to say?"

"I like her, Mel. She..." His voice trailed off.

"Makes you happy, doesn't she?" She remembered that feeling. There was nothing quite like it and she missed it. Missed it bad. But she was happy for Parker. Of course she was. When they were all in high school, the poor boy used to follow Nikki around like a lovesick puppy dog. Okay, maybe not quite like that, but he had the biggest crush on her back then.

"She does. I...we need to talk."

"We do? What about?" She didn't like the sudden change in his tone.

"I got a letter from my brother."

And with those words, Melissa was just sucker-punched. Her first thought was why? Why did he get a letter and not her? But the next thought explained it all...of course he would. They were brothers, and close brothers at that. And she'd asked him not to mail her letters. She'd had a good reason at the time, to try to contain the rumor she'd allowed to spread, to protect her daughter...but it'd been the wrong decision; she knew that now. As her mother loved to say: *you make your bed, you lie in it— even if those sheets threaten to strangle you in the night.*

"Is he...is Wade okay?" It had been nine long years since her husband had left her but the sound of his name, the memory of their love...it still hurt. Really hurt.

They'd been high school sweethearts and married as soon as they both graduated. Of course, it helped that she was pregnant at the time...but who was she kidding? It wouldn't have mattered; they would have married, pregnant or not. She used to think nothing could come between them but she'd been young and foolish then.

A deep sadness set in and she wished she could turn back time because now she knew better.

She'd always wanted the happily-ever-after, the kind of romance Becky and Matt had and once upon a time, she'd honestly thought she had it. Until life threw her a curveball and she ended up raising their daughter alone.

"We need to talk. Tonight? Okay?"

A shiver of dread rolled over Melissa's body at Parker's words.

"Just tell me if he's okay."

She heard Parker sigh. "He's never going to be okay until he's home. We both know that."

"Soon. One more year," she whispered into the phone. Why did she whisper? There was no one around.

"That's what we need to talk about. Tonight, okay?"

When she hung up the phone, she knew she wasn't going to like their discussion. Only because she had a feeling she knew what it was going to be about.

For nine years, she'd been living a lie and soon, everyone was going to find out.

Chapter Four

Nikki

She put the finishing touches on a website project she was working on for a local photographer, and closed the lid of her laptop. Done. And just in time, too. Ryan would be home from school and she needed to hurry to the store to pick something special to cook for dinner, which was crazy: they'd had dinner together almost every night for weeks and it was never anything special. Heck, if she was cooking, it wasn't ever going to be anything special. She'd mastered the art of convenience cooking, which in her book was good enough. As long as it was healthy, quick, and Ryan would eat it, she was happy.

But as her relationship with Parker developed, she found herself wanting to impress him a little bit and tonight, Ryan would be spending the night at his dad's house, which meant... She laughed at her own ridiculousness as she collected the coffee cups that always managed to find their way to her desk. She wasn't a teenager anymore; she shouldn't be feeling the butterflies she was feeling. But she was. Things with Parker were going well —very well—and it had been a long time since she'd felt the way he made her feel. But they barely had any time to spend together, and Nikki insisted that Parker not stay the night when Ryan was home. After all, she didn't need to field those questions. Not yet.

But Ryan wouldn't be there tonight.

She let the thought dance around her brain for a minute and she indulged in the idea of what that exactly would mean. Nikki was still indulging the idea when the screen door slammed open.

"Mom! I'm hungry."

Nikki turned around at the exact moment her son slammed into her with a bear hug. At almost eleven, she was lucky he still liked to give his mom hugs, and she'd gladly accept them. It wouldn't be too much longer until he was too cool for hugs. She didn't want to think about those days and how much she'd miss them. "Grab a snack, but not too much. You're heading over to your dad's tonight and—"

"Becky's cooking!" Ryan whooped and did an impressive fist pump. She ignored the little twinge of jealousy. He certainly didn't get that excited for his mom's cooking. But the jealousy vanished almost as soon as it appeared. Who was she kidding? Nikki would get that excited for Becky's cooking, too. She was the best cook in Halfway—hell, probably the state—and whatever she cooked up for a simple Friday night dinner would be a hell of a lot better than whatever she picked up at the store to heat up.

But it didn't matter what was on the plate. Not tonight. Not with Parker coming over for a night alone.

With Ryan at his dad's, it meant they'd finally have a night alone together. Their first. Which was why she was so stressed about what to serve. It should be perfect. All the details should be perfect for something so special and romantic. Not that Parker would complain about what was served.

Nikki laughed. Parker was way too smart for that.

"What's so funny?"

She turned to see her son staring at her with a question in his eyes. Ryan liked Parker. He always looked forward to hanging out with him, and Parker was careful not to try to take the place of Ryan's dad, whom Ryan himself was just getting to know. But he acted like more of a friend to her son, which was exactly what he needed. But despite all that, Nikki still wasn't ready to talk to him about her relationship with Parker. He was too young to understand. At least that's what she kept telling herself.

"Nothing." She handed Ryan a cookie from the box. "Here. One cookie." Distraction was always the best technique when it came to Ryan. She'd talk to him about Parker. Just not yet. Not when he was still adjusting to life in Halfway and spending time with his dad and Becky. No, Ryan had enough going on without worrying about yet another change in his life.

And that was getting ahead of things. Nikki hadn't even spent the night with Parker; she needed to stop thinking too far in the future. Marriage was off the table. At least for now.

But she wouldn't rule it out. The thought bounced through her head the same way it had been for the last few weeks and a smile came to her face. No. She definitely wouldn't rule it out.

"When you're done with your snack, go pack your bag. I'll drop you off after I stop at the store."

"Okay." Ryan shoved the cookie in his mouth. "Are you—"

"Don't talk with your mouth full."

Ryan rolled his eyes but dutifully chewed and swallowed before he continued. "Are you hanging out with Parker tonight?"

She could feel the blush on her face, which was ridiculous

because she was talking to her eleven-year-old son. As casually as possible, Nikki nodded. "He said he'd come by for dinner. I'm going to pick something up before I drop you off. Is that okay?" She'd been waiting for Ryan to somehow object to their relationship, not because he didn't like Parker but because it had always been the two of them and secretly she worried Ryan might resent that.

"Yup." He shrugged. "But don't tell him about the new Lego I got. I want to show him when I'm finished building it."

"Deal." Nikki smiled. She had nothing to worry about. "Now go grab your bag. I want to get going."

* * *

The grocery store was busy, which wasn't unusual since Greta Wilson started her new dinner campaign to encourage the people of Halfway to eat healthy and it didn't have to taste bad. And it didn't—not when Greta prepared it and Nikki bought one of her pop in the oven dinners, which is exactly what she hoped to find today. Greta's cooking wasn't quite Becky's, but it had Nikki's beat.

"Do you need any snacks for school or anything?" Ryan had his eye on a stack of sugary cereals. He looked up at his mom hopefully. "Not a chance. But I'll get you granola bars if you need them."

Reluctantly, Ryan left the cereal boxes alone. "Okay. But can I choose them?"

"Sounds good to me." She took the basket from her son. "I'll tell you what—it's so busy in here and I want to get you to your dad's as soon as possible, so why don't you go get them and find me some milk, too, okay?"

His face split into a smile. He loved being independent and

189

it wouldn't be long before he was, time was going so quickly. "Yes! Can I get some—"

Nikki pressed her mouth in a thin line.

"What?" Ryan shrugged. "I wasn't going to ask for soda or anything. But..."

"No."

"What about those pudding things?"

"Fine." Nikki tried to look serious. "Now go. I'll meet you in the deli."

He didn't need to be told again. Ryan took off in the opposite direction and Nikki shook her head. No doubt he'd come back with all types of things she would have to say no to. It was almost impossible to keep his sugar intake down.

Without wasting any more time, Nikki headed straight to the deli. It was already late in the day, but with any luck there might be a lasagna or a chicken and dumplings or one of the other delicious meals Greta usually prepared. But when she reached the case with the big *Bring Dinner Home* sign over the top, there was only one package left. Chicken rotini. It wasn't her favorite, but it was a lot better than trying to whip something up on her own.

Nikki reached for the package at the same time as another hand. They both grabbed it at the same time. "Oh, I..."

Her words died on her lips when she saw the other hand belonged to Melissa Tait-Rhodes.

"Can you believe it's the last one?" Melissa smiled, but it didn't quite reach her eyes. "Ever since we ran that piece in the *Herald* about Greta's fabulous dinners, it's been harder and harder to get one. Sometimes I think I should have just kept it to myself."

Nikki chuckled politely. Neither woman took their hand off the package.

"I guess we have a bit of a situation," she said. "It's not like we can share it." The only person she planned to share her dinner with was Parker. But something told her that wouldn't be an argument to use in this particular situation. Melissa definitely was touchy about her relationship with Parker.

"I think I got here first."

Really? Nikki had to swallow the retort before it slipped out. "I'm not sure about that."

Melissa blushed, obviously realizing how her comment sounded. "Look," she said softly. "I would really owe you. I'm in a bit of a time crunch and...I'm sure if it's just you and Ryan, you could get by with something else tonight or—"

"Ryan's going to Matt and Becky's tonight." Nikki wished she could take the words back as soon as they popped out. Especially when Melissa's eyes narrowed in question.

"Surely you weren't going to eat all this by yourself?"

Nikki pulled her hand back and contemplated what and how much she should say. Melissa had never come right out and said anything, but Nikki had the distinct impression that Melissa wasn't a big fan of her relationship with Parker. It was no secret that Parker spent a lot of time with his sister-in-law and niece after his brother had abandoned them, but nobody she'd spoken with seemed to think it was a romantic relationship, and Nikki couldn't believe it was. But why then did Melissa seem so standoffish with her? Over the last few months, Nikki had tried to be friendly with her, even going so far as offering to help her out with the Halfway Pumpkin Festival, but either Melissa wasn't interested in being friends, or there was some other reason she pulled back. Either way, Nikki didn't think the other woman would be very happy to hear she was supposed to be sharing a meal with Parker.

"No," Nikki said, finally. "But you and Abby...maybe a pizza would be a more popular choice?"

Melissa drew her hand back as well and left the packaged

meal sitting alone in the cooler. Both women eyed it before they looked at each other once again. "Thanks for the suggestion," Melissa said, and Nikki tried to pretend she didn't pick up on the attitude in her voice. "But pizza won't work. Parker's coming over tonight and I—"

"Wait." That got Nikki's attention. "Parker?"

"Yes. I was speaking to him just a bit ago. He hasn't been around much, you know?"

Nikki knew the comment was aimed at her but she wasn't going to take the bait. "But tonight?" He couldn't be having dinner with Melissa and Abby. Not that she'd normally care. They were family after all, and even if she got a bit jealous sometimes...that wasn't the point. The point was, she had a romantic evening planned for them. And Parker having dinner with Melissa was definitely not part of that plan. "Are you sure?"

Her question caused a shift in Melissa's demeanor. She pulled her purse up on her shoulder. "Of course I'm sure. Why?"

Nikki didn't want to do it. She didn't want to tell Melissa that really Parker was having dinner with her; she didn't want to give the other woman any more reasons not to like her, especially when it would be so much better if they were friends. But, there didn't seem to be any help for it. She took a breath and tried to look as friendly as possible. "Because Parker's having dinner with me. We kind of have an evening planned."

She didn't know what was worse: the look of resignation on Melissa's face, as if she already knew what Nikki was going to say, or the hurt in her eyes she tried so hard not to show.

"I'm sorry, Melissa. I would absolutely reschedule, but Ryan's with Matt and Becky tonight and...well, it's kind of—"

"No." Melissa held up a hand. "I get it." She turned to leave, without the rotini, and suddenly it was the last thing Nikki wanted for dinner.

"Hey, wait." Melissa stopped and turned. "Why don't you take it? I actually think pizza will work. And—"

Her cellphone rang in her purse and interrupted her. She held up a finger in apology before she dug it out. *Damn.* "It's Matt. I'm sorry, Melissa. Just give me a second. I have to take this."

The other woman nodded and Nikki half turned away to take the call.

"Matt? What's up? I'm just going to be—"

"Nik, I'm so sorry for such late notice, but we have to cancel on tonight."

"Cancel?" Aware that Melissa probably listened in, Nikki lowered her voice. "Why? What's up?" She didn't say it, but it better be important for Matt to cancel. Especially last minute. Besides the fact that she was disappointed, she knew Ryan would be really upset. He loved spending time with his dad and stepmom.

"Becky's sick. Like throwing up sick and I'm sure Ryan could come, but—"

"No, no. I really don't need Ryan exposed to the flu."

"I know. I'm so sorry, Nikki. I hope Ryan's not too disappointed. We had an *X-Men* movie marathon planned. If Becky's doing better tomorrow, I'll come get him and take him out for the day, okay? Maybe we can even pop in on Levi."

Nikki smiled, because Ryan adored Levi Jenkins. The older man had been a friend of her mother's and had stepped in as a grandfather figure for Ryan. "Sounds good. He'll like that. Tell Becky to feel better."

She hung up and turned back to Melissa, who now had the chicken rotini dinner in her basket.

"That didn't sound good. Everything okay?"

Nikki shrugged. "Becky's not feeling well, so it looks like there'll be three of us for dinner after all." She glanced down at Melissa's basket. "I guess it'll be pizza."

"Pizza?" Ryan chose that moment to appear, his hands full of snacks he'd picked up on the way. Nikki noticed he'd forgotten the milk. "Who's having pizza?"

"We are." Nikki took the items from his hands, eyeing his choice of granola bars but she didn't say anything as she put them in the basket. "Looks like Becky is pretty sick, so your dad had to cancel on tonight. Sorry, buddy."

Ryan's face fell. "That sucks."

"It does. But he's going to take you out and spend the day with you tomorrow as long as Becky's feeling well enough to leave alone."

"Cool." Young boys were easily swayed, and Ryan perked up almost at once. "And I get to hang out with Parker tonight."

Nikki could almost feel Melissa bristle, and when she looked up, the other woman didn't look pleased. "That's really too bad," Melissa said.

With her romantic evening a bust, it would be easy for her to cancel on Parker altogether so he wouldn't have a conflict with Melissa. But when she saw the rotini meal in Melissa's basket, it sparked something spiteful in her. Something she wasn't altogether proud of, but she couldn't help it.

"Well, we should run." Nikki smiled sweetly. "But we really do have to get together early next week, Melissa. I worked on a few designs this afternoon I'd like to show you."

Melissa nodded. "I'm pretty busy with everything, but I'm sure I can make time."

The two women regarded each other for a moment, neither willing to turn away first. Finally it was Nikki who broke the moment, excused herself, and with Ryan in tow, went to pick out a frozen pizza.

Chapter Five

Melissa

Parker, how could you?

Melissa felt bad for Nikki and her son, for the letdown about to come their way when Parker canceled on them. It was really too bad. Her brother-in-law needed to manage his time a little better. Especially now that there was Nikki's son to think about. Kids didn't react well to change and the little guy had been through enough lately, with his grandmother passing away, moving to a new home, and finding out about his new dad.

God knows, Abby had been through enough. She knew how rough it was as a single mother to raise a child alone, especially one having to adjust to things out of their control. She really needed to give Nikki a break, be nicer. If things were getting serious between her and Parker, then one day, hopefully not too soon, Nikki would be family.

Part of her wanted to call Parker and be the better person—tell her brother-in-law to come over tomorrow and spend the night with Nikki instead. But that part warred with her concern over Wade. Parker wouldn't have mentioned the letter unless it was important.

Was Wade okay? He had to be. He was a tough guy. The only times Parker mentioned any letters from Wade was when something serious happened—like when he'd been in a knife fight or when he turned down possible parole.

Her husband was in an out-of-state prison for falling asleep at the wheel and killing a little girl—a girl the same age as their daughter. His mistake had cost them so much but she hadn't made things any better. She'd let people think her husband had left her, and in a way, she supposed, he had. But somehow it seemed better than letting people think he was a murderer. What kind of woman—mother and wife—did that make her?

Her heart jumped to her throat. *Oh God, let him be okay. Please, let him be okay.*

The first few months when Wade had been sentenced had been a living nightmare. She didn't remember much of the first half year but she knew she kept her focus on her daughter throughout the day but then at night, she'd crumble, cry herself to sleep and then wake up mere hours later in a panic, worrying about Wade.

Everyone had assumed she struggled because he'd left her, and they all tried to get her to take time off, offered to help her with the printing and even with Abby, but Melissa refused to wallow. She needed to stay strong, plus she needed the money. She was now a single mother and couldn't afford to take any time off, especially considering she was self-employed.

Any time anyone offered any words about Wade and how they *understood*, she would stop them. Nobody understood. How could they? She hated that she'd let the rumor start, but it was a lot easier at the time than having to explain how Wade couldn't live with the guilt of killing a little girl his own daughter's age and so instead of fighting for them, for their life, he went to prison without a word.

She'd always said Wade was her hero, her knight in shining armor.

Careful of fairy-tales, her mom used to say. *There's no happy endings in the real world.*

No truer words had ever been said.

By the time she made it to the cash register, her basket of food had grown from the pasta she should have let Nikki have, to include a Greek salad, a bag of potato chips, a tub of brownie chunk ice cream, and several bars of milk chocolate coconut. So much for eating healthy.

"Any more of those left?"

Greta Wilson was at the cash register and packed the pasta in a brown bag.

"Last one, Greta." Melissa smiled at the older woman and forced thoughts of her husband out of her mind.

"Ever since you placed that article in the paper, I'm running out before the dinner crowd is over." Greta shook her head. Her light purplish gray curls swayed with the movement. She reached for the glasses that hung down around her neck and propped them on the edge of her nose. "Time for me to start making more, I guess."

"I knew it would work." Melissa watched as a faint blush bloomed on the woman's face. Greta had hemmed and hawed for weeks about letting Melissa write an article about her meals but finally gave in when Melissa promised her that they'd see an increase in business.

Come on, home-cooked food you didn't slave over? A sure win anytime.

"I was thinking we could start adding weekly menus in the paper?"

"We could." Melissa thought it through. "That's actually a

great idea, and I think I have the perfect spot for it too. Or we could stick it in with all the flyers?"

Greta shook her head. "Easier to get lost with the flyers, isn't it? Besides, if we do weekly, I'm sure you could give me a deal, right?"

It took every ounce of strength for Melissa to not roll her eyes. A deal? On top of what she'd already be giving her? How was she to make any money then?

She could almost hear her father's voice in her ear: *take care of the people who will in turn take care of you.*

"Oh, I'm sure we can work something out." Melissa winked. "Why don't you come by the office and we'll take a look at the layout and whatnot." The topic of menus gave her an idea.

"Greta, would you happen to have any extra pumpkin recipes I could use for the festival this year?" She leaned forward and lowered her voice. "Norma wants to create a recipe book and I know everyone would love anything you could add."

Greta winked at her. "Norma already asked. I've got a file folder to hand in whenever you're ready for it."

Melissa smiled. "Awesome. How about I stop by and pick it up tomorrow? Around lunch time?"

"That will work. Or...I can come by before lunch, bring you something to eat and we can discuss the menus at the same time? I'll figure out the next two weeks' worth of menus tonight. And your total is twelve dollars even."

Melissa glanced down at the two paper bags and then at the cash register.

"Are you sure you got everything? That seems pretty cheap." The pasta itself was ten dollars.

Greta leaned close. "The pasta is on the house. And I slipped an extra chocolate bar in there for Abby, too."

Melissa reached for the older woman's hand. "You're too good to us, Greta. Thank you."

Greta waved her hand in the air, as if to shoo her away, but Melissa caught the faint glean of tears in her eyes.

"Well, someone needs to help take care of you, don't they? I see that little girl of yours handing out those flyers. You've done good in raising her all by yourself. Wade would be proud."

This time it was Melissa's turn to blush. "She's a good kid." And before things got too awkward, Melissa grabbed her bags and blew a kiss to Greta before she left.

Abby was a good kid. Melissa was proud of her, proud of the young woman she was becoming and hoped that not having a father around wasn't a huge hindrance. Thank God for Parker. At least there was a male influence, someone she trusted and loved in her life. And Wade would be proud. He would.

Which brought back her run-in with Nikki. She loved Parker; he was part of her family and even though Abby missed seeing him...the right thing for her to do would be to call him and give him an out, suggest another night or something.

She went to reach for her phone at the same time it rang.

"Hey Abs. What's up?"

"We have no sugar."

"And we need sugar because..."

Her daughter groaned. "To make brownies, hellooo."

"Don't we have a mix or something in the cupboard?" The last time she headed into the city, she stockpiled a whole bunch of ready-made mixes because they were on sale.

"I want to make homemade ones, Mom."

Melissa scrunched up her nose. "I just left the store, Abby. I really don't want to go back in. Mrs. Wilson was there and I...I kinda made her cry."

"Great." The exasperation in her daughter's voice was quite evident. "Fine, I'll use the mix. Just hurry up. Uncle Parker will be here soon."

On her way home, Melissa contemplated calling Parker to

cancel officially and give him a way out of the situation he'd obviously created, but by the time she pulled up into her driveway and went to dial his number, she stopped herself. Parker told her they needed to talk about Wade, and in all honesty, news about her husband was more important than sharing pizza with Nikki. She knew Parker would agree with her. He'd be there.

* * *

For the umpteenth time, Melissa caught Abby eyeing the clock and letting out a long sigh.

"Are you sure he's coming? Check your phone again. Maybe he left a message."

Melissa already held the phone in her hand and was dialing Parker's number.

"How about I just call him." She held the phone up to her ear and caught her daughter watching her intently. "And he's not late," she added.

The dinger on the oven went off, giving Abby something to focus on rather than her phone call. The brownies smelled amazing and with the way Melissa's stomach was all knotted up, she could use the chocolate.

"Hey, what's up?" Parker answered the phone.

There was a happiness to his voice and it was nice to hear.

"Just checking in. How much longer do you think you'll be?" When he didn't answer, she added, "I just need to stick dinner in the oven to heat up, so no rush."

"Mel..."

Maybe it was the way he said her name or the fact that he hesitated...but that's when she knew.

He chose Nikki over her.

"I thought you said we needed to talk? That you," she

glanced over at Abby and lowered her voice, "got a *letter* we needed to talk about."

He sighed.

"I know, I know. But I forgot...well, not really forgot but just..."

If he were here, standing before her, she would have probably laughed at him. He forgot, it was obvious, but who did he forget about? Her or Nikki?

"Nikki, right?"

Abby raised her head and took a step towards her. She opened her mouth to say something but Melissa quickly shook her head, earning her a frown from her daughter.

"I'm sorry, Mel."

"I'm not the one to be apologizing to."

"I know. And we do need to talk. Can I stop by now?"

Melissa rolled her eyes. "What? We're good enough for you to drop in on but not to stay for dinner? If you come, you're eating with us. I didn't just fight over the last pasta dish at the store for nothing, you know." She attempted to keep her tone light while at the same time making her point.

"But I can't—"

Melissa quickly cut him off.

"You can and will if you do."

She knew it was a low blow, considering he'd already made his choice, but he could have manned up. And the letter must be important; otherwise, he wouldn't have mentioned it.

This was her husband they were dealing with.

"What did the letter say, Parker?" If he wasn't going to come and talk to her in person, he could over the phone.

"No. I'd rather tell you in person."

Oh God. Melissa's stomach dropped and she gripped the edge of her seat for strength.

"Is he..." Her voice faltered. "He's not..." She couldn't say the words. Not because her daughter was in the room with her but because saying it out loud would make it real and it couldn't be. Wade couldn't be dead; she would know it. Know in her heart, in her soul. He couldn't be.

Her hands were cold and a numbing sensation swept through her body.

"Mom? Mom, are you okay?" Abby ran across the room and knelt down in front of her. Melissa reached out and grabbed her hand.

"Dead?" Parker's voice calmed her racing heart. "Oh no, no Melissa. He's not. He's okay, trust me, he's okay."

If Parker were here, right now, in front of her, she would hit him. Hard on his chest with her fist and then cry with relief. Instead, she leaned forward and hugged her daughter. Tears pricked her eyes as she fought hard not to cry.

"I'm okay, Abby, I'm okay," she whispered into Abby's ear.

"Is she there? Oh, I'm so sorry, Mel."

Melissa took a few deep breaths, filling her center before she stood up and headed into the kitchen.

"Enjoy your evening with Nikki." She popped the pasta dish into the oven to heat up. "Drop by later tonight if it's still early enough, okay? Whatever you have to tell me can wait till then."

Right now, all she wanted to do was have a nice dinner with her daughter and then eat the pan of brownies. That's all she wanted to think about. Not Wade being dead. Not Parker choosing Nikki over his family. Not the fear of one day having to tell Abby the truth about her dad. Nothing. Just pasta and brownies.

"Better yet, just drop by tomorrow, okay? And bring breakfast."

"Are you sure?" Parker asked.

"No. But enjoy your pizza."

"Okay. Hey, how do you know we're having pizza?"

Melissa bit her lip. Should she tell Parker how she basically grabbed the pasta dish from Nikki or just play dumb? Would Nikki tell on her?

"'Cause I'm a single mom with a kid and it's a Friday night. That's what we normally always have." It was a good save—enough of one that Parker didn't even comment.

"Thanks, Mel. Say sorry to Abby for me, okay?"

Melissa looked at her daughter and saw the frown on her face.

"No way. I'll leave that up to you for tomorrow. Oh, and Parker? Don't you dare tell Nikki about any of this."

Melissa didn't even give him a chance to agree when she hung up the phone. She wasn't sure where that last thought came from and wasn't even sure why she mentioned it. Of course he wouldn't say anything to Nikki. They weren't that close—they couldn't be. Besides, Parker would never betray her. Not like that. He'd talk to her first before he mentioned anything about Wade to his new girlfriend. She knew that deep down.

When she looked at Abby, Melissa expected theatrics but her daughter proved her wrong once again.

"Guess Uncle Parker isn't getting any brownies tonight, is he?"

Melissa hugged her daughter to her side and kissed the top of her head. "Not even the crumbs."

"His loss." Abby flung her hair over her shoulder and then sat down at the table.

Totally his loss. But if that was the case, then why did Melissa feel as if they were losing out somehow too?

Chapter Six

Nikki

Nikki's plans for a romantic evening with Parker may have gone out the window, but Ryan was excited for the chance to throw the football around the yard with someone who didn't constantly drop it. It's not that she didn't like football, but...well, she didn't like football. She pulled the kitchen curtain to the side and watched for a moment while Parker easily caught Ryan's toss and instead of throwing it back at him, pretended to charge the boy and score a touchdown. Ryan tackled Parker's legs, and he fell to the ground in an exaggerated move.

She chuckled and let the curtain drop. It made her happy to see how much Ryan liked Parker. It made their relationship so much easier and Nikki had worried about it because she'd never before brought a man home to meet her son. But Parker was different than the few men she'd dated before they had moved back to Halfway. Very different. And Ryan was different now, too.

The boy had adapted better than she ever thought possible to life in a small town and the family that came with it. More than adjusting, Ryan thrived as he got to know his dad and step-mom. Not for the first time, a pang of guilt flashed in her chest when she thought about all the years they'd lost because she was too young and stupid to think things would work out.

But that was in the past and Nikki was done looking behind her. She was all about looking forward and to the future. Maybe even a future with Parker.

She laughed at herself. She was getting way too carried away. It was still new.

Not that new.

No, not *that* new. But still. They had a lot to discuss and there was no point rushing things. Except dinner. Her stomach growled to remind her that she'd skipped lunch again in favor of getting her projects finished.

Leaving the window, and the boys playing outside, Nikki checked on the pizza, put the oven to broil to finish it faster, and set the table. She made sure the beautiful bouquet of flowers Parker brought her from his family's flower shop were displayed perfectly. It was such a treat to have someone bring her fresh flowers. Especially when she knew he went to the trouble to arrange them himself to include her favorite lilies and Gerber daisies. Every week he brought her a different bouquet, and they were always a little different, but some little detail in each one let Nikki know he was thinking of her.

The back door crashed open as Parker and Ryan bustled inside. "I'm starving, Mom. Is dinner—"

"You're not starving. Children in Africa are starving."

"Really, Mom?" He rolled his eyes and shook his head to let her know how ridiculous he thought she was. "Okay fine," he tried again. "I'm really, *really* hungry. Is that better?"

"Much." She tousled his hair. "Now go wash up."

The second he was out of the room, Parker pulled her in close and wrapped his arms around her. The chill from the outside air clung to his clothes, and when he wrapped his arms around her, she inhaled the manly scent of him that never failed to make her stomach flip.

"You're cold," she protested, but not very hard.

"I should let you warm me up." His grin was both playful and sexy at the same time but it was a good idea, so she stood on her tiptoes to press her lips to his.

Parker's hand cupped her cheek while his thumb stroked lazy circles on her skin. It was a slow, deep kiss and Nikki could have lost herself in it except for the fact that she knew Ryan would be back any second and the smell of—

"Is something burning?" Parker pulled back, smelling the pizza at the same time she had.

"Oh no." She darted across the kitchen and flung open the oven door. A cloud of black smoke billowed out and she turned instinctively away. Nikki was just about to grab the potholder when Parker rushed forward, a dishtowel in hand, and yanked the now charred frozen pizza from the oven and tossed it on the stove top.

Tears pricked at the back of Nikki's eyes. She'd ruined dinner again. It was becoming a very disturbing trend. But a frozen pizza? Surely she should be able to handle that.

"Don't worry." Parker reached for her hand. "It's just a pizza."

"It's not—"

The screech of the smoke detector cut her off. Ryan walked into the room with his hands over his ears. "What's that noise?" he yelled to be heard. "And that smell?" He pulled one hand from his ear to cover his nose, but then realizing how loud it still was, his hands fluttered, unsure of where they should go.

He looked so funny and with the smoke in the air, the alarm still shrieking overhead, and the burnt pizza smoldering on the stove top, there was nothing else to do. Parker and Nikki looked at each other and laughed. Nikki laughed so hard that the tears that had threatened only moments earlier rolled down her cheeks and she had to clutch her stomach in an effort to contain herself.

Ryan looked between the two adults, confusion and pre-teen attitude all over his face. "You're both crazy."

That only made her laugh harder.

"Well," Parker said when he was able to pull himself together. "Who thinks we should go out for dinner?"

* * *

It was late by the time they got back from the restaurant and got Ryan to bed. He was wired after too much soda, a rare treat, and the addition of a piece of chocolate cake. It's not that Nikki was strict with him about sweets, but because she never baked, there just wasn't the selection of fresh goodies that other kids had. Unless he was at Becky and Matt's house. Becky could bake. She was amazing with her food blog and constant stream of new recipes. Nikki felt a pang of guilt as she thought of her friend. She probably should have called her to make sure everything was okay and she was feeling better. It wasn't like Becky to feel so bad that she canceled a date with Ryan. She loved Nikki's son as if he was her own. Nikki glanced at the clock. It was probably too late to call and check in on her now. Besides...

Her gaze drifted to the kitchen, where Parker was opening a bottle of wine for them to share. She'd been looking forward to their time alone together all night. Oh, who was she kidding, all day and even longer than that. She was more than ready to focus on Parker for a little while.

"Hey, I thought I told you to relax while I got some wine." He chastised her, but it was all good-natured.

"I am relaxing." She took the wine with a smile and sat on the couch. "If I'm not at my desk working, that's relaxing in my book. Thank you for this." She raised her glass in a toast.

"To us."

"And a night alone." She laughed ruefully. "Sort of."

They clinked glasses and each took a small sip. "You know I'm okay with this, right?" Parker was suddenly serious, the teasing gone from his voice.

She dismissed him with a wave. "Oh, of course. Every single, eligible man in town wants to be spending their Friday nights cleaning up burnt pizza and listening to stories about how much ten- and eleven-year-old boys like to fart." She shook her head as she remembered their dinner conversation. "I'm really sorry." She took another sip of wine because it was easier than meeting his gaze.

She liked Parker. Really liked him. But she also knew it wasn't fair to assume he'd be okay with jumping into life with a single mom. It was a lot. And as much as she wanted to throw herself over to him blindly and put her heart out there, she also had to be practical.

"Seriously, Nikki. I...would you look at me please?" His voice was gentle but firm and she did as she was asked, putting her glass down before she looked up into his kind eyes.

"I really am okay with all this. I actually kind of like it."

"Okay, now I know you're full of it. What man prefers a night of this," she waved her arm around, taking it all in, "in favor of a romantic night complete with lingerie?"

"There was lingerie?" He raised his eyebrow and Nikki swatted his arm.

"I guess you'll never know now."

"There's always later." Parker put his own glass down and scooted over on the couch so there was no longer a gap between them. He took her hands in his and pulled her close, giving her a kiss that left more than enough room for promises of later.

But it would also lead to promises that she couldn't keep. At least not with Ryan in the next room. Reluctantly, she pulled back and picked up her wine glass again as a defense.

"Tell me about your day." It was a lame segue, but she genuinely did care. Resigning himself to the fact that sitting next to each other on the couch was as close as they were going to get, Parker settled in and regaled her with tales of high school students that made her laugh in memory of the way they used to behave not that long ago in that very same school. Sometimes it seemed like forever ago that Nikki had been seventeen and carefree, and other times it felt like just yesterday.

"I've talked long enough. Tell me about your day? Anything exciting happen in the world of web designing?"

"You joke, but it's actually a very exciting business. I tried out three new fonts today, and discovered a new site for background images."

"Big day." He grinned.

"I also did some work for Melissa and the *Herald*."

"Melissa?"

Nikki nodded. "Yup, she threw me a few jobs. Nothing too major. But just enough to help her out, I guess."

"Why don't you seem so sure?"

"I just don't think it will lead to much is all."

"Why not? You do great work."

"Maybe. But Melissa..." Nikki bit her bottom lip, not sure how much she should say.

"What's up? What aren't you telling me?"

"I just don't think Melissa likes me is all. She's...well..."

"What? That's crazy. Why wouldn't she like you?"

"Because she has a thing for you." Nikki spit out her secret worry before she could stop herself.

She half expected Parker to be surprised, or maybe even upset. But instead, he laughed. *Laughed.*

"What is so funny?" She smacked him on the arm with a pillow. "It's not funny."

"It is," he said when he finally was able to contain his laughter. "It's hysterical. She's married to my brother, Nikki. She does not have a thing for me, I assure you."

"Was."

"What?"

"Was married to your brother," she corrected him.

Parker waved his hand, dismissing her concerns. "She doesn't have a thing for me."

No." Nikki crossed her arms. Now that she'd voiced her concern, she was not going to let Parker dismiss it so quickly. "She does. Think about it, Parker. How long has it been since Wade left? Years. It's not unusual for her to want to look for other companionship. And you've been so good with Abby and helping her out around the house."

Parker's face shifted. He was no longer laughing. In fact, his face held no trace of humor at all.

"That's not it, Nikki. You're way off base."

"I don't think I am." She hated that she sounded like a jealous girlfriend, which was exactly what she was. But now that she'd said it aloud, the worry seemed to take on a life of its own.

"Nikki, you have to listen to me on this. Please."

She shook her head. He was too defensive. Something was going on between them. She knew it. Hadn't she deep down known that whatever was going on between them was too good to be true? He reached for her but she pulled away and jumped up off the couch.

"You need to stop, Nikki." He stood in front of her. So close she could feel the heat coming off him. "You have to trust me on this. It's not the way you think."

"Then how is it?"

He opened his mouth to say something and for a moment, she thought she might get the truth of whatever he was worried about. But then he shook his head. "You just have to trust me," he repeated. "Please."

She thought about it for a minute. Trust him. She should. She had no reason not to. But she also knew what she saw with Melissa. The woman had feelings for Parker, that much she knew for sure. How could she ignore all that and just blindly trust whatever he was saying?

"No." She couldn't. She would not open her heart up to that kind of hurt. And never mind her heart. She would not do that to Ryan. She had to protect Ryan. "I don't think I can do this, Parker. Not if there's someone else's feelings at stake. It's too messy. And I can't do messy."

"It's not messy." But she saw the doubt in his eyes. It was messy. And if it wasn't already, it would be.

"Okay. It's a little messy," he admitted. "But not in the way you think." He took a deep breath and exhaled hard.

Something in his voice made Nikki question whether she really wanted to know or not. Suddenly, she wasn't so sure anymore.

Parker took her hands and gently led her back to the couch so they sat and faced each other. "I want this to work, Nikki. And I know I need to be one hundred percent honest with you if that's going to happen."

She nodded and waited for him to drop the bomb that would implode their relationship.

"Things with Melissa and Abby are complicated. I've always felt a certain responsibility towards them because they're family."

Nikki looked up sharply.

"Not because there's anything romantic going on with Melissa," he added quickly. "There never has and there never will. She loves my brother."

"But he left her," Nikki protested. "How could she still be clinging to that after all these years?"

Parker shook his head. "No. He didn't leave her. Well, not by choice anyway. About nine years ago, Wade was driving a truck in Oregon. It was late; he'd been pushing his schedule and he probably should have pulled over to get a bit of sleep. But he didn't. He doesn't remember everything that happened, but he must have shut his eyes for a moment because the next thing you know, his truck went over the center line and hit a minivan."

Nikki's hand flew to her mouth and her lips moved silently in an effort to ask the question she already knew the answer to.

Parker nodded as if she'd spoken. "He hit a family. A little girl wasn't wearing her seat belt," he added before she could ask.

"Was she...did she..."

"By chance, one of the first on the scene was Nyah Henderson. She was a paramedic and was actually on her way back to Halfway from visiting her mom in Oregon. Do you remember her?" Nikki shook her head although she did have a vague recollection of the woman, but they'd never been friends. "Ironically, Nyah was Melissa's best friend growing up and she did everything she could." Parker refocused on the story. "But the little girl didn't make it. She died on the way to the hospital. Wade was charged with vehicular homicide. Sentenced out-of-state for ten years in prison."

Nikki sucked in a breath. "But I don't understand. Why would Melissa tell everyone he left her? What about Abby?"

"Abby was the reason. In Melissa's eyes it was better to have her daughter and everyone else think that he left her than for Abby to know her father had killed someone."

"But it was an accident."

Parker shrugged. "It wasn't my call to make."

Chapter Seven

Melissa

After tossing and turning half the night, Melissa dragged her exhausted body out of bed, wrapped herself in her thick house-coat and made her way downstairs, careful to avoid the squeaky sections of the stairs so not to wake Abby. She had a few bottles left of her favorite wine, a piesporter from Germany, and even though she'd tried to save them until her next trip into the city, she decided to open one up. The wine would accomplish one of two things: actually help her to get to sleep or calm her down.

The calm would be nice.

She'd gone to bed seething thanks to Parker standing her up, again. She'd tried hard not to—she knew where he was, after all —but it took everything inside her to not send him a text or call his cell before she went to bed. He'd picked Nikki over her, and she got it. She really did. He deserved to find someone who made him laugh and smile and think about a future...if anyone deserved that, it was Parker.

But what about her? She knew that made her out to be

a whiny crybaby but still...who did he think he was, calling and saying he needed to talk to her about Wade and then standing her up? Not only stand her up after making a dinner date with her daughter...but afterwards, too.

She'd tried to take Abby's mind off the disappointment and they'd had a long talk before bed about how life was going to change for them all now that Nikki was in Parker's life...but this stuff was for adults to figure out, not kids.

Melissa curled up in her favorite two-person chair, wrapped herself in a blanket she'd knitted for herself last winter and sipped at her wine.

What she needed to do was stop thinking about Parker. Stop relying on Parker. Stop expecting...what? To not put them first in his life? Not to be there, helping them like he'd promised Wade? She wasn't being fair, and she knew that. But to be honest, she didn't want to be fair. That was allowed, right? Tonight she gave herself permission to be completely self-centered, to only be focused on herself and no one else. Just for the night.

Tomorrow she'd put her big-girl panties on, pretend life was normal and move on with her life.

Except, how could she move on when the clock was ticking? Wade had a year left of his sentence. A year left in prison where he could be seriously injured or worse—killed. A year of separation and loss...loss of love, of life, of being a family.

She had a year to figure out what to tell her daughter. She'd made her bed, years ago, when she concocted the lie in order to protect their daughter...and now she needed to figure out how to fix things.

Abby was going to hate her. She knew it. And she didn't blame her. Nothing she said, no matter how many ways she tried to explain herself...her daughter would never forgive her for forcing her to live a lie and for keeping her father away from her.

"I've screwed up big time," she whispered into the quiet room.

She'd brought down the journal where she wrote letters to Wade. She'd tell him things in there, share what her day was like, keep him in the loop of what was happening in town. This was her ninth journal—one for every year. Originally she'd thought to save them and give them to Wade when he came home, but then decided to share them with him every year. At first, he'd welcomed the journals: he'd pore over them and ask her to clarify events or details whenever she visited him. Then, after a few years, she saw the look in his eye, read the desperation there and realized reading the journals probably hurt too much. She offered to stop bringing them and even though she could see that he wanted her to, he didn't. It was his only link to her and Abby, he'd told her.

Her heart ached when she thought of Wade. She hated the life they'd been handed. Hated how things had worked out. Hated that the guilt of his actions ate at him so much that he refused to try to get an early release. Hated that by staying in the prison, it made things harder for her, financially. He could never go back to being a truck driver, but he could work on trucks as a mechanic, something he'd been handy with before prison. He'd even taken on training while in prison to be a mechanic, so when he was finally released, hopefully he could get a job.

Not having to worry about the finances all the time would be nice. So would having him home.

Sitting here, alone, made her admit something she tried to always stuff deep down inside.

As much as she loved Wade, sometimes she even hated him.

Melissa reached for her iPad and opened up her social media tabs. It was too early, or too late, depending on how you looked at it, for most of her friends to be online so she just scrolled and liked various posts she saw on news about babies and cute puppy photos and so was surprised when she caught Becky's message to her.

Can't sleep? Becky asked.

Melissa took a photo of her wine glass and posted it. *This might help,* she said.

Why are you up? Becky wasn't one to have issues sleeping. In fact, all through high school, Becky would often be the first girl to fall asleep at any of their slumber parties.

Not feeling that great, restless, and don't want to keep Matt up.

Everything okay? She really prayed that everything was fine.

I...well... If I ask you something, do you promise to keep it between us?

Now that piqued Melissa's curiosity. *Of course. You know that.* She thought about her friendship with Becky and how she'd been the one person always there for her, especially in the beginning after Wade...left. In all these years, she'd leaned on Parker as her support, but maybe she'd been wrong. Maybe she could have leaned on Becky.

Actually, there were no maybes about that sentence. She could have and she knew it. Becky would have been the voice of reason for her, helped her think things through properly and would have been there as a support.

That first year, when everything had happened, it all remained a blur. A blur she liked to forget.

Mel? You okay?

Absolutely. I'm here for you and I promise. Whatever you ask is between us, Melissa reiterated.

I thought morning sickness was only in the morning.

Melissa gave a little squeal of happiness. Was Becky pregnant? Of course she was; otherwise, she wouldn't be asking.

Are you...? She wanted to play it cool, not make too big of a deal until Becky did.

Yes. But shh, okay? Keep it between us for now.

Ok. Wow. *Didn't you have morning sickness with any of your other pregnancies?* From what Melissa knew, Becky had been pregnant a few times but always lost the baby early on. She knew she and Matt really wanted a child of their own. The last time they'd had coffee, they'd talked about Ryan and how he filled a hole in their lives and heart and made them realize they wanted more children.

Not like this. I feel like I'm going to die. When does it end?

I've heard the more sick you are, the better the pregnancy. Fingers crossed? She remembered being told that when she was first pregnant.

That's what Dr. Richards said too.

Melissa could almost hear the agony through her friend's words. She'd been sicker than a dog with Abby—in fact, her morning sickness lasted all forty weeks—but she wasn't about to tell Becky that.

It'll get easier. Can you keep anything down? Maybe she could put together a care package and drop it off tomorrow.

Matt says we should buy stock in a cracker company.

Ouch. If she were to read between the lines, that didn't sound so good.

It'll get easier. Promise. Just have Matt rub your feet, massage your back and keep the house clean for you. How about I bring some homemade chicken soup to you tomorrow? It's good—promise. It's the only soup I can make. Despite all her soup cookbooks and attempts to make the best homemade soup she could, they never tasted good. Other than her chicken soup.

If you stay, we could have girl time! It's been too long.

Girl time. That sounded promising and the perfect opportunity maybe for Melissa to confide in Becky about Wade. She needed someone to talk to and help plan his return home. Who was she kidding? She needed someone to help her out of the hole she'd dug herself into and it didn't look like Parker was that person anymore.

It's a date! I have something I need to tell you anyways. There. She'd done it. Now she couldn't back down even if she'd wanted to. Becky wouldn't let her.

Is this the deep dark secret you've been keeping for years and can't bear the weight of anymore? Please tell me it's something good?

Deep dark secret? How did Becky know?

Chapter Eight

Nikki

After Parker had left the night before—late, considering neither of them was in a hurry for him to leave—Nikki had lain awake for hours to think about what he'd told her about Melissa and Wade.

It was crazy. All of it was absolutely insane. But as the hours ticked by and she tossed and turned, slowly Nikki came to some sort of understanding about why Melissa would rather the world think Wade had left her. It was a no-win situation for her, and as a mother, Nikki could relate to wanting to protect her child as much as possible from the fallout of the accident.

And it made so much sense about why Melissa wasn't entirely pleased with Nikki's presence in Parker's life. Not only had he assumed the role of the male figure for Abby, he'd also in a way assumed that role for Melissa, too. And even if it wasn't romantic the way Parker claimed—and Nikki believed him—it was still a relationship and it would need to be respected.

At least that was the decision Nikki came to right before she finally drifted off.

The next morning, she didn't have time to think about the whole Melissa and Parker situation right away. Ryan was up and tore down the stairs for breakfast before he headed out to spend the day with his dad.

"Slow down, buddy." Nikki shook her head. She smiled and she stepped out of Ryan's way as he raced through the kitchen for the second time. "What are you looking for?"

"I want to show Dad the new app I got the other day and I can't find my iPod."

"I'm sure it's here somewhere." The truth was, Nikki had no idea where it might be. Ryan always misplaced his things. It could be anywhere. "Where was the last place you saw it?"

Ryan rolled his eyes. "Can you just text it, Mom?"

"Text it? Since when do you have text? And why didn't I know about it?"

"Mom. Seriously." Ryan reached past her at the sink and grabbed her phone. "Parker set it up for me last week. Don't worry—it only works on the Wi-Fi."

Nikki watched as Ryan used her phone to send himself a text message. "Wait, we have Wi-Fi?" She didn't mean it to come out as dumb as it sounded. She knew she had Internet access. But she'd just assumed it was confined to her computer and her desk. There'd never been a reason for Wi-Fi in the house because she did all her work at her desk. "Why?"

"Because it's 2014. That's why."

Nikki couldn't help it; she laughed. "That's true. But seriously, how did it happen and...why?"

At the beeping sound across the room, Ryan smiled triumphantly as he dug his iPod out from the depths of his school bag. "Because I needed text, obviously." He grinned and in that moment looked so much like his father that it took

Nikki's breath away. Ryan had really come into his own since they'd moved to Halfway, and she knew that Matt was a large part of that. As was Parker, who'd been such a good influence in more ways than just the Wi-Fi scenario.

"Well, it's probably a good thing," she agreed. "I guess this means I can take my laptop and work from the couch now."

Ryan looked at her as if she'd lost her mind. "I guess."

"And I can get a hold of you and call you down for dinner."

Ryan rolled his eyes again.

"And..."

"Okay, Mom." He held up his hand and Nikki laughed. "I get it."

"I was just pointing out all the benefits of Wi-Fi is all." She smirked. "I was agreeing with you."

"Whatever." They both turned at the sound of a truck when it pulled into the yard. "That's probably Dad."

Sure enough, it was Matt's truck. He hopped out of the cab of his truck and made his way to the front door, where he knocked once before Nikki waved through the window for him to come in.

"Hey Dad!" Ryan rushed across the room but stopped himself before he gave his father a hug. He fist bumped him instead and Nikki felt a little tug in her heart. He was growing up so quickly. "I just need to grab a few things and we can go, okay?"

"Sounds good."

"We can text you to tell you to hurry up," Nikki chimed in with a grin that got yet another eye roll, this time with a sigh as Ryan ran off. She laughed as he left the room.

"What was that all about?"

"Apparently Parker set us up with Wi-Fi and Ryan was trying to convince me why it was so great, so I was helping." She added the last word with another giggle.

"Seriously? You didn't have Wi-Fi? You do realize it's—"

"2014. I know."

"And you're a web designer. Aren't web people usually up on this kind of thing?"

"There was no need for it." Nikki waved her hand to dismiss the conversation. "Anyway, how's Becky feeling?"

Matt got a strange look on his face and glanced away. "She's fine."

"Fine? Last night you said she was really sick." Without asking whether he wanted one, Nikki put a cup of coffee in front of Matt. He accepted it with a nod of thanks. "Must have been a twenty-four-hour thing then, huh?"

"Must have been."

She watched him closely. His left eyebrow twitched up and he rubbed his nose. He'd never been a good liar. He was definitely keeping something from her.

She shook her head and with a sigh, put her hands on her hips. "Spill."

"I don't know what you're—"

His protest died on his lips when he saw the way she looked at him. "How do you do that?"

"You're way too easy to read." Nikki laughed. "Now tell me what's going on."

Matt shook his head. "Can't." He held up a hand to ward off her protests. "But Becky can. I think she's having a bit of a girl's day." He used his fingers for quotes. "Why don't you head over there later? If you don't have any plans, that is." He gave her a side-glance that implied a whole lot more than words could have said.

"If you're talking about Parker..."

"You know I am." Matt took a sip of his coffee and smiled behind his mug. Once again, Nikki marveled at how easy it was between them now. She never would have guessed it could be so good after everything that had happened. "You two are getting pretty serious, aren't you?"

Nikki shrugged. The truth was, she didn't know. She'd like to think so and most of the time she did think so. But they'd been together awhile now and she was just finding out about Melissa. And even though he'd told her, Nikki couldn't help but feel a little let down that he'd waited so long to say something. If he felt as serious about her as she felt about him, wouldn't he have been totally honest with her by now? And if they were serious, then wasn't it time their relationship moved forward? At least a little bit? She sighed and exhaled hard.

"Well, that doesn't sound like the sound of a woman in a happy relationship." Matt put his mug down and met her eyes. "Wanna talk about anything?"

"Not really," she lied. She did want to talk. But there was no way she could tell Melissa's secret to Matt. No, she'd have to talk to Melissa about that. And then maybe she'd feel some sort of reassurance that things with Parker really were as platonic and *helpful* as he'd said they were. "But I will go see Becky today." She forced a smile to her face. "Parker's helping out at the flower shop and I don't really feel like doing any work. This will be a great excuse to get out of the house."

Before Matt could pry any further, Ryan bound down the stairs. "You two have fun. Matt, I'll call you later about dropping him off."

"Okay, Mom. But you know you could call *me* if I had a phone?"

Nikki shook her head and it was her turn to roll her eyes. "Keep dreaming, kiddo. Go. Enjoy your day."

"You too, Nikki." Matt gave her one last look before he offered her a friendly smile and headed out.

. . .

***

She hadn't been invited to Becky's house, not really. But it wouldn't matter. Their friendship was back on solid ground now after so many years, even if it was different. Nikki was sure Becky wouldn't mind her crashing a little get-together. *Since surely her invitation must have gotten lost,* she thought with only the slightest air of annoyance as she pulled into the yard at the Christmas tree farm and saw Melissa's car parked out front of the house.

When Becky opened the door, she looked surprised to see her. She also looked as if she'd been crying. But she recovered quickly from her shock and pushed open the screen door, before she pulled Nikki into a hug. "What a surprise. It's good to see you."

"Well, Matt said you were feeling better." She stopped herself before asking her outright what was going on, but added, "And he said you were having a bit of a ladies' day and I should come out. So here I am."

Becky's face split into a smile. "Of course you should come out. I'm glad you did. Come in. We were just going to try some coffee cake that I made for the blog. Would you like a piece?"

"Would I? Of course." Nobody turned down Becky's baking. Nobody.

Nikki followed Becky into the kitchen where she expected to see a few women, but it was only Melissa at the large oak table. She quickly wiped her eyes and gave a smile anyone could tell was forced. "Nikki. Hi."

"Hi." Nikki glanced between the two women. What was going on? "Is everything okay here? I hope I didn't—"

"No. I was telling—"

"I just told her—"

Melissa and Becky spoke at once.

"You were both telling secrets?" Nikki tried to smile, but she couldn't help the prick of jealousy she felt. Becky was telling Melissa her secrets now?

"Well, I just..." Melissa broke out into tears.

"She is just so happy with my news," Becky covered quickly. It was clearly a distraction. And it worked.

Nikki spun her head around to see Becky lit up in a smile, her hand on her stomach.

"No."

Becky nodded.

"Oh my God!" Nikki flew across the space and pulled her friend into a tight hug before she quickly released her. "I'm sorry. I shouldn't."

"I'm not going to break, Nikki." Becky laughed and twisted out of Nikki's arms. "But there is a very good chance that I'm going to be sick, so don't squeeze too tight. This morning sickness is going to kill me."

"I keep telling her it's a good sign," Melissa said. "It means the baby's healthy."

"I know, I know." Becky waved Nikki over to the table, where she poured Nikki a cup of tea. "And of course that's my first concern. It's always my first concern." Nikki nodded. With Becky's history of miscarriages, of course that was the thought on everyone's mind. "But I'm past the three-month mark now and it can stop any day."

The women all nodded sympathetically, although for Nikki, her pregnancy had been so easy, she thankfully hadn't experienced any morning sickness at all. Of course, it could be different if she got pregnant now. That thought came out of nowhere. She certainly hadn't thought of more children, but that was before things started to get serious with Parker.

Maybe...she shook her head to clear the idea. There'd be time to think about all that later.

Thinking about Parker reminded Nikki of what he'd said the night before about Melissa. She glanced across the table right as Melissa lifted her head to meet Nikki's gaze. Her red rimmed eyes reminded Nikki that she'd burst into tears only a moment ago. "Is everything okay, Melissa? You look like...well, is there anything you want to talk about? I'm really sorry about everything with Parker yesterday. I didn't realize that Wade—" Nikki stopped herself abruptly before she said too much.

Melissa narrowed her eyes. "Didn't realize what?"

"Oh, just that...well, you know..."

Nikki could have smacked herself. She'd said too much. Way too much. And judging by the way Melissa glared at her, she thought so too.

She reached for a piece of the coffee cake and quickly stuffed some in her mouth. "This is really good, Becky," she said through a full mouth. "Is it a new recipe?"

"What do you know?"

Melissa's voice was hard. Nikki swallowed the cake before she turned back to face the other woman.

"What did Parker tell you?"

Nikki glanced quickly between Melissa and Becky. "Maybe this isn't—"

"She knows everything." Melissa's voice was clipped tightly. "Because I told her. It was my story to tell. Not Parker's."

"He was worried about you is all," Nikki said quickly. "And he didn't want me to think that—"

"So it was about you." Melissa stood. The chair scraped loudly in the room as she shoved it back. "It wasn't about me at all. Or what was best for my daughter. I should have known." She pulled her purse strap over her arm. "Thank you for the tea, Becky."

Nikki jumped to her feet. She couldn't let Melissa leave. Not when she was so upset. The problem was, she didn't know what to say to her to make it okay. "Melissa, don't go." She took a step towards her. "I know it must be so hard what you're going through and Parker's been so great to help out with Abby and everything. I didn't realize that our relationship made that harder and I'm really sorry. I—"

"You have no idea what I'm going through." Tears spilled down Melissa's cheeks, but it was easy to see they were tears of anger. Nikki took a reflexive step back. "You have no idea at all," Melissa said again before she walked past her.

Nikki flinched when the front door slammed. She looked at Becky, who simply shook her head. That hadn't gone at all the way she'd hoped, and she had a feeling that things were only going to get worse.

Chapter Nine

Melissa

How dare he!

Her vision clouded from tears, Melissa gripped the door handle to her vehicle and bent over. An agonizing sob tore through her body.

Parker had no right. No right. How could he betray her like that? How?

"Melissa, wait!" She heard Nikki's voice call her from the house.

Hearing Nikki's voice forced Melissa to push down everything she felt. She was not going to let that woman see the damage her words had caused. So she made herself stand but she didn't turn.

"Please, I'm sorry. I didn't mean..."

Melissa heard the lie in Nikki's voice.

"Didn't what? Come on, let's be honest here." She turned and faced the woman her brother-in-law had betrayed her trust for. "Why did you come out here today? Now? Did you know I was going to be here? What? You couldn't stand the thought that I'm friends with Becky, so you had to come out and get in the middle of that too?" She spat the words out, uncaring whether what she said was the truth or not.

"Of course not!" Nikki's eyes grew round and the shock on her face told Melissa she'd gone too far, that she'd been unfair with her accusations. "Matt said..." She turned towards the house. "Becky...I just... God, I'm so sorry."

Melissa shook her head, Nikki's pleas falling on deaf ears.

"Let's make one thing clear, shall we? What happens in my life has no bearing on yours. I do not care if you are dating Parker or even sleeping with him. Hell, I don't care what you are to him. To me, you're nothing. Understand? NOTHING." Melissa barely restrained herself from screaming at Nikki.

"That's not fair." Nikki visibly strengthened in front of Melissa and walked towards her. "You're hurt. I get it. But you don't get to lash out at me because of it."

"Really? You're going to tell me what I can and can not do? Next you'll be telling me the mistake I made with Wade, right? Like you can talk." Melissa wiped at the tears that continued to run down her face, hating herself for showing any weakness to Nikki.

Melissa didn't understand where this anger was coming from and there was a part of her that felt horrible for taking it out on Nikki. She was about to apologize for her anger but stopped at the fury she saw in Nikki's gaze.

"I made a mistake. But at least I owned up to it. And I'm doing all that I can to correct it. You have no right to throw that in my face. And I'm trying here, Melissa. I'm trying. You're mad. I get it. But Parker didn't betray you. You placed him in a difficult position...or did you never think of that?"

"What are you talking about?" What position did she place Parker in?

"Couples don't keep secrets from each other." Nikki's voice had lowered as she said the words, the space between them shortened.

Melissa looked over to the porch; Becky stood there, her arms wrapped around her body. She thought about her conversation with her friend, not just the understanding she'd received but the honesty too.

You've made a mess of things, Mel, Becky had said. And she was right. She knew that. But still...Parker had betrayed her. The least he could have done was talk to her first, tell her what he intended to do. Give her a heads-up that his girlfriend knew her deepest and darkest secret.

"This wasn't Parker's secret to tell." Melissa sighed, the anger that had filled her suddenly gone.

"Wade is his brother too. Did you ever think about how hard it must be for him to pretend his own brother had run off, abandoning his family?"

Melissa shook her head and looked up into the sky. The tears had stopped but now the pin pricks of a headache were there, piercing into her skull. Of course she'd known it was hard for Parker but he'd agreed.

He'd agreed.

She must have whispered the words because she caught the sheen of tears in Nikki's eyes.

"Of course he did. He loves you. You're his family." Nikki's hand reached out, as if to touch her, to offer comfort, but then it fell back to her side and in that moment, Melissa realized that Nikki wasn't the enemy.

Nor was she a friend either, though.

"Then I guess I need to talk to him. But he should have come to me first, given me a heads-up that he was going to tell you."

Nikki nodded and then winced. "That's kind of my fault."

"Excuse me?"

She shrugged and the skin around her cheeks went red. It could have been from the cool wind but Melissa didn't think so.

"I thought..." Nikki's gaze dropped to the ground. "I thought maybe you were interested in him, as you know, more than—"

From deep inside her, a laugh rippled through Melissa's body until she was doubled over and forced to grip her knees. The idea that she was...her and Parker...no. God no.

"He's..." she couldn't stop the laughter, "oh my God, Nikki. He's Parker. Parker. My husband's brother. Oh my God."

She knew she must look a sight, from crying to laughing, but she couldn't stop herself. She let the emotional roller coaster take hold, work through her body until she was left struggling to take a breath.

"Everything okay?" Becky tentatively asked.

"I have no idea," Nikki said softly.

Melissa glanced up and saw both of them looking at her with concern filled faces.

"Melissa?"

She tried to smile at Becky but ended up only shaking her head as she kept filling her lungs. In and out. In and out. When she knew she wasn't going to burst out in tears or laughter, she reached for Becky's hand and squeezed.

"Nikki thought I had feelings for Parker."

She wasn't sure how she expected Becky to react to the news, but it wasn't for her to agree, that's for sure.

"Can you blame her? I'm sure there are others in town who wonder the same thing."

Melissa's eyes grew round and she wanted to deny, to argue her stance but then thought better of it. She'd dug this grave herself.

"I never...that's not what I—"

"I realize that now," Nikki said. "But it's what I thought. So

Parker came to your defense. And I get it...that's what I meant to say earlier, or at least, what I was trying to say. I understand." Her words came out in a rush as if she expected Melissa to go off on her again, and Melissa felt a smidgen of remorse.

"I'm," she swallowed hard, past the lump in her throat, "I'm sorry. For losing it like that, for saying—"

"Please." Nikki reached out and grabbed Melissa's hand. "Please, don't apologize. I handled it wrong, when I came out."

Melissa shook her head. "We both did."

"So we're all good now? Please? Can we go back inside where it's warmer at least? Besides," she gave Melissa a pointed look, "we're not done talking."

"Why don't you two go back in and I'll just come out later to pick up Ryan, okay?" Nikki backed away but Becky stopped her.

"Not going to happen. Stay. Both of you. You can help me figure out how to fight this morning sickness and then we can work on a plan on how to fix the mess Melissa made." She turned to Melissa. "If you're okay with that, which you have to be, because you're not dealing with this alone. Not anymore."

Melissa welcomed the hug that Becky enveloped her in. "Thank you," she whispered into her friend's ear.

"Only if Melissa is okay with me staying." Nikki stood off to the side, her arms crossed.

She looked guarded and Melissa knew it was her fault. She'd said some horrible things. And still kind of meant them. Kind of. But it wasn't fair of her to be mad at Nikki...her anger needed to be directed to Parker. But then, that wasn't even fair, was it? What if Nikki was right? She'd never really thought about how Parker felt in all this. He'd agreed with her decision to lie about Wade, but she'd never really asked him why he agreed. Was it just for her? For Abby?

She felt sick to her stomach as she realized that for nine

years, she'd made him carry out the lie. That wasn't okay. She was a horrible person for doing that and she owed him a huge apology.

But not only him...her daughter too. What kind of mother did that? Made her child think her father had left them? That wasn't okay either.

"Melissa?" Becky's voice was muted, as if in a fog. "Nikki, help me get her into the house before she passes out."

She let herself be walked back into Becky's home and forced to sit down. Moments later, a warm mug was pressed into her hands and the heat of it swept through her body. She hadn't realized just how cold she'd been.

"I'm sorry," she whispered. She stared at the wood table, unable to look up.

"You have nothing to be sorry for," Nikki said to her.

Warm hands settled on her shoulders and gently kneaded the tight muscles.

"Of course she does. She's screwed up big time and you were quite rude to Nikki."

Melissa raised her startled gaze up and looked at Becky, who gave her a sad smile.

"Well," Becky said. "You have and were. Let's be honest here."

"It's okay, I mean it," Nikki said. "I handled it wrong and really shouldn't have said anything. I just wanted you to know that I got it, that I understood, and here I go again."

"No, no. It's okay. Becky's right. I've screwed up and I need help to fix this. And I was rude. I could have listened to you at least without blowing up and I didn't mean that stuff...you know, about you meaning nothing to me." Melissa dropped her head in shame.

"Seems to me we used to have blowups like this quite a bit when we were younger, too. Remember? We were both hotheads." Nikki pulled out a chair and sat down while Becky kept quiet and cut pieces of coffee cake.

"My mom used to tell me I should have been born a redhead." Melissa smiled at the memory. "I do need to talk to Parker, though."

Nikki nodded. "Yes, you do. But don't get mad at him, okay?"

"No one is getting mad at anyone today. Got it? And if anyone is going to be emotional—it's going to be me. Hello? I'm pregnant, remember? So...can we bring the conversation back to me? Melissa, we'll deal with you later." Becky handed out the plates and sat down.

"So...morning sickness, mood swings, and amped-up sex drive. Anything else I should be ready for?"

Chapter Ten

Nikki

It had been just over twenty-four hours since the emotional confrontation between Nikki and Melissa and as far as Nikki was concerned, it could be longer until she saw Melissa again. A lot longer. Nikki was still licking her wounds when it came to the hurtful things the other woman had said to her and try as she might, and damned if she hadn't tried, she could not forget the vehemence in Melissa's voice as she told Nikki she didn't matter to her.

Not that she should be surprised. Of course she didn't mean anything to Melissa. Why would she? They'd never really been friends and just because she was...well, whatever she was with Parker, didn't mean that Melissa had to think of her as anything other than what they were. Acquaintances. Maybe it had been too much to wish that they'd be friends. Or maybe she just needed to cut the other woman some slack; she was obviously going through some things. Things that Nikki couldn't possibly understand. And hadn't she been just as defensive when she'd been hiding her own secret not that long ago?

Despite all the ways she'd tried to justify it in her head, Nikki still couldn't get to a place where she felt good about the way she'd left things with Melissa. Even after Becky—bless her —had dragged them both back into the kitchen in an attempt to bond over coffee and cake, it was still awkward, and Nikki had made her excuses and gotten out of there as soon as she could.

She shook her head clear for the umpteenth time and tried to focus on her work. She needed to stop thoughts of Melissa and Parker from interfering with her work or she'd be in real trouble if she couldn't meet her deadlines. She was just about to plug her earphones in and drown out her inner thoughts with some mindless pop music when her phone rang.

Parker.

Again.

She'd avoided his calls and he knew it, which meant he'd gotten her voicemail—a lot. Enough that his voicemails sounded concerned. Nikki knew it wasn't fair to make him worry about her or them, but she didn't really know what to say to him at the moment. On the one occasion they had spoken, she'd managed to avoid any mention of anything really by rattling on about how much work she had to do and how she really needed to focus if she was going to get her jobs done before the Pumpkin Festival. It wasn't totally a lie. And if she was totally honest with herself, she wasn't even totally clear why she was avoiding him.

With a sigh, she dropped her earbuds on her desk and picked up the phone.

"Hi."

"Nikki, how have you been?" She could hear the mix of relief and worry in his voice, and guilt clawed at her.

"I've been really busy." The lie came easily, and she hated herself for it. "It's been kind of crazy."

"Really?"

"Yes, really." Parker wasn't an idiot and she was a bad liar. Nikki squeezed her eyes shut.

"Nikki, what's going on? Why are you avoiding me?"

"I'm not—" There was no point avoiding it any longer. "Okay, I am."

"Why? I thought what we had going was...well, I thought we had something."

"We did. We do. We..." She rubbed the heel of her palm into her eyes. She was screwing this up. And for what? "We do," she tried again.

"Then what is going on with you? Nikki, I don't have the time or the inclination to play games. I need you to be honest with me, and I thought what we had going on was worth that."

"It is," she said quickly. "I just think it might be a good idea for me to back off for a little bit, just until you get things sorted out with Melissa." There, she'd said it. What she'd been thinking ever since Melissa blew up at her.

"What are you talking about?" She could hear the frustration in his voice and part of her, a big part, longed to take it all back and make all of the drama between them disappear. "I thought I told you there was nothing going on between me and Melissa. I explained it all to you. I told you it's my brother and—"

"I know. And I get it, I really do. But when I said something to Melissa, she totally—"

"You said something to Melissa?"

"Yes, I went over to Becky's and she was there. I was just trying to let her know that I understood and—"

"Shit."

Nikki waited for him to say something else. After a moment, he finally asked, "Did she freak out?"

"That's an understatement." Melissa's hateful words

replayed in her memory again. "I'm pretty sure I made it, whatever *it* is, worse. I just need to back off for a bit, Parker. Until you figure out whatever is going on with Melissa, I'm going to steer clear. I don't deserve the things she said to me, and I understand she was upset and probably totally taken off guard, but I didn't deserve it and I'm not putting myself in that position again."

"Okay," was all Parker said.

"Okay?"

"I get it, Nikki. And I don't blame you. I need to talk to her. I've actually been putting it off for a few days, but there are a few realities Melissa's going to have to face very soon. And having you in my life is one of them."

A warm glow bloomed in her chest.

"I'm going to go talk to her right away," Parker said. "As for you, we're still on for the Pumpkin Festival, right?"

She smiled, even though he couldn't see her through the phone. "Of course."

"Good, then get your work done. I'll see you soon."

***

After talking to Parker—something she should have done right away—it was as though a load had been lifted from Nikki and she flew through the remaining design work she had. With a free afternoon stretching in front of her, Nikki decided to head down to Main Street to grab a coffee and maybe even one of those pumpkin spice muffins from the bakery she kept hearing about. It was a beautiful day. The air was crisp, but not cold yet. Montana could be unpredictable with the weather and Nikki knew enough about living in Halfway to know that it could change in an instant. It was best to enjoy every warm autumn day as if it might be the last, because it very well might be.

Which was why after she got her coffee and muffin from Muriel, she went right back outside to the town square and found a bench to enjoy her snack on.

"It's a lovely day, isn't it?"

Nikki looked up to see a vaguely familiar woman on the bench next to her.

"Sorry, I didn't mean to interrupt your quiet time," the woman said. "I just thought you looked like you were enjoying the day as much as I am."

Nikki swallowed the piece of muffin in her mouth. "No," she said. "You didn't interrupt me at all. Hi." She gave the woman a wave. "I'm Nikki Landon. Are you new to town? You look like I should know you."

The woman laughed. "I'm sort of new," she said. "My name is Nyah Henderson. I grew up in Halfway, but I moved away and...now I'm back."

Nyah? Melissa's best friend from school, the one Parker told her about.

"You were friends with Melissa Tait-Rhodes, right? Or, I guess it was just Melissa Tait back then." Nyah nodded. "You were a few years ahead of me in school, but I'm—" She stopped short of saying they were friends now. "I know her," she finished lamely.

Nyah's face closed up, and then a strange expression crossed her face. "I was," she said after a moment. "We didn't really keep in touch after I moved away and then...well, we haven't really seen each other for a long time."

Nikki nodded in understanding. It wasn't that long ago she was a stranger to her childhood best friend, too. Her relationship with Becky had taken a lot of mending, but she had a feeling that the reason Nyah and Melissa were no longer in touch had something to do with the accident and Wade, not that she was going to mention it. No way—she'd had enough experience getting in the middle of Melissa's business. Whatever went on between her and Nyah was none of her business.

"Coming home can be hard," Nikki said instead. "I recently moved back to town, too. Are you moving back?" she asked, realizing she'd just assumed. "Or just here for a visit?"

"No, I'm back for good."

"You don't look really happy about it." Nikki joked in an effort to lighten the mood. "I mean...well, I don't really know what I mean."

"No." Nyah smiled. "It's okay, really. To be honest, I wasn't very excited about moving back. I mean, I loved living and working here when I did. I was a paramedic for the county, but I left almost ten years ago to live with my mom in Oregon, and I never thought I'd be back."

"So then what happened, if you don't mind me asking? I mean, it's not every day people move back to Halfway. It's a great town and all, but there's not really a lot going on here."

"It's true." Nyah laughed again, which was nice, because Nikki could tell she was loosening up. "And like I said, I never thought I'd be back. But my dad's retiring and he offered me the practice. It's a great opportunity and—"

"Wait," Nikki interrupted her. "The practice? Your dad, is he—"

"Dr. Henderson. Yes," Nyah finished for her. "I'm going to take over the practice."

Nikki wasn't sure why she hadn't made the connection herself; after all, Halfway was a small enough town that she should have heard about it by now, but then again...she'd been pretty wrapped up in her own stuff for the last bit. And there was one other thing. "Wait. I thought you said you were a paramedic."

"I was." Nyah's face grew serious again. "But years ago there was a patient I couldn't save because I didn't know enough. I didn't have the skills and...anyway, it doesn't matter. But I went back to school, and I've been practicing in Portland for the last little bit."

Nikki nodded. "Well, I'm probably the last to know." She laughed at herself. "I usually am. But welcome to town."

"Thanks. But I think you're probably the first to know. Dad didn't announce anything yet and we just made the decision, so here I am." She raised her arms in the air. "Truth be told, I'm actually enjoying the relative quiet before people find out I'm back."

"Well, I'm glad to be the first to know then. And you're just in time for the Pumpkin Festival this weekend. It's going to be a big deal. This is actually the first year they pushed it back so it was closer to Thanksgiving. People are really excited." That was an understatement. The whole town was spooled up about the festival. The citizens liked nothing more than a good festival to plan for.

"I remember the Pumpkin Festival," Nyah said. "As a kid, we'd pick out the perfect pumpkin to decorate our porch with. Only back then it was before Halloween, so we'd carve them. What did the kids do this year if the festival was so late?"

Nikki chuckled as she remembered the pumpkins Ryan had brought home from Matt and Becky's farm. "Oh, there were pumpkins. If you ask me, pushing the dates back gave everyone a good excuse to grow twice as many pumpkins this year. Remember, we're talking about the people of Halfway here."

"True. Any excuse for a party."

"Exactly."

As much as Nikki enjoyed the conversation, it was getting late and if she was going to make it home in time for Ryan to get off the bus, she needed to get on her way. With her muffin and coffee finished, Nikki stood. "I should go. But it was so nice to meet you, Nyah. Welcome back to town."

"It was great to meet you too, Nikki. Thank you for making me feel so welcome."

Nikki's smile was genuine. "No worries. I know exactly what it feels like to come back after being gone for so long. And trust me when I say it'll get easier."

Nyah nodded. "Maybe we can do this again?"

"Absolutely. I'm sure I'll run into you this weekend at the festival. We'll exchange information then, okay?"

The women parted with promises to get phone numbers and have another coffee, and as Nikki walked away, she thought about how nice it would be to have another friend in town. Especially one who knew what it was like to be an outsider in their own town. Of course, that feeling had passed for Nikki and it would pass for Nyah, too. Especially when she started to run into her old friends.

But she hadn't been very enthusiastic about running into Melissa again. The thought hit Nikki as she walked through her front door. And if she had been the first person to know that Nyah was back in town, that meant that Melissa didn't know yet. And if what Parker said about Nyah being the paramedic to respond to Wade's accident was true, things were about to get a whole lot more complicated in town and just in time for the Pumpkin Festival.

Chapter Eleven

Melissa

As she took in a deep breath, Melissa slowly straightened her back, not enjoying the aches and pains from being bent over for so long. She should have Abby out here to rake the last of the leaves in her backyard, but she'd sent her daughter off to deliver flyers before dinner and took the job on herself.

She needed an excuse to work off the brownie she'd eaten at lunch today.

A horn briefly honked before a car door slammed. Curious, Melissa made her way to the side of the house. Parker headed towards her front door.

"I'm over here," she called out.

Parker stopped and headed her way. Melissa returned to the pile of leaves she created earlier and leaned the rake against the house. She was glad Parker was here—she could use the break.

"We need to talk."

Parker stood there, his arms crossed and the fiercest frown she'd ever seen him wear. What was his problem?

"Well, hello to you too." If anyone was going to be upset, it would be her. First he'd stood her up and then betrayed her. She'd picked up the phone numerous times to call him and ream him out, but every time she did, Abby would enter the room.

Besides, she'd managed to calm down somewhat since her outburst at Nikki. She still didn't appreciate Parker telling his girlfriend before giving her a heads-up, nor had she liked how Nikki had brought it up, as if it were something they could bond over...but she didn't want to dwell on it anymore. She couldn't. Even though things had been awkward between them before Nikki had left Becky's, Melissa had apologized for her words.

She had a mean bite when it came to words and she'd been pretty hurtful.

"You need to apologize to Nikki." The true anger in Parker's gaze shocked Melissa.

"Excuse me?"

"You heard me, Mel. I want you to apologize to Nikki."

Melissa crossed her own arms, copying him, and gave him a frown to match his own. Two could play at this game.

"What for?"

His brow rose. "You know what for."

She snorted. "If anyone owes anyone an apology, it's you to me." She stepped closer to him and had to stop herself from poking him in the chest.

She was not going to get angry. She was not going to get angry. She was not...

"Don't turn this around on me. I don't know what you said to Nikki, but it was uncalled for."

Melissa shook her head in confusion. What she said? When? The last time she spoke to Nikki had been at Melissa's and she'd already apologized. Over and done, in her book.

She said as much to Parker, who looked confused.

"You know me, Park. I blow up but then I own up. I said I

was sorry. I knew I'd gone overboard. You can't tell me she's still upset about it?"

He shrugged. "Not everyone forgives as easily."

"Well, if she's going to be part of this family, she'd better learn. If she's got an issue with me, then it's up to her to come to me—not you. She's a big girl; I expect her to act like it." Inwardly, Melissa sighed. Sensitive much? It had been over twenty-four hours. Enough time that Nikki obviously stewed in her hurt and then dumped it on Parker, expecting him to take care of it for her.

That's not how Melissa dealt with things at all.

"Fair enough. At least talk to her, okay? She's important to me and I...I want her in my life."

Melissa nodded. "I figured as much if you went and betrayed my trust to her."

Parker reacted as if she'd slapped him, and in a way, she just had. And it felt good. She wasn't one to hold her punches; she said it like she saw it and if she was wrong, then so be it. But in this case, she wasn't.

"I know. I'm sorry." Shamefaced, Parker uncrossed his arms and reached out, as if he wanted to give her a hug.

Like hell he would. Not until he explained himself. She wasn't upset at him, not anymore, but she wasn't going to let this go either. Besides—he'd been the one to tell her they needed to talk and then he'd left her worrying for days on end about Wade. That wasn't fair.

"I know she's important to you, and I get that. I really do. But it wasn't your secret to tell—not without giving me fair warning first."

Dejected, Parker dropped his arms and grunted as he sat down on the steps of Melissa's back porch. She joined him.

"He's my brother. Sometimes I think you forget that." Parker's voice was low and she almost missed his words.

She wanted to deny his claim but she didn't. She couldn't because he was right.

"Oh, what a tangled web we weave..." Her voice trailed off as she worried her hands. "Asking you to keep my secret for this long was—" She struggled to find the right words. Wrong? Hard? Difficult?

"What you needed." Parker finished for her. "And I was the one who agreed. Maybe I shouldn't have. Maybe I should have fought with you on it." He shook his head. "It's easier to look and judge our actions, and we can't do that either." He gave her a sad smile and in that moment, Melissa realized just how much of a strength he'd been for her in the past nine years.

"I've made such a mess out of things," she admitted. The realization of that weighed heavy on her. She was in so thick she had no idea how to climb out of the hole she'd dug for herself. She'd talked with Becky and strategized a bit, but bottom line, there was only one way to repair what she'd done. And that was to be honest.

"You...we...made mistakes. And we're running out of time to fix it."

The way he'd stressed the last bit caught her attention.

"What do you mean, we're running out of time?"

Parker sighed before he rubbed his face with his hands. And then messed up his hair. Then stood up. Those three actions in a row only meant one thing.

Now she was really worried.

"Parker? What's going on? You told me we needed to talk... is Wade okay?"

"Has Abby talked to you yet?"

Confused, Melissa shook her head. "About what?"

Parker paced a straight line in front of her, his focus off in the distance and his hands stuck deep in his pant pockets.

"Parker?"

"Is she here?"

Melissa shook her head.

"Maybe we should wait then."

Melissa pushed herself up from the stairs, her hands fisted as she stepped in his path and forced him to stop.

"Enough. For days you've had me worried, stressed that something is wrong. Do. Not. Play. This. Game. With. Me." Her chest hurt as her emotions strangled her. The air in her lungs seemed to cut off and her heart pumped faster. Black dots danced before her and she stumbled. If it wasn't for Parker catching her, she would have fallen down.

"Sit. Take a deep breath. In and out. In and out." His hand pushed her head down towards her knees and Melissa focused on breathing just like he told her to.

"You need to tell me, Parker," Melissa finally said after the dizziness passed.

Parker sat on his heels in front of her. Concern and pity filled his gaze as he reached for her hands and held tight.

"She knows," he said quietly.

Melissa shook her head. No. She heard him wrong. She had to have. He was talking about Nikki, right?

"Abby knows about Wade, Mel. They've been writing letters back and forth for the past year or so."

Melissa's world dropped. She felt as though she were sucked into a black hole that stretched out until there was nothing.

He couldn't have just said that. How? How could that be possible?

"I don't understand. How? How could she know?" She bit down hard on her lip, hoping the pain would stop the flood of tears that threatened to fill her eyes.

"It's my fault."

"I'm sorry?"

Parker dropped her hands and stood. "It's my fault. She was

over one day after school and found a letter from him on my table."

"When?" Cold dread filled her heart.

"Over a year ago," he reminded her.

She slowly nodded her head, taking in what he'd just said. Her daughter had known about her father for the past year and said nothing. Nothing. What did that mean?

"Why didn't she tell me?" Wait...she had a better question. "Why didn't you tell me?"

Parker rubbed his hand through his hair again. "I don't know. I should have and I'm sorry. But I didn't think anything of it. She saw the envelope and asked me about it. I tried to make it sound like it was nothing and she left it alone. I thought it was over, that she believed me."

"You should have told me."

He nodded. "I should have. I didn't find out until last month that they'd been writing."

Melissa was so confused right now. Abby and Wade had been writing for over a year because her daughter found a letter from her husband on her uncle's table but everything was kept hush-hush until last month?

"You're not doing a very good job of explaining yourself, Parker, and I'm about to get really freaked out. Abby will be home any minute and I want to know all the facts before I talk to her about this."

"She hasn't told you anything?"

She shook her head. "Nothing. We've talked about Wade sparingly, here and there, but nothing to grab my attention and make me question anything."

He pursed his lips in thought. "I only found out about it because Wade mentioned it briefly last time he called."

"What did he say?"

"That he enjoyed getting to know his daughter again."

Those words hit her heart like a ton of bricks. It carried the weight of guilt: she was the reason Wade didn't know his daughter like he should. She'd made so many mistakes. So many.

How could he ever forgive her? Abby must hate her too.

"Why didn't you tell me sooner?"

Parker sat back down beside her and put his arm around her. Melissa leaned in and rested her head on his shoulder. She couldn't have asked for a better family with him in her life. He reminded her of Wade in so many ways. The ache in her heart intensified and she felt as if she were going to break into pieces if she wasn't careful.

"I should have and I'm sorry. I wanted to talk to Abby first, find out her side of the story. But then—"

He was cut off by Abby's sudden appearance at the back door.

"Hey, Uncle Parker! Here for dinner finally? Or are you going to take us out to make up for standing us up?" Abby wrapped her arms around his neck and gave him a hug.

"Hey, Mom." She winked at Melissa before she plopped down on the deck behind them. "So, what's the plan?" Her earbuds hung from her neck and they could faintly hear her music before she turned her iPod off.

"Hey, Abbs. I'm not sure what we're doing for dinner..." Melissa looked at Parker, who only shrugged.

"I'm in the mood for a good burger and fries. What do you think?" Parker angled his body to look at Abby, who grinned.

"But first, I think it's time we all had a real solid family chat. What do you think?"

Parker's words drained the smile off of Abby's face.

"What about?" Her voice was timid, quiet even. Melissa rested her hand on Abby's knee and squeezed.

"We've got some secrets happening in this family." Melissa managed to squeeze the words out. "But I think maybe," she wiped at a tear that ran down her face, "maybe we should talk about them. What do you think?"

Abby slowly nodded her head before she clasped her hands together.

"This is about Dad, isn't it?" Abby said.

Both Melissa and Parker nodded.

"I'm sorry I kept him from you." Melissa wanted to reach over and give her daughter a hug, to soften the blow of her own betrayal but she didn't. She wanted—no, she needed—to know how her daughter felt right now before anything else.

"Yeah. I get it. I mean...it wasn't okay and I was angry at you —like really angry, Mom—for a long time, but Dad explained it all. So I get it."

No way she was getting off that easy. And Wade explained it all? For her? Why would he do that?

"What did your dad say, honey?"

Abby finally raised her gaze from her hands and blinked.

"I don't hate you, if that's what you're worried about. Not anymore."

And just like that, Melissa was sucker-punched in the gut. Her daughter had actually hated her. Just like she expected.

"But it's cool," Abby continued. "Dad said you were only trying to protect me, that if people really knew what had happened, it would make things really difficult for both of us here. And he's right, right?" She looked at Parker this time. "Kids would have bullied me about having a murdering father or tease me that he was in jail. Right?"

Parker nodded. "But not your friends. They would have stood by you."

"I know. But how do you explain something like that? I mean...it's kind of hard to live with. My dad killed a little girl. She would have been my age by now."

"It was an accident, honey." It killed Melissa to hear those words come out of Abby's mouth.

"I know. But still. She's dead because of him."

Melissa had lived with this knowledge for nine years and in all that time, the pain of what had happened never dissipated. She could only imagine looking at it from a teen perspective.

Black and white.

He fell asleep at the wheel and killed a little girl the same age as their own daughter. The guilt had been too much for him.

There was no gray.

In this case, Abby was very much like her father.

"I understand if you're mad at me, Abbs." Melissa gave her daughter the permission that maybe she needed.

"Yeah. I was mad. Angry. I mean, you told me he left us. You lied, Mom. You lied to me."

Melissa nodded. There was no escaping that truth.

"But I get what you did. I'm not giving you an excuse, just saying I understand. I was young. I wouldn't have understood it and all you wanted was to protect me, right?" Her voice pleaded with Melissa to agree. Her gaze told her she wouldn't understand if Melissa said otherwise.

This time Melissa did get up from her spot on the step and sat next to her daughter. Her arms wrapped around her and when Abby leaned in and relaxed against her, Melissa couldn't stop the tears that fell.

"That's all I've wanted to do, honey. Protect you. Keep you safe. But I messed up. I should have told you the truth a long time ago." Melissa ran her hand down Abby's long hair. The action soothed both their hurting souls. "I shouldn't have kept this a secret from you."

"Yeah, you should have. Told me, I mean. You can buy me a new laptop to make up for it though." The twinkle in Abby's gaze had Melissa laughing.

"Not on your life, kiddo. Save your money, you know that." But good try. She'd give her that.

"Abby, about the letters..." Melissa wasn't sure what she wanted to ask or not ask. These letters, they were private, between Abby and Wade, and yet...

"I should have told you about them. Dad told me to, but... this was my little thing with him, know what I mean?"

Melissa sighed. She got it. She did.

"Sounds like you're getting to know your dad pretty well?" Parker asked.

Abby's face lit up like a Christmas tree. "He's cool. He's been telling me all sorts of stories, of things he's learned and the people he's met. They're not all bad—some just made stupid mistakes like him. I just can't wait to actually see him."

"That could work. We'd have to fill out some forms and it will take time but..." As much as Melissa hated the idea of taking Abby to see her father in prison, this was the least she could do. Even though they had a year before his release, she wasn't going to ask her to wait that long.

"What? Forms? No." Abby leaned forward, the excitement on her face almost palpable. Melissa's heart clenched and she knew whatever her daughter was about to say was going to rock her world, and not in a good way.

"I mean when he's here, next weekend."

Chapter Twelve

Nikki

The last week had been a kaleidoscope of emotions for Nikki: from a high with Parker when he finally opened up to her about the truth of everything, to the low of being berated by Melissa. She didn't care what the other woman had gone through—no one deserved to be spoken to that way. Nikki had gone through her share of drama herself, and she would never lash out like that at someone who was trying to help. At least she hoped she wouldn't. Either way, Melissa was important to Parker, so she'd do her best to let it go. But she wouldn't forget.

Not anytime soon anyway.

She glanced at the clock for the dozenth time. Parker had called to say he was going out for burgers with Melissa and Abby, so clearly they'd talked about whatever they'd needed to talk about. She hated to admit it, but it stung a little more than it should have to be left out of that conversation. Logically, she knew it had nothing to do with her. But if she was going to be part of Parker's life for the longer term, then she would be family, too. And whether Melissa liked it or not, she'd have to be part of those conversations, too.

She pulled the tray of brownies out of the refrigerator where she'd put them to cool. Becky had given her the recipe and in her quest to have at least one home baked item that she could actually prepare successfully, she'd attempted the recipe. Becky had assured her that they would turn out. As she looked at them, Nikki had to admit that Becky might have been right. Of course, nobody had tasted them yet.

Baking had simply been a distraction. An effort to clear her mind of the doubts about Parker and their relationship that kept creeping in and niggled at the back of her mind. Thoughts that she didn't want to think about, and questions she wasn't sure she could answer. But she'd need to face things soon. Parker promised he'd be by for coffee and dessert before Ryan went to bed. Which meant he should knock on the door any minute now.

"Ryan? Are you in your pajamas?"

Nikki could hear him sigh from the living room. "Can I just wait till after? I mean—"

"Forget it." She left the kitchen and stood in front of him on the couch. "It's a school night and I'm already letting you stay up later than I should."

"Dad would—"

She held up a finger to silence him. "Forget it. Don't think for a minute you can play that card with me."

He pushed her a little bit more every day, which she assumed was a normal developmental thing as he got older, but still, she didn't have to like it.

Ryan flipped the cover over on his tablet and tossed it on the couch next to him before he stood up.

He was getting so tall. Not her baby anymore, and soon he'd even be a big brother. Would she ever have another child? It was a thought she'd had more than once when things started to get serious with Parker. But they'd never spoken about the future in such specific details and she realized that she had no idea whether he wanted children of his own. It was just another question to put on her growing list.

"Besides," she focused her attention back on Ryan, "you know your dad and Becky wouldn't let you stay up really late either. And I'm letting you have chocolate before bedtime, for goodness' sake." She tried to make a joke. Ryan just rolled his eyes, but she could see the glimmer of a smile he was trying to hide.

"I'm not a kid anymore, Mom."

"Don't I know it." She pulled him into a bear hug, and when he didn't immediately protest, she squeezed tighter.

"Okay, okay." He finally wriggled free. "I give. I'll go change."

Nikki released him and smiled triumphantly. "That sounds like a great idea."

The knock on the door distracted both of them. "Go quick," she said to him. "And double-check that your homework is totally done."

He sighed again, but did as he was told. If sighing was the worst of it, she could handle that. It would be a small miracle if that was where his rebellion ended, though. But for the moment, she would take what she could get and she certainly didn't need any more conflict in her life at the moment. Not even of the eleven-year-old boy variety.

"Hey there," she said to Parker as she pulled the door open and let him in. He looked tired, his eyes rimmed with red and his hair all mussed. "Everything okay?"

Parker nodded and kissed her on the cheek before he forced a smile to his face. "Yeah. It's all good. It was a long night, but the three of us talked and now everybody knows everything. I thought Melissa would be more upset when she found out—"

"What?" Nikki knew she probably shouldn't interrupt, but something about what Parker said didn't make any sense at all. "I don't understand. What did Melissa find out? And why would she be upset about it?"

Parker squeezed his eyes shut for a second, as if he was trying to gather his thoughts. "It's kind of a long story, but basically all three of us were able to sit down and hash things out. So now Melissa knows everything."

"Wait." A chill crawled down her spine and her stomach rolled. "Didn't she already know everything?" Parker glanced away and the feeling grew in intensity. "It was her story, right, Parker? So what didn't she know?"

Nikki wasn't entirely sure she wanted to know the answer, but she also knew she couldn't handle any more secrets. The niggling doubts she'd been trying to push away crashed full force into the foreground again. If he was hiding something else from her, she wasn't sure if—

"It's complicated, Nikki." Parker ran his hands through his hair again and mussed it further.

"I'm listening." She didn't even bother leading him into the living room. She stood frozen to the spot, needing him to talk. "I'm sure I can follow along."

He looked as if he was going to object to her sarcasm, but instead he said, "Abby's known the truth about her dad for the last year or so. She's been secretly writing him letters and they've been—"

"She what?" Nikki shook her head, letting the information process.

"I know it sounds bad."

"It does. How did that happen? I thought the whole point of Melissa's elaborate lie was to protect her daughter."

He nodded. "It was. But about a year ago, Abby stopped by my house to pick up some cans and bottles for a fundraiser and I didn't even think...I mean, I wasn't expecting her so I wasn't ready. Right before she got there, I'd picked up the mail and dropped it on the table. There was a letter from Wade on top of the pile. She saw it and of course there were questions."

"Of course." Nikki could hardly believe what she was hearing, but she forced herself just to listen.

"She asked me all kinds of things and I did my best to answer them without giving too much away, but she's a bright kid and when she dropped it, so did I. She never said anything more about it, so I thought it was all good."

"Wait." Nikki's brain raced as she tried to process what he told her. "Abby found out her father, the one she thought had left her and her mother, actually didn't, because she found a *letter*? And you're telling me that you smoothed this all over by answering a few questions?"

Parker nodded, but still Nikki couldn't make sense of things.

"She didn't freak out? Cry? React in any way to finding out her dad was actually in prison instead of off living another life somewhere?"

"Well...yeah." Parker shrugged. "Of course she did. But I dealt with it. We talked. I explained things to her, and she was fine."

"And you didn't think it was important that Melissa know that her daughter knew the truth about the huge secret she'd been trying to keep for most of her daughter's life?"

Parker tugged on his hair again. "Nikki, it wasn't like that."

"It sure sounds like it." She could hardly believe it herself, but Nikki actually felt a whole lot of sympathy towards the woman she had been full of animosity for only a few minutes earlier. "This is all crazy." Nikki turned away, not sure what she needed to do or say. Every doubt and concern she had about moving forward with Parker flashed in her head as if they were lights on the Vegas Strip. "This was just another secret you were keeping from me." She looked at him, trying in vain to find some sort of understanding in everything.

"Nikki." He reached for her hand, but she pulled it away. "It wasn't like I was keeping it from you. It was..."

"But you were. You told me everything about Melissa and Abby last week and...well, I thought you told me everything. But still, there's secrets. I can't..."

"Come on. Don't do this."

She took a step back. "No. I just need to think."

Parker looked so tired, so defeated, and she hated herself for having anything to do with that, but she had to think about Ryan, too. She couldn't bring any more drama into his life. Not with everything she'd just put him through. "I don't think I can do this right now."

Just speaking the words caused a physical pain to bloom in her chest.

She wanted him to say something. She needed him to say something. Anything. Finally, after what felt like an eternity, he opened his mouth to speak again, but before he could say anything, Nikki noticed his gaze travel over her shoulder and his face morphed.

Ryan.

She forced a smile on her face and turned to see Ryan. He watched them from the doorway with a wary expression on his face. "Are we going to have brownies?" he asked after a second.

"I would—"

"I don't—"

Nikki and Parker spoke at the same time. She dropped her head, and without looking at Parker, Nikki tried again. "Parker can't stay, buddy. But you go ahead and have one, okay?"

Ryan glanced between them one more time, but the lure of a

chocolate brownie was too much and soon he turned and disappeared again.

"Don't do this, Nikki." Parker grabbed her arm and spun her around so she faced him.

Tears pooled in her eyes and she blinked them back. She couldn't cry. She needed to think straight and think about the bigger picture. Ryan deserved more than secrets, lies, and drama. She shook her head slightly.

"No." Parker's voice shook. "This isn't a deal breaker. This stuff with Melissa and Wade, it's not my load."

"But it is." She forced her voice to stay even. "They're family and that's important, but I just don't think I can do this right now. Not with the secrets and the..." She drifted off and looked at her feet.

"Nikki, I love you."

The pain in her chest intensified, and she could no longer keep her tears at bay. They spilled hot and silent over her cheeks. Every fiber in her body yearned to look up and pull him into her arms so she could tell him that she loved him too.

But she had to remember Ryan.

"Parker." Her voice cracked. "I..."

"Okay. I get it." He glanced down at his feet briefly before he nodded once. In a move that shattered her heart, he turned and walked out the door.

Chapter Thirteen

Melissa

Wade was coming home.

Melissa's heart continued to skip beats every time she thought of her husband returning home.

What would he think of the house? Of the changes she'd made? Would he approve of the updated look to their bedroom, even though it was more feminine than anything else?

Would he care that she'd put on a few extra pounds since the last time he'd seen her?

Nine years was a long time. She swallowed past the lump in her throat. Way too long.

She alternated between feeling happy—ecstatic, really—that they would finally be together again to thoughts of dread and fear.

Would their marriage survive? Had it survived? Sure, in name they were still legally bound, but what if he'd found someone else to love? What if he realized he'd fallen out of love with her?

This time her heart didn't just skip a beat; it stopped altogether.

He was going to leave her. She knew it. He'd be crazy not to. She'd lied and told everyone he'd left her. What had she been thinking? How could he ever forgive her?

She hated how insecure she was right now. Hated it.

Melissa held the phone in her hand and checked the clock for the umpteenth time. Abby told her that Wade would call some night this week, between nine and ten o'clock, to talk to her. She could only imagine the conversation.

Did he realize he was coming home the weekend of the Pumpkin Festival? He always loved this one, more than any of the other seasonal festivals the town put on.

She'd been looking forward to the festival this year but now...now she wasn't all that sure how she felt.

"Do you think he'll call tonight?" Abby plopped down on the couch and tucked her knees to her chest.

Melissa shrugged.

"Can I talk to him? I wonder what his voice sounds like. I mean, I know in my head, at least I think I do...but what if it's different than what I remember?" Abby's lips quirked into a smile.

"Of course you can. You should. He probably...he's probably really looking forward to seeing you." That was probably what he was excited about the most. He must be nervous too... jumping back into his old life.

"He misses you too, Mom."

Tears pricked in Melissa's eyes. She was really tired of all the crying she'd been doing. Time to grow up, pull on her big-girl panties, and deal with life instead of waiting and crying. She couldn't handle any more crying.

"I have a question." Abby sat up straight and curled her legs beneath her. She pulled a blanket across her legs and fiddled with it before she'd look Melissa in the eyes.

"Shoot." Hopefully it was a question she could handle.

"Can I start telling my friends? I mean...is it okay if I tell them? Or would you rather wait till Dad comes home and people find out on their own? And what do I say? Should I tell them he's been in prison or just that he disappeared and now he's come back?"

Well...that was more than one question and she had no idea how to handle it. None.

"What do you want to tell them?"

In all her talks with Becky and Parker, this question had never really been answered. She couldn't really make a decision until she'd spoken to Wade. She'd made one decision on his behalf and made a mess of things; she didn't want to do that again.

"I'm not sure I want to tell the truth. Sometimes it's okay to lie, right?"

And here's where she failed in Parenting 101. She should have taught by example that it was never okay to lie, and here she'd done the exact opposite.

So much for mother-of-the-year award.

The phone rang right before she attempted to answer Abby, thankfully.

One glance at the number confirmed it was Wade.

With her stomach now in knots, she thrust the phone to her daughter, taking the chicken way out.

"Hello?"

Melissa caught the way her daughter's hand shook moments before her eyes welled up in tears and she could barely contain the sobs as she struggled to say hi to her father.

Melissa went to sit beside her daughter and held her close.

She could hear the gentle murmurings of her husband's voice on the other line as he tried to comfort their daughter.

"I love you, Dad," Abby was able to say before she handed Melissa the phone and then buried her face in her mom's shoulder as her body shook.

"Hi, Wade."

"Mel. It's so good to hear your voice. Abby...she's all grown up, isn't she?" Wade's voice broke, which in turn broke her own heart.

"That she is. Wait till you see her. She's probably as tall as you are."

"I can't wait. I'm...are you okay that I'm coming home early?" The way he hesitated, as if worried about how she'd respond, told her the answers to all her other questions. He wanted to come home. Not just home, to Halfway, but to her.

"I'm more than okay with it. I miss you." Those had to be the most inadequate words she'd ever spoken.

He breathed a sigh of relief into the phone. "I miss you too, Mel."

Neither one said anything for a few moments, as if worried to break the connection between them but she knew his time would be running out.

"When do you need me to be at the prison?" Suddenly the need to be with him, to see him, touch him and be touched by him, to be held in his arms after such a long time apart was overwhelming.

"Mid-morning if that's okay." He cleared his throat.

"Is there anything you need from me? Anything you want me to bring?"

"So much." Wade chuckled, a sudden lightness to his voice. "But nothing more than seeing you and Abby."

She could only imagine the things he would want after being in prison for so long. New clothes and shoes for sure.

She would put together a little package for him and give it to him...

"Wade, I'll bring Abby, but we'll need to stop at a hotel overnight." Her hands shook at the idea of spending a night with him, side by side, in bed again.

"I know," he whispered. "Let's drive as far as we can and then stay someplace nice. With fluffy blankets and room service maybe? But as far from this place as possible, please?"

Melissa nodded before she realized Wade couldn't see her.

"Mel, I've got to go. I can't wait...I can't wait to see you. Whatever happens...I'm just glad you're still there."

"See you soon."

She hung up and thought about the last words he said. *Whatever happens.* What did he mean by that?

There was a knock at the door and before she could dwell on her thoughts further, she went to answer it.

When she turned on the porch light and saw who was on the other side of the door, she almost wished she'd ignored the knock.

* * *

Nyah Henderson.

Melissa was tempted to slam the door shut in the woman's face. She'd once needed her best friend, and she hadn't been there for her. So why now?

What was she doing here? Why? Why was she here? Why was she back in town after all these years?

The last time she'd seen this woman—her ex-best friend— had been after everything with Wade.

One minute she was there in her life—best friends, soul sisters till the end of time—and the next minute, Nyah had disappeared and wouldn't return any of Melissa's calls or emails.

She'd never felt so abandoned. But it had been years since she'd last thought about her old friend. Too many years.

"What are you doing here?" Melissa kept her voice down, not wanting to alert Abby.

"I wanted you to find out from me, not from anyone else." Nyah bit her lip, a tell she'd always had, even when they were in high school. The woman was nervous. Good. She should be.

"Find out what?"

"Can I come in? So we can talk?"

Melissa shook her head.

Nyah sighed. "I'm back. For good. My dad needs me, and I was, well, I'm tired of running away."

Melissa found that a bit hard to believe. Running was all Nyah seemed to know how to do.

"Is your dad okay?" Dr. Henderson had to be close to retirement. He'd been around forever.

Nyah shrugged. "He's tired. Ready to slow down. That's why I'm here. To help him do that."

"Do what? Run his office? You're not practicing medicine." She wouldn't dare.

Nyah winced and shook her head.

"How is Wade?" From the way Nyah blurted the words, Melissa knew she hadn't meant to say it.

"Now? Now you want to talk about my husband after all these years? Why not when I needed to? I sent you so many emails, tried to call so many times but you just ignored me."

"I'm sorry." The regret in Nyah's words and demeanor were evident. And softened Melissa's heart. Somewhat.

Once, Nyah had been a medic and had by luck or misfortune been the first on the scene at Wade's accident. She'd been traveling back home from visiting her mother in Oregon and had actually been the one to call Melissa about the news.

She would never forget that phone call or the way Nyah

sounded as she told her there'd been an accident and a little girl had died.

With a sigh, Melissa pushed open the screen door for Nyah to come in. If they were going to do this, they might as well do it in private, away from prying eyes.

"Hey, Mom. Can I...oh, sorry." Abby rounded the corner, the rim of her eyes bright red.

"What do you need, hun?"

"Nothing. Just going to have a shower." She ran up the stairs and into the bathroom, and slammed the door behind her. Poor girl was probably embarrassed to have been caught crying by a stranger.

"Wow, she's really grown up."

Melissa nodded. "Funny how that happens." She led the way into the living room and waited for Nyah to join her.

"Wade is good. He's coming home this weekend, actually." Melissa decided to just lay it out there.

Worry and relief flashed across Nyah's face. It was funny how well she could still read her old friend.

"I heard some rumors..." Nyah visibly swallowed but didn't bother to finish her sentence.

Melissa nodded. "I'm sure you did. Let me guess...it's about Wade, isn't it? About my mistake, my lies?"

She searched Nyah's eyes, waiting for...what? Whatever she'd expected to see, the compassion and understanding Nyah gave her wasn't it.

"You probably just reacted in shock, Mel. And wanted to protect your daughter. Don't be too hard on yourself."

Melissa snorted at the advice.

"Trust me, I know," Nyah said softly.

"Reacted? Yeah, you could say that. I was in shock. I know that now. But it doesn't excuse my actions." Any more than it excused Nyah's that fateful night, but Melissa didn't say that. "I led everyone to believe he'd taken off and left not just me, but everyone. His friends. Those closest to him. And I made his brother live a lie too. Nice one, huh? But even worse—I kept my daughter away from her father. Nice reaction there." The words just tumbled out and when they did, a weight lifted off her shoulders. A weight she didn't realize she'd carried. It felt good to admit what she'd done to someone other than Parker or Becky.

For a moment there, it was as if the past between the two, the years when they'd lost touch for whatever reason, just melted. She wanted to ask Nyah where'd she gone, why she had disappeared so suddenly and at a time when Melissa needed her the most.

Losing her best friend like that, with no word, no explanation, had almost killed her. She had no one to turn to, no one to talk things through, other than Parker.

It had hurt. More than she'd wanted to admit. For years, Melissa waited for Nyah to contact her, to come home and see her dad. Whenever she'd run into Dr. Henderson downtown, she'd ask about Nyah, see whether she was coming home for the holidays but eventually she stopped asking.

And now she was here.

"We all make mistakes, Mel." Nyah's voice dropped. Melissa caught the way she gripped her hands, how white her knuckles were.

Mistakes. Yes, they all made them. Wade's mistake was falling asleep, costing a family to lose their little girl. Nyah had made a mistake in trying to do something she wasn't equipped to do, and her inexperience unfortunately didn't save a life. Melissa made the mistake in not telling the truth and letting her daughter grow up thinking her father had abandoned them. Her.

The heaviness of that weighed on her.

"Where've you been, Nyah? Why did you come home now?" Melissa turned the conversation.

Nyah bit her lip, obviously struggling to find an answer.

"That's what I wanted to come and talk to you about."

In that moment, Melissa knew, whatever Nyah had to say, she didn't want to hear it.

Chapter Fourteen

Nikki

"Mom, hurry up. We're going to be late."

Nikki stared at her reflection for half a second longer before she pulled her hair into a ponytail and turned away. There was no point. She was never going to be able to cover up the bags under her eyes, or get rid of the redness. Anybody would be able to see she'd been crying, but she didn't care. She had been.

And why shouldn't she? She'd basically kicked out the best thing that had ever happened to her because she couldn't deal with the reality of the situation.

She grabbed her sweater and made her way down the stairs, where Ryan waited to go to the Pumpkin Festival. The very last thing she wanted to do was go to the festival. What she really wanted was to climb back into her bed, pull the covers over her head and forget about everything, especially the Pumpkin Festival and Parker Rhodes, who would be there.

Not only was Parker going to be there, but he was helping Becky and Matt organize a "Welcome Home Wade" surprise at the festival, which she only knew about because Becky had called and asked her whether she'd help out. Apparently Melissa and Abby were headed up to the prison to pick Wade up and as a way to welcome him back to town, and to basically tell everyone in town the truth and turn it into a celebration.

Nikki wasn't sure how she felt about celebrating something like a prison release, but it would be good for Abby and Melissa to have Wade back and that's what was important. It would be good for Parker, too.

Parker.

Nikki hadn't been able to think of anything or anyone but Parker for the last few days. His face, and the hurt and confused expression he'd worn, haunted her. And she missed him. A lot.

"Mom, you look like you haven't slept in days."

Ryan scared her, shocking her back into the present and reminding her that she needed to rally and pull herself together, for the sake of her son. The festival was important to him and that's all that mattered. Not Melissa, or Wade, or even Parker. It was all about Ryan. It had to be.

"Thanks, buddy." She tried her best to put a smile on her face and a joke in her voice, but judging by the look Ryan gave her, she'd failed. "I've had a little trouble sleeping lately is all." She might as well go for honesty.

Unexpectedly, Ryan took her hand as they left the house. He rarely took her hand anymore now that he was older. She gave it a squeeze.

"Does it have anything to do with Parker and your fight?"

Nikki's stomach rolled and she froze in place. "What are you talking about?" She couldn't even look at her son as she spoke. He wasn't a fool, and he'd see right through her terrible acting.

"Mom." Ryan tugged on her hand. "I'm not a little kid anymore. I know you had a fight and I know you're sad. I'm also not blind." He gave her a look that basically said *you look terrible,* and she flinched. "Whatever happened, you're obviously not happy, so just fix it." He moved to keep walking, but stopped at the last minute and turned back to her again. "But first, you might want to brush your hair or something."

She couldn't help it; Nikki laughed. Kids had a way of seeing through the bullshit and putting things into perspective. "I look that bad, huh?"

"You know how I used to tell you that you were the prettiest girl in the world?"

Nikki nodded, but her stomach clenched at the memory of her little boy not that many years ago. She also braced herself for the open honesty of a pre-teen who no longer wore rose-colored glasses when it came to his mother.

"Well, I still think that." Nikki breathed a sigh of relief. "But it wouldn't hurt to put some makeup on or something."

She laughed again. "Okay. I see your point. Can you wait one minute?" Nikki grabbed the door handle, full of a new energy. Maybe Ryan was right; a little makeup couldn't hurt. Maybe if she at least tried to look better, she might actually start to feel better. She could hope, anyway.

* * *

By some miracle, they were only running a few minutes behind, but even so, by the time Nikki and Ryan got to the Pumpkin Festival, things were already well underway. Her heart squeezed a bit at the thought that she was supposed to be there with Parker. She was supposed to be doing a lot of things with Parker. But that was before all the lies and secrets. She shook her head and tried to push the thought of Parker out of her head. At least for the moment. She wasn't stupid; she wouldn't be able to avoid him.

"Hey," Ryan called out. "There he is!" Panic filled her. She wasn't ready yet. She thought she might have a few minutes to get acclimatized before she ran into him. "Levi!" Ryan waved his hands in the air.

Levi?

Nikki could have laughed at her own ridiculousness. Ryan was excited about meeting up with Levi, her late mother's dear friend who'd become a sort of grandfather figure to him. She smiled a genuine smile and followed Ryan over to where Levi stood with a cup of apple cider.

"It's good to see you." She allowed herself to be pulled into a warm hug. "It's been too long."

"Well, you've been busy with a certain young man," Levi said. "Just the way a woman your age should be. I'm glad to see it, too."

Nikki shook her head and glanced at Ryan, who rolled his eyes and volunteered the information she didn't feel like sharing. "They had a fight," he said. "And Mom's being dumb about it."

"She is, is she?" Levi lifted a furry eyebrow at her, and it was Nikki's turn to roll her eyes.

"Totally. All she does is cry and sleep and she won't talk to him." Ryan crossed his arms over his chest. "It's dumb."

"Ryan, it—"

"It certainly sounds dumb." Levi cut off her protests. "But sometimes adults do dumb things. Hey, why don't you go get some of those pumpkin spice muffins that Muriel is selling over there?" Levi handed Ryan a twenty, and he didn't have to be asked twice.

When Ryan was gone, Levi turned to her, and Nikki knew she wouldn't be getting away very easily. "So are you going to tell me what happened with you and Parker, or do I have to guess?"

The last thing she'd wanted was to talk about it, but now that she had the opportunity, getting it all out seemed like the best option she'd had in days. "He lied to me," she said quickly. "Well, not really lied, but...kind of withheld the truth."

Levi nodded knowingly.

"What?"

"I'm just agreeing with you."

"Agreeing with what?" Nikki eyed him carefully.

Levi nodded sagely like old men tend to do. "You seem to have it all figured out, is all. You've made your decision."

Nikki knew he was up to something. She knew the older man well enough to know that he was definitely going to have an opinion about things. But she also knew he wouldn't volunteer that opinion unless she asked.

"Okay, what? I know you're dying to tell me what you think."

Levi chuckled a little before his expression grew serious again. "I know Parker. He's a good man. I also know the secrets he's had to keep for almost a decade and that can't have been easy. He's sacrificed his own life for that little girl and her mama. He didn't have to do that. But he did."

She hadn't looked at it that way before. But wait...

"You knew? How did you know about Wade?"

Levi smiled. The skin around his eyes crinkled up as he did so. "I think a lot of folks around here knew the truth. Secrets are hard to keep in small towns."

"But nobody said anything?"

He shrugged. "Melissa had her reasons for doing what she did. And whether you agree with them or not, they were her reasons. People respect that. She needed it, so if anyone knew the truth, they kept quiet. Because that's what family does. And Halfway? We're a family. You should know that by now."

Nikki nodded and let what he said roll around in her brain.

"But Parker?" Levi continued. "He gave them everything. That is, until you came along. It couldn't have been easy, and I think you need to cut the man a little slack. He didn't tell you everything, it's true. Not because he didn't want to, but out of loyalty for Melissa and Abby. And don't you think that's a good trait to have in a man?"

Nikki nodded again, because there was no way she could disagree. "Still, Levi...the lies....I just can't—"

"I agree, lying is not okay, but don't you think before you throw it all away, you should talk to him about it? Give him the benefit of the doubt? Don't you owe it to everyone, yourself included?"

She thought about that for a second, but she didn't have to think for long. She knew what she should do, what she *wanted* to do. "You're right, Levi." She reached up and kissed his cheek. "How did you get so smart?"

The older man blushed. "Years of experience, my dear. Now why don't you go find that young man of yours? I'll keep an eye on Ryan."

They both looked over to where Ryan happily munched on a fresh muffin. He wouldn't need much looking out for and they both knew it.

With one more smile for Levi, Nikki turned and headed into the thick of the festival. She wasn't exactly sure where they were setting up the surprise for Wade, but it wouldn't be too hard to find. Judging by the excited whispers from people all around her, Wade's homecoming was literally the talk of the town.

It didn't take long for her to find Parker. He stood on a ladder and pulled one end of a banner up on the stage. Matt held the other end, with Becky between them to direct the whole affair.

Matt was the first one to turn and see her, but as soon as he did, Parker followed suit. His face immediately turned up into a smile, but it quickly faded into a look of cautious surprise.

Nikki smiled in return, in a way that she hoped was encouraging. "Hi."

Becky turned at the sound of her voice, lifted her hand to wave and say something, but her mouth opened and shut like a fish out of water and she turned to Parker. Obviously, word of their breakup had gotten out.

Parker held his end of the banner in mid-air. "Hi."

As she looked around at everyone watching her and waiting for a reaction, Nikki knew this was not how she wanted to do things. Not that there were a lot of options, but still. "Can we talk?"

"Absolutely." Parker dropped his end of the banner and was down the ladder so fast that Matt cursed in his wake, but he didn't seem to notice as he focused totally on her. "Why don't we go behind the pumpkin carvers' booth? It'll be quieter there."

"No problem, Parker," Matt called behind him. His voice dripped with sarcasm. "I got this. You—"

Nikki turned just in time to see Becky smack her husband's arm and she stifled a smile.

"I'm glad you came," Parker said as soon as they were out of sight from their well-meaning, but nosy, neighbors. "I've...I've missed you, Nikki."

He moved to reach for her hands, but she saw him pull back, uncertain of how she'd respond. She knew she'd caused that uncertainty, and she hated herself for it because at that moment, she wanted nothing more than to hold Parker's hands.

"Parker, I—"

"Nikki—"

She pulled back and laughed a little, all at once nervous.

"You go first," Parker said. "I want to hear what you have to say."

She nodded. So did she. The truth was, she had no idea what she would say. She took a deep breath. The last few days had been miserable just thinking she'd ruined everything with Parker. All she really needed to say was that she missed him, that she...

"Okay," he said when she still hadn't spoken. "I'll go first." She nodded. Maybe that was best. "Nikki, I'm so sorry I kept everything from you. It was never my intention to lie to you, but I—"

"I understand." The moment the words were out of her mouth, she realized they were true. She did understand.

"You do?"

She nodded. "I do. I think I always did, but Ryan...I had to think of him and everything he's been through already...well, honesty is really important to me."

"I know." He took her hands then and pressed them together in his own. His warmth filled her. "I know what you've been through, especially with Ryan. It wasn't my choice to keep it from you, but Melissa and Abby, they're—"

"I know," she said again. "I understand and to tell you the truth, your commitment to them is honorable. It couldn't have been easy for Melissa." The same feeling of understanding she'd had for the other woman passed through Nikki. She still smarted a little from the words Melissa had said to her, but she could relate to her and her need to protect her daughter. After all, hadn't she carried out a similar if not different deceit not that long ago when it came to Ryan and Matt? It might be awhile until Melissa and Nikki could call each other *friends* but at least she could let go of the anger, and that was the first step. "I know you did what you did out of love and loyalty for your family, and that's what makes you so amazing."

Parker squeezed her hands tighter and pulled her closer to him. In the background, they could hear the excitement of the crowd as people gathered to watch the expert pumpkin carvers just on the other side of the tent. In years past, it was Nikki's favorite part of the festival, to watch them take ordinary pumpkins and turn them into works of art, but at that moment, all she wanted was to be in Parker's arms.

"I'm sorry, Parker." Tears pricked at the back of her eyes. "I was scared and—"

He silenced her with a kiss. Tender, and warm, it was all she needed to know that things would be okay.

"Believe me," he said when he finally pulled away. "The only thing I want from this moment on is to be honest with you and build a life with you."

Was he saying what she thought he was saying? There was only one way to know for sure.

"And by *build a life,* do you mean—"

"Get married?" He smiled and squeezed her hands. "I know it's not the most romantic proposal in the world and I planned on having a ring and flowers and—"

"Yes." She cut him off. "Yes. Yes. Yes. I'll marry you." Sure, he hadn't officially asked her, but she also knew what she wanted, and she was sick and tired of letting anything get in the way.

Parker pulled her into his arms and kissed her thoroughly. When he finally pulled away, there were tears in Nikki's eyes, but this time because she was happy.

"Nikki Landon, I love you, and I refuse to spend another day without you—"

His words were lost as Matt ran around the corner. "It's time," he said, totally unaware of the moment he'd interrupted. "Melissa and Abby just got here. With Wade."

Chapter Fifteen

Melissa

Melissa's body drummed with nervous anticipation. Flashes of that awful day when she'd arrived home, over nine years ago and panicked to Greta Wilson that she was all alone now, that Wade had just up'ed and left them...it all overwhelmed her and she couldn't get her body to stop shaking.

"It's going to be okay, Mel." Wade reached across and grabbed her hand. He threaded his fingers through hers and squeezed tight.

"I have so much explaining to do," Melissa mumbled. Would people forgive her for never correcting the misconception, for actually going along with the idea Wade had left them, her and their daughter for no good reason, when it was the furthest thing from the truth?

"We'll deal with it together," Wade said.

"Just tell the truth, Mom. Everyone will understand." Abby blew a bubble and popped it.

The truth. Last night in the hotel room, they'd all played a game of Truth or Lie. After they'd ordered in pizza and chicken wings—an odd combination for a first night out of jail dinner—rather than watch a movie, Abby had come up with the idea to play a game. But not just any game...something that would help them all become better acquainted.

She'd raised a smart girl, that's for sure.

The game had gone well. At first, things were very light, and it felt good to laugh together as a family. But then, the tone became a little more serious, and real feelings were displayed through their statements until the laughter turned to tears.

The night ended with a pact between the three of them to always tell the truth.

"I will, Abby. I promise." Melissa looked at her daughter through the rearview mirror and gave her a sad smile. "But it's going to be tough at first; I'm not going to lie. I don't even know how to explain what I've done."

"There's nothing to explain," Wade said.

"Sure there is. No matter what my reasons were...I basically gave up on you. I thought it better to consider you deadbeat than tell the truth. I punished you for over nine years because of a small mistake."

Wade shook his head. "It wasn't a small mistake. I killed someone. I knew better. Knew I was tired and I should have pulled over hours before."

Abby sighed. "How long do we have to keep beating ourselves over this?"

Melissa had no reply and when she glanced at Wade, apparently he didn't have one either.

"I bet you people already know. Do you really think you could have kept something like this a secret for so long?" Abby leaned forward. Her hands rested on both her parents' shoulders.

"No one knows, honey." Melissa would have known if

others had found out. Becky hadn't even known...and if Becky had no idea, then no one did.

"Don't be surprised, that's all I'm saying."

"Why do I have a feeling you're not being completely honest with us?" Wade half turned in his seat to face Abby.

From the rearview mirror, Melissa caught the slight shrug of her shoulders. Something was up. Did people actually know? Had they actually gone along with Melissa's lie? Why? Why would they do that?

"What are you looking forward to the most, Dad? Being home, I mean." Abby quickly changed the subject.

"Being home home, or just home in Halfway?" Wade asked.

"Halfway. You know the Pumpkin Festival is happening. Are you looking forward to the pumpkin pies? Or seeing old friends? Or..."

"Hmm, pumpkin pie." Wade exaggerated the action of licking his lips, before he put his hand out, surprising Melissa.

"Can you pull over here?" Wade's voice hitched.

In front of them was the Halfway sign. Melissa slowed down, and pulled over onto the gravel shoulder until she came to a stop right in front of the sign.

"What's wrong?" Melissa put the car into park.

Wade shook his head and opened his door, getting out, and walked closer to the sign. He just stood there, his hands jammed into the pockets of the fall jacket Melissa had bought him.

"What's wrong with Dad?" Abby asked.

Melissa bit her lip and didn't say a thing. But she got out of the vehicle and went to stand beside her husband. They stood there, staring at the sign, no words spoken between them. When Melissa finally glanced up to look at Wade's face, she saw that he was crying.

"Some days I wondered if I'd ever be able to come back," he whispered.

Melissa wrapped her arm around his waist and rested her head against his shoulder. "This is your home."

"We'll see." Wade sucked in a deep breath and let it out. They walked back to the car and continued on their way, the silence between the three of them thick.

"Where do you want to go first? Home or the town park?" Melissa slowly drove through the streets of Halfway to let Wade take in the sights of his hometown.

"We should get it over with, don't you think?" Abby spoke up.

Get it over with, as if it were a hard task to accomplish.

"Parker is probably waiting for you," Melissa said quietly. She wanted the decision to be his—whether they head home and hide away for a few more hours before people searched them out or to face everything now, while they themselves were still fairly raw emotionally.

It would take a long time for them to heal as a family. There was no way nine years of separation could be erased overnight.

"No more hiding," Wade said.

"No more lying," Melissa added. This time, she reached for Wade's hand and squeezed.

Touching him, having him here beside her, although it remained slightly awkward at the best of times, it still felt right. She felt whole again. Seeing him yesterday as he walked out of the prison, all those walls she'd built around her heart crumbled. When he reached her side and engulfed her in a hug, held her tight against him as he wept in her arms, the cracks in her soul began to heal.

Whatever was about to happen was going to happen. Whether it was today, tomorrow, or the next day. They couldn't run and hide from it. This was their life now.

Wade gasped as she drove down Main Street. She could have pulled over anywhere to park, but she knew it would be better to head towards the town park and face the music, so to speak.

And she really hoped there would be music. Country, specifically.

As she pulled up, Melissa's eyes teared up at the sight before them. A banner had been raised that said "Welcome Home" and beneath it stood everyone, all their friends, waiting for them.

For Wade.

"Oh cool! Look, Dad—"

Wade cut her off.

"Did you know about this?"

Melissa wasn't sure how to respond. Wade sounded stressed, panicked almost.

"I thought you told them all I took off? This looks like everyone knew..."

Melissa swallowed hard and took a really long look at all those who waited beneath the banner.

It was everyone. The whole town practically stood there, in a large group, with large grins on their faces.

They knew? Everyone knew? How?

Melissa's chest tightened as her hands gripped the steering wheel. What was she going to do? How was she going to handle this? She'd expected a few people; she knew the story Becky was going to tell everyone—how she'd overreacted and let a rumor start that basically grew out of control and then only wanted to protect Abby from knowing her father had killed a small girl her age—but...this looked as though there was more to the story. She didn't expect people to be there, welcoming him home. She kind of expected to lose friends, to have people talk behind their backs...to blackball them from the community.

"I think everyone is waiting for you, Dad." Abby got out of the vehicle and then went to open Wade's door.

Melissa watched him. Would he be okay? Was he okay?

Could he handle this? Should they have just gone home, let him reacclimatize himself to his new life before throwing him in the mix?

Her husband wasn't the same man everyone remembered him to be. His body thrummed with tension; his muscles were more defined, his features sharper. There was a steel to his gaze that he never had before and even though he'd engulfed her in his arms when she first saw him, there were times, if she went to touch him unexpectedly, that he jerked away.

But they hadn't been together long enough to know how much more of him had changed.

Was he still the fun-loving, friend-focused man he used to be? Everyone wanted to be around him, ask his advice, hear his stories. Would they now?

"Are you going to be okay?" she asked him.

"Are you?"

She gave him a sweet smile. At least that hadn't changed—him always placing her first. But right now, this wasn't about her. It was about him, and she would be his strength if he needed her.

"We're together again, as a family. That's all that matters, right?" She leaned over and placed a soft kiss against his lips before she pulled back and opened up her door.

She stood there for a few moments and gazed around her. All of Wade's old buddies from school were there. Greta Wilson held a plate of cookies in her hands beside Norma Grant. Becky and Matt rushed over to Wade and gave him hugs and pats on the back. Parker stood there, off to the side with Nikki and when he gave Melissa a slight nod and raised brow, she smiled. He wanted to know if things were okay and they were.

Off to the side stood Nyah, and Melissa quickly glanced away. She wasn't quite ready to deal with her old friend and the news she'd told her that night at her house. She'd come back to town to help her father, who was ready to retire. But not to work in the office side of his practice. To run it. Nyah had gone on to become a doctor. The guilt she'd felt over Wade's accident had propelled her to right her wrongs. Good for her. But where she was now a successful doctor, Wade had spent nine years in prison, their family torn apart and his future uncertain.

Melissa wasn't too sure yet how she felt about that. But it wasn't something she was going to deal with now. Her attention needed to be on her family.

Abby was glued to her father's side, as she should be. When she went to join them, Wade immediately placed his arm around her waist but Melissa wasn't sure whether it was for support or to show that they were a family, united. Did it really matter, though?

Melissa took in a deep breath.

Wade did the same thing.

"This was probably my favorite festival out of them all. I dreamed about being here, smelling the pumpkin treats, seeing the fall decorations, drinking a cup of hot chocolate and seeing your cheeks rosy from the brisk wind," Wade said quietly.

Melissa was reminded of the festivals they used to go to, together. Wade and Parker would be a powerhouse team, dealing with the pumpkins and all the kids' games while Melissa would help wherever she was needed. Her favorite times during the day were when she could sneak away and bring Wade a cup of hot chocolate.

"Then I'm glad you came home today, of all days." She snuggled in closer and smiled up at him.

"Me too."

"This is a sight for sore eyes. We've missed you." Levi Jenkins came over and slapped Wade on the shoulder. "Good to see your family back together, the way it should be." Levi gave a deep nod of his head and backed up, letting others take his place.

One by one, people came up to hug, shake hands, or just express their happiness at Wade's return. The whole time, Melissa was ready to defend herself, her actions, her words if anyone said anything, but no one did. Not once.

Finally Parker came up and without any words, the brothers launched towards each other and held tight. Wade finally broke down and his body trembled with his sobs while Parker squeezed his eyes tight and held on. Everyone around them backed away, to give the brothers their privacy, except for Melissa and Abby. She knew that Wade wouldn't want her to leave. She had this innate feeling that he needed her close to his side.

There was nowhere she'd rather be.

"We're going to be okay, aren't we, Mom?" Abby had tears in her eyes as she watched her dad.

Melissa wrapped her arm around Abby's shoulder. "We'll be more than okay, love. We're not alone anymore."

"You never were."

Melissa turned and smiled at her friend, who appeared behind her. She gave Becky a hug and whispered *thank you* into her ear.

"Oh, this wasn't my idea." Becky's smile was secretive.

"I don't understand." If it wasn't Becky's idea, then whose was it?

Becky twined her arm through Melissa's and pulled her off to the side.

"You've never been one to hide your emotions very well, you do realize that, right? We all knew something wasn't right when you came home all those years ago without Wade." Becky leaned her head on Melissa's shoulder.

"Why didn't you say anything?" They'd known?

Becky shrugged. "We're all family, aren't we? You needed to deal with this your own way, so we let you. As a community. We've always had your back, Melissa. Always."

"Who found out?" The idea that everyone knew, that she hadn't kept her secret...that had her world spinning more than she'd thought possible.

"My mom and Levi, with the help of Mrs. Wilson. You can't pull a fast one over them. But once they found out, they worked hard to make sure you never knew."

Melissa shook her head. Greta Wilson knew? Norma Grant?

"So when you told me you'd take care of his homecoming..."

Becky pulled away and her face shone with the brightest smile Melissa had ever seen.

"Oh, I just told my mom Wade was coming home and she took care of the rest. You know how she is!"

Shocked and amazed, Melissa didn't know what to say, so instead, she sought out Norma and gave her the best hug she could give.

"Thank you, Norma. I don't understand, but thank you."

Norma held on tight for a moment. "Enough with all the hugging now. That's all you guys have done since you arrived. It's time to get on with the activities, don't you think?" Norma's voice was a bit gruff but Melissa wasn't fooled. The older woman had tears in her eyes.

"I can't thank you enough," Melissa whispered.

Norma grunted. "Of course you can't. Do you have any idea how hard it was to go along with your silly little lie and not tell you it wasn't necessary?" Norma shook her head, a slight frown on her face. "If your mother had been here...she would have done the same thing. Protected you and your daughter. So that's what we did. And, that's why you're going to give me a good deal on the cookbooks for the Tree Festival next month."

Melissa laughed. Give her a good deal? Melissa wasn't making money on it as it was.

"For you, anything," she told Norma. She'd figure something out. Maybe she could talk to Nikki about doing the layout instead of outsourcing it, saving money in the long run.

And on the subject of Nikki, Melissa looked around for the woman and found her off to the side, organizing the bake table full of muffins and pies.

"Need any help with that?" Melissa asked.

Nikki shook her head. "I think I'm only making a mess of Norma's handiwork." She peeked over at Norma and gave a small smile.

"Parker tells me I owe you an apology." Melissa shuffled her feet and glanced behind her at her husband. Her heart flopped at the sight of him, as he stood among his friends. He looked lost but at the same time, happy. She couldn't even imagine what he was going through.

"So you're only apologizing because Parker said to?"

"What? No." What was with the attitude? "I already apologized, at Becky's. I thought we were okay, but apparently we're not. But we need to be. For our men's sake. We used to be friends."

Nikki's eyes flashed with something—regret, maybe—before she, too, glanced over towards their men. "We've both made our share of mistakes when it comes to our children and those we love, haven't we?" she said quietly.

Melissa just waited. There was obviously something on Nikki's chest that she needed to say.

"I don't like being left in the dark, especially when it made me feel...like I couldn't be trusted. But Parker, he's the kind of man you want on your side and..." Her voice trailed off.

"And to trust with your heart?" Melissa hazarded a guess on

what she was going to say. "He's a good man and deserves to be loved by a woman like you."

She'd watched Wade last night, in bed. There was a moment, when he'd been sleeping, that he'd let his guard down —only a moment—but she caught sight of the man she'd fallen in love with, her Prince Charming. She lost her heart all over again and knew, that no matter what happened today, tomorrow, or even next year, she needed him by her side.

She wanted Parker to have that too. And if he could find that kind of love with Nikki and Ryan, then she wanted that for him.

"Can we start over?" Melissa asked.

When Nikki nodded, Melissa felt a rush of peace flow through her. "Good, because I know Wade is going to want to spend a lot of time with Parker, which means our family needs to be a close one. Wade has missed out on a lot and I don't want any tension between us to affect his relationship with his brother. I know I made mistakes, but—"

"We both made mistakes, for the right reasons. There's no judgment from me, Melissa. From one mother to another, we'll do everything and anything for our children, so trust me when I say, I get it."

"Mom!"

Melissa turned and caught Abby waving at her. "I'm being summoned."

"Here." Nikki pushed a plate of assorted pumpkin baked goods into her hands. "Take this for Wade."

"Thanks, but why don't you come with me and give it to him yourself?" Melissa pulled Nikki along with her until she was back at Wade's side.

Parker wrapped his arm around Nikki and smiled at his brother.

"Is that who I think it is?" Wade looked from Nikki to Parker and back to Nikki. "It's about time."

Melissa chuckled as Parker's cheeks blared bright red and Nikki glanced down at the ground with embarrassment.

"Are you ready to walk around? Grab some hot chocolate and see how your town has changed in the past few years?" Melissa stared up into her husband's eyes and melted from the look of love he gave her. His hands still shook and she could tell he was beginning to feel overwhelmed but he hid it pretty well.

"Please," he leaned down and whispered.

"Abby?" She glanced over at her daughter, who stood beside a group of her friends from school. "Should we ask her to join us?"

"I've got her," Parker said. "We'll meet up with you guys later. I think," he glanced around and lowered his voice, "there's a dinner planned for later, but if you're not feeling up to it, just say the word."

Wade thought for a moment. "This is all a bit overwhelming, so as long as it's low-key with not too many people..."

Parker shrugged. "Pub food with pool and friends who want to catch up. Everyone else has made casseroles and desserts and dropped it off at the house already. Becky took care of that."

Wade nodded. "That doesn't sound too bad."

"Whoa, wait a minute. What doesn't sound bad? Going to the pub later or the fact you won't be eating my cooking for a while?" Melissa pretended to frown, but in reality, anyone's cooking was better than hers.

"Don't worry, Dad. I'm taking cooking in school and Mrs. Wilson has already agreed to teach me how to make some of her casseroles. You won't have to eat much of Mom's cooking." Abby piped up among laughter from everyone around them.

Melissa rolled her eyes and caught the smile from Nikki.

"At least I'm not the only one," Nikki leaned over and

mumbled for Melissa to hear. "I manage to burn frozen pizza on a regular basis," she admitted.

"Did I hear that right?" Wade asked. "We both managed to find women who can't cook? Didn't Mom warn us about that?" he said to his brother who laughed and pulled Nikki close to his side.

"Good thing we know how to cook then, isn't it?" Parker agreed while both Melissa and Nikki pretended to glower.

"Come on." Melissa tugged on Wade's hand. "Let's go for a walk."

Not only could they use this time to help Wade adjust to the surroundings better, to see how their small town had changed and greet people on a one-to-one basis rather than in a group, but they could spend some quality time together, just the two of them.

Nine years without Wade in her life had been horrible and God knew she'd made plenty of mistakes in those years. But thankfully she had a town full of friends who loved her and supported her no matter what. Once she thought she was all alone except for Wade, Abby, and Parker. But now she knew better. She'd never really been alone. Family wasn't always grafted through blood; sometimes it was through laughter, tears, and understanding. Halfway was her family, her community, her strength—and she would never forget that.

NEW YORK TIMES & USA TODAY
BESTSELLING AUTHORS

STEENA
HOLMES

and ELENA
AITKEN

HALFWAY
to christmas

Introduction

Christmas has always been one of the busiest times of the year for the women of Halfway, Montana, and this year is no exception.

It's barely been a year since Nikki Landon and her son, Ryan returned to town. But a lot has happened in such a short time, and this year, with her new love by her side, the holidays are set to take on a whole new meaning.

Despite how busy Becky Jennings and her husband Matt are running their tree farm, Christmas has always been a time for love, laughter and...baking. Now, with a baby on the way, their lives are about to change—but is all the stress starting to take its toll?

Melissa Tait has spent the last nine years celebrating the holidays without her husband Wade. Now that he's returned, the whole family has a lot of adjusting to do. But is it too much?

After ten years away, Nyah Henderson has finally returned to Halfway to take over her father's medical practice. As happy as she is to be home, small town life can be tough. Maybe the holiday season is just what she needs to find her way?

Join the women of Halfway, Montana as they celebrate love, friendship and the benchmarks of life this holiday season while learning some hard life lessons along the way.

Happy Reading!

Chapter One

BECKY

Becky Jennings swung her legs as she sat on the bed of Matt's pickup truck, her hands wrapped around a thermos of hot chocolate, and giggled as she watched the men drag the monstrous Christmas trees behind them.

It was the perfect day for a big tree-cutting party. There was a slight chill in the air along with a light dusting of snow but with the sun shining bright, it almost could be deemed as a warm day. Almost.

"How could they seriously not be freezing?" Melissa Tait muttered beside her.

"Freezing or not, that's a sight I'll never get tired of." Becky sighed.

"What? The sight of our sexy muscle men walking toward us?" Nikki nudged her in the shoulder and smiled.

Becky shook her head. "No, it's the sight of those muscle men struggling with the trees they're dragging behind them that

I'd pay to see over and over and over." She giggled as Matt stumbled in the snow. "Where's my camera phone when I need it?"

"I don't know—Parker seems to be having no issues and Wade seems to be doing fine on his own." Melissa swung her legs out in front of her. "Thanks for inviting us, by the way."

Becky smiled and linked her arm through both of the girls beside her. "It feels like old times, doesn't it?"

"Someone's getting sentimental with her pregnancy," Nikki teased.

Becky rubbed her swelling belly. "I'm always sentimental. I don't know what you're talking about. Everyone keeps warning me of pregnancy hormones, but so far, I've been fine."

"Oh really?" Nikki's brows rose. "So that little shouting match we interrupted earlier was normal? Along with the outburst of tears when you hugged Melissa and Wade earlier?"

"Or how about the way you threatened Matt with the spatula when he tried to sneak some whipped cream before we left?" Melissa added.

Becky's cheeks reddened and she knew it wasn't from the wind. She wrinkled her nose and stuffed back the flood of tears that always seemed to come at the worst times. She blinked a few times and kept her gaze straight so the girls wouldn't notice.

"So I'm a little emotional." She huffed before she smiled.

"Can you believe I'm actually pregnant? I still can't. I mean, I know I am," she rubbed her belly again, "but you know, right? You know?"

"We know," Nikki and Melissa said together.

Becky pulled them in for a closer hug. "So stop busting my balls about being hormonal." She winked at Nikki before she nudged herself to the end of the pickup bed and shimmied off before she made her way toward Matt.

The snow was quite deep, she'd give him that. A few times,

she caught the way his feet would sink until the snow was close to his knees.

"Guess we didn't do a good enough job with the sled to pack down the path, huh?" Becky smiled up at her husband and despite the scowl on his face, she kissed him.

"Kiss me like that some more and it won't matter," he said just as she pulled away.

"Later, tree man. That's for later." She smacked him lightly on the chest before she looked over his shoulder at the tree she'd picked.

"It'll all be worth it," she said to him.

The look on her face told her otherwise.

"You just had to pick the biggest tree in the field, didn't you?" Matt grumbled. "You do realize it's more than double the size of what the other two picked, right?"

"But it's beautiful, don't you think?" Becky gave him the sweetest smile she could. It really was a big tree and probably too big for their home, but the moment she'd seen it, she knew she wanted it.

"She's got you wrapped, man." Wade Tait laughed. He hauled a fair-sized tree while his daughter, Abby, dragged a Charlie Brown-type tree behind her.

"I know." Matt leaned in for another kiss, which Becky was all too happy to give him.

Becky led the way back to the pickup where she stood off to the side while everyone else helped to load the trees. She'd been given strict orders not to do any type of heavy lifting and she had no problem following them.

"I've got a nice chicken and dumpling stew simmering for lunch," she reminded everyone.

Today was going to be the perfect day. She had it all planned. She loaded everyone up with some fresh homemade hot cocoa and sugar cookies before they trudged through the snow to find their perfect trees. Becky had filled a container with some treats for along the way, which was a good thing considering they'd been out here for half the morning already.

"Ryan and I are still building our gingerbread houses, right, Becky?" Abby asked, a hopeful gleam in her eyes.

"I cut out all the pieces you'll need yesterday so we should be ready. You up for it, Ryan?" Becky asked.

Ryan was holding the tip of his tree he'd picked with Nikki up while Parker stood on the bed of the truck.

"Will there be cookies to eat?" Ryan asked eagerly.

"Will there be cookies to eat?" Matt gave his son a playful punch in the shoulder. "As if you had to ask. Becky has a special tin set away with all your favorites. I wasn't even allowed to touch," he grumbled playfully.

"It's a big tin." Becky shrugged her shoulders as Nikki gave her a look.

Thanks, Nikki mouthed.

You're welcome, Becky replied.

Ryan's eyes lit up as he caught the exchange. "I won't eat them all at once, Mom."

"Sure, sure." Nikki shook her head.

Becky couldn't wait for this Christmas. This would be their second one with Ryan in their lives and the last one before their own baby was born. Their family continued to grow and Becky couldn't be happier about it.

She glanced over at Melissa and Wade, who stood off to the side. They appeared to be having an intense discussion and ordinarily Becky wouldn't have thought much about it, except, she'd noticed there seemed to be a tense vibe between the two of them all morning.

"They're fine," Matt whispered into her ear. He wrapped his arms around her and held her tight. "Wade is still adjusting to being home after so long."

She turned in his arms and frowned. "I know. I thought they'd be happier, you know?"

"Give them time. I'm sure it's hard going from being a single parent for so long to having to share the responsibility. Melissa's known for liking things to be a certain way, we all know that, and Wade...it's gotta be tough. Just give them time and love."

"I just want them to know they're not alone. None of us are. Not anymore. That's what today is about, you know?"

Matt touched the tip of her cold nose. "I know. Now, how about we head home before you turn into an icicle?" His stomach grumbled loudly.

"Oh sure, use me as an excuse, why don't you. Can we hurry though? I've never had to pee so much in my life," Becky complained.

She hopped up into the truck like a graceful elephant and moved over into the middle. Eventually Nikki joined her while Melissa climbed into the back. Wade, Parker, and the kids remained in the truck bed with the trees.

"We might head home early," Melissa said quietly to Becky.

Becky half turned in her seat and shook her head. "No way. I've got a whole day planned. You're all going to help us decorate our tree and we've got a mean game of Scrabble to play after dinner." She gave Matt a look.

"Wade's a little sore and his pills are at home." Melissa stared out the front window, not quite meeting Becky's eyes. "Plus I've got an order at the shop I really should work on."

Matt's hand squeezed Becky's leg moments before Becky was about to call Melissa on her lie. She let out a breath instead and attempted a smile.

"I've got some warm compresses we can heat up if it's his shoulder and he can snag Matt's comfy chair. Stay for a little bit at least, okay?"

"I don't know." Melissa hesitated. "I'll have to talk to Wade."

"Becky, didn't you mention you needed me to run into town for a few things for dinner?" Matt squeezed her leg again.

"What? I—" She stopped as Nikki kicked her foot. "Right. Yeah, I have a list. I can't believe I forgot them." She had no idea what it was she forgot but she went along with whatever Matt was doing.

"I'll ask Wade to pick them up. Think he'd be okay with that, Mel?" Matt asked.

"He might. Thanks." Melissa relaxed in her seat and Becky turned back around.

She looked over at her husband but he gave his head a small shake. Did he know something she didn't?

Once back at the house, everyone helped to bring in Becky's enormous tree while she directed its placement. Thankfully Matt had done an excellent job in cutting it down and it was the perfect size, with enough room for the new Christmas star Becky had picked up at a flea market earlier.

She clapped her hands with excitement as the tree was secured into the tripod and watched as Abby knelt to wrap the tree skirt she'd made years ago around the base.

"Before we get into decorating, how about some hot lunch?" Matt said. "I don't know about anyone else but I'm starving. These muscles," he flexed his arms, "don't come cheap, you know."

"Let me throw the biscuits in the oven and we'll be ready in a few." Becky watched the couples in the room to gauge their reactions. Nikki and Parker stood off to the side, arms wrapped around each other, while Melissa and Wade stood a few feet apart, their arms tightly crossed over their chests.

What was going on with them?

"Melissa, do you think you could help? I've got some apple cider in a crockpot you can hand out, if that's okay?"

She didn't miss the look of relief on her friend's face.

"I can't tell you how happy I am you guys were able to join us today," Becky said once they were alone in the kitchen. She set the timer on the oven and wiped her hands clean.

"Thanks for inviting us. Really." Melissa reached for a cup and filled it with cider. Becky pulled out a tray from the cupboard and placed the cups on there as Melissa filled them.

"Well, I'm all about traditions and Christmas is my favorite season. What do you think about making this an annual thing...a big tree-cutting day? Next year, we can all head to your home and decorate your tree—or Nikki's. Christmas is meant to be shared with those you love."

Melissa gave her friend a little side hug. "I love the idea." Melissa smiled.

Becky added a plate of cookies to the tray while Melissa continued to pour the cider.

"Are things...okay? Between you and Wade?" She hoped she wasn't being too forward in asking.

Melissa bit her lip. "Things are...good. It's different, you know? Wade being home and back in our lives. It hasn't been easy. I think—"

"Mel?" Wade stood at the doorway that linked the living room to the kitchen. "Can we talk?"

"Sure."

Becky tried really hard not to listen in as the couple spoke but their whispers were hardly quiet.

"Matt asked me to head into town to pick up a few things. I might be awhile," Wade said.

"We were supposed to do this as a family, Wade. You promised Abby," Melissa hissed.

"I won't be long. I just..."

"You promised not to go there during our family days. You promised!"

Becky kept her back turned and filled the remaining mugs with cider. She didn't like the anger she heard in Melissa's voice. Where was Wade going?

"I won't be long. I promise. A couple hours, max."

"Whatever." The dismissal in Melissa's voice was loud and clear and Becky winced.

She heard the sound of steps retreating, a door closing, and a soft sobbing. Becky immediately turned to find Melissa huddled in the corner, her face covered by her scarf as she quietly cried.

"Oh honey." Becky went over and wrapped Melissa in a hug. "Are things okay?"

Melissa shook her head. "Sorry." She rubbed her red-rimmed eyes and sighed. "Sorry. It's fine. I'm just..." She breathed in deep and slowly let the air back out. "It's fine. Wade will be back."

"I couldn't help overhearing. I'm sorry."

Melissa snorted. "It's not like I was quiet or anything. I just hope Abby didn't hear."

"Are things okay between you two?"

Melissa shrugged. "Like I said, it hasn't been easy. We've been going to family counseling and apparently this adjustment phase is quite normal for ex-convicts."

"Is there anything I can do?" Becky felt helpless. A feeling she didn't like.

Melissa shook her head. "Thanks. I appreciate that. But just being a friend, doing...this...is all I need."

"Being a friend, that I can do. Just remember you're not alone, okay?" She'd remind Melissa of that daily, if she needed to. Melissa had a tendency to do things on her own, like for the past ten years when she lied about Wade being dead to protect her daughter from the truth.

"Did you guys get lost or something?" Nikki came into the kitchen and pulled the oven door open moments before the alarm went off. "There, now I can say I helped. I saved the biscuits from their burning death." Nikki grabbed the potholders and pulled out the pan. The delicious smell of fresh bread filled the air.

"See, Ryan. I don't burn everything," Nikki called out teasingly.

"You didn't bake them though, Mom," Ryan yelled back.

Becky rolled her eyes. "Parker does know you don't cook, right?"

Nikki shrugged. "I cook. As long as it's pre-made by either you or Greta Wilson, I'm fine."

"Uh huh." She handed Nikki the tray of cider. "Why don't you hand these out while I get the bowls for the stew ready?"

"You got it. You'd better hurry up, though. The natives are getting restless."

Becky didn't miss Nikki's questioning glance at Melissa before she left.

Becky had no idea what was going on but she didn't feel it was appropriate to continue prodding Melissa either, not when anyone could walk in and overhear their conversation.

"You and I are overdue for a good ol' girly chat, I think," Becky said.

Melissa nodded her head. "Let's make it a date then. You can give me some pointers on how to handle your mother this year. She's driving me nuts with the Tree Lighting festival. I wish you were organizing it again this year."

Becky laughed. "Like that was going to happen. As long as my mother lives and breathes, she will continue to run that festival regardless of what you or I have to say about it. You do realize I was just her puppet last year, right?"

"I figured."

"She's not bad though, is she? Extra grumpy or harsh?"

Melissa shook her head. "No, nothing like that. She just can't make up her mind."

That didn't sound like Norma at all. "Want me to talk with her?" she offered.

"No. I'll be fine. Oh, don't forget that article you were writing for the paper. It's due Tuesday."

Article? Becky's brow furrowed as she thought about what she obviously promised.

"You do remember, right? You were going to do a thing about homemade stockings, I think."

Becky smiled. "Right! I do have that written down. I just thought it was for my website. Oops."

"Do you want to reschedule?"

Becky shook her head. "No. I'll have it done, don't worry."

"I'm not the one to be worried. Norma wanted me to post her article on changing the lights on the tree but I told her the spot was taken. Specifically by you, so..."

"So basically you're telling me I want to make sure it's done otherwise I won't hear the end of it from my mother. Got it." Becky groaned.

Melissa's cell phone rang so Becky headed into the living room, where everyone else was.

"Things going okay?" Matt went to her side.

"Just peachy." She took a look at her tree and pushed everything else to the side. Today was about being with friends and family, of placing smiles on faces and starting new traditions.

"What happened to all the popcorn I made for the tree?" Off to the side was a large bucket of popcorn she'd filled last night. Except, the bucket was no longer full.

"Don't look at me." Matt held up his hands. "I told Ryan not to eat the popcorn, but he's a growing kid."

"Ryan." Becky gave her stepson a mock glare as she placed her hands on her hips. "I wanted to string that for the tree."

"I'll help make more." Ryan held his hands behind his back and attempted a somewhat innocent look.

It didn't work.

"His father is just as much at fault," Nikki said.

Becky flicked a popcorn kernel stuck between the hem of Matt's sweater and t-shirt. "I see that. Guess I know what you'll be doing after lunch, eh?"

"I'd better help too," Abby volunteered. "I didn't realize it was all for the tree."

Becky couldn't keep the smile from growing on her face. "That settles it then. While the moms relax after lunch, the rest of you will be put to work. I don't know about you," she turned to Nikki, "but I'm exhausted. Picking out the perfect Christmas tree is a lot of work."

She sneaked a glance behind her while everyone laughed to find Melissa at the counter, her hands in a fist as she stared down at her phone.

"What did you say to Wade before he left?" she whispered to Matt.

He shrugged. "Not much. Just mentioned I had to run into town to pick up a few things and he volunteered to do it for me. Which I figured he'd do anyways. Why?"

"That might have been a mistake." She didn't like the look on her friend's face. Her face was flushed and she kept blinking as if warding off tears. "Maybe you shouldn't have gotten involved."

"He was just going home to get his pills and take a little nap. His shoulder was killing him, he said." Matt leaned past her to look into the kitchen. "Is she okay?"

Becky shook her head. "I'm not sure home was where he was headed."

Chapter Two

NIKKI

If Nikki hadn't been in the holiday mood before Becky's big tree-cutting festivities, the day of apple cider, freshly baked treats, and of course, tree trimming certainly did the trick. The truth was, she'd been looking forward to the Christmas season more than usual this year. She looked across Becky and Matt's spacious living room to where the men and the children were stringing a giant bowl of popcorn to use on the tree.

This year, Christmas was going to be different. Not only did she have Ryan, who was still young enough to actually want to do all the traditional holiday things with her, but she had Parker, too. Her heart warmed just watching her fiancé and her son together. It still amazed her how well things had worked out after she came back to Halfway.

This time last year, Nikki wouldn't have even been able to imagine such a festive scene full of love playing out. A tear came to her eye and she wiped it away quickly before anyone noticed. She'd been really emotional lately and although she hoped that meant what she thought it did, it was way too early to tell anyone else.

"My feet are killing me. Here, hold this." Becky appeared next to her and handed her a tray before she sat heavily onto the couch next to her. "Oh, that feels so good," she moaned. "I swear, I'm not even that pregnant yet and this baby is doing a number on my feet. I didn't think it was possible to swell so much."

Nikki laughed. "It'll get better." She put the tray full of cookies and squares on the coffee table in front of her.

"You're lying."

"I am." Nikki laughed harder but then added, "But you'll love every minute of it, I promise. How could you not?"

Becky's hands went to her stomach. "Right? I still can't believe it."

"Well, believe it—you're finally going to be a mama. And I couldn't be happier for you." The two shared a quick hug and Nikki had to blink hard to keep the persistent emotions at bay.

Over Becky's shoulder, Nikki spotted Melissa pacing by the kitchen window. She was trying to look busy, but it was clear to anyone who bothered to notice that she was waiting and watching for Wade to come back from town.

"Hey." Nikki pulled out of her friend's arms. "Do you think Melissa is okay? I mean, I know they've been through a lot, but do you think Wade's settling in okay?"

Becky shook her head and then shrugged. "Honestly? I don't know. I mean, they seem okay. Mostly. But every once in a while..."

Her gaze drifted to their friend, too.

"I know what you mean," Nikki said. "I just wish there was something we could do to help make it easier."

"Maybe we can."

Becky had that look in her eye. That look that Nikki had

come to be wary of in the past. That look that meant she may have just gotten herself a little too involved in Melissa's life. Not that sometimes meddling wasn't warranted. It was. Especially if it could help ease some of the suffering their friend was obviously going through.

Reluctantly, she looked at Becky. "Okay, I bite. What are you thinking?"

Becky laughed, no doubt because of the worried look on Nikki's face. "Oh, relax, Nic. It's not a big deal. And I promise I'm not planning some elaborate scheme that's going to get us involved in the middle of their domestic life."

Nikki raised her eyebrow.

"Seriously, I'm not." She lightly smacked Nikki's arm. "I'm not. Get that look off your face."

Nikki joined in Becky's laughter. "Okay then. What?" It didn't matter what Becky said, Nikki knew she was going to regret getting involved. But at the same time, she couldn't sit by and do nothing.

"All I'm thinking is that we distract them."

"Distract them?" Nikki reached for the shortbread on the tray in front of her. "What exactly do you mean by that?"

"With Christmas," Becky said, as if it clarified everything. "We'll just keep them all really busy with the holiday season and they'll get so wrapped up in everything they'll forget that they've been apart for the last ten years."

Nikki took a moment to mull it over. But only a moment. "That's your plan? That's it?"

"Don't knock it. I think it could work." Becky helped herself to a cookie as well. "And I realize it's not a big, fancy plan, but it doesn't need to be. Not really. I mean think about it—this will be the first Christmas they've been together in a very long time."

"True."

"And maybe they just need to remember what it's all about. Besides, the magic of Christmas and all that."

She hated to admit it. She really hated to admit it...but... "I think you might be onto something."

Becky flipped in her seat and stared at her. "Seriously?"

"Seriously." Nikki laughed. "It's actually so simple it could work. Christmas is a magical time. And maybe this year..." She drifted off before she could give away her secret but it was too late. Becky was way too perceptive.

"This year what?"

"Nothing." Nikki pointed to the men and children who were starting to drape the popcorn on the tree. "I think the guys need help." She moved to stand up but Becky grabbed her arm and pulled her back down.

"I don't think so."

Nikki glanced in Parker's direction in hopes he'd look over and rescue her from spilling the secret they'd promised to keep for a little bit longer. Although, she couldn't for the life of her remember why they weren't telling anyone yet.

"Nikki..." Her friend shook her arm, and Nikki looked around for a distraction of any kind.

"Melissa," she called to the other woman and used Becky's momentary distraction to jump up from the couch. "You have to come over here and try some of Becky's cookies. They're amazing."

"Nice," she heard Becky mumble behind her, but Nikki only laughed.

Melissa smiled, but even from across the room, Nikki could see it was forced. Becky was right; they had to do something to put a genuine smile on their friend's face again. "I'll be right there," Melissa said. "I'm just waiting for the hot chocolate. It's almost ready."

Nikki glanced back at Becky with a smile, but her friend

only shook her head. She may have bought herself a few minutes' reprieve from Becky's interrogating, but Nikki wasn't naive enough to think it would last long.

"Here you go." Melissa appeared with a tray of hot chocolate. She distributed them to the men and children before she joined the women on the couch.

"Thank you." Becky took a mug and wrapped her hands around it, inhaling deeply. There was no secret: she loved her sweets and the pregnancy only seemed to enhance their friend's cravings. "It smells delicious."

"It's going to be even better with a bit of this." Melissa poured a shot of Irish cream in Nikki's drink before she could stop her. "Sorry, Becky, none for you," Melissa said. "But have some extra marshmallows." She tossed some into Becky's drink and they all laughed. All except Nikki, who stared at her own drink.

"Maybe I could just get some extra marshmallows," she said slowly and put her mug back on the tray. "Instead of the Irish cream."

Melissa looked at her in confusion and she had a feeling she knew exactly how Becky was looking at her, but she dared not look. She was treading on very dangerous ground if she had any hope of keeping her secret from her way too perceptive friends. "But you love Irish cream in your hot chocolate," Melissa said. "I just assumed you would—"

"Oh my God."

Nikki could feel Becky next to her practically jump in her seat but still she wouldn't look. She needed to deflect the situation and fast.

"I do." Nikki grabbed her mug back. "In fact, I think I changed my mind." She clutched the warm drink and inhaled deeply. It did smell good, but there was no way she was going to drink it.

"Really?" Becky sounded disappointed and Nikki finally risked a glance in her direction. Her friend narrowed her eyes. "Try it," she challenged.

Dammit. She should have known Becky wouldn't let it go so easily. Pregnant women had radar for other pregnant women and more than that, they always seemed to want others to be pregnant with them.

Nikki put the mug down with a sigh. "I'm actually not in the mood for—"

"I knew it!" Becky jumped up so quickly her own hot chocolate splashed all over her lap. The commotion alerted the rest of the room and Parker looked over at them. Nikki caught him giving her a quick shake of his head, but there wasn't really any help for it. Not if Becky was on to them. "You're pre—"

"We're getting married."

"What?"

"You're what?"

The women stared at Nikki, their mouths open. She glanced to Parker for help but he was bent over chuckling and absolutely no help at all.

"Wait," Becky said. "We already know you're getting married." She grabbed Nikki's hand and held up her engagement ring that Parker had put on her hand at the Halfway Pumpkin Festival. "That's not a secret."

"No," Nikki said slowly. "But the fact that we're getting married on Christmas Eve is a secret."

"What?" Becky shrieked. "But that's so soon! How can you do it so quickly?"

"And why?" It was Melissa who asked. She glanced up at Parker, who'd moved and stood behind Nikki with his hands on her shoulders. "What's the rush?" She tilted her head and looked at them suspiciously.

Thankfully, it was Parker who answered. "We just don't

want to wait any longer," he said. "And everyone is already together at Christmas. It's not going to be a big, elaborate ceremony. Just something to celebrate our love. And of course you're all going to be there."

"Of course." Becky waved her hand. "That's a given. And it's going to be fantastic. That's a given, too. But seriously, we have so much to do. I still don't understand what the rush is, but we'll do our best and you know I'll be in charge of the food. Let's start planning right now."

"Actually," Nikki said. "We have most of the plans made. We were planning on surprising everyone with the ceremony." When Becky looked disappointed, she quickly added, "But of course I want you to help with the food and all the other details."

That seemed to appease Becky. Parker kissed Nikki on the forehead and backed away, smart enough to know when to make his exit. The second he was out of earshot, Becky leaned in so the three women were in a semi-circle, and whispered, "Okay, tell me the truth. Are you pregnant? Is that why you're getting married so quickly?"

There was no help for it. With a sigh, Nikki came clean. "No." Becky immediately sat back, crossed her arms, and used her eyes to gesture to the mug of spiked hot chocolate she still hadn't touched. "Well...maybe," she added and then quickly held her hand up to quiet her friends before they reacted. "We don't know. So don't say anything, okay?"

"Is that why you're moving up the wedding?" Melissa asked. "Because there might be a baby?"

"Yes and no." Nikki shrugged. "Honestly, I just want to be married already and make it official. But..."

"But you can't have a baby out of wedlock." The minute the words came out of Becky's mouth, she slapped her hand over it. "I mean...that's not what I...oh, Nikki, I'm sorry. I didn't—"

"It's fine." It was no secret that Nikki's first child, Ryan, was born out of wedlock but that was a very different scenario. Nikki had been too young, and she'd made a mistake. A huge mistake that they'd all finally moved past in order to be a family. But even though it wasn't the most tactful way to say it, Becky was spot on. "Yes," Nikki continued. "I want to do things right this time. And..." Her hand when to her stomach. "There's no time like now to make it official."

"So you are preggo?" Becky slapped her knees. "I knew it."

"Simmer down. I don't know anything yet. I was talking to Nyah the other day and—"

"Nyah Henderson?" Melissa's face was pinched in a scowl.

Nikki nodded slowly. She knew there'd been some tension between Melissa and Nyah—who'd been Melissa's best friend once—and she didn't know all the details of their falling out, but since Nyah had come back to town to take over her father's medical practice, Nikki had gotten to know her and she'd made a new friend.

"Is she your doctor?"

Nikki glanced quickly between her two friends, but Becky only shrugged. She looked back to Melissa. "She's the only full-time doctor in town right now. I have an appointment with her in a few days to confirm what I already think is true."

Melissa made a snorting noise and pushed herself up from the couch. "Well, I hope she's better with babies than she is at saving lives." Before Nikki or Becky could say anything else, she left them and went back to the kitchen, where she resumed her position at the window, watching for Wade, who still hadn't returned from his errands.

Chapter Three

MELISSA

Melissa stared at the page in front of her and frowned. With the Tree Festival just around the corner, literally days away, she was getting tired of having to make change after change after change, all because Norma Grant couldn't get the schedule right.

Everything felt off. Not just this project, but so many other things too. It was supposed to be Christmas, the time of miracles, of happiness and joy and... all that other stuff generally associated with the season, but Melissa couldn't get with the program.

She needed to get with the program.

Not only was her shop overrun with printing Christmas letters, Christmas cards, Christmas flyers, and anything else under the sun having to do with the season but it was the first Christmas with Wade at home.

Their first Christmas as a family after so long. Melissa should be excited, thrilled to have him home and a part of their lives again. Except...that joy, that level of excitement for the holidays that would normally be there—it wasn't.

She wasn't sure whether that was her fault, Wade's, or both.

Probably both. She couldn't lay the blame all at his feet.

"Hey, Mom." Abby dumped her backpack on the floor and stamped her feet on the front mat. "It's getting kind of cold out there and the snow is starting to really come down. Anything need to be delivered before I head home?" Abby rubbed her hands over her rosy cheeks.

"I've got nothing." Melissa set the page down and stood, stretching as she did so. "How would you like to start playing around with graphics and helping me with layouts?"

"Really?" Abby's eyes widened. "I thought I had to wait till the summer?"

Melissa shrugged. "I could use the help and you've got a great eye."

Abby winced. "I told Dad I'd come right home if you didn't need me. I just saw him." Abby looked everywhere but at her, Melissa noticed.

So she'd stopped in at his work before coming here. Melissa wasn't all that sure how she felt about that and instantly realized that it shouldn't matter.

Of course Abby wanted to spend time with her father, which was...understandable, right?

Of course it was.

Which meant her jealousy was completely out of line and totally off-base. It made sense they would want to spend time with each other; they had a relationship they needed to develop and strengthen.

"I'm probably going to run a little late, so would you mind starting dinner?" Melissa forced a smile on her face.

"Again?" Abby frowned. "You will be home for dinner though, right?" She picked up her bag but hesitated.

Melissa nodded. "I'll be home. Why don't you ask your dad to make his special spaghetti sauce?"

Abby's eyes sparkled as she walked through the front door. Ever since Wade's return, one of Abby's favorite things to do was cook with her dad. Apparently Wade had worked in the kitchen at the prison and discovered he enjoyed cooking.

Melissa really shouldn't complain. She hated to cook.

For the next hour, Melissa played with the template, adjusting the lines, changing graphics, and the handful of other issues Norma had pointed out and printed off a copy. Hopefully it passed inspection this time without any new major changes. She'd promised to drop off this sample on her way home and if she left now, she might have time to stop at the store for some garlic bread.

She sent Abby a text with her idea.

At the store now with Dad. Got it.

Just as she was packing up, Becky entered carrying a box.

"I'm so glad I caught you." Becky set the box down on the counter. "On your way home?"

Melissa eyed the box. "I am...I hope?" *Please don't say Becky was there with a last-minute project. Please...*

"I was playing around with some recipes today and need your opinion. There are six kinds of cookies in here but I only need three or four for Nikki's wedding. Which ones do you like the best?"

The moment Becky opened the box, the sweet aroma of freshly baked butter cookies had Melissa groaning.

"There's more than six cookies in here, Becky." She snagged a thumbprint cookie and bit into it. The cookie literally melted on her tongue.

"I know. I had to make full batches, of course. I figured Wade and Abby would enjoy them. Oh, that reminds me, I hope you haven't done any Christmas baking yet with Abby."

Melissa shook her head as she licked the crumbs off her finger. "I haven't had a chance."

"I could use some help for Nikki's wedding. I thought maybe you and Abby would like to come over?"

"Me? Bake?"

Becky laughed. "Well, maybe Abby could do the baking then while you enjoy a glass of mulled apple cider? I'll ask Nikki and Parker to join us too. It'll be fun."

"You're going to rope the guys into baking as well?" Wade would probably enjoy it.

Becky snorted. "Are you kidding me? They can help Matt out in the barn. Matt just picked up a new toy that needs some work. He's eager to show it off to the boys."

No doubt when Becky said a new toy, she meant an old truck that was rusted in a million places and needed some work.

"Don't tell Wade, but I think Matt was hoping to tempt your husband into helping him. He mentioned something about rebuilding the engine from scratch, I think."

Melissa groaned. "Wade would be in heaven, you know that."

Wade loved to work on old junkers and make them into something new. One of his old friends had offered him a job at their shop fixing cars and it had been a blessing in disguise. Wade would never be able to drive transport again, so this was the next best thing.

"So, Saturday? You'll come? I promise you'll go home with a tin or two of baked good as well."

Melissa pulled out her phone and checked the calendar. "It should work. Lorraine has the weekend shift and as long as your mother behaves...which reminds me." She handed Becky a folder. "Would you mind dropping this off at your mom's? I promised her another sample of the flyer to hand out at the festival. Hopefully she'll approve this one and not make any more scheduling changes."

She munched on another cookie or two while Becky looked at what Melissa had worked on.

"The festival is this weekend. What is she thinking?" Becky frowned. "This should work." She closed the folder. "Isn't this what was approved last month?"

"There's a few changes to the schedule and Norma didn't quite like the graphics I used."

"But I picked those graphics out." Becky shook her head.

Melissa just smiled at her. Working with Becky last year on the program while Norma was in the hospital had been a...nice reprieve from past years.

"I'll talk to her." Becky held the folder tight in her hand. "Honestly, it's not difficult and no one really looks at these anyways other than for the timing of events. I'm not sure why my mom is so fixated on this, but I'll take care of it, okay?"

Melissa sighed with obvious relief. She followed Becky outside and locked the door behind her. "Thanks for the cookies."

"Email me tonight with your favorites, okay?"

Melissa waved good-bye and slowly made her way home. She loved the quietness of Halfway in the evenings and if anything could help to rekindle that Christmas feeling, it was the sight of the town itself. Every building was covered in lights and homemade wreaths the school sold as a fundraising program for their troops overseas. Every yard held a snowman or snowdog or snow something and everything just looked...pretty.

As she pulled up into her own driveway, Melissa stared into the lit windows and knew that the scene inside was one she'd dreamed about for ten years. So why was she having such a hard time adjusting? She knew that's what it had to be...they were all learning to adjust and it was harder than any of them expected it to be.

It wasn't just learning to adjust to sharing her home with a man; it was having to share her daughter as well.

For ten years, it was just the two of them. They had a routine, a rhythm of how things worked at home but with Wade there...everything changed. Melissa couldn't remember the last time she'd spent alone time with Abby and yet Wade seemed to get a lot of it. When Abby had something exciting to share, Melissa wasn't the first person she came to anymore; when she had questions at dinner, it was Wade she was turning to...and Melissa knew that was probably normal and exactly what Abby needed right now, but...

The moment she opened the front door, her knees almost caved at the smell of garlic.

"Please tell me dinner's ready," she called out. She placed the box of cookies down on the counter and went over to the stove, sniffing the bubbling pot of sauce.

"Just about." Wade snaked an arm around her waist and gave her a kiss. "Welcome home."

"Hi..." Melissa replied, a little dazed as she peeked over his shoulder to see their daughter there, a smile stretched wide across her face. "Um...what's going on?"

Abby basically danced on the spot while Wade's smile continued to stretch.

"Anyone want to fill me in?"

"Can I tell her? Can I, Dad?" Abby begged.

Melissa pulled back from Wade's hold. "Tell me what?"

"Go ahead, kiddo. You tell your mom." The timer on the oven went off just then, so while Wade pulled the tray of garlic bread from the oven, Melissa stood by her daughter and waited.

"Remember that contest I entered awhile ago with my drawing? The one for that trip to California to see the Pixar studio? I won!" Abby squealed as she launched into Melissa's arms.

"No way! When did you find out?" Melissa could hardly believe it. In the fall, Abby's art teacher had mentioned it, suggesting Abby send in one of her drawings. In total, twenty kids would be selected from various schools and truth be told, Melissa had all but forgotten about it.

"My teacher just called. Mom, this is amazing, right?"

"So amazing!" She quickly hugged Abby again. "So, when is the trip?"

Abby shook her head. "The beginning of January." She squealed again. "We're even going to Disneyland!"

"That soon? That's only like," she mentally calculated the weeks, "less than a month away." Talk about short notice. "Is your teacher sure? That doesn't give us a lot of notice."

"I asked the same thing," Wade mentioned. "Ms. Hill said the news had come in last month but somehow the school misplaced the envelope. She'd just received a call from the studio confirming if Abby was able to come."

"Not by herself, right?"

"I can go, right?" Abby looked from her to Wade. "Dad said I could."

Melissa's head whipped around to where Wade stood, cutting the garlic bread. "Dad said, huh? Without talking to me about it first?"

"Like we're going to say no." Wade didn't even look up. "This is a once-in-a-lifetime chance, Mel."

Once-in-a-lifetime chance. So if she said no, that made her out to be the mean parent?

"But..." this time Wade did look at her, "you're right. I should have waited."

Melissa didn't say anything as she helped to dish out dinner. All through the meal, Abby talked about the studio and the movies made from there and how excited she was and Melissa knew that somehow she'd have to find a way to get her there.

After Abby disappeared up to her room to call her friends with the news, Melissa grabbed a rag and wiped down the counters while Wade finished drying the dishes.

"You're not mad at me, are you?" he asked. "About Abby's trip?"

Melissa sighed. "No, I'm not mad. I just..." She shook her head. "How is she going to get there? One of us will need to go with her, I assume."

"I'll go."

Melissa scowled. "You can't go." Thus the joys of being married to an ex-con. "You're not allowed to leave the state without permission and you'll never pass the police check needed to be a volunteer at the school."

"Why do I need to pass a volunteer check if it's my daughter?" He leaned his hip against the counter and flung the towel down.

"It's through the school, Wade."

"Well, that's just ridiculous. She's my daughter. I should be able to take her if I want to." He breathed in deep and Melissa could see the frustration mount on his face.

"Wade." She reached out and took his hand. "There's no point in getting upset. I'll take her."

He frowned but pulled her close. "I'm sorry," he said. "I want to take her, to experience this with her. I've missed out on so much and I...it just sucks."

"I know." She looked toward the stairs. "You have missed out on a lot but that just means we'll have to make new memories, I guess."

"Maybe I can talk to my parole officer and get permission to join you when you hit Disneyland? There's nothing stopping me from doing that, right? Maybe we can stay longer, make it a family vacation."

Disneyland. That was something she'd always wanted to do with Abby but could never afford it, not on a single income. Hope grew in her heart at the idea.

"Talk to him and see what you can do." She glanced over at the box of cookies. "In the meantime, we've been invited to Becky's this weekend to help get a start on Christmas baking plus help her make desserts for Nikki's impromptu wedding."

"This weekend? Are you going to have time?" Wade asked.

Melissa shrugged. "It's Christmas. Things are always busy this time of the year. Besides, Melissa let it slip that Matt bought some junker of an old truck and was hoping you'd look at it with him."

Wade's eyes sparkled. "What kind?"

Melissa snorted. "You expect me to know?"

"I'll have to give him a call and find out." He stepped away from Melissa and reached for his coat.

"Where are you going?" Why did she even bother to ask? Maybe it was because one day she hoped he'd give her an answer she wasn't expecting.

"I won't be long, Mel."

"You always say that." She began to wipe the counter again, this time in small tight circles while her fingers clutched at the cloth.

"He needs me and after...I can't just leave him, you know?"

Melissa's lips thinned as she struggled not to reply. Did she know? Hell no. How could she? Without fail, every night Wade would leave her—leave them—to go spend time with someone he'd met in prison. Someone who supposedly helped save his life.

"I don't know, Wade. I wish you would explain it to me.

Why do you leave, every night, to go sit with him? What do you do? Do you talk about stuff? Rehash the past? What?"

"We don't say a word," Wade said quietly as he shrugged on his coat. "You know that."

"I don't believe you," Melissa argued. It didn't make sense.

After the first month of being home, Wade started to disappear in the evenings and during the afternoon on the weekends. He never really told Melissa where he went until she cornered him one night.

"Charlie needs me, Mel. He was the only guy who was there for me in prison, the only one who..." He swallowed hard. "He had his tongue cut out because he stood up for me." Wade visibly shivered. "I can't leave him now. Not now."

Melissa stood there in shock. She hadn't known. Wade never said... "I had no idea," she whispered.

Wade's shoulders dropped as he stuck his hands in his pockets. "I didn't want to tell you, didn't want to bring that into the house. My time...that doesn't need to be part of us, you know."

Melissa went to her husband and held him, while guilt ate away at her heart. She'd argued with him, gotten angry at him for leaving night after night and had no clue or thought to really ask why he left. She should have asked, should have made him tell her.

"Your time there is a part of us, though," she said to him. "It's part of who we are now and if we're going to make this work...there needs to be honesty. You," she swallowed, thinking of all the things he could tell her, "don't have to tell me everything but, I thought you went to see him because you...needed to or something. I wish you'd told me, Wade."

"He's dying," her husband blurted out. "He's dying but he won't accept treatment, other than some pain meds, no matter how often Nyah comes—"

Melissa stepped back at the sound of that woman's name.

"Nyah?" she asked. "Nyah comes over? Nyah's there when you're there?" She struggled to breathe past the instant wave of anger that washed over her. She could feel it, the heat, rising up. "You're seeing Nyah?"

Wade shook his head. A bewildered look covered his face as he struggled to figure out why she was so upset. She could read it on his face, his lack of understanding. How could he not understand?

"She comes to check in on him," he said. "He doesn't have much time left but refuses to go to the hospital, so I asked her to come see him."

"So she's there while you're there? She couldn't go during the day, while she's working? She has to make a house call while you're there, with her?" By now Melissa's hands visibly shook and her chest hurt from a rapid heartbeat.

Did he not see the wrongness of this? Did he not think to tell her? To mention it at least?

"What do you have against Nyah?"

"What do I...I..." Melissa spurted. "You can't honestly ask me that and pretend you have no idea?"

"I'm asking." There was a sense of stillness about Wade that she'd noticed shortly after he came home. He became like this if they argued or he was upset. Almost as if he were checking himself, not allowing his emotions to get the better of him. Or, he was about to explode. Like the calm before a storm.

Melissa drew in a breath and let it out slowly. She could pretend to be calm too.

"If she'd known what she was doing that night, we wouldn't have lost ten years of our life together. Abby would have had her father to lean on; we might have had another child. I resent that she's back and a part of the daily life here. I resent that she's masquerading as a doctor when we all know it's a lie. She never should have come home."

"Mel, it wasn't her fault. None of this," he spread his arms out wide, "is because of her. It's because of me. Don't you think I know that? Don't you think I live with that, day in, day out?" He squared his shoulders. "You can't blame her. That's not fair to her or to us." He walked away from her, his hand on the handle of the door. "You're right. I should have told you. I should have done a lot of things and I regret so much. But don't ask me to stop visiting Charlie, because that's not a regret I can bear. Okay?" He looked at her over his shoulder.

"I lost you while I was in prison. I lost everything, even myself. But Charlie, he was the only one who stuck by me. I won't let him die alone, not even if it means having you angry at me."

Before Melissa had a chance to reply, he left and closed the door firmly behind her. She watched him drive away as she stood in the front window and wished for the chance to right the wrong she'd just committed.

Chapter Four

NYAH

More coffee. There needed to be more coffee if Nyah Henderson had any hope of getting through the day. She drained the last of her mug and looked to the office door, where she knew the coffee machine was only a few feet away. What were the chances anyone had made a fresh pot?

At two in the afternoon?

Not very good.

There was no help for it. If she didn't get at least a little bit more caffeine in her system, she was never going to make it through the afternoon and she had patients to see. Exhaustion was not an excuse for...well, anything.

Nyah pushed herself up from her desk and the patient files that always needed to be updated, and went out to the small staff room to brew another pot. This one extra strong. She hadn't meant to stay out so late the night before, but she hadn't expected Charlie to be in such a bad way. There were so many reasons she probably shouldn't be doing nightly house calls to the old man's home, but he was in such pain and with no way to communicate or any family. The man had no one. Well, almost no one.

He had Wade Tait.

Every single night when she got there to give Charlie his pain meds and change his IV bags—the poor man couldn't keep any food down—Wade was there. She couldn't quite figure out the relationship between them. It's not as if they had any conversation. After all, Charlie couldn't talk since losing his tongue in prison. He would occasionally scratch out some messages on his whiteboard, but from what Nyah could tell, they didn't even do that. Wade was just there. He just sat by his side and...was there.

It was touching and easy for Nyah to see how it would be comforting to the older man. Sometimes just having someone nearby, not talking, not even touching, could be the greatest comfort. And if she was one hundred percent honest with herself, she, too, found comfort in Wade's presence. Which was the strangest thing that could possibly have happened. The man had every reason to hate her, and the first time she ran into him at Charlie's house, she'd almost turned around and walked out. It was her fault he'd ended up in prison.

Sort of.

But that was a long time ago. Before she'd become a doctor. Before she'd known better. She'd done the best she could at the time with the knowledge she had. That was the message years of therapy had finally pounded into her head. And she believed it too. The little girl's death was not her fault. It was a terrible accident. She'd tried to save her life, and she'd failed. It was an accident. That was all.

That knowledge, and the constant self-talk Nyah did with herself, was all it took to stay that first night when she'd found Wade at Charlie's bedside. But every night that passed since that she stopped by and Wade was there, it got easier and easier. The thing was, Wade didn't seem to blame her. His wife Melissa? That was a different story. But Wade was at peace with his past and although she didn't know the details of it, Charlie clearly had something to do with that as well.

"Poor Charlie," she muttered to herself as she poured herself a cup of the freshly brewed coffee.

"Charlie?" Lana Porter, the nurse who'd been at the Halfway Clinic as long as she could remember, came around the corner, almost scaring her into dumping the coffee down the front of her blouse. "Charlie Renton? How is he? Did you see him last night again?"

"Every night." Nyah poured a generous dose of sugar into her cup. The combination of strong coffee and a hit of sugar couldn't hurt. Not when she was dragging this badly. "But I don't know for how long," she added ruefully. "He's not doing well."

"Your dad must be so proud of you taking care of old Charlie. It's just what he would do. You're a good doctor, Nyah. We're lucky to have you." Lana patted her hand. "Not many doctors would give up their personal time every evening to help out a lonely old man."

"He's not just lonely." Nyah took a sip of the scalding coffee. There was no time to let it cool. She needed caffeine, stat. "He really doesn't have anyone else and he's dying. I have no idea how he'd be able to get himself in here every day and the hospital is no place for a man like him to die."

"You mean an ex-con?"

"I mean, a...yes." Nyah nodded. "I mean, I know there must have been a reason he went to prison, but he served his time and a hospital bed would be just like a prison. He deserves to die at home and if I can help make that a little easier, that's what I'm going to do."

The nurse smiled kindly. "Like I said, Nyah. You're a good doctor. But more than that, you're a good person. I'm glad you're back."

Lana's words warmed her through. It had been awhile since anyone had said those words to her. Well, if she was honest with herself, no one besides her father had told her they were glad she was back. And that was only because he was itching to hand over the practice and go traveling. The truth was, there weren't many people in Halfway who would have a reason to be glad to have her back. It's not as if she were Miss Popularity when she was growing up and her closest friend, well...she'd done a good job ruining that friendship. Nyah forced a smile when she noticed that Lana still stared at her. "Thanks," she muttered and hid her discomfort by taking another sip of coffee.

"Feeling better?" Lana gestured to the mug in Nyah's hand. "Because you have a full afternoon."

"I do." Nyah nodded. "Who's next?"

Lana produced a file from nowhere and handed it to her. "Nikki Landon. She's here for a physical and..." The nurse's eyebrows wiggled. "And a pregnancy test. Maybe that's the reason for the quickie wedding."

She had to remind herself they were in a small town, where everyone knew everyone else and definitely knew their business. She would have chastised Lana for her unprofessionalism, but Nyah knew for all the older nurse's joking and inappropriateness, the information would never leave the office. She talked big, but Nyah was confident Lana would never cross the line.

Nyah took another big swallow of coffee and reached for the file. "Thanks, Lana. Room two?"

Lana nodded and took the mug of coffee out of Nyah's hand with a sympathetic smile.

There were only a few hours left in the workday, a handful of patients and then she could go home and hopefully have a nap before she went to Charlie's place again. It was bound to be another late night again. The poor man. Fighting cancer by yourself, unable to speak, she couldn't imagine...no. She shook her head. She needed to clear her head and focus on the present and her patients.

Nikki Landon, specifically. She flipped open Nikki's chart and smiled a little to herself. She didn't know Nikki very well. At least not yet, but she'd been one of the people to welcome Nyah back to Halfway with open arms. It hadn't been much, but it had definitely been enough to give Nyah a bright spot in what was otherwise a touchy transition.

She knocked lightly on the door of exam room two before she turned the handle. "Good afternoon, Nikki." The other woman was perched awkwardly on the exam table and fidgeted with her cotton gown. Sitting in an exam room with one person wearing a thin, practically see-through gown wasn't necessarily the best way to nurture a new friendship, but it was the only way to further the doctor/patient relationship, so it was Nyah's job to make it as comfortable as possible. For both of them. "It's nice to see you again."

"Thanks, Dr. Hende—"

"Nyah," she interrupted her. "Please, just call me Nyah."

Nikki's smile was warm, and she could see some of the nervousness melt away. "Okay." She nodded. "Nyah. It's good to see you again, too."

Nyah flipped open the file even though she'd just looked at it. "From what I can see, you're here today for a..." She glanced up and let Nikki finish the sentence, which she did with a broad grin.

"A pregnancy test. I mean, I did one last week at home, but those home tests...you know...sometimes they're not very accurate and I needed to...well, you know."

Nyah laughed a little. "I do know. And we'll confirm everything, but first, let's get some information."

The two women chatted easily for a few minutes while Nyah gathered as much information about Nikki's cycle as she could, took her blood pressure, and listened to her lungs. Before she handed over the specimen cup, Nyah was already fairly positive what the results would be, and ten minutes later, in the little lab room when Nyah ran the test, she confirmed what she already knew. This time when she knocked on the exam room door and entered, Nikki was fully dressed and sat in the chair.

"Well, I have your results." Nyah tried her best to keep a straight face, but there was no help for it; the smile crept across her face. "Congratulations, Nikki. You're pregnant."

Nyah wasn't sure whether she expected Nikki to cheer or dance or laugh or what, but she was not prepared for what she actually did. She lurched out of her chair, grabbed the wastepaper basket and threw up. Nyah stood by for a moment, stunned, before she jumped into action. She went to the sink and wet a washcloth with cold water before she pressed it to the back of Nikki's neck. She rubbed small circles on her back. "Are you okay?"

Nikki nodded slightly, but didn't lift her head up. She threw up one more time before Nyah handed her a handful of tissue.

"I'm fine," she said finally. "Could I have some water?"

"Oh, of course." Nyah jumped up and fetched the water. "Here you go. Sip slowly and just relax." She waited another minute before she said, "Well, that wasn't really the response I expected, but I guess it was a fairly appropriate one."

Nikki laughed. The color had returned to her face and she looked remarkably better. "I guess if the test didn't confirm it, the morning sickness just did."

"Have you been pretty sick already?" Nyah wrinkled her brow in concern. If Nikki was suffering too much from morning sickness, she'd definitely want to monitor it. But Nikki only shook her head.

"Not really," she said. "I mean, once or twice. But nothing terrible. Yet," she added. "With Ryan, I didn't get sick until I was almost two months along. It was so strange. And then I was sick into the second trimester. I guess my body likes to do things a little differently."

"Don't worry about it," Nyah said with a little laugh. "There really aren't any rules about pregnancy. Despite what everyone would like to believe. Every body is different and every baby is different. I'm sure you'll see some similarities between this one and your first pregnancy, but..." She trailed off, giving herself a minute before she broached what could be a sensitive subject. "I think you'll notice that now that you're, well, older..."

Nikki laughed. "I am older than when I had Ryan. Quite a bit older. And I'd like to think I'm wiser, too."

"Either way." Nyah smiled. It was so easy to talk to Nikki; the more they spoke, the more she liked the woman. "It will be different. Having a baby in your late teens is significantly different from doing it in your late twenties. I don't anticipate any complications or anything like that, but just be prepared for some differences."

"Oh, I know it will be different." A sudden tear slipped down Nikki's cheek and she made no move to wipe it.

"Nikki?"

"Oh, I'm fine." She waved her hand. "It's just that it will be different this time because I won't be alone." A gentle sob escaped her and it quickly morphed into a laugh. "I'm such a mess." Nikki wiped her eyes. "I'm just so happy."

To anyone unfamiliar with what pregnancy hormones could do to a person, Nikki's behavior would have seemed insane, but to Nyah, it wasn't only normal, it was heartwarming. She didn't know all the details of Nikki's first pregnancy but she did know it had been an accident involving her best friend's boyfriend at the time. Nikki had left town and not said a word, until recently. Now, as far as Nyah knew, they were all friends again and Ryan had a large extended family. Funny how things had a way of working out. She let her mind drift for a moment to her own situation. Would she ever be welcomed back by her best friend? Correction. Her former best friend? Nyah, too, had stayed away from Halfway for far too long because she'd hurt her best friend. She had a lot in common with Nikki. Maybe her story would have a happy ending, too.

"It's okay to be a mess." Nyah handed her the tissue box. "You have every right to be. After all, it's an emotional time and there are the hormones to consider. It's totally understandable. And you're right: this time will be so different for you. I'm sure you're going to enjoy every moment. Does Parker know?"

Nikki nodded. "Everyone kind of knows. Well, not knows-knows but Becky kind of guessed the other day and Melissa and the kids were all there and—"

"Melissa?" Nyah couldn't help but feel a twinge of jealousy and hurt. She wanted so bad to make things right between them again. She missed Mel. She'd missed her for years. As if there was a hole in her heart where their friendship had been. "How is she?"

Nikki stood and straightened her sweater. "She's, well...she's okay."

There was no way Nyah believed that, but it wasn't the time or the place to push the issue. She wrote out a prescription for prenatal vitamins and walked with Nikki to the front desk. "I'd like you to schedule another appointment for next month." She turned to Lana behind the desk. "Can you see that Nikki gets that appointment, Lana?"

"Absolutely, Doc."

She smiled and shook her head at Lana's formal tone before

she turned back to Nikki. "I'd really like it if we could maybe grab a coffee or something before then," she said. "I mean, if you have time. I heard about the wedding. I know you're crazy busy and—"

"Nonsense," Nikki interrupted her. "Of course I have time. And you know you're invited to the wedding."

A warmth bloomed in Nyah's heart. She hadn't thought she'd be invited to the wedding. The sentiment was so touching, it almost made her cry. "Thank you," she managed. "I didn't expect that."

Nikki waved her hand. "Of course. In fact, Becky's having a little gathering at her house to do some Christmas baking and prepare a few things for the wedding. Would you like to come and help out?"

Nyah couldn't have hid the smile if she'd tried. "I'd love to! That would be so great."

"Fantastic. I'll call you with the details, okay?"

Nikki turned to Lana to confirm the details of her next appointment and, eager to get back to work, Nyah grabbed the file the nurse handed her for her next patient. She headed down the hall with a new pep in her step and a smile on her face. Things were going to be okay after all.

But the smile fell from her face the moment she opened the file in her hands.

Abby Tait.

Melissa's daughter?

Knowing how her ex-best friend felt about her, something must be really wrong if she was bringing her daughter to see Nyah. Of course, she was the only doctor in town. Either way, Nyah didn't have a good feeling as she took a deep breath and knocked on the door of exam room one.

Chapter Five

MELISSA

Melissa's stomach knotted as she watched her daughter sit on the exam table, her face pale.

When the school nurse had called to say Abby had fainted, not once but twice while at school today, Melissa dropped everything and rushed over to pick her up.

"How are you feeling now, hun?"

Melissa stood by Abby's side and held her hands. The nurse had given her a banana to eat and mentioned it might be a simple case of low blood sugar.

Simple? Unlikely.

"A bit better now. I have a headache, though."

Melissa attempted to smile. "Collapsing on the floor and knocking your head on your desk might do that to you."

Abby grimaced. "I've never fainted before."

"I know. You scared me." Melissa squeezed Abby's hand, not wanting to let go.

"Did you call Dad?"

Melissa frowned. Had she called Wade? No. To be honest, she never thought to.

"I'll call him once we know what's going on, okay?"

Abby dropped her head and sighed.

Melissa was about to say more but the door to the room opened.

"Good afternoon, Abby." Nyah Henderson walked in, a smile pasted on her face and her gaze directed toward Abby.

"Hi," Abby said quietly.

"I don't think we've met before." Nyah held out her hand. "I'm Dr. Nyah. I grew up in Halfway and now I'm back working with my dad, Dr. Henderson."

Abby shook Nyah's hand. "Dr. Henderson is your dad? Cool. Did you know that, Mom?" Abby looked toward her.

Melissa nodded.

Oh, she knew. She knew and didn't like knowing there was no other doctor today for them to see.

She met Nyah's gaze and held it, not backing down despite knowing her daughter would no doubt read the hostility there.

"So." Nyah cleared her throat and looked away. "It says here you fainted and hit your head. Mind if I take a look?"

Melissa watched as Nyah carefully felt around Abby's head and then looked at her eyes and breathed a sigh of relief at the smile on the woman's face.

"Other than the obvious headache you must feel, anything else I should know? Any thoughts on why you fainted?"

Abby shook her head. "I just felt really weird, cold and tired all at once. It hit me hard. I wanted to get my sweater but the next thing I knew, I was on the floor."

"Hmm. This happened just after lunch, right? Can I ask what you ate?"

Abby shook her head. "Nothing. I had a few club meetings and everything was running kind of late."

Melissa didn't like the sound of that. "Abby, you ate breakfast at least, right?" She'd left early and Wade said he'd take care of getting her off to school.

With her daughter's hesitation, Melissa knew. "So other than the banana that the nurse gave you, you've had nothing to eat today?"

"I'm not starving myself, if that's what you think." Abby stared down at the floor.

Melissa ground her teeth together.

"That's good to hear," Nyah said. "Is this the first you've felt like this, minus the fainting, or has it happened before?" She glanced at Melissa, who shook her head.

As far as she knew, this was the first.

"It's been going on for a month or so now, but..."

"A month?" Melissa rubbed the back of her neck. "You've been feeling like this for that long and haven't said anything?"

"Can you describe how you've been feeling?" Nyah's voice was very calm, the complete opposite to everything Melissa felt at the moment.

Her daughter was sick. She must be. Yet she'd said nothing... nothing...to her about it.

To make matters worse, she'd never even realized.

Abby breathed in deeply and squared her shoulders. She reminded Melissa so much of her father right then.

"I get shaky sometimes and it's like I'm in a...brain fog. Sometimes my eyes...wiggle. Does that make sense? It feels like they won't focus on anything, as if they're in hyperdrive or something," Abby explained.

Melissa watched Nyah make notes and she wondered what she was writing.

"Do you notice if these symptoms disappear when you've eaten or do they happen close to a meal?"

Abby shook her head. "No, it's more like if I skip a meal or wait too long. I try to snack. Dad said that it was healthy to snack during the day on veggies and stuff, so I try but..." She looked to Melissa. "I swear I'm eating. I swear."

"I believe you. I watched you eat half the cake you made the other night when you thought I was reading," she teased lightly.

"Cake." Nyah sighed. "Do you know how long it's been since I've had a decent cake that wasn't flat or full of eggshells? Baking has never been one of my talents." Nyah gave Abby a big smile and Melissa found herself slightly thankful that Nyah didn't seem to be blowing this out of proportion.

"Here's what we're going to do. Are you ready?" Nyah waited till Abby nodded. "I'd like to do some bloodwork and a sugar glucose test. As well, for the next week, I'd like you to keep a food journal. Basically, list what you eat and how you feel throughout the day. For instance," Nyah sat down in the empty chair off to the side, "write down your breakfast and then note if you get a headache or feel tired, or your hands shake a little. Note the time and if you can, how long it lasts for."

"What will that do?" Melissa asked.

"A few things. We'll be able to see if maybe she's reacting to something she's eating, as well as take note if it's her sugar levels, which I suspect it might be. Your body can only handle so many skipped meals before it starts trying to protect itself and if it's a drop in sugar levels, what her body is doing is crashing. It's called hypoglycemia."

Melissa swallowed hard.

"Is that like diabetes?" Abby asked, the horror in her voice loud and clear.

Nyah shook her head. "Almost the opposite. It means your body doesn't have enough sugar to use as fuel. The solution is to eat. Crackers and cheese, fruit, nuts, a protein shake, smoothie... that kind of thing."

While Nyah filled out a form, Melissa wrote a note on her

phone to look into hypoglycemia and find out what it was all about. This was the first she'd ever heard of it.

She took the form for the bloodwork and sugar test from Nyah and helped Abby off the exam bed.

"In the meantime, you need to be eating, every three to four hours, okay? And I don't mean filling up on cookies tonight at the festival either." Nyah winked. "If the dizziness and shaking doesn't go away even after eating, come back in, but let's try this first." Nyah patted Abby's back as they went to leave the room.

Melissa turned. "So she's fine, right?" she asked. "Or should I take her up to the hospital to have one of the ER doctors look at her?"

Nyah glanced at her watch. "Considering I'm headed there in an hour, you'd be wasting your time. But if you want a second opinion, I can mention it to Dr. Jordan if you want. I'll see if he can fit her in before his shift ends tomorrow."

Melissa looked Nyah in the eyes. "It's not that I don't trust you—it's just..."

"You're protecting your daughter. I get it." Nyah nodded. "Why don't you take her in for her bloodwork tomorrow? She'll need to fast and she'll be at the hospital for a few hours since they need to monitor her through a few tests. I'll have Dr. Jordan look over her results and if I'm off-base, then I can hand you off to him. You can trust him. He's good."

The words Nyah didn't say rang loud and clear. Melissa's distrust hadn't gone unnoticed.

* * *

Melissa decided to wait until Wade was home to tell him about their daughter's fainting spell.

Probably not the wisest decision on her part.

"You okay, Abs?" His massive arms were wrapped around

Abby and he kissed the top of her head. "Why haven't you said anything?"

From the glares he'd continued to throw Melissa's way, she knew he was upset.

"I'm okay, Dad."

Melissa felt helpless as she stood there and watched her daughter take comfort in her father's arms.

"Does the school have my number too? I'd like to be called if something like this happens again." His lips thinned in an angry line.

"Probably not, but we can get you on there," Melissa said quietly. Just one of the many ways she needed to make Wade a part of Abby's life officially.

"Mom didn't want to bother you. Honestly, I'm okay." Abby stepped back, breaking his hold, and stood between them, as if a referee.

"I can take you to the hospital tomorrow." Wade looked Melissa in the eye as if to make sure she heard him.

This...this wasn't easy. The joint parenting after having to do it alone for so long was...an adjustment to say the least. It wasn't as if she didn't want to, as if she didn't appreciate her husband stepping up and wanting to be a real partner in all of this...but it was hard to let go.

"You can't miss work," she reminded him.

"The Tree Festival starts tonight."

As if she needed to be reminded. She groaned.

"Correct me if I'm wrong but it's going to be a madhouse for you tomorrow with reprints and the newspaper and everything else," he pointed out.

He was right. It was. Which meant there was no way she could take hours away from the shop.

"We can wait till next week," Abby suggested.

Both Melissa and Wade shook their head. "Not happening,

love," Wade said. "I don't like hearing you haven't been feeling well and not telling us. We'll get this figured out. Besides, Nyah said she thinks it's something simple like sugar levels, right? There were a few guys in prison who had that. Working in the kitchen meant I took care of their meal trays and made sure they came in for snacks."

"So you'll take me then, Dad?" Abby munched on some crackers and cheese Abby had prepared after they came home.

"No doubt we'll run into my boss tonight. I'll make up the time if I need to, don't you worry."

"Whoa," Melissa jumped in. "I'm not sure if we should go tonight. Maybe Abby should take it easy for the night. We can watch movies or something instead." As much as she would hate to miss the opening night of the festival, there was no way she was going if Abby wasn't feeling up to par.

"I'm fine, Mom. Promise. Please, can we go? Please? This is Dad's first one in a long time. Our first one as a family," Abby begged.

"Your mom's right, kiddo. If you're not feeling well, it's not worth it. We can go tomorrow or the next day. You're more important."

Melissa mouthed, *Thank you.*

"What will it take for you to trust that I'm okay?" Abby asked.

Melissa looked to Wade. He apparently knew more about this than she did.

"How about you finish up the cheese and crackers then have a bit of a nap? You look tired. I'll make some homemade soup to warm our bones before we go out. If you're still feeling tired or have a headache, then we'll try again another night, okay?"

Abby rolled her eyes, grabbed her plate of food and began to eat.

Thirty minutes later when Melissa had gone up to check on her, Abby was fast asleep, curled up beneath a cozy blanket.

"I remember a few of the guys always needed to sleep after they had an attack." Wade was in the kitchen, chopping up vegetables, when Melissa told him about Abby.

"An attack?" She didn't like the sound of that.

"Headaches, shakiness, that kind of thing. Some guys spaced out completely, too, or couldn't get the right words out. Everyone reacts different but the one thing I remember is they all needed to sleep after. Sucked when it meant someone else had to pick up their slack." Wade finished chopping up the carrot and then set the knife down.

"You really should have called me, Mel."

"You're right, I should have. I'm sorry, it's just..."

"You've been doing this for so long by yourself. I know. But you're not alone anymore." He reached out for her and she stepped into his embrace. "I'm sorry you were alone for so long," he whispered as he held her.

"Be patient with me, okay?" The adjustment period to Wade being home was a lot harder than she thought it would be.

"Remember what you said to me the first day I got back?"

Melissa nodded. "One day at a time. As long as we do it as a family, we'll figure it out."

"Exactly. As a family. You won't be alone anymore, I promise." He tilted her face up for a kiss.

"Gross."

Abby had her eyes covered.

"That wasn't a long nap." Melissa stifled a grin as Wade kissed her again.

"Seriously?" Abby groaned. "Do you have to do that in public?"

Wade chuckled. "You think this is in public? Wait till

tonight when we're at the festival. I plan on smooching with your mother all night under the mistletoe."

Abby's eyes widened with delight. "So we're going? Sweet! Is the soup ready?"

By the time they made it to the festival grounds, the park was packed. Cups of hot chocolate were being handed out while the school band played carols in the music pavilion off to the side.

"How come you're not up there playing?" Wade asked.

Abby snickered. "Have you heard me play the trumpet? Mr. Alexander says I need a few more years of practice before I'm ready for my debut."

"Is that so? Have you tried other instruments? What about the flute or..."

"The guitar? That would be cool, right?" Abby couldn't seem to contain her excitement while Melissa groaned.

"Who knows, maybe Santa will bring one."

"Really, Dad?" The look Abby gave her father had Melissa laughing.

"Yeah, like really, Dad?" Melissa nudged him in the side. Santa? Seriously? He thought their teenage daughter still believed in Santa?

"Sorry." Wade held his hands up in mock surrender. "Get with the times, right?"

Abby rolled her eyes before she took off after one of her friends up ahead.

Melissa linked her arm through Wade's as they followed along but at a more leisurely pace. She watched as Wade took it all in—from the displays and lights to friendly hellos from friends who stopped them along the way. When they eventually stopped by a fire pit to warm their hands, Wade handed her his coat, which she gladly put on. It was colder out than she'd thought.

"Where's Abby?" She'd kept her eye out for her daughter but lost sight of her over half an hour ago.

Wade nodded toward the large tree in the center of the park. "She's in a group over there. I've been keeping my eye on her."

"Aren't you cold?" She buried her hands into the oversized pockets on Wade's coat.

"I did suggest the extra sweater, if you remember." His own hands were buried in his oversized pullover. "How about I go get us another warm drink? Stay here and keep warm."

While he was gone, the phone in the pocket of his jacket buzzed. She was going to ignore it but...curiosity got the better of her. She shouldn't look...she knew that...and yet she couldn't help herself. It was probably one of the guys from the body shop and she could keep them on the line until he got back.

And then she saw Nyah's name on the display screen.

For one brief second, she considered answering it, demanding to know why Nyah would be calling her husband.

The temptation was there but she didn't give in to it.

She hit the Ignore button.

Why was Nyah calling Wade? And why was her name and number programed in her husband's phone?

"What's with the frown?" Wade returned with two cups of hot chocolate.

She sipped on hers while she debated whether to tell him about the call.

In the end, she decided not to. If it was important enough, the woman would leave a message for Wade to listen to later. For now, this was her time with her husband and she wasn't going to allow that woman to interfere.

Tonight was about remaking memories, building their relationship and focusing on the future.

"It's almost time for the lights to come on." Wade couldn't contain his grin. "Do you know how many times I thought about this? The simple act of the lights turning on, the sounds everyone makes the moment it happens. I would imagine us standing over there," he pointed toward the pavilion where the band continued to play, "and you'd snuggle in close as we stood there."

"By the pavilion?" Of all the places for them to stand, why there?

"I also imagined our daughter playing in the band." He shrugged.

Melissa reached for his hand and led him over to where he'd indicated. Abby stood with her group of friends, just off in the distance but headed their way.

"It's almost time." Abby reached for Melissa's cup and went to take a sip but stopped as Melissa's brow rose. "Okay, okay. I'll go get my own."

With Wade's arm around her, Melissa snuggled in close as they watched everyone gather round the tree. The phone in her pocket buzzed, which Wade must have felt.

"Did someone call?" he asked.

Melissa just shrugged but he didn't notice.

As he listened to the message, the arm around her shoulders slipped and he stepped away from her.

"What's wrong?"

"It's Charlie. Nyah..." He struggled with the words. "She found him unconscious." Wade closed his eyes. "I need...I need to be with him." His voice was hoarse, as if he were close to tears.

"Now?"

He nodded. "Nyah says there's not much time. I...I can't...he shouldn't be alone, Mel. I just...I can't."

Before she could even say a word, Wade turned and walked away, headed toward the north section of the park. She ran after him.

"Wade, stop." She grabbed his arm and pulled. "Where are you going?"

"To Charlie's. It's not far, a few blocks maybe. I can't let him die. Not alone." His voice broke.

"I'll come with you."

Wade shook his head. "No."

"I want to." For whatever reason, he remained adamant about keeping that part of his life from her.

"I said no."

Melissa took a step back at the harshness of his voice.

"I mean it, Melissa."

She took another step back as she stared into his hollow gaze. Who was this man in front of her?

"When will you be home? Abby is—"

"Tell her I'm sorry," he interrupted. "I'll explain when I get home, okay? I don't know when that will be." He turned and walked away from her.

Melissa watched him walk away until he was too far for her to see in the dark anymore. By the time she turned, the tree was lit and her daughter stood there, all alone.

"Where's Dad?"

"He got a call and had to run. He'll meet us at home."

"Who called?"

Melissa swallowed past the lump in her throat. "No one important."

She lied.

She pasted a smile on her face and pulled her daughter into

a tight side hug. "I'm in the mood for some gingerbread cookies. Think they'll have them out yet?"

Tradition was to save the best homemade gingerbread anyone in Halfway had ever tasted until after the tree was lit.

Apparently she wasn't the only one lying today. Wade promised she wouldn't be alone again, and yet, here she was.

So much for making new memories.

Chapter Six

NIKKI

Just as it had been the year before and every year Nikki could remember from when she was a kid, the town square was lit up like a magical winter wonderland. The Tree Festival had always been her favorite, which was saying something because Halfway was known for having a festival for every possible occasion, and they were all amazing. But the Tree Festival had always held a special place in Nikki's heart. She'd missed it when she'd been gone.

You don't have to miss it anymore. She smiled at the thought and warmth filled her. Oh, how things had changed in only one short year.

"You look happy." Parker squeezed her hand a little tighter.

She leaned over and kissed him on the cheek. "I am happy." She was about to pull away when he wrapped his arms around her and spun her.

"Good." Parker kissed her thoroughly. "All I ever want is for you to be happy and if I can be the one to do that for you, well... that makes me happy, too."

Nikki swatted her fiancé on the shoulder. "You know you're the only one who could make me this happy."

It was true. From the moment Parker came into her life, she'd been ridiculously happy. Not that it had all been sugar and sunshine. It hadn't. They'd definitely had their share of bumps along the road, but there was no doubt in her mind that now that Parker was part of her life, and they were all going to be a family, everything would be okay.

"I'm just checking, babe." He kissed her on the tip of her nose and she giggled.

"That's so gross." Together, they turned to see Ryan holding a snowball and shaking his head. "Seriously, you guys are way too gross."

"You think that's gross?" Parker slid a hand up Nikki's cheek. "I'll show you gross." Before she could object, he dipped her backward and his lips crushed hers in a stage kiss that was totally over the top and completely put on for Ryan's benefit.

She couldn't help it; Nikki giggled. Try as she might, she couldn't contain the laughter and soon Parker lifted his head and joined her in the laughter. A second later, there was a wet thunk against Parker's shoulder as a snowball hit him.

"Hey!" He pulled away from Nikki and reached down to make his own snowball before Ryan could rearm himself. "You think you can out snowball fight me? You're crazy, kid." Nikki shook her head and smiled as Ryan let out a screech and took off running toward the sleigh rides with Parker in hot pursuit.

She straightened her coat and headed toward the food and baking stands. No doubt the boys would get tired of running from each other in a few minutes. She might as well get some snacks ready.

The Tree Festival was known for the bounty of treats and

fresh baking stands, including the best gingerbread she'd ever tasted. When she found out she was pregnant, Nikki had promised herself she wasn't going to let her pregnancy be an excuse to eat everything she wanted, but this baby was definitely craving sweets and the smell of the gingerbread wafting over to her was too strong to be ignored. Surely one cookie wouldn't hurt. Besides, she was going to make sure her boys were well fed for the holidays and that meant she was going to be staying far away from the kitchen herself. She was good at a lot of things, but cooking and baking was definitely not on that list.

She got in the growing line and turned to see whether she could see Parker and Ryan yet. She caught sight of them by the tree; Ryan was still doing a good job staying away from Parker. Nikki laughed again. It warmed her heart to see them getting along so well. They really were going to be a great family.

"What's so funny?"

Nikki spun around to see Melissa and Abby in line in front of her. She'd been so caught up in her own life she hadn't noticed them. A flash of guilt went through her. That had been the problem lately. She'd been so preoccupied with everything going on in her own life she hadn't been there properly for Melissa and she definitely looked as though she could use a friend. "Oh, it's nothing." Nikki waved her hand. "I was just making sure the snowball fight hadn't escalated too badly. Ryan decided it would be a good idea to take aim at Parker."

"Oh, that was bold," Melissa said.

Nikki cocked her head and examined the other woman. She was trying to sound light, but Nikki could tell there was some-thing going on; she didn't seem like herself. She did a quick scan but didn't see Wade nearby. It wouldn't take many guesses for Nikki to figure out what was bothering Melissa.

"It was," Nikki said. "Especially since Parker isn't likely to give up soon." She laughed, hoping to lighten the mood. Maybe if she just forced some lightness into the air, Melissa would smile, too. She wasn't so sure her plan would work, but it seemed like a better idea than getting into a deep discussion with Abby there, so she kept going. "It turns out Ryan thinks it's gross when Parker and I kiss," she continued the story. "So he took aim."

"I totally get that," Abby said. Nikki noticed Melissa tense as her daughter spoke and she wondered again where Wade was. "I think it's totally gross when my mom and dad kiss, too."

Nikki nodded. "Maybe it's a universal kid thing."

Melissa smiled but it was easy to see that it was forced. Nikki's heart ached for her friend and not knowing what she could do to make things better.

"Hey, Abby. Maybe you should go help Ryan out a little?" Nikki suggested spontaneously. "I'll help your mom pick out the gingerbread. Besides, the line isn't moving very quickly."

Abby glanced at her mom and then back to the tree, where she'd been watching Ryan lob snowballs in Parker's general direction, and then back to her mom. "Can I? I mean, it looks like Ryan could use a little help. He's not a very good shot."

Melissa laughed before she quickly swallowed and grabbed Abby's arm. "As long as you're careful. Are you feeling okay?"

"Mom." Abby rolled her eyes. "I'm fine. I promise I'll come right back and have a snack, okay?"

For a moment, Nikki thought Melissa might object again, but she nodded quickly. "Okay, have fun. Oh, and don't beat them too badly."

Abby didn't wait around for any further advice; she took off running, stopping only to scoop up some snow as she got closer to the guys.

As soon as she was out of earshot, Nikki turned back to her friend. "Is everything okay?" Melissa's face fell and Nikki quickly added, "With Abby? You seem worried." She wanted to add that Melissa seemed worried about a lot of things, but it didn't seem like the time or place to get into a deep conversation.

"Oh, she's..." Melissa stuffed her hands deep into the pocket of the coat she was wearing. Wade's coat by the looks of it. Nikki wondered again where Wade was. "She'll be—" Tears sprang from her eyes and she looked away so Nikki couldn't see. Melissa sniffed loudly and wiped her face with the sleeve of the coat. "I'm sorry...I just..."

"No." Nikki wrapped her arm around her friend. "I should be sorry. I wasn't trying to make you upset or anything. We don't have to talk about this right now."

Melissa shook her head. "It's fine. Really. I'm just...well, there's a lot going on is all." She forced a smile through her tears.

"You can say that again," Nikki agreed with her. "It's a crazy time of year and with everything else your family is going through...well, I don't blame you if you're a little out of sorts. Don't be too hard on yourself, okay?"

Melissa nodded and wiped her face again.

"Looks like it's finally our turn." Nikki pointed to the ginger-bread. The line had finally moved and she breathed a sigh of relief to have something to focus on. When the women were done picking out their cookies and paying for them, they moved to a bench near a fire pit where they could warm up and wait for the snowball fight to be over.

"I'm sorry," Melissa said. "I didn't even think to ask you about the wedding plans. What a crazy time of year to get married. I don't think I could do it."

Nikki laughed. "I know. It is crazy. But then we thought, it's always going to be crazy. There's never really a good time to go ahead and get married, you know? So why not do it when every-thing is already busy and we have a million things going on?" She laughed again. "Besides. We really just wanted it to be simple and festive. Christmas Eve is perfect. I can't wait."

Melissa reached over and squeezed her hand. "You deserve it, Nikki. It's going to be beautiful."

For a moment, all Nikki could do was stare at the other woman. She had so much going on in her own life. Her world had been turned upside down in the past few months, but she was still looking out for others. Nikki's heart could have burst from the love she felt from this woman who'd only recently become her friend. Melissa deserved to be happy, too. She only wished she knew how to help her.

"You're going to be at Becky's tomorrow, right?" It was the only thing she could think of. It wasn't much, but maybe surrounding Melissa with friends and family would help get her through the tough times.

"I mean, I need all the help I can get when it comes to baking." She laughed at herself because it was definitely not a secret that she was a mess in the kitchen. Melissa looked as though she was going to object, so Nikki added, "I will not take no for an answer. It will be fun and super festive and you can bring the whole family." She patted Melissa's leg and jumped up. "Sometimes it just helps being around friends. I'll see you tomorrow, okay? I'm really looking forward to it."

* * *

"You know I love spending time with you, Nikki." Parker drove their SUV down the highway toward Becky and Matt's tree farm the next day. "But I have a pile of papers to mark before school lets out for the holidays, never mind the list you made for the wedding. I could probably be a lot more productive at home today. Besides, I think Ryan said something about wanting to do a little Christmas shopping."

"I did."

Melissa turned and looked at Ryan in the backseat, who

grinned from ear to ear. It didn't seem to matter what Parker said these days; Ryan would agree wholeheartedly with him. She simply shook her head and turned back to Parker.

"I know you have a million things you should be doing." She slid her hand on his leg. "I do. And I really appreciate you coming with me today."

He put his hand over hers. "I know you do. I'm just not sure why I needed to be here today."

Nikki glanced quickly behind her again, but Ryan seemed to be immersed in whatever game was on his tablet. "I'm hoping that Melissa and Wade come," she said. "I know Matt has that... project or whatever it is in the garage, and I thought maybe you guys could talk and bond and—"

"Meddle."

"Not meddle." She smacked his arm lightly. "Just...be a friend."

Parker laughed, but his smile was kind. "Of course, we can go and do what guys do in the garage. I have no problem with that at all. Just don't ask me to bake anything."

"I'll be the taste tester," Ryan piped up from the back. "I'm good at that."

"Yes you are," Nikki agreed. Her attention was drawn to Becky and Matt's driveway as they pulled into their yard. She hadn't been sure Melissa would actually come, but there was her car. Nikki breathed a sigh of relief. Everything would be okay. She knew it. And if it wasn't, she'd try harder.

A few moments later, after having sent Parker and Ryan straight to the garage to find Matt, and hopefully Wade, Nikki knocked and walked into Becky's house.

"It smells so good in here." She inhaled deeply. The air was full of a yummy mixture of cinnamon, sugar, chocolate and that general yummy sweetness of Becky's baking.

"Did you leave anything for me to help with?" She walked

through the living room and into the kitchen where Melissa stood at the sink, her arms up to the elbows in suds. "Hey, Melissa. I'm glad you came."

She turned so quickly, suds flew from her hands and onto Nikki. "Oh, I'm sorry. I didn't hear you come in." Melissa blushed. "I was daydreaming."

Nikki laughed and wiped the bubbles from her sweater. "No problem. I know how that can be. Where's Becky?"

"I'm here." Becky came through the door, completely hidden by an oversized box she was lugging. Nikki moved quickly and grabbed it from her.

"You should not be carrying stuff like that," Nikki said. "What's in here anyway?"

Becky sank heavy into a chair and wiped her brow with the sleeve of her sweater. Nikki watched her closely. She didn't look right. It was probably the stress of all the baking on top of the holiday business, but still... "It's just some tins and jars and things that I need to put the cookies in," Becky said. "I meant to get Matt to grab it but he's busy in the garage and I didn't want to bother him."

"I'm really sorry Wade didn't come," Melissa said and Nikki jerked her head up to look at her. Wade didn't come? "He had a long night last night and I don't think he was really in the mood to be social."

"That's what friends are for." Becky tried to come off light and carefree, but Nikki noticed her heart wasn't in it. Something was going on with her. "Friends don't judge," Becky continued. "We're just there for each other."

"That's right." Nikki put the box down on the table and went to the sink to pour a glass of water. She handed Becky the glass. "Drink this. You don't look good."

"Thanks." She half-heartedly protested, but took the glass

and drank deeply. "And here I thought I was pulling off this pregnancy thing pretty good."

"You're doing great with pregnancy." Nikki's hands instinctively rested on her own stomach. "But I think you should rest. Carrying boxes probably isn't a good idea."

"What!" Becky put the glass down and pointed at her. "What about you?"

"Oh my goodness," Melissa said from behind her. "I'm a terrible friend. I totally forgot to ask."

Nikki's head swung between the two of them. Of course she hadn't seen anyone since her appointment with Nyah and therefore hadn't confirmed anything with her friends, but...she nodded and the women all let out a whoop of joy. "It's true. It's official. I'm pregnant."

"Oh Nikki, that's fantastic." Melissa wrapped her in a quick hug before she spun her to face Becky, who took a moment longer than Nikki would have expected to get out of her chair. Nikki crossed the distance and went to her for a hug.

"I'm so happy for you." Becky's words were muffled into her shoulder. "How far along are you?"

Nikki noticed her friend grab her own stomach and a flash of pain—or maybe it was worry—cross her face. She ignored the question and eyed Becky suspiciously.

"What?" Becky said after a moment. "I want to know details. How pregnant are you? I want to know if our babies are going to grow up like sisters or be each other's first love."

She couldn't help it; Nikki laughed. The thought had definitely crossed her mind, too. It would be fantastic for their babies to grow up with each other. Just the way they had. Only without any of the drama in between. "Well, Nyah said I was—"

"Nyah?"

Nikki looked at Melissa, whose face was screwed into a tight ball. There was definitely something going on between the two women, but for the life of her, Nikki didn't know what it was. The two women always struck her as so similar. They could probably be good friends for each other again if they'd just let whatever grudge they were holding onto go. "Of course, Nyah," Nikki said. "She's the only doctor in town right now."

"Her father is still supposed to be here." Melissa crossed her arms. "I don't understand why Nyah has to—"

"Did someone say my name?"

All three women turned to see the doctor rush through the door. "I knocked." Nyah bustled into the room. "But no one answered so I figured I should just come in. I know how it can be when everyone's in the middle of something. Anyway, I'm so sorry I'm late. I was up with a patient last night and it wasn't a good situation."

Next to her, Nikki heard Melissa make a sound she couldn't quite decipher, but when she turned to look, Melissa was back at the sink. "Don't worry," Nikki said with a smile. "I was late, too."

"I'm just glad you're here." Becky pushed up from her chair and took a step toward Nyah.

Just as Nikki was about to mention how pale she looked, Becky gripped her stomach and folded in half.

"Becky!"

Chapter Seven

BECKY

"I want to go home," Becky begged.

Matt sat at her side, holding tight onto her hand, and shook his head.

Nyah stood at the foot of her bed, arms crossed, and she shook her head.

Even her mother, Norma, who sat on the chair off to the corner, shook her head.

"Oh come on," Becky muttered. "I need at least one of you on my side."

"If you go home, you won't rest. We all know that." Norma pounded her cane on the floor. "You'll be in your kitchen, baking up a storm and stressing yourself out. That's not good for the baby."

"You don't know that."

Matt laughed. "You're kidding me, right? You're probably already thinking about how many batches of cookies and squares you need to make for Nikki's wedding."

Becky didn't argue because he was right. "I promised her I'd take care of the food. You can't celebrate a wedding without—"

"HA!" Norma shouted out. "I knew it. You're not the only one in town who knows what they're doing when it comes to baking, girl."

Becky shifted slightly beneath the thin hospital blanket. "I know, but..." She rubbed her belly softly.

"You need to put yourself and your baby first right now." Nyah only said what Becky already knew.

"You're on bed rest and I have a feeling this will be your life for a little while." Nyah gave her a weak smile. "I'll let you go home, but in a few days. We have an obstetrician who will be here tomorrow and we'll do a few more stress tests in the meantime."

"I'm fine, Nyah. Honestly." Becky struggled really hard to make her voice sound convincing.

The way Nyah's brow rose told Becky otherwise. Her shoulders slumped.

"Becky, Nikki will understand." Matt continued to grip her hand.

"I know she will but..."

"No buts." Norma stood and leaned on her cane. "You let me take care of the food. You have a stash in your freezer already, right?"

Becky nodded. She'd started early and today's baking session was about having extras, just in case.

"Good," Norma said. "I know more than enough women who will jump at the chance to add some extras, you know that."

"Mom, I think Nikki wanted to keep it small, you know?"

Norma snorted. "Does she really think she can keep something like this a secret?"

"What am I supposed to do on bed rest? Knit?" She really wasn't someone to sit still. There was still a lot to do, to take care of. She wanted to finish painting the old crib Matt had refurnished from a garage sale and put together the baby's room properly. That really wasn't something she could leave up to Matt.

"You've been complaining that you haven't had time to really work on your website lately. Maybe now you can?" Matt suggested.

She shrugged.

"Oh, come on." Nyah nudged her foot and smiled. "Bed rest isn't all that bad. You've got Matt, who will be at your beck and call, and you know you'll have lots of friends come out to keep you company."

"Wait a minute." Matt leaned back in his chair. "I think I might be with Becky on this...bed rest seems kind of hard core, doesn't it?" He winked at her.

"Well," Becky smiled, "now that you mention it..." She took his hand and squeezed before she leaned forward as a sharp pain tore across her stomach.

"Oh," she moaned through the tightness as Nyah had taught when they'd rushed to the hospital earlier.

"Becky?" Matt leaned forward and placed his hand on her stomach. "It's okay," he said. "It's going to be okay." He struggled to soothe her, to talk her through it.

As the wave of pain washed over her, Becky clutched at her belly. *Please don't let anything happen to their baby, please...*she silently prayed. As the tightness dissipated, she relaxed slightly and leaned back.

"Is the baby going to be okay?" she asked Nyah weakly. The fear of losing her child, of there being something wrong, scared her. If bed rest was what she needed to do to protect her baby, she'd do it. She'd knit baby blankets and booties and hats and...

"You're both going to be okay, I promise." Nyah leaned against the bed and lightly touched her shoulder.

Becky nodded. Yes, they were both going to be okay. They had to be. She refused to think anything else, to believe anything else.

"Mom, do you have any knitting needles I can borrow?"

Norma shook her head. "You tried knitting once, remember? A scarf. A simple project that ended up being full of nothing but holes." She came to stand beside the bed and touched Becky's leg. "Movies. Now is a great time to watch some of those movies you keep telling me about and maybe read some books."

"Movies? Books?" Becky repeated.

"I believe that's what you told me when I was stuck here, in this hospital." There was something that resembled a smile on her mother's face.

"I also came to see you every day." She rubbed the ache in her belly and tried to keep the pain off her face. She knew everyone watched her closely.

Norma nodded. "Guess that means I'll have to do the same. Now, I've got some people to round up to do some baking. I wonder if I can convince my grandson to make some cinnamon tea cakes. Everyone loves my tea cakes and they're perfect for a wedding."

"Ryan loves spending time with you," Matt said.

"Well, of course he does. I'm his grandmother." Norma huffed before she made her way out of the room. "Matt, I'll need you to take me home, please," she called over her shoulder.

Becky gripped her husband's hand tighter. "You'll come back, right?"

"Of course I will." Matt stood and kissed her. "You're okay? Really?"

Becky nodded and forced a smile on her face.

"How about I bring you a hot chocolate back with me and maybe something sweet to eat?"

"I'll take one of those too," Nyah said. "I'll sit here with you until Matt comes back. We can catch up and maybe you can help me figure out what I'm doing wrong with my cookies." She sat down once Matt left, after Norma called out to him again.

"Your mother is one tough cookie, isn't she?" Nyah mentioned.

"That's one way of saying it." Becky rolled her eyes. "If she can survive a car crash and hip replacement, I can survive this, right?"

"Of course you can. Now, I'm not an expert when it comes to pregnancies but, with medication we can bring down your blood pressure and with some rest and careful monitoring, you'll deliver a healthy baby."

The ease in Nyah's tone soothed Becky's fears—somewhat. After so many miscarriages, the fear of never having a child of her own was always there at the forefront of her mind. The fears had eased as her pregnancy progressed but now this...

"I promise." Nyah leaned closer. "Just think of this time as a way for you to be pampered for once. Knowing this town the way I do, they'll make sure you're taken care of."

Becky chuckled. "This will be hard for me. Normally I'm the one who likes to take care of others."

"Suck it up, princess." Nyah stood. "In all seriousness, I need you to promise me you'll follow doctor's orders. The heaviest thing you'll be allowed to lift is a cup of coffee or a plate full of cookies. No laundry, no boxes, no vacuum or shovel. I want you in bed or on your couch, feet up and drinking lots of herbal teas. Or hot chocolate."

Most days, that sounded like a small piece of heaven. But the seriousness in Nyah's gaze, despite the smile at the end, told her this was no picnic.

"So I'm really on bed rest then?"

Nyah nodded. "'Fraid so. At least until we do more testing and get you looked at by a specialist, okay?"

"You know I hate knitting, right?"

"Then don't knit. Do crossword puzzles or read a book or something."

Becky groaned. "Since you're stuck in here keeping me company, why don't you fill me in on how you are, what you've been doing and if you're glad to be back in Halfway or not."

Nyah sat back down in the chair. "Glad to be back? I really didn't have much of a choice. My dad...he kind of twisted my arm, you know? Family guilt and all that."

"Ha! Tell me about it. There's a reason your father and my mother get along so well." Becky almost felt sorry for Nyah. She understood all too well what family guilt meant. Her mother had used it on Becky almost all her life.

"I think my dad just missed me, which is fine. I was ready... to settle down, I guess. To come home." Nyah fidgeted in her seat.

"What did you do before you came here? I mean, you obviously went to school, but then what?"

"Oh...nothing too exciting." Nyah jumped up from her chair and paced a little. "Worked at a few hospitals, some emergency wards, you know...nothing too thrilling. I thought about joining up with Doctors Without Borders but..." She shrugged. "Tell me about you. I checked out your website and you've got quite the following."

Becky smiled. "It's been fun. I have a cookbook coming out soon." She knew Nyah wanted to change the topic.

"You do? That must be cool. Have you thought about doing baking lessons? I promise I'd be the first to sign up. I can't seem to bake anything edible, no matter how hard I try."

"Are you measuring properly?"

"I am. I even bought Cake Boss baking cups and pans."

Becky snorted. "Cheap ones from the dollar store would work too, you know."

"I need all the help I can get, trust me."

"Come out one day and I'll help you make cookies." If she had to rest, then she'd rest. But it didn't mean she had to be lonely.

"Did someone say cookies?" Matt walked into the room, a tray of drinks in one hand and a closed box in another. "I've got hot chocolate for the three of us and some goodies. As well as a message from Norma."

Becky sighed. No doubt her mother sent along instructions.

"She says to tell you she's got it handled and although the baking might not be as good as yours, it'll do Nikki proud." Matt handed her a cup of hot chocolate and then one to Nyah as well. "She also says you're to do everything to take care of this grand-baby of hers."

"She did, did she? And what did you tell her?" She sipped her delicious hot cocoa and sighed.

"I told her you were my number-one priority and that I'll be on hand to pamper you day and night."

Becky's heart swelled at the same time she felt her baby kick. It tickled but gave her hope. Everything was going to be all right.

Chapter Eight

NYAH

She adjusted her dress for the dozenth time and looked in the mirror at her hair. She'd had it cut short only two days earlier, and for the life of her, she couldn't get used to it. It was probably a mistake.

Much like moving back to Halfway was.

Nyah sighed and shook her head. No. It hadn't been a mistake and she couldn't let one bad experience taint it for her. Okay, it was more than one. It was a few experiences.

But it was one person.

Melissa.

Nyah couldn't change what had happened in the past. Lord knew she'd tried. She'd done everything she could to make amends because of her mistake on the side of the road. She'd spent the last decade dedicating herself to helping others, healing and honing her skills. She wasn't perfect. Far from it. But she'd learned to forgive herself.

If only Melissa could.

But it seemed to be just the opposite. Every time she ran into Melissa, her old friend seemed to hate her a little bit more. And it was hate. The way she looked at her, as if she blamed Nyah for everything that had gone wrong in her life.

It made Nyah's heart hurt. They used to be so close.

She sighed and grabbed her purse. Between Wade's friend Charlie and their daughter Abby getting sick, there'd only been more and more reasons for Melissa to resent and dislike Nyah. Not the other way around.

But she needed to stop dwelling on all the things she couldn't change, and she definitely couldn't change any of that. She needed to focus on what she could do something about. And right now that meant pulling it together and getting herself to the wedding.

Nikki and Parker wanted a small, intimate Christmas Eve ceremony, and Nyah had been shocked to be invited at all. The fact that Becky had more or less volunteered her as a medical escort so she could go to the ceremony was a minor detail. Nikki had issued her a personal invitation and whether the other woman knew it or not, it had meant a lot to Nyah to be accepted, even a little, back into the Halfway community.

She glanced at the clock over her fireplace as she grabbed her keys and the small gift she'd picked up. She needed to hurry if she was going to get there before Becky. Knowing that woman, she was probably already there and it would be killing her to stay seated and not oversee every detail for her friend.

As it turned out, Nyah was right. When she walked into the "Barn"—which wasn't really a barn at all, but an old historical building that had once been used by a dairy farmer that had been beautifully restored into Halfway's only upscale restaurant and the venue of choice for special events—the first thing Nyah heard was Matt's voice.

"Becky, sit down! Remember what the doctor said."

Nyah quickly hung up her coat and hustled across the room that was gorgeously decorated in pine boughs, silver and white bows, and frosted pinecones. It was a winter wonderland, and absolutely perfect.

"I know what the doctor said, but she—"

"Is right here." Nyah put her hand on Becky's shoulder. "And she absolutely agrees with your husband. Sit down."

Becky sighed and slumped back into the wheelchair they'd borrowed from the hospital for the night. "I know. I know. And I don't want to do anything to harm the baby, but—"

"I know." Matt bent and kissed her forehead and nuzzled her face in a move that was so sweet, Nyah felt as if she was intruding on a private moment. "This is crazy hard on you, Becky, and you're doing an amazing job. And you're going to keep doing an amazing job making that baby. Our baby."

Becky's hands cradled her stomach. "Our baby," she repeated.

Nyah tried to take a step backward and leave them to their moment, but Matt stopped her. "Nyah. Now that you're here..."

She smiled. "Yes?"

"Can you sit with Becky for a bit? I just wanted to go check on Parker and make sure he doesn't need anything."

"No problem." She grabbed the handles of the chair and gave Becky a quick spin, causing the other woman to laugh and reach out and smack her.

"Nyah!"

"Don't worry, I'm a doctor."

"I'm in good hands then." Becky smiled and Nyah couldn't help but notice how radiant her friend looked. Pregnancy, even a troubled one, definitely agreed with her. Or maybe it was that she was so in love with her husband. Either way, she looked fantastic. "Will you take me to look at the cake?" Becky tipped her head up and asked Nyah.

"Absolutely. Let's check it out." Dutifully, she turned the chair and headed to the front corner of the room. "I still can't believe you gave up making the cake," Nyah said. "I mean, I know you had to."

"Doctor's orders," Becky said pointedly.

"Right. And it *is* for the best. Besides, I'm sure whoever she found did a good job making the cake. Not as good as you would have," she added quickly.

The cake table was at the front of the room, next to an arch covered in pine boughs and twinkly lights where the ceremony would take place. Nikki and Parker had opted to have a simple "dessert style" wedding. There was nothing traditional about it. Guests would gather close to the couple and then, after a short ceremony, they'd mingle and feast on the sweets that had been prepared. Simple, elegant, and fun.

Nothing at all like the traditional wedding Nyah would have wanted. Not that she'd actually thought much about getting married since she'd been a little girl. Her whole adult life had been dedicated to medicine and she didn't see that ending any time soon. Although...she let her gaze wander over the beautiful room...it wouldn't be so bad to find someone to spend some time with.

"I can't believe it." Becky's voice distracted Nyah and brought her back to the moment.

Nyah shook her head and looked at the cake in question. It was beautiful: a white three-layer square tiered cake with delicate fondant sprigs of pine and red berries that decorated the edges. There was a dusting of what looked like sparkles over the surface, making the entire thing glittery. It was spectacular and she said as much to Becky.

"It's a Danny Spencer cake."

"Who's Danny Spencer?" Nyah asked, although judging by the tone of Becky's voice, she probably should have known.

"He's the most amazing wedding cake, or any cake at all, baker in Montana. Probably the Western states, actually. He's like Cake Boss, only...not a celebrity. I was hoping to interview him for my blog."

"Well, maybe Nikki knows him and can get you a phone number or something?" Nyah shrugged and looked around, the cake or the baker not holding her interest at all. The room was starting to fill up with guests. It was true that they'd wanted to keep it small, but these things had a way of growing. Especially in a small town. She saw a few people she recognized. The longer she was in Halfway, the more people she was getting to know again. It was nice to be part of a community again. She waved as Sarah Kingsbury, who owned A Cut Above, the salon where Nyah'd just had her hair cut, waved at her. Behind her, the door opened and Wade and Melissa walked in with Abby.

Instinctively, Nyah turned away. Her heart raced and she forced herself to take a deep breath and stay calm. She got so rattled around Melissa. She only wanted to fix things between them. She turned around slowly and risked a glance. Melissa stared in her direction. Nyah smiled and raised her hand for a small wave, but Melissa had already turned to something Abby was saying and hadn't noticed.

"We should probably go get you a spot right up front," Nyah said to Becky, needing a distraction. "The ceremony is supposed to start soon."

Becky laughed. "Come on. Nikki's never on time for anything."

"True." Nyah laughed along with her as she wheeled her friend to what would be a prime spot to both see Nikki walking down the aisle and to witness the exchanging of the vows.

Right after they got in position, a justice of the peace appeared from a back room with Parker, who looked very handsome in his coat and tie, and Matt right behind him. Matt took charge and made a quick announcement about the ceremony before acting as an usher and directing everyone where they should stand before he joined Becky and Nyah. He took his wife's hand and gave it a sweet kiss right as the music started to play. Nyah turned along with the crowd to see Nikki dressed in a shimmery white gown. It was simple and form-fitting, her pregnancy not giving anything away yet; it fit perfectly. The fabric had a shimmer, almost a glitter that sparkled as she walked. In one hand she held a beautiful mixture of white blooms, with sprigs of pine tucked among the petals. In her other hand was Ryan's.

Nyah's hand flew to her mouth to hold in the sob that threatened to escape, but it was a cry of joy and she wasn't the only one. All through the room, guests noticed the same thing Nyah had. The look on Ryan's face as he escorted his mother was one of pure love and adoration. He looked every bit like the proud young man Nyah knew him to be as he led his mother to her future husband.

"Hi," Nikki whispered to Parker as she stopped in front of him.

"Hi there yourself." Parker leaned forward and kissed her on the cheek. "You look amazing." Before she could respond, he looked to Ryan, who watched them very seriously. "Thank you," Parker said to the boy.

"For what?"

A little giggle went through the crowd, but Parker didn't take his eyes off Ryan. "For taking such good care of your mother until you could both find me and allow me to be part of your life."

Nyah didn't even bother to try to stop the tears that flowed down her cheeks.

Nikki turned and handed Becky her bouquet. Parker took her free hand in his and the other in Ryan's to form a small but unified circle in front of the justice of the peace. The ceremony was perfect. It didn't matter if the entire town was in attendance; the only people who mattered were Nikki, Parker, and Ryan as the three of them stood together and recited vows that included them all as a family. It was the most beautiful wedding Nyah had ever been witness to. When finally the officiant declared Nikki and Parker husband and wife, Parker pulled his bride into his arms and kissed her while Ryan stood by and shook his head slightly in a way that made everyone laugh, before they opened their arms to include their son in a hug.

The crowd cheered and together, Nikki, Parker, and Ryan came to give Becky and Matt hugs and kisses as well. The fact that the five of them—soon to be seven—had managed to find their way through the hurt and heartache of their past was remarkable and gave Nyah hope that one day maybe she and Melissa might be able to see their way past their own troubled history.

Nyah wiped the tear from her eye and turned, looking straight into Melissa's eyes.

Was she thinking the same thing?

Nyah offered a small smile and much to her surprise and joy, Melissa returned it. Her old friend's eyes crinkled the way Nyah remembered from when they were young and her heart surged with love and hope. Maybe it was the season. Maybe it was the touching wedding. Whatever it was, it didn't matter because in that moment, as Michael Bublé's version of "I'll Be Home For Christmas" played and Nikki and Parker took to the floor for their first dance, Nyah's heart was full of hope.

Hope for the future. For love. But mostly, for the friendship and family she knew she'd have in Halfway.

ABOUT ELENA AITKEN

Elena Aitken is a USA Today Bestselling Author of more than fifty romance and women's fiction novels. The mother of 'grown up' twins, Elena now lives with her very own mountain man in the heart of the very mountains she writes about. She can often be found with her toes in the lake and a glass of wine in her hand, dreaming up her next book and working on her own happily ever after.

Subscribe to Elena's Newsletter and never miss a thing: https://view.flodesk.com/pages/603805efeeca3d548fe659e2

Series you may enjoy:
THE SPRINGS
CASTLE MOUNTAIN LODGE

Let's Connect
www.elenaaitken.com
Elena@elenaaitken.com

ABOUT STEENA HOLMES

Steena Holmes is a NYT and USA Today Bestselling Author with close to 3 million books sold worldwide. She writes Women's Fiction, Contemporary Fiction and Psychological Suspense. Listed as one of the top 20 women to read by Good Housekeeping, there's bound to be a story you won't soon forget in her catalog.

Join Steena's mailing list: https://www.steenaholmes.com/newsletter-sign-up/ and grab a free read - and if you're a fellow travel lover like her, come join one of her upcoming reader trips - like her Sweet Christmas in Paris tour!

Let's Connect!
www.steenaholmes.com
steena@steenaholmes.com